The Evidence Against You

GILLIAN McALLISTER

PENGUIN BOOKS

PENGUIN BOOKS

UK | USA | Canada | Ireland | Australia
India | New Zealand | South Africa

Penguin Books is part of the Penguin Random House group of companies
whose addresses can be found at global.penguinrandomhouse.com.

First published 2019
001

Copyright © Gillian McAllister, 2019

The moral right of the author has been asserted

Set in 12.5/14.75 pt Garamond MT Std
Typeset by Jouve (UK), Milton Keynes
Printed and bound in Great Britain by Clays Ltd, Elcograf S.p.A.

A CIP catalogue record for this book is available from the British Library

ISBN: 978–1–405–93456–5

www.greenpenguin.co.uk

For Clare, my agent, confidante, life coach and friend.
Without you, not only would this have been much
harder, it would never have happened at all

I

It was a wicked and depraved act, Izzy is thinking as she closes her curtains. That's what the judge said. She remembers his exact words from eighteen years ago. *It was a wicked and depraved act. You wanted Alexandra English to die, and you made sure that she did.*

Her father was standing in the dock, staring impassively at the judge, his gaze not faltering, his body completely still. He wouldn't even look across at her. Not as the guilty verdict was read out. Not as he was sentenced to life in prison. And not as he was taken away, either. Her final view of him was of his swarthy face in profile, hooked nose, dark hair covering his ears, eyes staring straight ahead.

It's the first week of May and the weather has warmed up so fast it is as though a switch has been flicked. Moths tumble around the lamp in Izzy's bedroom. She reaches to close the window, even though it's still stuffy.

Downstairs, she can hear Nick moving around. She draws the curtains and listens to him opening the dishwasher. He will have gathered up their plates and glasses from the living room and carried them all into the kitchen together in one towering pile. He likes to do things with – according to him – maximum efficiency.

A tree seems to shift in the darkness outside their bedroom window. Izzy is used to the palm trees, but Nick – somebody who likes to follow rules – couldn't believe it when he first moved across to join her on the Isle of Wight where she grew up. 'It's not like it's the *Caribbean*,' he kept saying. 'They're everywhere.'

'It's tomorrow,' she says now to Nick, still standing by the window, as he arrives in the bedroom. There is no point, Izzy reasons, not saying anything, though both she and Nick are good at pretending.

A strange expression crosses Nick's face. Something between a smile and a grimace. He runs a hand through his black hair. She has always loved how much hair he has; how thick and dark it is. He has two crowns at the back; a satisfying double whorl.

He's carrying a box of crackers and a plate. He's laid out four cheeses of exactly equal sizes. They've been doing this lately. Sharing a fourth, unnamed meal most nights in bed. Guilty pleasures, consumed after hours. *We ought to stop*, they keep saying to each other, but they don't, laughingly spreading another cracker for each other. *Just one more*. Izzy has gained four pounds. Everybody will think she is pregnant. Thirty-six, married and so of course pregnant.

Imagine if she was.

Nick goes back down to make a cup of tea. He always makes it the same way: brewed for a timed three minutes, and then the milk.

She wonders if she will miss this phase of their relationship, the crackers and cheese phase, when it's over. It will be replaced with another, she guesses: the long terrain of a marriage.

'Yeah,' Nick says quietly, walking back into the room and continuing their conversation. Izzy looks at him as he shrugs. He opens the box of crackers and passes her a knife, then she sits on the bed next to him. 'He might come looking for you,' he says, raising his eyes to hers. He's a police analyst, so his bluntness never surprises her.

'I doubt it,' she says. This is how she deals with it. A glimpsed news story – closed down. A friend asking a probing question – ignored. At least once a week, in the restaurant, in the bank, in the doctor's surgery, somebody asks her if she is *the* Isabelle English . . . she can never deny it. She is the image of her mother.

She reaches for a Hovis cracker and smothers it in butter. Nick smiles as she does it. She runs a gourmet restaurant, yet spends her time eating what Nick calls 'lovely crap'. Hovis biscuits spread with synthetic cheap margarine. Angel Delight. Chocolate coins. McDonald's on the way home. Hot dogs from a tin with a ring pull and an expiry date of four years' time. By day, she assembles artful salads with smears of balsamic vinegar across the plates. By night, she eats bite-sized chicken Kievs and wonders why on earth she owns a restaurant.

Nick avoids her gaze as he carves a slice of Wensleydale. 'It'll be what it'll be,' he says. It's one of his phrases. He puts topics to bed with these phrases. She used to think it was helpful, but she's less sure these days.

He sits back against the headboard. She had always said she wanted a bedroom like a hotel room and, after a weekend away for her birthday, she arrived home to a different room, as though she had walked into the wrong house. A high bed with a dark suede headboard, six duck-feather pillows piled up. Aubergine-coloured walls, a deep carpet. Everything. He'd done it all for her. He'd bought copper lamps from HomeSense and scented pillow spray and a leather ottoman that he placed at the bottom of the bed. And finally, she thought, looking at the hotel bed in her marital home, she felt safe. After everything that had happened, she had a home, had made herself a new family with

3

Nick, who showed her, in his own understated, indirect way, that he understood. He would not kiss her passionately after dates or confide in her late at night. But he would give her a beautiful bedroom.

And so for the first time in years she had felt happy, just for that moment. Happy and normal. Knowing that happiness was possible at all had helped her to nurture it, like a tiny germinating seed.

A spray of crumbs lands on the bed and Nick brushes them carefully into his hand and into the bin.

He pushes a triangle of Dairylea towards her and she opens it and eats it, neat, the soft cheese coating her teeth like plastic.

'But you'll tell me, if you hear anything,' she says to him, lifting her eyes to meet his. They ought to be practical, at least, and Nick will hear before she does. If her father does anything. If he causes any . . . trouble.

'Yep,' he replies softly, reaching and interlacing his fingers with hers. 'I'm not supposed to,' he adds. He knows the rules. Izzy isn't surprised: Nick is the sort of person who would buy a parking ticket on a Sunday *just to be sure*.

She gets up off the bed as she hears one of her neighbours outside. 'I'll just pop out,' she says to him.

Something akin to shame bubbles up through her as she descends the stairs. When she is running the restaurant, when she is laughing at Nick, when she is booking appointments and meeting suppliers, she is fully formed. Capable. Adult. But there are certain situations, like this one, where she regresses, where she tumbles back into something long forgotten. She can feel it happening. Nick doesn't know. Nick thinks she is relaxed. That she is whole. People at work don't know. Only she knows.

She unlocks the front door and drags the bin across the back alleyway. It's Wednesday, bin night. They live on the end of a set of four houses, isolated in Luccombe, only three miles from where Izzy grew up. The row of seventeenth-century cottages is set back from the road, and they share a flagstone access way. Bin night went from friendly nods to protracted chats to something more sociable, for Izzy's neighbours. A way to welcome the week, William said, when he rang her doorbell to ask her to join in their barbecue one night. Nick once told her that people don't do these things on the mainland. It makes sense, Izzy supposes. There are so many things the Isle of Wight is cut off from: specialist hospitals, universities, Category A prisons ... they are marooned over here, trapped with the natives, and so they engage in their own traditions.

Nick was working, so she went alone to meet the neighbours. God knows what they thought of her. Nothing, probably. But she thinks about them too much.

She hears them now as she reaches her bin. They're laughing about something, a burst of noise in the warm night. She nods to them as she wheels it past, trying not to look. Thea, Izzy's direct neighbour, is in a lightweight cardigan, flip-flops, her face showing the beginnings of a tan already.

'Busy day?' she says to Izzy. Her grey-streaked hair is held back by a single clip just by her temple.

'Yes. And you?' Izzy says with a smile. She hovers next to her, holding the warm handle of the bin. Middle-aged women are Izzy's favourite. The kind who wear sensible shoes and tunics and draped summer scarves. Who wear nice perfume and statement necklaces and arrange birthday lunches at Zizzi's with their grown-up children. These are the people that Izzy finds herself seeking out, over and over again, trying to catch hold of a memory. Something – anything. *Yes, that's right*, she will sometimes think as she talks to Thea, as she is given that most precious thing: a new, as yet unearthed, memory of her mother. A look she had once given Izzy. The way she instinctively reached down to stop her crossing the road. She is obsessed with the mothers of the world, taking perpetual care of people.

'Did you decide on the paint?' Thea asks.

'No,' Izzy says. 'Not yet. But I'm leaning towards the grey.'

'Good choice.'

Izzy nods. She wants to ask Thea to come help. They'll spend the weekend together, painting her kitchen and drinking pots of tea. But – for now – she continues to wheel the bin by them quietly and leaves it at the end of the path with theirs. She pauses again, listening to them.

'May, end of May, she'll be home, just as soon as her exams are over,' Thea is saying now, the conversation having shifted topic. 'She went to some Californian music festival instead of revising over Easter and is now stressed out of her mind. It's too hot to study, she says.'

It was warm the May Izzy's father was convicted, too. The air had the same heavy quality. 'It's a sweat box already,' she heard one of the prison van drivers say outside the court-room as they led him away wearing a suit and handcuffs. She didn't try to speak to him.

When Izzy walks back to her house, Thea has turned to William. He is holding a cup of tea and the vapour steams up his glasses as he sips.

'But then, after, she'll be back here, I expect, at least for a few years. She doesn't know what she wants to do.' Thea's smiling, her eyes crinkling, looking upwards at the sky as she thinks of her daughter coming home. 'I never knew what I wanted to do, either,' she adds. 'We can work it out. And in the meantime, she's the best company. We're both stupid at going to bed. We stay up together, buying rubbish on the internet.'

Izzy averts her eyes as she walks past. When she reaches her back door, her hand lingers on the doorknob.

She closes her eyes just briefly and stands, feeling the air on her skin. And then she allows the fantasy into her mind, as she always does at this time during the evening. Thea is her mother. She's visiting her for a short break. They've been out for pizza, shopping, the cinema. Wherever. She finds the feeling she likes, that safe, content feeling; the feeling of a cup of hot chocolate passed to her by a mother, the feeling of a log burner on a winter's day, a worn novel pressed into her hands – *you'll love this* – and enjoys it for a few minutes.

And then, of course, the guilt comes, as she thinks of her own mother, with her brilliant red hair and her huge, wide smile. Irreplaceable.

Her mother.

Murdered by Izzy's father, when Izzy was just seventeen.

After a few seconds, she goes inside. She locks the door, then checks it, just to be sure.

2

The third of May has passed as any other day would.

It is eleven thirty at night, and Izzy is hanging glasses above the bar which are hot from the dishwasher. They leave her palms pink and burning as she handles them, but she wants it done quickly so she can leave. The less time she spends at the restaurant, the better.

She never intended to end up here, running a restaurant, stuck on the Isle of Wight. But the ranks seemed to close around her after her mother's trial. The sea a moat, cutting her off from the rest of England. And the restaurant a memorial to her mother. At first it was nice to run it just as her mother had. Izzy would talk to her as she tidied up at night. Pretend her mother was helping her, sometimes – just out of sight, just out of earshot. 'Let's stick the stereo on and turn it up,' she imagined her mother saying, and Izzy would do just that.

But after a few months, it lost its shine. Her mother was gone, and Izzy was making food she didn't care about. Serving customers meals she didn't want to eat herself. Sweeping up, putting the chairs on top of the tables, putting the plates in the dishwasher. Listening to music but standing rigidly, alone. The same every night, no matter what. Even now, she manages it and cooks, just for some variety.

What does she want to do instead? The things she used to do, she supposes. Before her life derailed.

She checks her phone, which is lying on the wooden bar. Nothing from Nick. He's on a late shift tonight, so she'll pick him up on her way home. She wants chips and a battered sausage for £2.90 from the place near his work. Delicious curry sauce. The newspaper offcuts they come wrapped in. The white steaming bag that will sit on Nick's lap in the car. She looks guiltily at the sea bass leftovers she has instead. 'Not the sea bass,' Nick will say, gently mocking her. 'Not the nice, nutritious, home-made food!'

Izzy refitted the restaurant a few years after she reluctantly took it over, and changed the layout completely. The reception desk moved to the left, the cloakroom was gutted and changed into a booth. It didn't make sense this way around, but she had to do it. It couldn't have remained the same as when her mother ran it. She couldn't navigate the same route between the kitchen and the tables and the bar. Walking just like her mother. Looking just like her mother. It would have been too much, and not just for her. She ripped it all out, even though her cousin, the head chef, protested. Even though everybody asked her if it was the right thing to do.

But she has – secretly – kept so many things the same. The internal, private things. She would deny them if asked. But they are the same, deliberately so. The order in which she keeps the cutlery in the drawer: knives, forks, spoons (the only correct way). The print of the tea towels: gingham. It took her so long to find the right ones on eBay. Her mother used to keep a gingham tea towel tucked into her apron. Sometimes, Izzy catches sight of her own reflection in the windows and has to stop herself from calling out to her. Those touches that nobody else would recognize: they're just the same. She changed the layout of the restaurant to stop the gossip about the murder. But she kept the internal things for herself; to honour her mother.

Sometimes, as she reaches for a saucepan, she wonders if her mother was doing the same thing on 3rd May, nearly twenty years ago. Was she, too, sautéing onions in a pan, standing with one hand on her hip, on this exact spot, in 1999? Izzy doesn't know, can hardly remember the details before the murder, but she remembers the summer right before it. It is a memory that she has taken out and looked at so much that it has become crystalline and artificial. They were at the beach in Yarmouth for the day. One of those rare bluebird summer days when everything was dropped in search of sunshine. The beach was crowded with rainbow-coloured windbreakers and ancient-looking picnic blankets brought hastily out of airing cupboards for their annual outing. Izzy's mother had raced to the water's edge almost as soon as they got there. Izzy was seventeen and watched her, half fascinated, half embarrassed, curling in on herself. Her mother had taken her shoes and socks off and turned a cartwheel, leaving splayed impressions of her hands and feet in the sand. People were staring, but her mother didn't care. That was how she was. And she modelled it, for Izzy to be that way, too.

But then she was taken, before Izzy was fully formed.

On 31 October 1999, the night she died, was she cashing up, unknowingly for the last time? Izzy doesn't know what her mother's final movements were – nobody really does. All they know is that she went missing. Disappeared. Until she was found, of course, but by then it was far too late.

Izzy kept the restaurant name, Alexandra's, after a lot of thought. She would be recognized anyway, even if she changed it. It's because of the way she looks.

In the end, she kept it because of the sign. It had passed to her, under the terms of her mother's will. Her father, Gabriel, had painted it himself. Teal on light wood, the letters as sweeping and graceful as dancers. She remembers that the sign was laid flat on their driveway all summer when he was painting it, brought in hastily when rain started to fall. 'The sign! The sign before the washing!' he would shout. The smell of the wet grass, her feet damp, squeaking in flip-flops – it had been an exceptionally rainy summer – and the way he was always out, on the driveway, on his painting stool, by the time she got up. 'It's cooler in the mornings,' he had said to her with a smile. 'You should try it.' Her mother's cooking had become more elaborate as the wet, dreary summer went on. Her mother had been bored, Izzy guesses. Fresh blackberries baked in pies. Home-made pasta. All served up to Gabriel. Those were the ways they had loved each other. Through art and through food.

Izzy liked to observe it.

Before.

It wasn't unusual for somebody to arrive and say, 'Alexandra's: is this the one? The one where the owner was murdered?' Izzy would feel her jaw tense, and say, 'That one, yes,' wondering privately how her cartwheeling, fun-loving mother who wore the gingham tea towel and had belonged only to Izzy and Gabriel had become something so gruesome and public. They are voyeurs, but she would be the same, if it hadn't happened to her, she guesses. It's hard to know what it would be like to grow up without a macabre past.

It's silent now in the restaurant. One of the glasses is still swinging on the rack where she has just hung it, and its reflection catches the overhead lamp, scattering chinks of light over the bar as it moves.

As she lifts her head to look for her handbag, a peculiar feeling settles over her. A not-alone feeling. She listens intently to the silence, wondering at the small knot forming in her stomach, at the sensation of a gaze on her skin.

She looks at the windows. They're curtain-less, bare. From the outside, everybody can see everything she is doing, lit up, inside, alone; a moving doll in a doll's house. She's never thought of that before. Goosebumps break out over her shoulders and neck.

She stares at a movement in the window. A tree, a dog walker, a waiting taxi with its indicator blinking, her brain suggests. But Izzy knows exactly who it is.

There he is, his face pressed to one of the small Georgian windows. She would recognize him anywhere, even after eighteen years. The swarthy skin, sallow-looking unless he was on holiday. The heavy-lidded dark eyes.

She feels fear bloom across her chest. Her body tenses. It is 3rd May, the exact date she was informed he was to be released, and here he is, like clockwork. Of course he is. She didn't change the name of the restaurant: it is obvious it is Izzy managing it. It would have been simple for him to find her, laughably so. She has always known it might happen, theoretically. But it was easy to take a risk when he was still imprisoned. And it was so very easy to do nothing upon his release.

The door is unlocked. Adrenaline fizzes in her arms and legs as she realizes. Her only thought is that she needs to get across the restaurant to secure the lock.

But she can't move. She is frozen, staring at her father's face in the glass.

Her mind is a snowstorm of bad memories. Her grandmother saying to the newspaper reporter during the trial, 'He's as guilty as sin.' Overheard snippets about her mother's injuries, her *remains*. The forensics reports. The evidence against her father. An open and shut case. A condemned man, sentenced to life, led away in handcuffs that caught the sunlight like diamonds.

After everything, when she had gone to live with her grandparents, they had warned her that he would do this one day. She looked just like her mother, her grandmother said tearfully to her one night. The same red hair. The same pale skin. She should change her name, they said. Move away. He might come back for her. But she had never changed anything, had never wanted to. Here she is, not even hiding, in plain sight. And here he is, released from prison today and watching her through the window.

At last, she meets his eyes. She can't help it. There is something natural about it, like a plant turning towards the sun. His eyes crinkle ever so slightly – is he *smiling*? Izzy's mouth falls open in shock. Here she is, being greeted politely by a murderer.

Other memories crowd in. She thinks of the red bicycle he used to own, the way he joyfully commuted everywhere on it. She thinks of his myriad sporting hobbies, the way it was rare to have a conversation without him tossing a tennis ball up and down, or bouncing it on the tiled kitchen floor.

She thinks of the way they watched every single episode of *Dawson's Creek* together, the year she turned sixteen, when she should have been revising for her exams, their knees tucked up on the sofa, the ragged tartan blanket shared between them.

Later that same summer, he had whooped and swung her around on her GCSE results day. 'I only got Bs!' she'd laughingly said. 'Your Bs are perfection to me,' he had said, as excited as she was. There was no dampening of it. No dismissing of her teenage emotions. Just joy.

He must see her expression, because he steps backwards, and now she can see his face and upper body framed in the window, his arms raised up in a gesture of defeat. No, not defeat. A gesture of peace. *I mean no harm*, he is saying, palms to her. She stares and stares at him. His aged figure is skinny under his coat. Cheekbones protruding. Hair greyed out, as if he used to be in colour and is now in monochrome.

A second later, a letter slides through the box in the navy-blue front door. She looks at the white envelope caught in the bristles, still warm, no doubt, from his touch.

After a few seconds, she advances towards it, locking the door before she takes the letter. She hesitates, but she knows she will open it. The worst has already happened to her, when she was seventeen. So why not?

She peers out of the tiny window at the top of the door. The street is empty. She recalls his gesture, and she knows instinctively that he won't try to come inside, that he won't be waiting anywhere. But how can she know that? She thought her father would never have murdered her mother . . . and how wrong she was.

She stands by the locked door, hands shaking as she tears at the envelope, and begins to read.

3

She keeps her phone in her hand, fingers poised to dial, as she grapples with the locks on the front door of the restaurant. She's amazed at herself, at her lack of preparation for an inevitability she was in deep denial about. She is good at denial. Too good. She has never once read about his trial. Never even heard him out. She didn't need to. The evidence against him has surrounded her like smoke; she's breathed it in even as she's tried to ignore it. Her father's police interview. The DNA. The last text message he sent to her mother. Where and how she was found.

She drives to Nick's work too quickly, the street lights blurring around her like a long-exposure photograph.

Once in the car park, she catches her own eye in the rearview mirror. She had never realized how much she looks like him, having not seen him since she reached adulthood herself. Her grandparents took down every photograph of him. The ones Izzy kept are hidden away in her attic. Out of sight, out of mind.

Everybody has always commented on how much she resembles her mother – the long red hair, the green eyes – but the rest of her is her father. High cheekbones. Skinny, long limbs. She is half of him. At least, she hopes she is *only* half him. She thinks of the cross words she had with one of the waitresses recently, of the surge of rage she felt when another had called in sick. Was that normal? What if she is . . . ? No. She won't let herself think it. She is not like him. She is good: she tries to be good.

She gets out of her car and walks towards the lit-up entrance to the police station. She looks over her shoulder, just once, then pushes the door open. The metal handle is warm in the heatwave.

It is only once she's inside that she realizes: she hasn't looked over her shoulder like that for years.

She hasn't yet told Nick about the letter. It has always seemed to Izzy – on first dates before she met and married Nick, and upon being introduced to people – that if she says it out loud, it will be more true, somehow. *My father murdered my mother. He's doing time.* That is the way she says it, if she chooses to. Dispassionate and clear. But the older she gets – when surely she should be beginning to process it? – the easier she finds it to keep secrets, even from herself. She simply pretends. She pretends all sorts of things. She pretends Thea is her mother. She pretends she has two brothers, that they live abroad but that they're there for her, just like Nick and his family WhatsApp group. And, more than anything, she pretends that her father didn't kill her mother. And, if she ever gets angry, or annoyed, she pretends that this doesn't mean anything. That she doesn't have a temper. Because she *doesn't*. She knows that. But maybe her father thought he knew that too?

Actually, he came by tonight, she practises as she meets Nick in the reception of the police station.

He crosses the foyer to her, gives her a distracted kiss on the top of her head, and takes her hand. 'Do you have leftovers?' he says to her. He is well trained to expect leftovers. Sometimes, she wishes he wouldn't ask. That he would say,

'Fancy a pizza?' on the way home, instead. It's unfair on him, she knows. She has always appreciated his solid nature, his routines and his rules.

Perhaps if he hadn't asked about the leftovers, she might've told him. Two roads diverge in front of her, and she takes the easy one: something she and Nick often do. 'I was just thinking about chips,' she says instead. They walk three paces to the door.

Headspace, she decides. She'll give herself some headspace, and speak to him later.

But by the time she has decided to throw the sea bass away, and she has asked about his day – 'Nothing, just a series of tedious driving offences to look into' – it is too late. Time up. She can't bring herself to say anything. Nick would be astonished it wasn't the first thing she said, and so . . . the moment passes, like a train rushing through a station.

Nick puts his phone on the arm of the sofa when they walk in. The screen is intermittently lighting up and darkening again. Nick's sisters and parents text all day long. Photos of pets and children and the quote of the day signs on the London Underground. Nick hardly ever responds, but reads every single message almost the second it comes through. Izzy is waiting to be asked to join.

She can only imagine how the conversation would play out with his family if they knew about the letter. *Can you believe it???* Robyn would say. Dani would respond with a string of shocked emojis.

Izzy looks around her at their tiny cottage, not even big enough for a hallway. They bought it two years ago, having sold their terraced house too quickly, an offer within forty-eight hours. 'Oh shit,' Izzy had said when they accepted the asking price.

'It's fine,' Nick had said with a wave of his hand. 'It'll focus our minds.'

He drew a map on Rightmove, set up the filters: three beds. 'You know, just in case,' he'd said with a hopeful smile. Izzy had ignored him. She always does. Motherhood is fast approaching her, in her mid-thirties already, and she is not prepared for it. Her own father murdered her mother. How can she step into a parental role with such an ugly, gaping wound in her past? Victim and villain play out in her mind whenever she thinks of it. What if there's something awful running through her core, just like in her father, and parenthood – and all its stressors – exposes it?

They had spent their Saturdays viewing properties. Izzy was easily swayed by a granite kitchen, a well-placed skylight. 'No, focus!' Nick would laugh. 'It's on a massive road.' Or, 'No way! A notorious burglar lives near here.'

They'd been searching for four months, their buyers sending increasingly frustrated solicitor's letters, when they drove by the cottage in Luccombe. A home-made wooden sign stood in the garden, pointing at an angle. 'For SALE' it read, in shaky felt-tip pen. A mobile number was listed. Nick slowed the car, and Izzy looked across at him.

'We could just ring the bell,' she said, looking at the cottage's pink exterior, at the climbing wisteria, at the lamp-lit windows on the first floor.

'Flip you for it,' Nick said with a grin. It is exactly the sort of solution he suggests: something dispassionate, fair, logical. He was already angling his body, grabbing a pound coin out of the pocket of his jeans. 'Call it.'

'Heads.'

'Tails. Bad luck,' Nick said. He reached over and unlocked her door, then pointed to the house. 'Go and English them up.'

Izzy had blushed with pleasure. She loved how he had taken her surname — such a sullied name, marred by the media, the courtroom, her father — and made it light again. *English them up.* Just like her brave, hard-working, fearless mother.

The owner let her in, and Izzy turned and beckoned Nick inside. Before they'd seen the kitchen, before they'd been upstairs, Izzy said, 'I want to buy your house.'

During the conveyancing process, the seller became aware of *who Izzy was* but, luckily, didn't mention it. But as Izzy moved in and she moved out, Izzy felt her curious eyes appraising her. The island was divided into the natives who knew, and the tourists who had no idea about red-headed Alex English and her daughter. Izzy could spot a native a mile away.

She closes the door of the tiny coat cupboard now. There are so many impractical things about their cottage — the low ceilings, the uneven floor in the bathroom — but she doesn't care. She puts her shoes in the rack that they've had to squeeze in underneath the bay window. Nick has started his chips, perched on the arm of the sofa, using the wooden fork. As she looks at him, she thinks of the letter.

They said I was guilty. The press. Your mother's parents. The lawyers and the jury. And they no doubt told you that, too. But have you ever examined it for yourself?

I want to tell you my side of it.

Izzy had blinked. He was guilty. Of course he was. He had been arrested, charged and convicted. There was no doubt. That was the point: beyond reasonable doubt.

19

But . . . he knew her so well. Nearly twenty years on. Even just in a letter. He knew that she had not read about it. That she had kept it in a box in her mind.

By the time his trial rolled around, she had been living with her mother's parents for several months. Stilted, 1970s-style meals. Conversations that began and were snuffed out almost immediately like candles that failed to ignite. Sentences left hanging.

They drove her to his trial in their car on the day she was called to give evidence. She took a flask of coffee with her. Izzy is a believer in things like this: small pleasures, even when life is hard. Like little pinpricks of light in a dark sky. A hot cup of coffee every morning got her through those early days. Each morning coffee signalled another day done. One more step towards . . . something better, she supposed. She hoped.

The newspapers had speculated about how she had arrived with her mother's parents, what it meant. She had taken sides, they said. But she hadn't. Not by then. And maybe she never did, not explicitly, anyway. She just did what she had to do to get through those intervening years, behaving passively. She accepted his guilt stoically, like a child taking a spoonful of medicine every day. She didn't think about it, didn't question anything, looked forward each morning to her Mellow Bird's coffee with its four sugars and didn't realize, along the way, twenty coffees later, thirty, one hundred, one thousand, that, in not choosing, in doing nothing, she had chosen.

Let me tell you this, Izzy: I am innocent. It is not just something I said to try and get out of a prison sentence. Not a tale some lawyer spun.

The truth is, I didn't do it. I swear to you, Izzy, it wasn't me.

He had written out a mobile number. At first, she thought it was his. But then she read the text, looped carefully across the page, right along the fold of the paper.

Speak to the person who knows me best. I know you won't want to be alone with me. But maybe you can speak to him?

Paul Wakefield. Her father's best friend. Izzy hasn't heard the name for eighteen years. Paul used to call her father Tin Cup. It was a long-standing joke between them that Izzy had never understood. He was forever letting himself into their house, two tennis rackets held in one hand. 'Yes, Gabe can play out,' her mother once said laughingly. But she had always liked Paul, Izzy thought. He would help her with the company accounts, sometimes, late at night. They'd have a bottle of red.

Paul. With his steady job as an engineer, his little family, his holidays to the Costa Del Sol and to Disneyland. His whole, full, functional life. His own mind. His own judgement.

And he thinks her father is innocent. If he can . . . could she?

4

Another letter comes the next day. It is waiting for her when she arrives at the restaurant. A white envelope. Hand delivered, bearing her name on the front.

It is only one line long:

I promise, you won't regret speaking to Paul.

Izzy sighs as she folds it up and puts it in her pocket. Her instinct is to shy away from it, she thinks, as she slices a celeriac. Even when she tries to make her mind consider her father's guilt, it veers away from it, like two magnets automatically repelling each other. Eventually, years ago, she stopped trying.

She looks through the door and out into the foyer of the restaurant. She can hear two customers. 'Was she actually murdered *here*?' one says to the other, gazing around her. Izzy peers out at them. Locals. She can tell immediately. No rucksacks. No walking shoes.

Izzy looks back down at the knife in her hand, wishing she was somewhere else. Somewhere anonymous.

Three more letters appear over the next three days.

The first says:

Humour a man who's lost everything?

And the final one says just:

Please?

Izzy hesitates as she holds the final letter. *Please?* She folds it and catches something. A scent, maybe. A memory. Nothing concrete that she can latch on to, but something. Her father's broad smile. The way his eyes crinkled. The way he'd say, 'Fetch me a beer, will you?' to her, and she felt so grown up as she wrestled with the bottle opener while he waited patiently. But it's mostly just the smile. That's all.

Something bubbles up inside her in response to it. It's not hope, exactly. It's too premature to call it that. But it is *something*. A desire to take action, to do something. To break free of the routines and the island. To dare.

She'll speak to Paul. Only Paul. Not her father. There's no harm in it, she reasons as her hands shake. She keys in his number carefully, standing there in the restaurant where her mother once stood.

She leaps.

Nick notices that she is leaving early, as she expected he would.

'It's ten,' he says. There's no question in his voice, no concern on his face as he sips a coffee. He's just making an observation.

Izzy feels an unexpected flare of irritation rise up through her. Nick goes to work, comes home, eats dinner, and goes to bed. Sometimes, he sees his family. There are occasional parties, trips across the Solent to London that they have to plan

23

for. The ferry. The train afterwards. And she used to like that. That they were sequestered here, on the island, safe. The island that had seldom experienced murders. Until her mother. They had their routines here, safely hemmed in by the sea on all sides. Nick didn't need anything more, and that suited her as she rebuilt her life.

But now . . . today. About to see her father's best friend, she feels differently.

Nick's made her a coffee, which he proffers to her, his eyebrows raised. 'Mellow Bird's. Four sugars,' he says with a smile. He makes her the same drink each morning.

'I'm going to go shopping before work.' She shrugs, taking a few gulps of the hot coffee and putting her jacket on, even though she doesn't really need it in the warm weather. Acting casually is the best way, she decides.

'Okay,' he says. A faint frown crosses his features.

She doesn't often do this: go out alone. Even if people don't know who she is, she misinterprets their glances. The interested expressions that cross the shopkeepers' faces as they see the name on her debit card. *Everyone knows*, she finds herself thinking when out. Every shopkeeper. Every hairdresser. *They all know.*

It's amazing how Nick doesn't realize. How she can open herself so fully to him, late at night, lying on their big hotel bed, and tell him everything, and how she can now keep something so secret, and he has no idea; is unable to distinguish between the two. Nobody can, she supposes.

She thinks immediately, as she often does, of her father and the things he must have kept from her during the days when he was planning to murder her mother. Is she foolish to start to investigate? To be sucked in by a liar? She doesn't think so, but she doesn't know. And there's nobody she can ask. Even this man, standing in front of her, with complete access to everything her father has done.

'That's really nice,' Nick says. 'Good.' He smiles at her; a warm, genuine smile. He's glad she's getting out. She feels a fizz of pleasure in her stomach for this easy, kind man who wants the best for her.

'Have you ever looked my dad up?' she says to Nick.

He stares at her in surprise, his coffee cup halfway to his lips. 'Where?'

'On your systems, at work.'

He looks away, his mouth turned down, then straight back at her. 'No,' he says.

'But you could access his file . . . ?' She tails off. She knows it's unfair of her to ask. 'No, of course not,' she says to him as she pours the coffee into a flask.

He helps her, steadying the flask, his hand warm on her own.

It's a forty-minute drive west to Yarmouth, right across the island. Izzy loves how the character of the Isle of Wight changes, even by driving only a few miles. From the ancient-feeling woodland of Luccombe, to Yarmouth's pretty harbour, the lamp posts decorated with garlands of flowers. The air down here is fresh, despite the warmth of the sun, and smells of fish and salt. By the time she reaches the coast, the radio is saying it could be set to be the hottest early May on record. She listens, looking forward to the summer and the influx of *grockles*: the tourists who line the streets along the coast. Who hover around postcard stands and ensure corner shops stock less food and more Isle of Wight mugs, sticks of rock and tacky ornaments. Izzy prefers the natives to be diluted by the tourists: there is less chance, then, that somebody she meets will know who she is. She can move more freely across the beaches during the summer months, sand between her toes.

Paul has moved house, and he now lives in a Georgian semi on a quiet cul-de-sac. As he opens his door, her mind is suddenly crowded with memories. A picnic with their combined families on a village green one summer day. Izzy doesn't know why she remembers it, but she does. Paul had brought a cool bag full of cider, and Gabe had said, 'My kind of picnic.'

She remembers Paul turning steaks, standing under cover on the patio as it rained July rain. She remembers him taking them all out on his boat, at Nettlecombe Farm Lake, Izzy trailing a hand in the cold water which parted effortlessly around her fingertips. And here he is. The same blue eyes, the same full, round face. But his hair is white and there is a curve just at the top of his spine: the beginning of old age.

'Come on in,' Paul says with an understanding smile, and she's grateful for that: his warm greeting, in the coldest of circumstances.

He leads her into an old-fashioned, large living room. *A family home*, Izzy thinks, as she looks around. A teapot sits on the dark wood coffee table. The green carpet is freshly hoovered; Izzy can see the markings. A large family photo collage sits on the mantelpiece. One of his daughters' weddings. She resists the urge to go and pick it up and study it.

This is what she misses. She had the childhood, but it's this: the infrastructure of family life, in adulthood. Family doesn't end at eighteen. Izzy imagines her parents having attended her own wedding to Nick a few years back. Gabe would have liked the ceremony, even though Nick didn't want to deviate from the traditional vows. Her mother would have hit the dancefloor before anybody. She was like that: unapologetic about who she was. A great cook. A great dancer. The proprietress of Alexandra's. A fully rounded woman, Izzy supposes.

'Everybody's out,' Paul says to her, raising his eyebrows.

Izzy wonders how to say it. How to tell him. After a second's hesitation, she decides to plunge right in. 'My father has been writing to me,' she says, then swallows. She is circling the closed box where the case sits, unopened in her mind. The basics went in but, after that, Izzy shut it.

On Hallowe'en, 1999, her mother received a call to say her car – in for service – wouldn't be ready. She told a waitress she was going to take a taxi home from the restaurant because she figured Gabe would have been drinking. The taxi driver gave evidence to say she entered the house. That night, Gabe reported her missing. He didn't know she hadn't driven home, that there was a witness. She never came home, he said. Izzy was at her boyfriend Pip's, oblivious. Two days later, her mother's remains were recovered.

That is the story.

'What is he saying?' Paul says. He leans back on his blue sofa and crosses his legs at the ankles.

'He is saying that –' Izzy swallows. 'He is saying that he is innocent.'

Paul merely nods. There's no shock. No derision or doubt. And that's all it takes for Izzy to open the box. Just a crack. Just to look inside.

Could it be?

Her father murdered her mother. He was waiting for her. He had already threatened her once. These have been facts to Izzy for almost twenty years. The ferry leaves the island at five past the hour. There is always at least one T-shirt day in March. And her father murdered her mother. They're just facts.

But what if this one isn't?

'Do you believe him?' Izzy says, not quite able to believe she's truly here, opposite her father's best friend. The ground seems to move underneath her. What if she's been wrong? Is there any chance?

'Yes. I do. Because ... because I know him, I guess,' Paul says. He looks so relaxed, one arm along the back of the sofa, his eyes on her. 'And because the evidence was circumstantial.'

'Was it?' she says.

'Some of it.' He makes a gesture like weighing scales, then lets his hands fall back on to the sofa. He pauses, still looking at her. 'I'm surprised you're here,' he says.

'I ...' she starts, then stops. How can she explain it? 'Would you believe me if I said I'd really never thought about whether or not he is guilty?' she says.

Paul's expression opens, his eyebrows rising, his mouth parting slightly in understanding. 'I see,' he says slowly, fiddling briefly with his wedding ring. 'Yes, I would believe that. You.'

'And now it's – I don't know. I wonder if ... should I hear him out? Is it safe to?'

'You should do whatever you want to do,' Paul says. 'There's no rule book. I'm meeting him next Wednesday. We're playing pool. He says he got real good in prison.' He offers her a hot drink and disappears into the kitchen to make it. She can see his form moving behind a set of frosted glass doors.

Izzy thinks about what she wants to do. About what she believes. She casts about inside herself, but all she can find is other people's opinions. What does *she* think? Who is her father, really? What is the truth? To answer those questions seems to require impossible reserves that she can't find. Her cheeks heat up.

Unbidden, an image of her father being led into a Serco prison van with tiny blacked-out portholes lining its sides pops into her mind. She only attended the trial to give her evidence, and again on the final day, to see his sentencing. She stood on the pavement and watched the prison van drive away. From there, her father would go to HMP Belmarsh to begin his life sentence.

She closes her eyes as she remembers him. Swarthy arms, even though he had been in prison for months already. Black hair, just a few streaks of grey. His tall, rangy form that seemed always to have so much energy. His constant action. Hitting a tennis ball against the wall of the house while on hold to an insurance company. The way he'd race her to peg all of the laundry out in record time. An impromptu game of rounders on a summer Sunday night, the thwack of the ball against the bat, running through evening clouds of mosquitoes and through cut, sun-dried grass.

He appeared on the local news after his first police interview. His final days of freedom. Those messy days, those two days of purgatory, when her mother was missing and not yet found. He looked at the camera and said, 'No, I am not under suspicion.' His wedding ring caught the autumn sunlight as he waved his hand. His eyes flashed, the whites bright against his tanned skin.

'I often thought about Gabe's side of it,' Paul says as he arrives back in the living room, handing her a cup of coffee. His tea slops over the side of his mug as he sits down, and he grins and rubs at the spillage on the sofa. 'I'll get bollocked for that later, no doubt,' he says. 'Jane bought this sofa from some reclamation yard. She wipes it every night. It's practically her pet.'

But Izzy's not listening. She's thinking: *Gabe*. Everybody called him that. Even Izzy, by the time she was sixteen. 'I'm Gabe, and you're Iz,' Gabe once said to her. 'And we're the best of friends.'

'Anyway,' Paul says with a sad smile. 'I felt like, if only they could find that alibi . . . his acquittal would follow.'

Izzy feels cold with shock. 'What alibi?'

'The neighbour.'

'Who?' she asks.

'The one who was working casually for the summer. Windsurfing instructor? Or something. Moved right after your . . . after it happened. That was always the biggest part of Gabe's defence.'

Light is creeping, dawning, in the back of Izzy's mind. She remembers something . . . the neighbour. The police interview.

'What was his name?'

'David Smith? He talks about him often. Even now.'

Izzy spoke to the police during the two days when her mother was missing. 'So your father said that you left the restaurant that night at ten to go to your boyfriend, er . . .' the policeman consulted his pad, 'Pip's.'

'Yes.'

'He says that he spoke to a neighbour that night. David Smith.'

'David Smith?' Izzy said.

He'd said goodbye to her several days ago. 'See you,' he'd said casually, walking backwards down his drive to his removal van as she was coming home from school. She'd watched his back muscles flex as he hefted a box of books.

The van was already packed, and he had to nudge a chair to make the box fit.

'But he's moved.'

'We thought as much,' the policeman said, making a brief note. Then, his voice suddenly serious, 'When did he move? Your father is adamant they spoke. He said you'd vouch for that.'

She felt her mouth slacken in shock. An alibi. Her father was constructing an alibi. She had read about them, watched crime dramas featuring them, and here was her father, in the wake of her mother's death, asking her to corroborate his – in this, the most indirect of ways.

'When did Dad say this?'

'In his initial interview . . . yesterday.'

Izzy blinked. 'No – David . . . he moved.' Izzy had seen the removal van drive off. One of the doors hadn't quite closed because of all of his stuff. It had flapped as he drove down their street.

Izzy stared at the wooden table, overcome by the very particular feeling of having had a significant life moment without even realizing it.

As she left, she turned to the policeman. 'You won't tell him I told you the truth about David, will you?' she said.

'No. We won't. Don't worry,' he said.

She nodded. Surely her father was mistaken? At the time, she had hardly thought anything of it. The police were just following all lines of enquiry.

But then her mother was found.

Izzy stares straight ahead now, thinking of that alibi. She wishes, looking back, that she had understood much sooner. But the policeman's casual tone, his presumption, had fooled her, just for a moment.

'I looked into it a bit. David's tenancy ended on the first of November,' Paul says, running his finger over the rim of his mug. 'So the defence team thought he might've been there that night. They really tried so hard to trace him. But it was tough then. No Facebook, you know?'

'Yes,' Izzy says, her voice barely above a whisper.

What if . . . God, what if she was wrong? What if it hadn't been his final trip? What if David Smith actually moved out several days later?

The main part of his defence. And Izzy . . . she decimated that alibi. Did her father know? Is that why he has directed her to Paul? Not to protest his innocence but to let her know that he knows?

She shivers with the sinister thought. Surely not.

'The police were pretty sure your mother died that evening. The pathologist gave a window of between eleven and the early hours of the morning. Gabe says he was talking to David Smith for part of the evening and that David would be able to verify, because he was packing his van, that your dad didn't go anywhere at all. If only they could find him.'

Izzy sits, stunned, staring at Paul.

An alibi. Something to eradicate the doubt. What if her father had one? It is as though another door has opened, letting in just a chink of light. Could it be?

David Smith must be one of the most common names in the UK. But what if she could find him, and he could confirm he did talk to her father that night? It would change everything. Absolutely everything.

Where is he now? Would he even remember? She supposes not. Maybe he doesn't even know. The murder wasn't national news. If he left the island, he might never have heard about it.

They arrested her father two days after her mother went missing, within hours of discovering her body. Gabe never told her himself. She found out from the police. Her mother had been found. She had been murdered. Izzy's father was arrested at the scene. Even now, today, she still can't think about where and how her mother was found.

Izzy gleaned from overheard snatches of her grandparents' conversation that the prosecution at the trial had run parallel arguments against her father: both that he had planned to murder her mother and that it was a crime of passion. They moved fluidly between them, twisting, it seemed to Izzy, the facts to meet each. It didn't matter to them which was true: it was clear he had done it. It was clear to everybody that he had done it. The evidence against him was overwhelming. The jury had looked bored when she was cross-examined, their eyes on her but not looking, not really.

But what if . . . what if there is a different story? Another story? *One he has had eighteen years to concoct*, Nick would say, but Izzy doesn't agree.

That very first contact her father has made with her has opened up the door to something. To doubt. That's all. Just doubt.

Reasonable doubt.

5

Only her cousin, Chris, is still here in the restaurant with Izzy, stacking the dishwasher. It's late and her eyes are tired.

'How's things, anyway?' Chris says, his head bent as he stacks the plates in identical neat rows. 'Hardly seen you.' He is broadly set but meticulous, an easy multitasker. The perfect chef.

Chris's presence, to her, is the most companionable of anyone's, because he never asks anything of her. They used to sit together in silence against the apple tree outside the restaurant when they were teenagers, the one she'd had cut down five years ago. Then they were housemates for a few years in their twenties. Even now, they can wash up for an hour and say nothing, or talk non-stop. There is no bullshit, no tricky conversations: her apple-tree friend.

Their fathers are brothers. Estranged, of course; her father is estranged from everybody. There is just the faintest trace of Gabriel in Chris: skin that tans easily, something about the set of his jaw, the same distance between his eyes. You would never spot it if you weren't looking for it, but Izzy is. He moves with the same sort of energy, washing up and putting away, and prepping for tomorrow. His phone is on the counter. He's always recording his cooking on Instagram Stories. He likes social media unabashedly. Izzy will tease him about it, but he won't rise to it, is so assured that he doesn't even defend himself. When the restaurant's business boomed because of his Instagram following, he said nothing.

'Do you ever think about my father?' Izzy says impulsively, leaning her elbows on the table. Her mother used to do exactly this, she can remember it so clearly – pale arms folded upwards, face cupped in hands – and so she shifts position. What would her mother think of her trip to Paul's this morning? She was one of life's hard workers, a go-getter, so maybe she'd be proud of Izzy going forth and getting answers, finally. 'Don't just ignore it!' she would shout up the stairs when Izzy had received poor feedback, failed tests, handed in below average coursework. She had tried to teach Izzy, again and again, about facing up to things, but then she had died before Izzy had properly learnt.

Chris's movements don't stop, but his cheeks redden underneath his dark beard. 'Sometimes,' he says. He's wearing navy-blue Crocs, and they squeak on the floor as he moves. 'Yeah, sometimes,' he says with a little nod of his head. He rubs at his beard and then scrapes a plate into the bin.

'Me too,' she says. She appraises him as he rinses the plate, the water frothing over its surface.

'Especially at the moment,' he adds, darting a glance at her.

Izzy and Chris went to get their GCSE results together in the rain twenty years ago. She was wearing flared jeans that the damp rose up through. 'Nice seventies vibe,' her cousin had said immediately as he opened the door.

Her uncle Tony was behind Chris. 'Make sure he tells us his grades before he goes on the lash,' he'd said.

Izzy had liked that. Tony had always treated them as equals: adults entitled to celebrate, to commiserate; not teenagers deserving of admonishment. Even now, he works shifts at her restaurant and defers entirely to her seniority. He never pulls rank, or tells her what her mother would have done. The only thing he asked was never to work mornings – he's retired, and now a night owl – and Izzy has been happy to oblige. She prefers to work the same shifts each week: Wednesday through to Sunday, lunchtime and evenings. On working days, she eats cheese with Nick late at night in bed. She hates her job, but she likes the steadiness of the working week. And, luckily, Nick does too. When they're off, they're rudderless, meandering, wondering what to do.

'What do you want to do after?' Chris had said that day, as they walked together in the August drizzle. Her feet squeaked in her rubber flip-flops on his quiet street.

'Depends how good our results are.'

'No, let's do something cool, whatever they are,' he said.

'I want to go and sit in McDonald's and eat rubbish,' Izzy said honestly.

'I get it,' Chris said immediately.

She never got to do these things. She went to ballet school every Saturday, and on Tuesday, Thursday and Friday evenings. She was never idle, and nor would she eat rubbish. Her mother wouldn't let her. She was one of the most active people Izzy knew. She slept little, worked a lot. Never moaned, either. Izzy sometimes tries to channel her now, late at night in the restaurant when she is tired and feeling lazy, but her mother resolutely won't come.

'Then we'll do that,' Chris had said simply. That was how he was, too: mellow, willing to do whatever. Easy company, her cousin.

When she looks back up at him now he is staring at her, a

serious expression on his face. That look that says he understands her.

'What?' she asks.

'He'll come here,' Chris says simply. He stops what he's doing and stands there, looking at her, holding a plate in one hand, down by his side. 'You know he will.'

The memory of that rainy day they collected their GCSE results fades from her mind as she remembers everything that came after it: the murder trial, forensic reports, the appeal, headlines about their family. Their quiet suburban life, their family business: decimated. By what? By reporters. Police cordons. Crime Scene Investigators.

And murder.

'I doubt that,' she says vaguely.

Let's not talk of this, she thinks. *Let's just ignore it. Put it back in the box.* Why doesn't she tell him? She casts about inside herself, looking for the answer. Eventually, she stumbles upon it: it is because she doesn't want to be dissuaded. She wants to find out for herself. Finally. To find her own voice, amongst all of the others. She wants to *hope*.

She locks up with Chris a little later, after eleven. And even though she has company, she still checks over her shoulder. Now that Gabe is out, and she has seen him, she looks for him everywhere. Is she looking out of hope or fear? She doesn't know. She wants to see him, and she doesn't want to see him, all at once. A man on the street outside Tesco had his gait – his energetic walk from her childhood – but wasn't tall enough. Another man had his exact build, but blond hair. But Gabe, the real Gabe, stays respectfully away.

'I can't believe it's arrived. The day he's out. I sort of thought it would never happen,' Chris says as they walk across the car park. He has hay fever; his nose is red, and he rubs at it.

'I know,' she says. 'Eighteen years. It seemed endless then.'

Izzy shivers now in the warm air by Chris's car. He's unlocking it, the lights flashing and turning the bushes an amber hue, but he hasn't opened the door yet.

'It's amazing how much of the trial I remember,' he says, turning to her. He sneezes and gets a packet of tissues out of his pocket. 'Bastarding hay fever.'

Izzy looks down at her trainers, avoiding his gaze. The trial. Her father's police interview. Her mother's injuries . . . nausea rises up through her. She tries to swallow it down, to look at it dispassionately and, suddenly, she's sad for all the years she's spent in denial, not opening the box, not examining it. Because she doesn't know. She knows the basics, but none of the nuances.

'I almost wish I'd gone,' she says.

Chris looks at her in surprise. 'Why?' he asks. 'Trust me, you don't.'

'Because . . . because I don't really know why he was convicted.'

Chris kicks a tiny piece of gravel, sending it skittering into the undergrowth. They're totally alone out here. That's how the island is in the off season. Isolated. Izzy has a constant stream of waiters and waitresses who've moved out here alone. They're escaping things, she often thinks. They move on again after a few months, never making friends, never putting down roots. It seems amazing, to Izzy, that people come here to escape, when the worst happened to her here, but they do.

'Because he did it,' Chris says.

'Are you certain?'

Izzy's words seem to echo around them in the car park. She shivers as a gust of ocean air blows in.

'What?' Chris says, but it comes out as more of a guffaw. '*What?*'

'Like, do you ever think they might've got it wrong?'

Chris stares at her, a tissue clutched around his nose. 'You're serious?'

'Just theorizing,' she says.

Chris eyebrows are up near his hairline. He brings a hand down over his beard and rubs at it, then shakes his head, folding the tissue and putting it into a nearby bin. He takes his time over it, his eyes widening then narrowing as he thinks about what to say to her.

'Well, anyway, what do you think twenty years inside has done to him?' he says eventually.

'I don't know.'

He looks at her, saying nothing. 'Jeez,' he says, shaking his head. 'You always did surprise me.'

'Quiet. I'm your boss,' she says, trying to dispel the mood, but it doesn't work.

She can sense Chris is about to get into his car, to say, '*Anyway . . .*' and pull his keys back out of his pocket, but suddenly, he speaks again. 'It was one of the easiest murder prosecutions. That's what they said.'

She doesn't mind that Chris talks bluntly to her. She grew tired of the euphemisms her grandparents would use: 'since her passing', 'since he took her from us', 'since he went away'.

The details are drifting back to her like snowflakes. Pieced together from news stories she was unable to avoid, overheard conversations, things mentioned incidentally, years afterwards.

The Crown Prosecution Service's arguments.

A passionate relationship.

There was passion, wasn't there? She blinks and remembers coming home from a New Year's Eve party in 1998 – her mother was unknowingly entering the final year of her life – and interrupting them in the kitchen. They weren't kissing. What she interrupted was far more intimate.

'I think it's because your hair's stayed red, no greys,' her father was saying to her mother. His hips were close to hers, the two of them a blurred shadow in the corner of the kitchen. 'No, wait, it could be because you own more shoes than anyone I know . . . it truly is *incredible.*'

Her mother had her head back, Izzy realized, as her eyes adjusted to the dimness. Her throat was white, exposed. She was laughing. 'Let me count the ways,' her mother said sardonically, and her father laughed too. 'Maybe it's because I wash your underwear for you. Pay your bills.'

Her father's laughter intensified, and Izzy had slipped away. They had loved each other so much. It had been a source of comfort to her, her parents' marriage, like solid bedrock beneath her feet. But, apparently, it was poisonous. She had no idea, and she lived with them. What if Izzy's own marriage is? What if – one day – she lashes out, loses her temper? What if Nick does? How can anybody be sure?

A controlling relationship.

Her father liked to drop her mother places. 'I'll just wait for you,' he would often say when he insisted on taking her to her evening yoga class. 'I'll just wait.' It wasn't sinister: he was happy to idle. He always said it was when he was doing nothing that he had his best ideas. Izzy and Gabe used to go out, often late at night, to pick her up. She remembers their shared singalongs in the car. They both liked soft rock.

American rock. She introduced him to the Goo Goo Dolls. He played her the Eagles. Why were they doing that? They had two cars. Why couldn't her mother drive herself home?

She tries to view the memory with an adult's eyes, but can't. She can't make sense of it. It is like looking the wrong way down a telescope. What was normal then has informed what she views as normal now. A close marriage seems usual to her. But so, too, does tragedy. How can she possibly look back at their relationship without thinking about everything that happened afterwards?

Charm.

Her father was perfectly beguiling; he always was. Even his letter, written on plain A4 paper, the handwriting looped and childlike, has forced her to take action, to go and see Paul, to begin examining the evidence. She is already two steps down a path she never thought she'd take.

Temper. Control. Charm.

Her father was a sociopath. That is what the prosecution said.

Izzy draws her lips together.

She looks at Chris and wonders how convinced he would be of his own father's guilt. If it were *Tony's* trial.

She remembers Tony and Gabe together at a barbecue when she was a teenager. It was a Christmas party. 'A barbecue?' Gabe said when they arrived, seeing the smoke rising in the garden above the snow.

'Why the fuck not?' Tony had said in his jovial way. He opened a bottle of champagne and Gabriel effortlessly caught the cork. He was so co-ordinated, her father. It expressed itself in so many ways. His love of tennis, cricket, but in his art, too. His portraits, faces on miniature canvases, his pots, made on his potter's wheel. He was a true artist, multi-talented, as good at drawing a caricature as he was at whittling a face out of a piece of wood.

They'd lit a bonfire. The snow sizzled as the fire melted it away. They'd eaten hot dogs and Izzy had become light-headed on mulled wine. Tony had joined her by the fire after midnight. 'Here's to 1997,' he'd said. He lit up a cigarette, the rasp of the lighter loud in the night.

'Did you come over purely to make my hair smell?' Izzy had smiled, shifting away from him.

'No, came over for chats,' he said, taking another drag.

'Get that stink away from my baby,' Gabe had said, striding over and taking the cigarette clean out of Tony's mouth, stubbing it out on the ground. He was always so bold in his affection for her. Charming. He was charming.

But it is not only her father who is charming her. Not directly. It is the past, too. Imagine if he was innocent. Imagine, imagine, imagine. Her history would unravel differently, like a painting almost restored to its former glory. Her mother tragically taken from her, but not her father, too. She wouldn't have lost both parents in one evening; only one. Her tragedy would weigh half as much.

'Don't think on it, Izzy. It's enough to drive you mental,' Chris says now, touching her shoulder ever so lightly. He used to do that all the time when they were housemates. It meant lots of things to them: *Want a cup of tea?* and *Sorry everything turned out this way for us*. Both. Neither.

She shakes her head but doesn't say anything more. Her father is a sociopath. A murderer. It ends here. She will not let herself be charmed by him.

Later, Izzy hears Nick's footsteps on the stairs. She's in bed before him, tired from the events of the day, but also hiding away from him, not sure what to say. As he walks into their bedroom, she works up to the question.

'Do all criminals say that they're innocent?' she asks.

'Convicted?' Nick says, without missing a beat.

This is why Izzy loves talking to him. He can always keep up. Is usually three steps ahead of her. Where would she be without him? She can still recall the exact emotion she felt as they exchanged their wedding vows. They were each other's. Her past was behind her.

'Yes. People like my dad.'

'Oh yes, the vast majority of them,' Nick says. He begins to whistle as he gets a shirt out for the morning. 'Baljinder interviewed your dad.'

Izzy's lips draw a thin line. She doesn't know how she feels when she thinks about Nick's boss. He arrested her father, and he sees her husband every day. He must have a view. Do they ever discuss it?

'No exceptions?' she says lightly.

'Why?' Nick replies sharply. He hasn't missed what she's angling at.

'No reason . . . nothing.'

Izzy can sense Nick weighing up whether to say anything. He avoids confrontation more than anything else. He would rather be overcharged in a restaurant than query a bill. He slowly twists the knob on their wardrobe, evidently thinking.

'It would be insane for you to see him,' he says eventually. 'Insane.'

'I know. I know. I just wanted to hear about . . . I don't know. Someone innocent.'

'I had a guy once that I wondered about,' Nick says. There's relief in his voice. That he's said what he needed to say, and moved on. 'But there was no evidence against him except circumstantial. Like, zero. Mistaken identity, maybe. In hindsight. He had the same distinctive tattoo as this other serial offender.'

'Hmm. So if I went into a prison . . .'

Nick turns to her, eyebrows raised. 'Lots of them would say they're innocent. Yes. That they were framed. That their identical twin did it. They were nowhere near, in another city. Et cetera.' He catches her expression. 'Sorry,' he adds. 'Usually they just say that they don't know, but that it wasn't them. Even if they pleaded guilty, to be honest. That's the easiest defence.' He lifts his hands up. 'Don't know, wasn't me. Wasn't there.'

Izzy thinks about that alibi that she ruined and a strange feeling settles over her shoulders, like she's put on a cardigan of fear.

There's something about the set of his shoulders as he turns away from her. They look tense, braced. Is he *annoyed*? Maybe he wishes she was normal. That she didn't have this wound in her past. Maybe he has been pretending it hasn't happened, too.

'Identical twins . . . crazy,' Izzy says, wondering what, if she let him, her father would say to her. Would it be as outlandish as that? What is his defence? Not his rebuttal of the prosecution's evidence but . . . his real defence. The truth.

'Some of them, the scariest ones,' Nick says, shutting one of his drawers with his hip, 'even believe their own lies.'

6

Izzy sits in the kitchen of her restaurant before it's open, her nails tapping out a rhythm on the metal table. In front of her sit her phone, her father's letters, an instant coffee and a beef Pot Noodle which she will bury deep in the rubbish once she's finished it. Her stomach sinks as she thinks of what lies ahead of her this evening: a full shift. All the prep. All those meals cooked, eaten, the leftovers binned. Sometimes it feels so pointless to her. She's never much liked eating out, is always happier at home with Netflix and a tub of ice cream. But what could she do instead? She's too embedded here. The owner. The daughter of the founder. And could she really leave it? The place where her mother spent so much of her life? Izzy sometimes thinks she stays just to try and absorb any last vestiges of her mother that might remain here. The way she always erred on the side of sunny optimism. 'It'll be *fine*,' she'd say when her father worried about things. 'Lighten up.' She would never mind leaving late, coming in early, experimenting during her days off with new dishes.

Izzy wants to sit here and explore the feeling that overcame her as she saw her father. The feeling that arrived after the shock and the fear: the feeling of familiarity, of *oh, it's him*. The feeling of seeing the man who taught her to walk, to read and to write, how to draw a cartoon dog, how to say I love you and how to laugh at herself.

The jury in her father's case didn't think there was

reasonable doubt; the verdict was unanimous. But what does Izzy think?

She unlocks the front door, even though nobody's due yet. She enjoys the peace of the restaurant. Like being somewhere official after hours. A museum or a school. It's only when it's full and buzzing that she feels fraudulent; when it's full of the people who love Sancerre and foie gras and oysters, while she craves beans on toast and Vimto.

The kitchen smells of disinfectant. A single drip of beef sauce rests between her and the letters, and she dabs at it with the pad of her finger.

She picks up her father's first letter.

His handwriting. She would know it anywhere. Almost two decades' worth of shopping lists – *peas, peppers, cat food* – of Christmas cheques – *fifty pounds and zero pence only* – of notes by the bread bin – *Popped out for milk* – and gift tags – *To Izzy, my little lady: all my love, Dad* – and school forms needing signatures. Of birthday cards and passport applications and appointments scrawled on their shared family calendar. Of his paintings, initialled by him – *GDE* – in a hurried loop. Those words, that handwriting – his loopy *L*s, his giant *O*s – was the messy thread running through the middle of their lives together. She would always recognize it.

Suppose she called him. Anonymized her number. Told him she'd seen Paul.

He already knew where she worked. In some ways, the worst had already happened. If he became too demanding, or behaved strangely, she could simply tell the police: Nick. Her father would be recalled, restrained, kept away from her. What would Nick think of that? For some reason, as Izzy imagines it happening, she sees a look of distaste cross

46

her husband's face. That she's on *this* side of the law, with a criminal family, and not on his side.

She folds her father's letter neatly across the central line, running her fingertips along the sharp edge it creates, then opens it again. He has pressed hard with his pen, and the letters have scored the page.

Is it time to hear him out? Was seeing Paul a delaying tactic? A way of safely dipping her toe in the water?

Or is this insanity? She can't tell. She can't tell at all.

She spoons some more noodles into her mouth. She likes the very end of the Pot Noodle; she doesn't mix the powder in, so it is deliberately sharp towards the end, almost *too* tasty.

She opens Instagram listlessly on her phone and scrolls to her favourite family. Two parents. Six kids. They live in Napa Valley, California. Today, they're sitting on the porch together. She zooms right in on the photograph and studies it closely. The kids' little toes in their brown sandals. The just-touching knees of the parents, Bob and Sue. One of the children's hands is curled around Bob's thumb. The other hand rests casually on his knee, for balance. Izzy winces as she looks at it. That fat little hand, placed so casually, as though it is the child's own knee.

Family is everything is the caption. #FamilyOfEight.

She knows nothing about family, she thinks, as she likes the photo and closes the app.

But she could learn.

I want to tell you my side of it, he had written in his letter.

Perhaps, if she could understand it, she could put it to rest. Stop wondering whether his temper lurked behind their identical bone structure, too.

But what if he was innocent? *I swear to you, Izzy, it wasn't me*. She allows herself to imagine it for a second. Her mother would still be dead, but her father wouldn't have done it. The image is tantalizing. She and her father on a porch, next to each other. Her hand on his knee.

She struggles to shift the memories, like they are cobwebs across her face, to really see what is sitting beneath them. And there is something. It thrums with its own heartbeat: it is doubt. Not doubting her father, but giving him the benefit of it.

Izzy's hand twitches on the table. She could just do it, right now, in the empty, safe restaurant, a cup of coffee on the table in front of her. No. She's not going to. She gets up, circles around the kitchen, staring at the phone.

But . . . wait. She can't help it. She has to do it.

Why not? Why the hell not?

She presses the home button on her iPhone, and carefully keys in her father's number. And then, without any further hesitation, she presses 'call'.

7

'Izzy,' is the only thing he says to her, after she has said hello. His accent. She closes her eyes. The kitchen disappears. She can feel only her fingertips on the cool metal table, hear only his voice. She had forgotten. His parents are Irish; they moved to the Isle of Wight in their twenties, but never lost the accent. And so neither did he, despite visiting Ireland only occasionally.

'Oh, Izzy,' he says. She doesn't say anything back to him. There is silence for a few seconds, then a gasp.

'Hello?' she says.

'Sorry, sorry,' he says, his voice sounding strangled. 'I have wanted . . .' He draws a shaky breath in, then breathes it out. She can almost feel it tickling her ear and neck down the phone line, it is so visceral. 'I've wanted this for a very long time,' he says. 'Since . . . since you came to see me.'

Izzy went to see him on the first day she was able to: her eighteenth birthday. It is the final memory she has of her former self. The self that would want to do something and simply go and do it. The self who wanted a career in ballet. Who left the island whenever she wanted to.

It was a freezing cold late May, after the sweltering early May of his conviction. The spring flowers had bloomed in abundance and then withered in the frosts like fireworks let off too soon. She had looked up at the hail bouncing off the skylight in her grandparents' attic and wondered if her father was cold in prison.

Her grandparents thought she was with friends.

Her friends thought she was at ballet.

But the truth was, nobody really cared what Izzy did by then, not even on her birthday. The tragedy of the previous year had eclipsed everything. She could ask for whatever she wanted and get it. They'd go out for dessert, sometimes, even though her grandparents couldn't really afford it. Izzy winces to remember it. New trainers, expensive pointe shoes. She had them all, a series of items she thought would begin to part-pay the debt of her tragedy, but none of them did. Not even close. Everybody was sleepwalking through that horrendous spring. They had been present in body and absent in mind, lost in their grief. In the room with her, and looking at her, but not there, not really.

She got the ferry at eight o'clock in the morning. She'd sat out alone on the deck, on the blue benches, even though it was freezing and misty. The sea air tangled her hair and made her eyes feel gritty and dry. By the time she reached Portsmouth, her hands were red and freezing. She had nobody to remind her to take gloves. An umbrella. Spare change. A drink. The infrastructure of her life: parents. Her hands thawed out on the overly warm train to London. To HMP Belmarsh, where her father was waiting for her, amongst the murderers and terrorists and rapists.

It was a red-brick building with a hexagonal-shaped reception. She had to put her Nokia phone, her book that she had been reading on the train, and her house keys into locker number 101 in the foyer of the prison.

She was strip-searched next, staring dully at the wall as she removed her jumper. A woman's cool, professional hands skimmed her torso, which goose-fleshed in the chilly room. She put her top back on, and removed her trousers, so her legs could be rubbed down. That's how they did it: stripping in two parts. The indignities that sprang from her father's crime were plentiful, and still in free fall.

Metal detectors next. Just in case she had hidden something in her underwear, she supposed. A sniffer dog – a ginger and white spaniel in a fluorescent coat. Even the dog was on duty, serious, sombre. Standing silently next to the guard, not looking at her, not jumping up, not interested in being fussed. Staring straight ahead. Doing its job.

He had already been seated, waiting for her. He was in the corner nearest the door, flanked by two guards who were trying to look like they weren't observing. Other inmates had nobody near them, Izzy noticed, and swallowed.

He didn't look like her father. It wasn't only the sinister and unfamiliar surroundings: he looked wasted. That was the first thing she thought. Already skinny, he had gone beyond lithe. He was too tall to be that thin. His cheeks were sunken, two hollows the size of golf balls, ears protruding too much. Cheekbones forming precariously spindly bridges from his ears to his nose.

It had been less than a year since he had killed her mother.

She sat down opposite him, feeling both guards' eyes upon her.

'After my appeal, Iz,' he said, reaching his hands across the table for hers, and then withdrawing them before they'd reached halfway. 'We'll go away – bike riding somewhere. No, camping.' He was staring just beyond her. Lost in a fantasy.

'When is your appeal?' she said woodenly.

'All going through now, won't be long . . . barrister thinks we've got a good shot . . . and then we'll be away.'

Izzy stared at him, practising saying the words in her

mind. Her lips were moving slightly with her thoughts. 'I can't come with you,' she whispered.

'What?'

'I can't come with you. I can't even see you.'

'But – the appeal.'

'I can't . . .' Izzy said, drawing the sleeves of her jumper down over her hands. 'I can't.'

His head sank immediately down on to his chest. She could see the bones in the back of his neck: one, two, three nodules under his skin. When he looked up again, his face was red, his lips twisted in on themselves. 'Got it all worked out, have you?'

'No, I . . .'

'Mud sticks, does it?'

She stood up at that. 'Why did you do it?' she said.

'Think you know best, don't you?' He stretched his arms wide, like a bird of prey displaying its wingspan, right in front of her. 'Think you've got me all worked out. You're just like her. Just like your mother,' he shouted. '*Was*,' he added nastily, unnecessarily. He reached for the table between them.

She backed away. He was going to tip it on to her.

The guards stepped in, and that was that. The freezing ferry. The two-hour train journey. Those two separate consent forms. The sniffer dogs. Having her just-turned-eighteen-years-old body touched by strangers to check it did not house a mobile phone, knives, cocaine. All of it extinguished right there, along with the hope that – somehow – this had been a mistake. That he wasn't a monster.

She left quickly.

'Izzy,' he said, one last shout, as she was leaving. He added something else, but she couldn't hear what, not over the noise of the visitors' centre, the clunk of the locks, her own noisy, disturbed thoughts. Eighteen years and thirteen hours old, and look: look where she was.

He must have known, she thinks now, looking back, in light of the conversation with Paul. He must have known she ruined his alibi.

She shivers in her restaurant's kitchen. 'That visit was horrendous,' she says.

'I know.'

He says nothing more. He doesn't try to defend it. He doesn't apologize, either. They sit listening to each other saying nothing, just being.

'It's you, Iz,' he says eventually. His nickname for her. *Iz.* A soft, mournful sound, suffused with nostalgia from all the times he has uttered it. On her thirteenth birthday – 'My little Iz, a teenager!' and on GCSE results day – 'God, good luck, Iz' – and countless other times.

'It's me.'

'You run Alexandra's,' he says softly.

'Yes,' she replies.

'It was easy to find you.'

'I know.'

'It took me two hours.'

'I sort of knew you would,' she says.

They lapse into silence again.

'My husband doesn't know,' she says. 'He's a police analyst.' She says it almost to warn Gabe, but he doesn't seem to rise to it, doesn't acknowledge what she's said.

'I don't know where to start,' he admits.

'I know.'

He takes another shaky breath. 'I bet they screwed it all up for you. In your little head.'

Izzy narrows her eyes at the strange choice of words.

There's something off about it. Something condescending. Just as he wouldn't allow her her own view then, the only time she visited him, he won't permit it now, either. She's thirty-six, but he's still parenting her. Controlling her.

'Who?'

She hears a dog barking in the distance and wonders where he is. She hears a thump, a window closing, maybe, even though it's chilly. She guesses he might like to have the windows open these days.

'Her parents.'

'He died,' she says. 'Mum's dad.'

'I know,' Gabe says. 'Paul passed it on to me.'

'And Mum's mum isn't . . .'

'Isn't what?'

'Well, she's eighty-six,' Izzy says. She picks up a spatula and turns it over in her hands.

'Do you know,' he says, 'they say prison stops you ageing? Ironic really.'

'Does it?'

'No booze. No parties. No hard living. Hardly ever seeing the outside: no sun. I'll probably outlive you.'

Izzy's hands still over the spatula. What does he mean by that? No. Nothing. It was just a flippant remark. Nothing.

He takes her pause for scepticism, and says, 'I did have the stress of being innocent.' But he says it so quickly. Defensively. 'Anyway,' Gabe continues. 'You got my notes? How's about a meeting?'

'Yes. I did. And I . . . I'm calling because . . . because I only want to know why,' she says simply. 'I can't meet you.'

'You want to know why what?'

'Why you killed her. What happened.'

He says nothing, then says, 'Okay.' His teeth are gritted.

She can tell in that way families have of interpreting each other. A kind of shorthand, a code. A million clues filter into it: his tone of voice, the beat before he answered, how loudly he said it.

'And then at least I'll understand. And try to move on,' she says, thinking. Just the other day, she had been chopping vegetables, and the prattle of the other kitchen staff had been irritating her. She'd gripped the knife too tightly, wanting to fling it across the room. What if she had? Was she transforming into somebody who couldn't control herself?

'You'll never understand,' he says, and there is something almost snide about it. Angry.

She messes with the spatula. Of course he's angry. It's only natural. And he's not angry *with her*. Just . . . with the world. She imagines what her mother would say. Her tough, strong mother. 'You're delusional, Izzy. He's a killer,' she might say. Or, 'Hear him out. I loved him.'

'But I'll tell you. From the beginning,' Gabe says.

'Okay.'

'But, Iz.'

'Yes?'

'It wasn't me. I swear it. On my life. On yours. Before God.'

'*God?*'

'Yeah. I read everything I could in prison. The Bible. The Qur'an. Everything.'

'Right.'

'So when I tell you I'm swearing before God, I mean it.'

She looks down at the table, her eyes damp. He had always been an atheist; a closed-minded, scientific type who would compare God to the tooth fairy. But here he is: changed. Of course he is changed.

She had become obsessed with reading about wrongful convictions on the internet during the trial. '*He* is not one of *those*,' her grandmother had said. 'He plotted to murder her, and then he did it, and then he has denied it, so far, for every day of a five-week trial.' There was something compelling about her grandmother's green eyes – so like her mother's – meeting hers, telling her something she believed so completely, that a court and a handful of lawyers and twelve members of the jury were using their time to investigate, to deliberate. Of course he had done it: why would they bother otherwise?

The night after he was convicted and sentenced, Izzy read an article about him in the *Isle of Wight County Press* – 'Savage Wife-Killer Gets Life' – shredded the paper, and moved on. And then the money came from her mother's parents, the money that had reopened Alexandra's. And life began again. Not the life Izzy had really wanted, but a life nonetheless. And she took it.

But today. Today, she remembers those wrongful conviction articles.

'So what happened, then?' she says.

'I have no idea. As I said in court.'

The oldest defence in the book. *It wasn't me. I don't know.* Just like Nick said.

'But I do know some things which might help us. Let me tell you my side of it,' he says. His voice is louder. The Irish brogue has been rubbed off from around the edges, softened, as he has become more animated.

'All my adult life I've believed you were guilty,' she says. 'You never wrote. You never wrote to say all this.'

'I haven't wanted to mess with your head. Until now – until you were older, and I was out. But I'll keep coming here. Until you listen.'

Izzy cocks her head. Is it a threat? Or is it what an innocent man would do?

'I mean . . . I didn't mean that how it sounded,' he says quickly. 'I'll never come back again, if you want.'

And that's what does it. His apology, combined with the fact that he came to the restaurant on the day of his release. Desperation and restraint. Putting her first, even though he doesn't want to. Parenthood, she supposes, thinking of the Instagram family, of the way Thea still organizes her life around her adult children even though she is in her fifties. It's a lifelong job.

'The evidence against me starts on the night of her murder, but the story starts earlier. Iz, let me tell you it. The story. And maybe you can tell me what you remember, too. We can meet and talk about it. Piece by piece.'

8

PROSECUTOR: You had several rows before you murdered your wife, didn't you, Mr English?

GABRIEL ENGLISH: I didn't murder her. We did row.

PROSECUTOR: Your daughter, Isabelle, heard the end of one row, as the jury heard four weeks ago.

GABRIEL ENGLISH: Yes.

PROSECUTOR: And were you angry with your wife?

GABRIEL ENGLISH: Yes. I . . . I was. But I didn't kill her.

June 1999: four months before Alex's murder

Gabriel

Your mother said she had something to tell me, but I was distracted by her hair. I loved it when she wore it that way. Scooped up messily, loose red strands resting against the softest part of her neck. When we went out – though I can't now recall a single recent date – she always wore it down and straight, but I loved this tangled mess. I couldn't stop looking at it as she was talking to me. When I painted her, I used burnt sienna mixed with raw sienna. A dash of burnt umber. Sometimes cadmium yellow deep, if she was in the sunlight.

We were in the basement of the restaurant, next to the wine rack.

She turned and put something into her handbag. And . . .

ah. Her hair was held up with a breadstick, taken from the bar at the front desk. I felt a pleasurable expansion in my chest.

'So . . .' she said, turning around to face me. 'It's just something that's becoming a bit tricky and you – I guess you need to know about it.'

'I'm all ears,' I said.

Alex leant back against the wall. It was dim and cool in the basement. It smelt of old stone. I loved it when she stood like this. Arms behind her, looking up at me shyly. And there we were, like it was 1970 again, and she the girl I met on the beach. (Do you know the story of how we met?) Still all that chemistry, even after all that time.

The lines around her eyes pleated together as she frowned at me. She had turned forty-five the previous year; we'd celebrated right here, in this basement, with a few candles and a bottle of white, late. It was the frown that alerted me. Something bad was coming.

'I didn't save up for everything here,' she said, gesturing to the basement around us. 'I didn't . . . I didn't have the savings I told you I did.'

'What?' I said. I was panicked, I guess, disbelieving, but maybe she would have said I was angry. Her face instantly began to close down, just the way she closed up the restaurant. Backroom lights first, that frown beginning again across her forehead, moving to the front. Her eyes darkened next and then her hands dropped down by her sides.

'I paid the rent deposit in cash but I put everything else that month on a credit card so I could do that.'

'Which credit card?'

She bit her lip. 'Yours.'

'*Mine?*' I patted my pockets, looking for my wallet. Sure

enough, the card was missing. I'd never have noticed. I didn't use it. My vices were plentiful, but they didn't include spending money.

'I opened your statements. So you wouldn't see.'

I started to panic properly then, running my hands through my hair. We'd taken out a twenty-grand business loan to start up the restaurant the previous year. An overdraft on top of that, which we'd already burned through. Alex had said she had ten thousand saved from her previous events. Catering for weddings, for parties. 'So you didn't have any money saved?'

'No.'

'Why did you say you did?'

'I wanted to open as soon as we could, I . . . I thought it would be easy to repay it once we started making a profit.'

'So the debt is . . . how much more debt is there?'

'Well, I maxed out your card.' She winced. 'So then I opened two more cards. And now I'm paying the interest on one with the other.' Her eyes were damp.

I'd never been one to worry about money, not too much. *It's only money*, my mother and father used to say. They'd spent their youth travelling around Ireland, racking up debts, never paying them off, and it hadn't harmed them. The debts would die with them, they always said laughingly while my father opened a beer.

But this was . . . shit. This was bad. She'd opened the restaurant only recently – as it turned out, a year before she died – and, already, we were in more debt than we'd ever been in our lives.

'What's the total?' I said.

She met my eyes briefly, then looked away again. I knew she wouldn't know. She was wild, your mother. A loose cannon. She'd always spent money with no regard for anything. She'd buy all sorts. Dehumidifiers. Once, a ton of fruit someone was selling by the side of the road. She couldn't resist. But more than that, she just didn't think sometimes. On holiday once, she jumped off a cliff and into the sea. She'd chat to strangers at bus stops late at night. And then this.

Debt.

Debt upon debt.

Alex's green eyes were wide now. 'I don't know . . . forty? Fifty thousand?'

'Jesus Christ.'

'We needed so much stock . . . the pans and the knives and all the equipment. I just typed your credit card into so many websites . . . to buy it all. It didn't feel like shopping. It felt like . . . I don't know.'

'*Shopping*,' I said nastily.

Your mother was a shopaholic. Shoes, candles, new tyres for the car 'because they were on offer'. She even managed to spend money sitting alone in our house, without the internet. Remember the time she paid a window cleaner? We'd laughed about it then – 'Nothing like the shopping buzz,' she'd said – but it wasn't funny any more.

'You lied to me. About having enough money to set up.'

'Yes,' she said, looking directly at me. And I still loved her then. Her freckled nose. The beautiful red hair, full of breadstick crumbs by the end of each day. And her directness, too. She loved me enough to stop lying then, at least. 'I thought I could – I thought I could make it work. If I really tried.'

You know, Izzy, right at the beginning of our marriage, we used to count how many beds we'd slept in. I don't know why we started, but we did. It became a long-standing joke. Sometimes we'd recite them. A hotel in Paris. Paul's house at Christmas. The Travelodge before we went to Glasgow that time. The sofa bed at her parents'. There were hundreds of them, by the time she died. A dossier of our marriage, of the number of times we'd slept skin-to-skin. 'Oh, we forgot one,' she would say sometimes. 'That blow-up airbed in France, the one that deflated by midnight.' And now, so many beds later, and she'd been lying to me.

The restaurant was swallowing money that first year like a hungry bird.

'We forgot about VAT,' your mother had said one night. 'And we need a computer system for the bookings.'

We'd inched into our overdraft, without me knowing that there was already too much debt to hope to pay off. Six months ago, we'd been solvent, and now . . . what were we? One step away from something scary, that's what.

'Are all the cards at their limit?' I asked.

Your mother nodded slowly, swallowing, her eyes wet. 'We can't pay the mortgage,' she whispered. 'We can't pay the rent here.'

I reached out to touch the wall of the basement, steadying myself. It had been painted white by me. I'd bought a pot of paint for £28.95 from B&Q and painted it in the sweltering heat the previous summer. At the end of every coat I'd had to wipe my face with my T-shirt.

'I'll . . . I'll sell some of my paintings.'

'*Gabe*,' she said, and I knew exactly what she was saying with those raised eyebrows. My paintings sold for next to nothing. 'You need to get a painting and decorating job.'

I gritted my teeth. It was just too much, Iz. Your mother was always telling me what to do. Hang this picture frame up, even though it's close to midnight. Shower, you're filthy, covered in paint. Help me strip the bed. I don't know. Life seemed sometimes to be so hard with her, your tempestuous, hard-working, slave-driver mother.

I told you I'd tell you my story honestly.

She started to pull a white hoody on. I was sure it was actually yours. I'd always been in charge of the household washing. Tiny white Babygros moving through the system, from drawers to the machine to the tumble dryer. I'd always loved it. Toddler outfits, like adult outfits in miniature: tights with three-inch-long feet, tiny dresses. And now, look at this. She was wearing your hoody. You were seventeen, moving into adulthood: here was the evidence.

'I need you to get more work. You don't work a forty-hour week, do you? There's room in your life.'

I thought of where I'd been that day: painting a kitchen in the morning, then back for a late lunch at home. I'd made some pots on my wheel. Three bowls: for you, me and her. I was going to paint them green crystal 8650; a kind of mottled mint colour.

'You knew about most of the debt, anyway,' she said, chewing her thumbnail and looking at me.

'I didn't know about the debt on my own credit card,' I said tightly. 'I'll try and get some more work. I'll advertise.'

'What's the rent on the shipping container?' she asked, a dangerous edge to her voice.

I rented that container – a metal box, really, perched near to the beach – for £50 a month. I could store my potter's wheel there, my kiln, make as much damn mess as I wanted. I loved painting with the doors wide open, and I loved the way the light hit the inside of the container in the early evenings. The sea air infiltrated everything, and I'd come home smelling of oil paints, of turpentine, of linseed and salt. I loved the way the clay behaved in that shipping container.

More malleable, more workable, wetter. It centred more easily on the wheel. It was my luxury, my only one. I would sit on my wooden stool in there and just paint. Some artists paced, looking at their work this way and that, but I didn't. I sat perfectly still, with only the walls surrounding the painting, so I didn't get distracted. Or I'd sit at the wheel and just make pot after pot. Skinny, sexy vases. Fat, stout mugs with two handles; I'd leave them hanging on hooks to get the perfect, curvaceous shape.

'Fifty pounds a month,' I said.

'You could pause it.'

But I couldn't do that, Iz. For me, life was lived in order to experience joy. Sure, I painted some living rooms magnolia so I could pay the mortgage, but jobs shouldn't go any further than that, for me. Life was made up of bike rides, summer tennis matches, barbecues, catching the exact curve of your mother's neck in a portrait. I wouldn't let her, and the restaurant, take that away from me.

'No way,' I said.

'You're a lazy man, Gabe,' she said.

Her words were acid on my skin. My hairs stood on end with the shock of her attack. 'What?'

'You have never liked working.'

I took a step back, my palms up. That was totally unfair, and totally true, all at once. I didn't have the temperament for office jobs. I didn't like being told what to do, always being in the same place at 11.00 a.m. on Tuesdays. It wasn't for me. She was right, but she was wrong, all at once. No, she wasn't *wrong*. I had just thought that she loved that about me. That I was a free spirit. Her nomad, she once said. The person she had shared hundreds of different beds with: a life lived fully.

'This is your debt,' I said. 'How am *I* in the wrong?'

'Forget it,' she said.

I reached for her, to calm her down, to make her see sense, but she brought her arm up.

'Get the fuck off me,' she screamed. Her nostrils were flaring. 'Forget it,' she said tightly to me. She looked at me again, a hard stare, then picked up her bag.

'Anyone here?' you called. I saw you standing at the top of the stairs, one hand on your hip. So like your mother: skinny limbs, elegant neck. Your hair was back, off your face; you'd come from ballet. You were scowling, looking impatient.

'Here,' I called up to you from the gloom.

Your mother said nothing further to me. She reached down into her handbag, feeling for something. Whatever she'd put in there earlier was important to her. Was that a guilty expression that crossed her face? It was only later that I thought about it. She gestured for me to lead the way out, but I followed her.

Izzy

Izzy's ballet teacher agreed to drop her at the restaurant. Her mum and dad couldn't seem to get their act together for one of them to pick her up. When she was older, she thought, she'd rule her life like a well-run ship. Everybody would always be where they said they would be. There'd be none of this chaos.

'The pirouettes are really good,' Stephanie said to her in the changing room. Izzy was just pulling on a vest top over her leotard; she'd have a bath when she got home. They stepped out together into the summer evening. It was a Friday night, nine o'clock, and sometimes, at times like this,

Izzy felt like life was just beginning. The sky was clear, the moon low and big, and she could do anything she wanted to do.

'I've got my centre right,' she said. 'Just in time.' The audition was in November. Sometimes, it seemed like time was meted out around that, and only that, as though everybody else's future revolved around it, too. Every morning, she calculated how many days there were to go. It was currently one hundred and twenty-six. She imagined it every morning, too, as she put her hair up. The ferry crossing to London. The cold of the changing room. The unfamiliar ballet studio, a patch of rosin for dipping pointe shoes in, over in the corner, so they didn't skid. It would leave chalky marks over the sprung wooden floor. Her reflection in the mirror as she began the ensemble. The cut of the ribbons, tucked into her ankles: she had to hairspray the ends so they didn't fray, but it left them sharp. If she let herself, sometimes her mind would wander past the audition, and to the following September. *Ballet school*. Bunk beds, *jetés* on the roof terrace, performances and . . . more than that. Freedom, she supposed. Adventure. A career that might take her all around the world. Her boyfriend Pip was going to visit her every Friday, they had decided. If she got in. 'I'll get the train to you,' he had said to her cheerfully. 'I love trains.' That was how he was. Open-minded and optimistic. He loved nothing more than *doing*. Seeing things. New places. Travel. He found the good in everything. Even a seasonal traffic jam. 'Well, let's put some tunes on,' he would say.

Stephanie dropped her outside.

'See you,' Izzy said to her.

The lights of the restaurant were on, so Stephanie drove off, leaving Izzy alone. The restaurant was set back from the road, with a gingham awning and an outside area. The last of their regulars was just leaving. Izzy remembered his full name – Marcus Scott. That's how he always used to introduce himself to people. He had white-blond hair. Izzy liked him. He was always smiling, often chatting to the locals. He wasn't from the Isle of Wight, but had settled there a few years back, seemed to want to put down roots, make friends, unlike most of the people who came in to eat alone: they'd come in most nights for a few weeks and then move on, the transient trade of island life. Marcus would occasionally help carry sacks of potatoes into the kitchen for her mum.

Chris, who washed the pots, had already left that night. Her uncle Tony had picked him up. He'd started working in the restaurant alongside Izzy while they were studying for their A-levels. They would giggle into the washing up about her mother's neurotic outbursts.

Izzy crossed the car park. In the distance, she could hear the rustle of the sea against the sand.

She eased open the door to the restaurant. She could hear the murmur of her parents' voices as she weaved her way between the tables. They were downstairs, she realized, crossing to the basement door and pulling it open.

'Get the fuck off me,' she thought she heard her mother say.

There was a pause. Some shuffling.

She stopped, listening. She frowned, a hand resting on the door. Surely not.

'I said last time would be the last time, and I meant it,' her mother said.

'Don't talk back to me,' her father said.

'Anyone out there?' Izzy said as she went inside. She stopped as soon as she saw them. The silence. Their faces. They'd stopped speaking but their expressions remained the same. She knew them well. The air seemed to shiver with resentment.

'Here,' her father called to her, though she could see them plainly. Her mother reached down into her handbag. Izzy looked, and saw leftovers there, foil wrapped like a swan. Her father's eyes tracked her movements.

The atmosphere followed them out, despite her father trying to talk to her, and edged into the car with them. Her mother glanced over her shoulder and held Izzy's gaze, for just a second. Then she looked back at her father, who was staring at her mother. Her father was always staring at her. Whenever they went out together, all three of them, Izzy would be forever catching him looking at her mother: over menus; as he held doors open for her; gazing across at her in the passenger seat of the car. It had always been so clear to Izzy how much he loved her. He had never hidden that, never been embarrassed by it. 'Oh, I'm so soppy over her,' he once said to Izzy.

Nobody spoke on the way home. Something was amiss. Izzy thought about that appraising look her mother gave her often.

Izzy's mother went straight upstairs when they got home, and into the bath. Her father went into the kitchen. Izzy lingered in the hallway, not knowing what to do. She could hear her father on the phone.

'I'll sort it, okay,' her father was saying into the phone. His tone was off. It was tense and angry. The *okay* was gritted.

She heard him open the fridge, then close it again. He couldn't have got anything out of it. She moved to peer through the crack between the door and the frame. He was leaning against the kitchen counter, his chin in one hand.

'A few months,' he said. 'It'll take a few months.'

9

Izzy sits, the phone still held to her ear. She's stunned. She had forgotten all about that row that she overheard. She'd only remembered her parents kissing in the kitchen, the way they'd still held hands, sometimes. She'd completely forgotten that row that she recalled now because she heard Gabe's side of it first.

'I wasn't jealous,' Gabe says quickly.

She has to think of him this way: *Gabriel, known as Gabe.* He isn't *her father.* He isn't *Dad* to her. Not at the moment. Not yet.

'You were. Sometimes. You often said Mum was looking at other men.'

'That was banter,' he says easily.

'But I heard Mum say that night that it would be the last time. And then you told her not to talk back to you. I remember it.'

'*Izzy*,' he says. His tone is as sharp as acid. 'I'd never say those things. She was the loose cannon, not me. In fact, she once wrote me a letter apologizing for throwing a glass at my head.'

Izzy frowns. She hasn't imagined it. Has she? Now that she's pointed it out, she's unsure whether she's right. She thought she was. But surely he'd know? She was so young.

'You didn't row often, though,' she says. 'It was just that one time – right?'

'Things were strained,' he says down the phone. 'About the debt. I thought your mother had her head screwed on better than that. But I hadn't done it before. You're mistaken when you say she said that.'

Izzy shakes her head. No. They were happy. She's sure she's correct about that. Goosebumps break out over her arms. Suddenly, the phone is too warm against her ear. What if she's wrong? They *were* fighting. And it escalated.

'How often were you arguing?' she asks.

'I don't know,' Gabe says. And, again, his tone is off. Like there is a slowly simmering anger building. But surely she's imagining it?

'Look. Let's talk about something else. It's been so long since I've heard from you. I've hardly chatted on the phone at all for years, to anyone,' Gabe says, changing the subject.

'No prison phone calls?'

'It was in the main association area, you know? Two phones between seventy-five men. No privacy.'

'Wow.'

'I know. Hard to believe somebody isn't listening now. I haven't had a proper, normal conversation in years.'

Izzy closes her eyes as she imagines Gabriel in prison. She hasn't allowed herself to imagine it, not really. But now she can't help but ask. 'Did you talk much in prison?' she says.

He lets a little air out down the phone to her. 'There wasn't anybody I wanted to speak to,' he says.

'For eighteen years?'

'Criminals are criminals, Iz.'

'They are,' she says softly, thinking about Pip and how it ended. 'What happened to the debt?'

'Midland Bank took the proceeds of the house sale. That's why you didn't get it. The business loan was secured against the property.'

'They're called HSBC,' Izzy says, without thinking.

'Who?'

'Midland Bank. You know?'

'Oh.'

She blinks. Of course. Of course he doesn't know. He hasn't seen a high street for almost twenty years. It's a wonder he can remember anything at all.

'Anyway . . .'

'Gabe,' Izzy says, a thought occurring to her. A suspicious thought about one of his memories.

A momentary pause as he digests how she's referred to him. 'Yes?'

'You said it was you who painted Alexandra's cellar.'

'In the restaurant?'

'Yes.'

'But it was Tony.'

'Was it? No, it was . . . I remember . . .'

'Tony did it because you were working on something else. I still look at the poor job he did with the cutting in. It wasn't you. It wasn't neat.' She adds another sentence without thinking, 'I'll show you.'

Gabe laughs. 'Isn't the mind a funny thing? I was a painter-decorator . . . I must have just . . . transported the memory from Tony to me.'

Izzy frowns, saying nothing. There is something unconvincing about his tone.

'The point of all this is that we *were* rowing. But with reason, Iz. That's why I've told you. Nobody wanted anyone dead. It was just a marriage under strain, I guess. The things your parents don't tell you.'

'I see,' she says. But she doesn't. Not really. The more they speak, the more she's remembering. Rows. Cross words. Perhaps he was trying to portray their strained marriage – the mistakes her mother made – to show himself in a good light. But all it's done is make him look dangerous. Controlling. She's got to go. She's got to get off the phone to this man. To this abuser.

'My lawyers tried so hard to find my alibi, you know?' he says suddenly. Out of nowhere.

Izzy stops moving, sitting completely still, her back straight, her body cold. 'And they couldn't?' she says.

'No. No social media then. But, if only they could've. None of it would have happened, hey?' His tone is light. Deliberately so.

She holds the phone closer to her ear while she runs her fingertips over the letter. The kitchen seems to close around her. She shivers amongst the sterile countertops, the pans on the hooks above the table swinging like hanged men.

He remains on the line for a few seconds more, and she thinks of the words the press used to describe him. Monster. Wife-Killer. Sociopath.

She used to dream of him. He would arrive in her bedroom at her grandparents' house and kill her. She would wake up, sweat dripping between her breasts, dampening the small of her back, and feel whatever the opposite of relief was. It *had* been a dream, but it had also happened. Just not to her.

It's only when Izzy is in the car on her way home from Alexandra's that she thinks more about his memory of painting the basement. *Some of them even believe their own lies*, Nick had said. It had been Tony's work. Her father hadn't realized she'd known that, but she had. Not to mention the inconsistency between their accounts; the phrase she's sure she heard her mother say. Was he inventing things, exaggerating the good, playing down the bad? Having painted the cellar for her mother would make him sound . . . heroic, loving, maybe, he thought. Were all these memories merely stories, inventions? Gabe's flights of fancy? Or had he really just misremembered?

Izzy drums her fingers on her kitchen table at home, thinking. She has seen Nick think through cases hundreds of times. She'd bought him a shower whiteboard for his birthday, after he'd said he had his best thoughts in the shower. She reads the scrawls he makes on it. Sometimes it's as specific as someone's movements to a car garage and back once a week, every Monday at 9.00 p.m. Other times his musings are broader. Talking of *opportunity. Motive. Risk/Reward. Alibi.*

So what would Nick do?

She stares at the kitchen wall where they have hung a calendar up, finally, five months into the year.

What if she could investigate it herself? To decide whether or not her father's story of the debt is true, and then maybe – she closes her eyes in hope – to eradicate the doubt?

Say she looked into his case by herself. Into the evidence. She has boxes and boxes of evidence. She doesn't have to contact him. See him. Be alone with him.

The boxes had passed to Izzy's grandmother. It was only twelve years ago, when her grandmother moved, and Izzy moved out, that Izzy was finally able to get them. Her grandmother had guarded them, never allowing Izzy access, never discussing with her where they would end up when she moved. 'For the bin?' a packer had asked her, pointing to the stack of aged boxes with their mismatched lids. He was wearing light green overalls that looked like scrubs. He had braces, his hair gelled stiff. He couldn't have been over seventeen. He would have had no idea who Izzy was; who her father was.

'No, to keep,' Izzy had said quickly. She couldn't even explain why she wanted them. Maybe she knew, somehow, that one day she'd end up here.

She'd ask her grandmother, she reasoned. She wasn't stealing from an old lady: she was just taking what ought to have been hers. 'Can you do an extra trip?' she'd said, looking at the packer. He'd shrugged, not caring, and she gave him thirty pounds. That night, the boxes were delivered to the house she was moving into with Chris: every single company document from the time her mother ran the restaurant, all of her parents' personal files, and every piece of artwork Gabe had ever created.

She did check, later, with her grandmother. She had nodded, her eyes unfocused and glassy in the nursing home she'd moved into. Izzy felt a lurch of guilt. It was strong, but it was outstripped by the urge to keep the boxes of her father's things. Of the artefacts of her parents' marriage. And of their life before. A life where the future held sixtieth birthday parties, phone calls returned reluctantly to whichever parent had left her yet another voicemail. Fixed leaks and father-of-the-bride speeches and birthday cards sent lovingly through the post.

It had made sense to move in with Chris when her grandfather died and her grandmother moved into care. Izzy and Chris had found a two-bed they could afford that overlooked both the sea and Alexandra's in Luccombe.

'We can even keep an eye on our own workplace,' Chris had said. He'd been sitting on the sill of the Victorian sash window, his bare feet against the magnolia wall. He pointed. Alexandra's was just visible, up the hilly street and to the left.

'How sad,' Izzy had said in the tone of voice she reserved

74

for talking about Alexandra's. Perhaps it was contempt. Or maybe just the sardonic way you'd talk about a distant relative you are supposed to love.

'You're the boss. Always have to be on duty,' Chris had said, lifting his arms above his head. He'd said it without judgement or malice. Izzy *was* his boss, and he her chef, but nobody wanted it to be that way. Chris loved food just as much as her mother had – enthusing about wild garlic and artichokes – and he'd rather run the restaurant. Izzy would . . . well. Where would she rather be? She gazed at Chris's legs stretched out in front of him.

'You've got great turn-out,' she had said, pointing.

'Yeah?'

'Yeah. Almost flat. You'd have made a good dancer.'

He'd laughed at that. 'Trust me when I say I wouldn't.'

Later, they'd ordered their first joint pizza, drunk wine out of mismatched mugs, and Izzy had touched the boxes for the first time, taking them up to their loft while Chris held the ladder, not saying anything.

Later, she moved them to the cottage she'd bought with Nick.

Maybe she could unearth the boxes from the recesses of the cottage's loft. Start to go through them. Methodically, carefully. Just to be sure. Investigate it herself.

But what else can she do? Is there anyone she could speak to?

She stares at the calendar as she realizes what Nick would do. Of course. Who knows the most about her father's case?

His lawyer.

10

The next morning, Izzy is on the BBC news archive web-site. They began reporting online in 1997, and so what coverage there was of her father's trial is all there.

Matt Richmond. That was his name. Her father's solicitor was tall, almost as tall as her father. Bald, with dimples. He'd been in his late twenties at the time, which had privately worried Izzy, but he had an arresting presence. His shaved head and bright blue eyes. She can remember him well. He attended every single day of the trial, even though it was her father's barrister who was conducting the court proceedings. Matt had been so involved. Passing notes to the barrister. Leaning in close to her father, his head by the dock, listening to instructions as her father gesticulated.

Matt knows more than anybody.

She types his name into Google. *Matt Richmond lawyer Isle of Wight.*

She slowly dials his number on her phone. 01983 . . .

'R and G Solicitors,' a clipped woman's voice says.

'Is Mr Richmond available to speak to?'

The woman pauses, then sighs. Izzy hears clacking – nails typing on a keyboard, maybe.

'Not today, I'm afraid. He's in an all-day meeting. Could I arrange a call back?'

'Could I come to see him?'

'What is it regarding?'

'A past case he worked on.'

'And who are you?'

'I'm . . . I'm a witness, and I want to clarify something with him.'

'Mr Richmond isn't usually . . . what is it you want to know? I'll need to inform you of his hourly rates.'

'What are they?'

'Three hundred pounds per hour, plus VAT.'

Izzy swallows. How did her father afford that? 'He worked on my father's defence case.'

'And who is your father?'

Izzy closes her eyes. Is there any way she can't say? 'I . . . I just want to talk about the evidence.'

'I see,' the woman says, and Izzy thinks she detects a little sympathy behind her clipped tones. 'I'm sorry, but Mr Richmond does not routinely discuss cases with witnesses. Especially after the event.'

'I just wanted to find out something about my father's defence.'

'I'm sorry. Have you tried contacting witness support?'

'I just want to . . . to talk to the person who defended him.'

The woman pauses. 'No,' she says. 'I'm sorry, Ms . . .'

'Gainsborough,' Izzy says, using her married name. She always does in these circumstances, to avoid the speculation. 'Please,' she adds. 'I wouldn't usually ring and beg but . . . please.'

There's another pause. Five seconds, ten. Typing.

'Come in next Thursday. Eleven o'clock.'

Izzy skips the lunchtime service. She'll tell anybody who asks that she had a doctor's appointment.

Once she's made the decision to look into her father's case, the rest comes easily.

The loft hatch sticks as she tries to prod it open. In the end, she gets a chair and balances on it, but she still isn't tall enough. Eventually, she unearths a pair of pointe shoes that she keeps out for exactly this sort of situation – reaching things on high shelves, changing light bulbs – and puts them on. She rises up through demi-pointe, feeling the muscles of her feet contract. She stands on the ends of her toes in the shoes, the pose as natural and as easy to her as sitting on the sofa, and she is reminded of how strong her arms are, how good her balance is. She is grateful for her body that keeps these skills hidden, waiting patiently like an understudy until she calls upon them. She reaches the hatch easily, pulls the ladder down, takes the shoes off, and ascends the steps. They're covered with a layer of dust in which her bare feet leave messy impressions.

The attic is stuffy and too hot in the warm spring, the air close, like a sauna or a nightclub. The ancient beams of their cottage run across the roof, covered in cobwebs. Nick lined the boxes up against the far wall. He never said anything about them. He accepted her past in typical Nick style: with a shrug. It was easier not to have the conversation about their contents, so he simply didn't. No, that's not fair, she corrects herself: he accepts her for who she is. Doesn't he? She thinks of the set of his shoulders from the other night. No. He does. He *does* accept her. He answers all her questions about her father. Nobody else would do that.

She had been at the Isle of Wight festival for the first time, with friends, when they met. She had imagined sunsets and late-night chats around fires. A festival full of crap food. Sausage rolls and Pepsi Max cans and pizzas: heaven. She went to sleep at two o'clock in the morning, spread out in her borrowed single-person tent, listening to the relaxing sound of rain on nylon, and woke up at five with wet feet: the tent had flooded. She unzipped it, and tried to empty some of the puddled water out. A tall, pale, dark-haired man was sitting on the grass outside, nursing a coffee, a cynical expression on his face. The sky was oyster pink behind him.

'Rained on?' he asked, gesturing to her tent.

'Flooded,' she said irritably.

'Sleep in mine, if you want. It's not comfortable, but it is dry.' He gestured to two tents down. His purple tent was open, and inside she could see an invitingly warm, dry sleeping bag, half unzipped. A proper pillow. A little radio propped against a Tupperware pot. So ordered in the chaos of the festival.

'Do you really not mind?'

'Nope,' he said easily.

She didn't sleep in her tent for the rest of the festival. Nick was a great host. He brought her a proper coffee every morning, brown cardboard cup, white lid, plenty of packets of sugar. They'd slept side by side, the sleeping bag opened up to cover them like a duvet. His body was warm next to hers. She propped herself up on her elbow and looked at his sleeping profile in the night, and felt that feeling: *a significant person has just walked on to the stage of my life*. She was fascinated by him. By the way he had not a single contact in his phone because he knew everybody's phone number by heart – he has a great memory – by the snacks he'd brought – cheese in a cool bag, crackers – and by the way he stood and watched the bands play, not dancing, just nodding along, on the fringes of life somewhat, an observer, just like Izzy.

Within forty-eight hours, she had told him about her

father, in the almost total darkness of his tent, their hands entwined, the shipping forecast on low – 'I like to give my mind something to focus on,' he'd explained – and he'd shrugged. 'We all have our crosses to bear,' he'd said, and she was grateful for that, though she didn't admit it. She'd told him the way she told everyone else: factually, quickly, and then she'd moved on. He'd told her a few work stories, and that had convinced her: Nick was used to crime and darkness. To him, she was normal. And that was wonderful.

She wouldn't have been surprised, then, to know that they are now married, but she would be surprised to know that they were childless. That she hadn't processed and conquered her fears about what had happened to her parents. That she wasn't ready to move forward and have a family of her own. That the whole concept still felt alien to her.

She turns slowly now, looking around the loft. She glances at the open hatch and wonders why she didn't lock the front door. She should have thought about it, planned it out better, like Nick would. She'd love for him to help her right now. She stares at the hatch and feels the eerie sensation she has carried around since she was seventeen: it is loneliness, she guesses. But it isn't temporary. She is alone in the world, in this attic. She has tried to turn the feeling into self-sufficiency, and she succeeds sometimes, but other times it is just impossible, like trying to magic water into wine.

She turns and walks across the beams, balancing delicately, making her way to the first box. It's labelled *Bank* and so she starts there, removing the lid and putting it on the floor. Next to it is a box of her father's artwork, which she can't bear to open, not yet. She'll start with the bank statements: safety in numbers.

The box's cardboard sides are sagging, the Sellotape fuzzy and ineffective. It is strange how things become eroded even when kept safe, away from everything. Time itself has damaged it.

She breaks open a lever arch file. She flicks through the bank statements. July 1997. December 1998. She leafs through a few more before she realizes there is no order to them whatsoever. How was her mother running a business?

She spreads them out on the floor of the loft and sorts them into chronological rows. She works quickly in the heat, unclipping statements from folders and rearranging them.

The walls are insulated with fibreglass. Tiny particles of it drift down on to her arms which she rubs at, irritably, making it worse; like nettle stings. Soon, her chest is covered in sweat, and her arms are burning uncomfortably, but she carries on.

She finds the profit and loss account for the restaurant's first trading year and frowns at it. The outgoings are high – high wages, high food costs. She leafs through, looking for invoices, and finds a few, folded in half and stuffed into a plastic wallet. Her mother bought high-end food, and often. In small quantities, too. She sold the dishes for three times the price of the ingredients, not five or six. She paid twice the minimum wage. Izzy raises her eyes to the beams above her. No wonder they were in debt. A clutch of old recipes sits in the back of the folder. She opens it with interest. *Half a teaspoon of lemon juice*, her mother has written. Next to it, she's written *or a whole teaspoon – testing*. Next to that: *yes, a whole one*. The care that went into it.

An invoice for wine is next, the paper stiff and slightly yellowed. Her mother bought twelve bottles for £5 each but sold them for £30. Izzy never scrimps on wine: those who care enough to order expensive wine can tell.

Izzy sits back against a beam. So her mother was cutting corners. Wow. Izzy can hardly believe it. Her organized, fearless mother. Drowning in owning a business. Making strange decisions.

It is an odd feeling to objectively observe her mother's failings. She was only ten years older than Izzy is now when she died. Still, Izzy thinks, as she holds the invoice, it's nice to feel something that she once touched. Perhaps she was the last person to touch this very piece of paper. Except the police.

She becomes engrossed in the papers, not thinking about anything else, the hatch letting in a steady stream of cooler air. She wonders if she'll see what she wants to find: evidence of her father's truth, and not of his lies. The police took a cursory look at these statements but, by then, they had their man. But still. It's nice to look at them. To see if they tally with what her father has told her. And maybe – just maybe – she'll find something else, hidden here, waiting for her.

She looks back at the overdraft. She never felt or witnessed her parents' poverty herself. Maybe no teenagers did, back then. She had a cheap mobile phone, sometimes no new clothes for the entire school year. But hadn't that simply been how things were? She had had as many ballet lessons as she had wanted. New pointe shoes every other week because she broke them in too fast. Leotards and leg warmers and soft block shoes – shoes designed to transition from ballet flats to pointe shoes. The things she needed grew and grew. A pale blue leotard for her Advanced 2 exam. A piece of resistance rubber through which to flex her feet, to improve her arch. Ankle weights, to increase her strength when holding her legs in the air during *développés*. Surgical spirit to soak her toes in, to toughen the skin up.

Her mother gave Izzy the money for her ballet audition. Only her mother had really known what ballet had meant to Izzy. She got it. 'It's so healthy to be in your body and not in your head,' she had once said to her. The money had been in an envelope. It had been saved up, maybe. Weeks and weeks of saving twenty pounds here and there. Izzy winces to think of it.

Something makes a noise in the corner of the loft, a kind of skittering sound, and Izzy stops, the papers in her hands, not moving, not wanting to breathe. She waits for it to happen again, then exhales slowly when it does. It's just birds. They must be nesting somewhere up here. She hears a flapping noise, then a rustle, and then silence again.

She pulls a pile of statements on to her lap and begins leafing through them, laying them out on the floor, when she hears another noise. Her heart races. It's a voice.

'You can't think that way,' it's saying.

She stops, an ear cocked. It's Thea. Of course. She vaguely remembers the seller telling her once that the loft was shared, and divided up much later. 'Yes, yes,' Izzy had said impatiently, thinking that she didn't care about any of the flaws in that beautiful pink little cottage.

'Really,' Thea is saying.

Izzy scoots closer to the partition and listens, feeling guilty and voyeuristic, but unable to stop herself. Thea must be on the phone.

'I think that's a very sad thing to think about yourself.' Thea's voice is so maternal, so warm, so suffused with everything Izzy lacks that she feels her eyes moisten. 'And most definitely not true.'

Izzy still has the clutch of bank statements in her lap, but she's not looking at them any more.

'Don't make decisions when you're tired, sad or hungry, anyway,' Thea says.

Izzy shakes her head and looks down, studying the statements. £19,950 DR. Overdrawn. She sits back. Perhaps there *was* no money. Perhaps there was debt, like her father says. Perhaps that was why there were rows: perhaps the arguments were justified. Not domestic violence, but family life. A marriage under pressure. She sets the statements down, thinking.

Her phone starts vibrating on one of the beams.

'Hi,' she says, picking it up.

It's Nick. 'Where are you?' he asks.

'Why?' she says, though she knows it's incriminating.

'Free for lunch,' he says, sounding hurt. 'Thought I'd come by the restaurant.'

She closes her eyes. He hasn't done that for years.

'I'm not there,' she says. 'I'm at the doctor's.'

'Why?'

Her mind races. Not contraception – he knows she has the implant. 'I needed antibiotics,' she says lamely. 'Water infection.'

He pauses for just a split second. He can tell: of course he will be able to tell. 'Okay,' he says tonelessly. 'Don't worry.' And then, 'Too much Angel Delight and not enough fresh fruit. Cranberries.'

'Yes, maybe,' she says with a laugh.

He hangs up and Izzy sifts through to the credit card statements. There they are. Gabriel English's Halifax credit card: maxed out. Thousands and thousands. The minimum repayments made, and then missed, over and over again. Izzy's eyes scan over the numbers. She has always found maths easy, but uninteresting, same as running a restaurant. She turns the last statement over, feeling the imprint of writing on the back.

August – £250 extra jobs
September – sell car? Sell painting? Plus 80 extra hours' P&D
October – Get credit card in Tony's name . . . ask him.

It's her father's handwriting. She stares at it. And there it is. Tangible evidence.

A contemporaneous note, as the lawyers would call it. Evidence of him trying to solve their debt. Not evidence of his innocence, exactly, but of his version of events. Evidence of a reason for the rows doesn't make him innocent, she tells herself, but she likes looking at it anyway.

She grabs the rest of the statements and works backwards, turning them over, looking for more. There's nothing for two years, until 1997. Izzy had been fifteen. The paper feels thicker, older, underneath her fingertips, and she recognizes Gabriel's handwriting immediately.

Gone golfin' x
   PS: I picked Izzy up from dancing. She was so good. I saw her while I was waiting. She's the best in that class, hands down.

Her mother has written back beneath it. Izzy touches the letters, like relics she has uncovered from another time.

She's the best, full stop x

She looks at it for a few minutes longer, this glimpse into

her parents' marriage, and thinks how far back their lives go. She has lived for thirty-six years without children, but any child of hers would never consider that, just as she hasn't. Maybe there are more clues, hidden deep in the past. She brings the next lever arch file down, ready to search through, but pockets that note. That evidence that they *were* happy, that love note from her father to her mother, about their daughter.

11

Chris drums a rhythm on the table in the pub. They come here every Monday night to a quiz. The restaurant skips an evening service. Her mother kept the restaurant open seven days a week, Izzy learnt last night. All that heating, lighting, staff, food, and nobody ever does anything on a Monday.

They have only missed a handful of quizzes in over a decade. Even after Izzy moved out, and in with Nick, who never comes. 'Nick would absolutely boss this,' Chris once said during a particularly tricky round. 'He would find it boring for that exact reason,' Izzy said back. And it is true: Nick does find the pub boring. 'I can drink at home,' he says. 'With the television.'

Izzy and Chris attended their first quiz a few years after her father was incarcerated. Afterwards, at their house, Izzy ate frankfurter hot dogs when they got in, boiled in a saucepan, stuffed in cheap bread, and Chris laughed and said, 'Don't tell the manager.'

Chris picks up a biro now and writes their team name on the sheet. *Shazam for Robots*. It's a years-old joke between them. They won, one week, because they identified all of the robots in a picture round. Another team accused them of cheating and Chris said, seamlessly, 'Oh yeah, we just Shazam'd them,' while Izzy looked on, unable to stop laughing.

'Been revising?' Chris says. He sips his drink – he drinks endless Diet Coke – and pulls his phone out of his pocket.

Izzy's always liked his easy company, his small talk, but tonight, she wants something different. She craves a female friend. Wine, feelings, over-analysis. That's what she wants. Someone to whom she can say, 'My father is out of prison and says he didn't kill my mother.' Someone unconnected, open-minded. Everybody she has surrounded herself with is male, and most of them are involved: Chris, Tony. Nick wasn't there, but is a hardened cynic. Izzy has always shied away from having girlfriends. Tears and book clubs and probing questions. Denial is impossible around women. But now, she wants a friend. A true female friend.

'How's the love life?' Izzy says, flashing Chris a tiny grin.

'Gonna bin her off,' Chris says, drumming with one hand on the table. He reaches for a beer mat and fiddles with it.

'*No!* Why?'

'She used hashtag blessed on Instagram. Loser.' He picks up the beer mat and gestures, a kind of *what can you do?* He chucks it on to the table and it skids across and lands in Izzy's lap.

'I think that's forgivable,' she says, picking it up.

'Nope.' He opens Facebook and begins mindlessly scrolling through it. When they first moved in together, she couldn't believe how much he used his phone. It was off the charts. He had multiple chargers. Plugs that had five USB ports in them. A charging block so he could still use it in the bath – he loves to tweet from the bath – and long leads that stretched from the plug to his bed. 'It was that or move the bed,' he had said.

He slips into his own world now, as she takes the picture round from him. 'It's photos of James Bonds,' she says, passing it back to him. 'No idea.'

He scribbles a few names into the quiz-sheet boxes. She

sips her wine – house white, the cheaper and sweeter the better. When he's finished, he looks up at her.

'Take it you've heard nothing?' he says.

'From Gabe?'

'Yep.' He puts his phone down on the table, face up.

'No,' she says.

He's staring closely at her now, but his expression is unreadable, impassive. She looks back down at the table. She has isolated herself by not telling anybody, but the truth is that nobody understands. Nobody is here with her. She is alone with it, the reality of her father being out; she's forced to be. Chris's uncle killed his aunt, but her father killed her mother. It is incomparable. Chris doesn't understand. Nick doesn't understand. Thea wouldn't understand. The Instagram family wouldn't understand. Izzy herself doesn't: look at her, sleuthing alone in the attic. It is not understandable.

'Round one,' the announcer says. 'Question one.'

'We were talking last night about his trial. I guess because he's out. Dad was saying . . . do you think your dad will look him up?'

Izzy glances across the pub. The doors are open, but no breeze gets through. It's airless, like the middle of August in May. Two people must be smoking outside: Izzy can only see their long, sunset silhouettes thrown across the paving slabs. They're passing the cigarette between them. Shadowed hand to shadowed hand.

'I said, it's been almost twenty years. I mean . . .' Chris says.

'You said he'd come to see me.'

'You're different,' Chris says.

She feels a flush of pleasure: she's *different*. She's his daughter. It is just like how Thea would do anything for her

89

daughter Molly. Gabe will do anything for her. The thought arrives in her mind, fully formed, but she tries to suppress it. Of course it's not the same. Gabe doesn't care about her. Clearly, he doesn't.

'Dad's got in touch with Gabe's probation officer, anyway. Just in case.'

Izzy blinks. Yes. That friendly woman who, a year ago, had asked if Izzy wished her father to have any conditions attached to his licence regarding her. 'No, no,' Izzy had said, not wanting to discuss it, avoiding it, but inadvertently paving the way to this situation they now find themselves in. She had forgotten all about the probation officer until now.

'Your dad did?'

'Which country beginning with G . . .' the announcer says.

Izzy tries to tune him out. 'His probation officer?' she prompts, talking over the announcer.

'Shh,' Chris says.

He listens to the rest of the question while Izzy anxiously chews on the skin around her fingernail. *Stop it*, she tells herself. Usually, she'd change the subject. She's been playing it cool for eighteen years, after all. She covers up the way seeing families on the street makes her feel. She says, 'No, it's fine,' when people joke about killing someone, their faces falling as they realize who they're with. She never makes the point that everybody's problems could be worse: they could be hers.

But everything has changed since her father stopped by the restaurant. She isn't cool now. She is desperate.

'Probation officer?' she prompts, when it's quiet again.

'Yes. She keeps an eye on him for the duration of his licence.'

'How long's his licence?'

'Life,' Chris says. His eyes narrow slightly as he looks at her, his brows lowering into a puzzled frown, like he can't quite believe she doesn't know that. Not even Chris knows how deliberately she has avoided this topic. She closed her eyes whenever she saw the newspapers. The less known, the better. Until now.

Izzy stands up, needing to think. Needing to think somewhere he can't see her facial expressions. 'I'll get you another,' she says, tapping the side of his full glass as she gets up.

She stands at the bar. It's too warm in the pub. Her hair feels heavy against her neck. Her mother's hair. The exact same shade of red. Unmissable.

She can't believe she had forgotten that call she'd taken. That there is a *system* that governs her father's actions, his movements; something bigger than just father and daughter on the telephone. Something bigger than just her own private thoughts about it. She swallows as she orders a lemonade. Is he *allowed* to be contacting her? What does his probation officer think? Is he considered dangerous? Worthy of keeping an eye on, as Chris said? After all, Gabe has come to see her, and only her. 'He'll come for you,' her grandmother had said, and she wasn't wrong.

She puts Chris's Diet Coke on the table in front of him.

'Should keep me going,' he says, eyeing both glasses. 'Question four was about eggplants – easy peasy,' he adds.

'How did your dad contact the probation officer?'

'He rang the probation service.'

Chris shakes his head just slightly as question five is announced. Izzy looks at him closely. Something is off about his expression. 'Don't think on it,' he says to her. 'Everything's fine. You're fine.'

'Is your dad seriously just never going to see him again?'

'What . . . are you going to?'

'Well, it's a small island.'

Izzy thinks about how often she runs into people she knows. Almost every day. Everybody knows everybody. They won't be able to avoid him forever.

Chris frowns. 'What?' he says. 'What do you think . . . we're all going to go out to dinner together?'

'I just wondered what your dad really thought he was going to do. He could . . . I don't know. He could help him.'

'He's done your dad enough favours.'

'What?'

'Nothing.' Chris's forehead has turned red. He draws a deliberate circle on the answer sheet, not looking at her.

'What favours has he done?'

Chris shakes his head just slightly, infinitesimally. 'Izzy.'

'But what . . . I don't know what you mean.'

'Alright,' he says, putting the pen down. 'He said last night that he considered testifying for the prosecution and then didn't.'

'What? Why?' It feels as though the blood in Izzy's veins has slowed down. The pub seems silent around them. All she can hear and see is Chris.

He taps the pen on the edge of the table.

'What?' Izzy says again. It comes out shrilly, and Chris moves his head away from hers, rubbing at his ear irritably.

'Izzy, it's . . . Jesus, I don't know what the evidence was: I didn't ask. He clearly didn't want to discuss it. He's still . . . he's still massively hurt by it all. I don't know why you're . . . going on. You never usually want to discuss it. We've tried so many times with you and –'

'That's fair, isn't it?' she says. Her voice is raised and he's wincing, but she doesn't care. She tries to calm herself down. Temper, Izzy. Don't get angry. You'll only worry about it later. 'That I wouldn't want to discuss it?' she adds, more quietly this time.

'But why do you want to now?' he says.

She can't answer that. Not without revealing herself.

'Izzy, I mean . . . it was nearly twenty years ago. God. Let's just – can we please just let sleeping dogs lie?'

The quiz announcer says, 'What was the name of the actress who played Erica in *Friends*, who gave birth to Monica and Chandler's twins?'

'Well?' Chris says. 'You're the *Friends* fanatic.'

'I don't know,' she says tightly. How can he treat her so callously? Just drop that information into conversation, and refuse to elaborate? Is it just because it's history? She tries to look at it from her perspective, and then from his. He doesn't know she's seen Gabe. He doesn't know about her doubt. How adamant her father is. How convincing. How persistent he was with his daily letters, sent until she gave in. Chris is still where she was: ostensibly fully recovered from a long-ago tragedy. It has no part in his life now.

Chris is staring at her. His phone lights up, on the table, but his gaze doesn't stray.

'Anna Faris,' Izzy says. Then, 'Did you say it was for the prosecution? Not the defence?'

'Let's just do the quiz,' Chris says. She has annoyed him, which hardly ever happens. 'This is a twenty-year-old argument you're having with the wrong person,' he says, but not nastily. He says it gently, factually. And then he unlocks his phone, and begins scrolling anew, despite the signs up saying that phones aren't allowed at the quiz. Conversation over.

Izzy watches him, trying not to look like she's reeling. Wondering what her uncle's evidence was. Wondering how she will find out. And wondering why Chris is so bothered, so closed, so determined to shut the conversation down and move on. A blush stains his cheeks, above his beard. It takes several minutes to drain away.

She calls Nick once she's in her car. It's after eleven thirty. She often picks him up on the way home on Mondays if he's on lates. He answers immediately, on the first ring. 'Shall I come?' she says.

'Sure. Be done in half an hour.'

She opens her mouth to say something about Chris, but what can she say? Nothing Nick will understand. Not unless she tells him everything.

She drives along the coast. The Shanklin beach huts catch the moonlight and she opens the window to let in the warm, soft air. A hotel stands tall against the sea, bright white, lit with old-fashioned lanterns. Several of its windows are illuminated already. Here they come: the tourists. Ready to invade the beaches and the shops and Alexandra's.

Izzy gets to the police station at quarter to midnight. The conversation with Chris is swirling around in her mind. She wants to be closer to it all, somehow. Closer to the evidence. Closer to the authorities. She wants to call up his probation officer. Find each and every member of the jury. Go in and look at the police, doing their jobs diligently, day and night, and hope they got it right.

And maybe, by chance, see Nick's boss, who arrested her father nineteen years ago.

12

Nick emerges in the foyer with Baljinder, his boss, like she knew he would. They're close, even though Baljinder is a police officer and Nick is an analyst. Baljinder likes Nick's good memory and Nick likes that Bal brings cakes in most days.

'Let me know, though, soon as?' Bal says to Nick.

Nick nods, running a hand through his hair. 'I'm sure he's a garden variety lunatic.'

It's a typical thing for Nick to say. Izzy loves that about him. He is so sure of himself. She can become absorbed in that, too: if she is partnered up with somebody sure about life, then she is safe.

They stop walking when they see Izzy.

'I thought I'd wait inside,' she says feebly, looking from Bal to Nick and then back again.

'Here she is, your lady in waiting,' Bal says. 'How're you doing?' He looks at her warmly. He always seems genuinely interested in her.

'Let me get my bag,' Nick says, touching her briefly on her shoulder and disappearing down a different corridor. The dark wood door bangs behind him.

'Alright, thank you,' she says to Bal. The foyer smells of canteen food and sweat.

'Big week,' he says.

She likes that he just says it. That he doesn't avoid the

topic, as others might have. She looks up at him. He's thick-set, stout. Nothing like lanky Gabe.

'Yeah. I've had better weeks,' she says, wondering what would happen if she just told him. Just said it, right here in the foyer. *I've seen him. He says he's innocent. Why would he do that? Why would he bother still defending it after eighteen years, after time served?*

'I think Nick's pretty worried,' Bal says, checking his watch. 'He'd never say – you know him – but I can tell.'

'Is he?'

'Yeah, you know. Weird situation, isn't it?' Bal takes a packet of chewing gum out of his pocket and offers her one.

She shakes her head. 'You interviewed him, didn't you?' she says softly. 'All those years ago.'

He nods, not flinching, and she is glad of that. They only have a few minutes.

'I sat in on it. I was twenty-two. Green around the gills.'

'How did he . . . you know?'

Bal understands subtext better than almost anybody. He looks at her closely, his expression settling into something approaching earnestness. He puts a hand to his chin, his thumb moving rhythmically along his jawline. 'I was living with my dad, at the time,' he says. 'So it seemed . . . I don't know. Close to home, I guess. I felt for you.' He puts the packet back in his pocket and chews thoughtfully.

Izzy feels her eyes burn with envy as she looks at Bal. Imagine not having something so grisly in your past? How light you'd feel . . . sometimes, she mistakenly thinks that everybody has such a secret, such a thorny historical event, and remembers with a start that that isn't true. Not every-body has something that their mind returns to, even during happy moments. It is always waiting for her, like a cruel

96

safety net. Without it, she would be so free. She'd have two children. Two girls, she thinks. Redheads. And she'd never have to worry about them.

'He was . . . evasive, I suppose,' Bal says thoughtfully. 'It was a very easy case, though. Open and shut. So we weren't worried.'

Izzy feels her stomach clench. 'I see,' she says, though it isn't what she means. She doesn't see. She ought to know, but doesn't, not really. Not beyond the basics. 'Evasive in what way?'

'Maybe evasive is the wrong word,' Bal says. 'Callous, I suppose. Removed.'

'Callous.'

'So, for example –' he stops, putting his hand out just slightly towards her in a placating gesture. His wedding ring glints under the fluorescent lights. 'You sure you want to talk about this?'

'It was ages ago,' she says. 'I just . . . I guess with this week, I've been thinking about it more. But yes,' she says, straightening up and nodding. She can see a figure looming in the dim corridor that Nick disappeared down, and she wills Bal to hurry up.

'So, for example, when the evidence was put to him, I remember very clearly, he said: "Oh, so it was me, then?"'

'I see.'

'Like, he was being sarcastic,' Bal says. He takes off his glasses and begins rubbing them on his shirt. 'But I wouldn't usually observe that sort of detachment from an innocent person. Usually they're shocked and scared. Bewildered, really. He was . . . I don't know. Not shocked. Like he already knew. And I guess sort of belligerent.'

Izzy's polite smile is frozen on her face. She nods.

'Nothing like you,' Bal adds nicely. 'He was – I don't know.'

'Like he's got a personality disorder,' she says faintly.

'Exactly,' Bal says, like she has scored the right answer on a test.

'I know,' she whispers.

'It's not evidence, is it?' Bal says.

Nick is walking down the corridor. She can see the outline of his tall form.

'And you can't go to court on it,' Bal continues, holding a hand up. 'But it's instinct. And it's very powerful. Once you've been in the job a while – arresting people, seeing them convicted or acquitted, hearing their stories and the other witnesses' stories, for years, every single day – well, you get the instinct. I can't explain it, but you develop it. I had it, and so did my super. You *know* when somebody's guilty.'

'And you thought he was?' Izzy says, trying to decide how she feels about this: reassured or suspicious. Were people – *suspects* – interviewed fairly when gut instincts played such a role? But weren't instincts also part of the job, an important part?

'As sin,' Bal says softly, still looking at her.

For a second – just a second – she thinks she detects his eyes misting over, but then he blinks, and they look normal behind his glasses again.

She tries to remember the afternoon of her father's arrest herself. The news. The phone call to say he'd been formally charged. Her grandparents' faces. The rest is blank. Shock, she figures. She wonders if her father can remember his own belligerence. If maybe that was a form of shock, or something else.

98

'I see,' she whispers.

Bal's eyes flash and he looks at her more closely. Suddenly, she thinks she's gone too far. He knows, doesn't he? He knows she's doubting it all.

'If you ever want to talk more,' he says softly, as Nick emerges back into the foyer, whistling 'All About That Bass' under his breath, 'you can always call me.'

'Okay,' she says. 'I might.'

'Why has he been released?' Izzy says on the way home. They stop at a zebra crossing. A woman carries a sleeping baby in a sling, pyjama-footed legs swinging in the warm air. Izzy stares in fascination at the late-night moving tableau in front of them, at the dangling baby's arm. At the expression on the mother's face. To think Izzy, too, once had a linchpin with which to anchor her to the world. She wishes she could remember her mother more clearly. That she could separate her from herself. A mass of red hair and pale skin, the both of them. And she wishes, too, that she could cross a road with her mother, now. Going anywhere. Shopping – her mother loved to shop. To see a film. Just walking and talking.

'He would have been considered for parole, and they decided to give it to him,' Nick says. His eyes are closed. He crosses his legs, stretching them out in the passenger seat.

'Will he have conditions attached to his release?'

'Yeah. He can't re-offend. If he does anything, even the smallest crime – a bit of weed, whatever – he'll go back to prison for the rest of his life.'

'What if he approaches me?' Izzy says. An oncoming car's headlights dazzle her as she turns on to the country track that leads to their cottage.

'You'll tell me if he does, and we'll deal with it.' Izzy says nothing, and Nick adds, 'Yeah?'

'Yes,' she says, staring at the dark road ahead of them, finding it incredible that he can't tell. Her husband.

Nick's phone pings and lights up. 'Robyn's birthday in September,' he says. 'We going?'

Izzy shrugs. 'Yes, please,' she says, the heavy feeling in her stomach lightening momentarily at the thought of a birthday party.

September seems impossibly far away. More than a whole season. Still, the date will be marked on their calendar in red, and Izzy will look forward to it, that rarest of things: a family event. She'll buy a special outfit.

'But how did he come to be released?' she asks. She keeps thinking of Baljinder's words. *Callous.* 'Don't they test prisoners before they release them, these days? To make sure they are . . . safe?'

'Oh God, let's not . . .' Nick says, closing his eyes again as if to seal the matter. 'It's not good for you.'

'But I want to know,' Izzy says, glancing across at him. She is overcome with the eerie feeling that her husband might find her dysfunction – her avoidance, her denial – convenient.

'He will have had to present to a parole board to get out. He served eighteen years and six months,' Nick says, all in an irritated rush.

'What will he have had to show?'

'Lots of things . . . Adjustment. Willingness to engage with the community.' Nick reaches over, still with his eyes closed, and squeezes her hand as she changes up a gear.

See? Izzy says to herself. He is on her side. He is willing to explain things to her, to help.

'Are there set criteria?'

'Yes. Eight.' Nick rattles them off easily. 'Behaviour in prison, plans on release, danger to the public, why you were in prison, previous offences, the judge's statements at trial, the victim statement, and medical and psychological evidence.'

'What does the psychological evidence include?'

Please say it includes an assessment as to safety. Please say that.

Nick says nothing. She looks across at him again. He's frowning. She pulls on to their driveway. He's reluctant. It's obvious. And she knows why: it's tricky. It's emotional. She is not usually high maintenance in this way, and it is one of the reasons he loves her. *Sadly*, she finds herself thinking.

'A lot of it is about remorse,' he says, an edge to his voice.

'Remorse?'

'Less than it used to be,' he adds quickly, regretfully. 'But they still do take that into account.' He looks apologetic as he says it now, the annoyance gone.

'But he has always, *always* maintained his innocence.'

'Not in the parole hearing,' Nick says. 'I doubt.'

It is like an arrow has speared right though Izzy's chest. She feels winded. She says nothing after that, while she parks the car.

'I looked through some boxes,' she says, angling for a kind of hybrid of the truth. 'Did you know they were in lots of debt? That was his defence. That they rowed because of debt.'

'They were in debt?'

'Yes. *She* was. She took on loads of debt, then got him into debt herself.'

Izzy exhales softly. It's cathartic to discuss it, however obliquely, with somebody. She feels the muscles in her shoulders and back soften as the tension leaves them. Maybe she could tell him everything. Maybe he would help her look. The responsibility would be shared, halved. She'd have an ally. The feeling is new to her. She always deals with this stuff alone. No, she *doesn't* deal with it. She simply represses it.

Nick pauses, staring at her now, thinking, sucking his bottom lip in and out. 'Hmm. Did her life insurance ever pay out?'

'No. I don't think so, anyway. We got no money.'

Nick frowns again, sitting in the car as she switches the engine off. 'Usually it would pay out, but skip the perpetrator. So you would've got it. In substitution, instead of your dad.'

'Oh. I never did.'

Nick clasps his hands across his body. 'Well, then.'

'Well what?'

'The presence of debt makes it worse, does it not?' he says softly.

'Why?'

'Somebody in the insurance company obviously thought it was an inside job. That he killed her so he could use the insurance money to pay off the debts. It voided the policy.'

It's as though somebody has thrown cold water over her, right there in the car. 'What?' she says. But she knows what. God, how could she have been so stupid? Her father was rowing with her mother. That was bad enough. And now this: the debt isn't evidence of his innocence. It's evidence of his *guilt*. It goes to motive. And, worse, premeditation.

Nick's eyes look mournful, his brow lowered. 'That's what I would conclude. If it were my case.'

'I see,' she whispers.

They get out of the car and walk towards their house. The air smells of cut grass and manure. It's still warm, T-shirt weather. It feels eerie that outside is warmer than in, like the world has been inverted.

Nick slams the passenger door loudly in the quiet night. Apart from their row of cottages, there are no other houses around for miles. Izzy suddenly longs for a train, a crowded bus stop, a metropolis. Homeless people, commuters, *witnesses*.

Something shifts as they approach the house. She blinks, staring hard, keys in hand. A tree moves again, its branches passing in front of her window. She continues to look, but nothing else moves. Just that. It must just have been that.

13

Izzy is sitting in Thea's garden. It's her birthday. Thea invited her over the fence while Izzy was hanging out her washing, and she accepted the invitation immediately, with the awkward feeling that Thea didn't expect her to. Nevertheless, she's here, with a slice of birthday cake and a coffee and the sun warm on the tops of her legs. Izzy is thinking about wanting to confide in a girlfriend, and watching Thea move around the lawn, socializing, making sure everybody's drinks are topped up.

'Alright there?' Thea says to her.

Izzy looks at her bare feet as she walks across the grass. She sits down next to Izzy and stretches her legs out in front of her. Her heels are cracked and her toenail polish chipped, but she doesn't seem to care. Did Izzy's mother use to wear nail polish? Izzy feels her chest heat up: she can't remember. She has no idea. Shouldn't she know?

'Fine, fine,' she says to Thea. 'Though, I wanted to ask you something . . .'

'Shoot,' Thea says, her smile broad. She tilts her face up to the sun. 'I never thought I'd get such a hot birthday. I'm not usually so lucky.'

'My father contacted me,' Izzy says.

Thea knows who she is – everybody does – though they have never directly spoken about it. Izzy is ashamed to feel a spark of something powerful ignite inside her. She *likes* shocking Thea by braving the topic. She likes the widening of Thea's eyes. The way she scoots her chair closer to Izzy, even if she is merely after a salacious slice of gossip. Izzy hasn't thought beyond this: this attention. She basks in the glow of it, though she knows it is unhealthy, that she is trying to fill a void.

'Wow,' Thea says. 'How?'

'By letter. He wants to meet.' Izzy sips her coffee.

Thea's eyes are wide. She has no idea what to say. Izzy recognizes the expression very well. Thea looks distractedly over her shoulder. Two of the guests are struggling to open a bottle of prosecco.

'I'd love to talk more about this,' she says to Izzy, and Izzy's shoulders sink with disappointment. The brush-off. 'Maybe another time?' Thea says gently.

Izzy nods. Of course. It makes total sense. Of course she shouldn't speak to her neighbour about this. But, even so, Izzy is filled with the feeling she calls loneliness again. Everyone has a family except her. She is free-floating, here, in Thea's garden. She's looking for something in the wrong place. Intimacy, she supposes. She briefly wonders whether she's supposed to be getting that from somewhere else. Her husband, perhaps? But she suppresses the thought before it can take root.

Izzy is quiet and withdrawn for the rest of the party and, later, Thea says to her, 'Well, we're going to have some supper now with just close family,' and even Izzy knows that is her hint to leave. She has outstayed her welcome, hoping to continue the conversation. Needy and aloof, all at the same time, always both together, a curdling, ugly combination.

She lets herself into her house via the back garden. It's completely silent. Nick is at work. She imagines, as she often does, what it would feel like to have a family waiting inside. Busyness. People. Toddlers banging wooden spoons on saucepans, grumpy teens texting, their feet up on the kitchen chairs, and babies snuffling in their sleep. The stuff of life.

But how could she do that? What sort of a partnership would they make, she with her mother issues and Nick with his . . . with his what? How closed off he is, she supposes. It's the first time she's really admitted it to herself. But she can't deny it, not now she's tried to confide in her *neighbour* rather than her husband. She boils the kettle, getting a mug out and making a second coffee. She tries to imagine it. Properly this time. Bringing a baby home. Caring for it. But what if she and Nick began to argue? What if she shouted at the baby? Lost her temper? What if what happened to her father during his forties happened to her? What if it's lying in wait, until then? No. She spoons coffee into the mug. She can't do it.

She looks at her phone and imagines it lighting up constantly with texts. Siblings, parents, nephews, nieces.

The row her father had with her mother leaves her mind. She forgets his lies. All she can think of is this feeling inside her. This hollow feeling. This lonely feeling as the party continues next door – *family only* – while she stands alone, making coffee for one, thinking about traits she might have inherited.

Maybe she could speak to him. Maybe she could meet him. Maybe everything would feel clearer, and less muddy. He is suddenly a pinprick of light in the darkness. Her father. Her dad.

She picks up her phone, and dials.

*

They arrange to meet at a café at the beach the next evening. Nick is on lates, and Izzy will get Chris to cover for her at the restaurant. Her father has a job interview, he says, and he'll see her after that.

He's there before her, looking furtively around him. She's pleased he's nervous. But he's also just – she sighs with pleasure, not able to stop herself – her dad. Look at him, there at the table. Her *dad*.

He's ordered a bottle of wine, she's surprised to see, and it sits on the table in front of him. The café is ambiently lit: candles line the windowsills in glass jars that refract the light across the wooden flooring. It's pleasantly busy, to her relief. Folk music plays softly in the background.

Gabriel is wearing an anorak. As she approaches him, she sees it still has the price tag on, dangling down from the hem: £12.99 from Matalan. He isn't sitting normally. She doesn't quite remember his body language, but this isn't it. He's hunched over. He's wearing unbranded trainers and jogging bottoms that gape and flap around his ankles. He looks cold and tense, here in the pretty café.

She sits opposite him and looks out to sea for just a few seconds. The horizon is completely flat, the sky a deep blue. If it wasn't for a cooling breeze, it could be the height of summer.

'How have you been?' he says softly. He hasn't removed his coat. He is just staring at her, his white hair messed up around his temples.

She can't answer that – how could she possibly? – so instead she says, 'This is a very strange situation.'

He nods, the ghost of a smile on his face, glancing down at the table. When he looks up at her, his eyes are wet. 'You're so big,' he says to her. A statement from father to daughter after almost twenty years apart.

'Oh, thanks,' she says, surprised how easily the teasing rolls off her tongue.

His face stretches into a grin that makes her insides twist. There is just a glimpse of Gabriel there, hidden deep underneath the too-thin face, the missing tooth, five along. The white hair. The prisoner's pallor.

'You grew more. After I was taken,' he says. *Was taken.* She notes his use of the passive voice. 'You're so tall.'

'I did,' she says. 'I grew another few inches when I was eighteen.' She casts about for something to say, something to break this awkward, loaded meeting, to distract herself from his unwavering gaze. 'Your friends used to call you Tin Cup,' she says, thinking of the memory that popped into her mind earlier. Why did they? She suddenly wishes to know everything, absolutely everything, about his history. Before her. Perhaps it'll help.

He blinks, then the grin appears again. 'They did.'

'I don't remember the friends. Who were they?'

'Let me see,' he says. He drums his index finger on the wooden table. 'Tim, Dixy, Allo-Allo, Greg. Paul. Tin Cup . . . it's a movie reference. Do you know . . . ?'

'No.'

'No. You're too young. Kevin Costner played a golf prodigy. I was good at golf. And most sports, I guess. They used to draw the short straw on who got to play me,' he says.

Izzy shifts on the wooden chair. 'Will you start playing again?' She wonders if he could even kick a ball against the yard in prison. Probably not. She winces as she thinks of her father, her gregarious, messy, creative father, locked up.

He always had so much stuff. Was always doing so many things, forever a project on the go. His shipping container was chaos, but in the centre of the oils and the discarded canvases, the overalls and the lumps of clay, there would be a painting rising up from the mess like a statue. He had enjoyed his life, plain and simple: he and his friends used to play tennis every Wednesday in the summer. Badminton in the winter. Golf some Sundays, when they weren't hungover. Yes. It's all coming back to her now. He was known as Tin Cup to his friends.

He finally removes his coat, even though he still looks cold. It fires a thought off inside her mind, like the first bubble in a boiling vat. Where does he live? Does he have any money? Do people *remember*?

'How was the interview?' she says.

'Didn't get it. I was late. Taxi didn't show.'

'You should've called.'

He throws her a strange look. 'Next time, can I call you, then?'

'Yes,' Izzy says, but she feels uneasy, suddenly. Her casual offer of a lift has been grasped by her father like a life raft. 'But you withheld your number,' he says. He proffers his mobile to her, and she keys it in, not knowing what else to do in the face of his persistence.

'I didn't want the job, anyway.'

'You could call back, explain why you were late . . . they might make an exception.'

'Nah.'

'But if you were working –'

'Leave it, alright?' he says, his voice thunderous in the café.

'Sorry.'

'I'm sorry.'

Her eyes meet his. He doesn't look away, so she does, instead.

'Anyway, it was just shelf stacking,' he says, fiddling with the menu on the table. A blush is colouring his cheeks.

She finds her face heating up, too. Her father was no academic. He only ever had handyman jobs, painting, decorating, but his tastes were firmly middle class. He liked Brie and red wine and discussing art – he loved Francisco de Zurbarán and Caravaggio. He liked to buy pork and apple sausage rolls from M&S Food and posh burgers for barbecues. He liked that they owned an upmarket restaurant, even though he never worked in it himself. He had a wide pretentious streak that she had loved.

'Going to any interview is a great first step,' she says brightly.

'They asked where I'd been for the last eighteen years. Then it all came out. I'll have to lie, I guess? Next time.'

'What's the advice? Your . . . from the people helping you.'

He laughs now, a bitter sort of laugh. More of a *huh* sound. 'My cellmate got released two months before me. Know where to?'

'No.'

'Finsbury Park. Just gave that as his postcode to the probation officer. They were fine with it. Though they made sure he bought a tent.'

'That's . . . horrendous,' Izzy says, staring at him, this fascinating familial specimen she's sharing a table with. How is it ever going to work? Even if he is innocent. Even if. How will he find a life? Build one from scratch? What are the ingredients for starting over? Does he want something, maybe? Help . . . money?

He's still staring at her. He hasn't taken his eyes off her. 'You're so like her,' he says. 'Do you know? Do you remember?'

She nods. 'Yeah. I remember her. Of course I do.'

Her eyes meet his. He looks . . . how does he look? There's a kind of hunger in his expression. So why does she feel fine here, alone with him, in the dimness of the café? It is because of him, she supposes, and the way he makes her feel. The way fathers make their daughters feel: safe.

'Me too,' he says softly. He gestures to the bottle. 'You want to share? It's nice,' he says. 'Though maybe too upmarket for your tastes.' A tiny grin.

Of course. Of course he remembers. Memories spring forward, scenes she hasn't thought of for years. Heinz baked beans and sausages, shared in a single bowl, during *Dawson's Creek*. A 99p Sainsbury's kids' pizza, proffered to her like a gift one evening. He knows her tastes. He made her, she thinks, as she watches him. He made her, and so he knows her – still – better than anybody.

She flags a waitress down, gets a glass, and pours the wine. It dribbles out of the bottle like blood. She takes a sip. He's right. It's too rich.

'Order something else,' he says, catching her expression. 'What do you want?' He rummages in his pocket and her heart constricts when he pulls out a handful of coppers. 'You order at the bar.'

'It's fine,' she says, hoping he hasn't spent the last of his money on an impressive bottle of wine.

Gabriel sips from his glass. 'Nothing like a fine red on a warm night,' he says, but the sentence sounds strange to her. Constructed, somehow: fake.

'Did you ever drink in prison?'

He gives a tiny laugh, a little sniff. 'No.'

'Not at all?'

'No.'

'I thought prison was a law unto itself.'

'Oh, it is. It's easier to make things other than alcohol. Fermenting is beyond most prisoners.'

'Like what?'

'All about Spice these days.'

'Spice?'

'Legal high or, at least, it was. Manufactured into liquid. Sprayed on to a faked child's painting which is brought in; they can get it past the guards.'

'And then what?'

'Ripped up and smoked, like tobacco. They would get off their bloody faces on it.'

'On their kids' paintings?'

'Most of them didn't even have kids, Iz. All fake.'

'Did you ever try it?' A sickly feeling settles in Izzy's stomach. The old Gabe was so against drugs. And now look at him – roughened around the edges by prison life.

'*No.* Spice was the least of my worries, anyway,' he adds.

'Yeah?'

'During my fifteenth year, I was moved to this open prison, shared a room with a guy named Steve. He was in for embezzlement, from work. He was doing an Open University course in social media, whatever that is – I never really got the hang of it. Anyway, in open prisons we had rooms, not cells. Like . . .' he gestures one hand upwards, trying to find the word, 'like halls of residence, I guess.'

'I didn't go to university.'

'No, I know. Paul said . . . Jesus, Izzy, of all the things I thought you'd end up doing, it wasn't running a fucking restaurant. You used to exist on cheese toasties.'

She has to laugh. 'Still do.' She likes the swear word. He

would never have sworn in front of her when she was seventeen. But here they are, two adults, a bottle of wine between them.

'Yeah, I . . .' he scans her face, searching, she guesses, for an explanation. 'I was surprised.'

'What did you think I'd do?'

'Ballet,' he says immediately. 'Teaching ballet, or dancing . . . didn't you?'

She shrugs awkwardly, not looking at him. Nobody knows about the ballet. Not even Nick. 'I'm good at running a business,' she says eventually. 'Better than you and Mum.' She flashes him a grin. 'What happened to Steve? In the open prison?' she asks, and she remembers now. Their chats were always full of layers, digressions, asides. They meander and undulate like linking rivers, dividing far apart and then coming back together.

'Oh, he was training in the gym. Bench pressing. This other guy, Danny, was spotting him, then moved, so Steve dropped the weight. Bar crushed his windpipe. Danny set it up. Denied it, but I saw the whole thing. Blood everywhere.' Gabe makes a slitting motion across his throat while staring directly at her.

Izzy scoots her chair backwards, away from him, feeling herself pale.

'Sorry,' he says quickly. 'Been inside too long. I've become . . . I don't know what's normal now.'

'Why did he do that?' Izzy says, ignoring that sentiment. She can't go there herself. It's *not* normal to have witnessed these things. He must be changed, inside, because of it. Made worse. Blackened.

'Wanted him dead. Always had.'

'Jesus Christ.'

'Yes. That's the thing in there. They're already serving. They have nothing to lose. Lawless place. Fucking lawless.'

Think of what the years inside have done to him. She hears Chris's warning again. She had thought of the monotony, the pain of being in prison, but not the other things. Who has Gabriel associated himself with for the last eighteen years? Not people who drink nice bottles of red in a seaside café, seemingly. And so, whoever he is now, he has her phone number, programmed in by her, willingly.

'Sorry for telling that story,' he says suddenly, putting his wine glass down and slopping wine on to the table. He doesn't clear it up, doesn't even look at it.

'It's fine,' Izzy says tightly, wanting to move on. To get away, really: she shouldn't have come here.

'I've forgotten how to converse normally,' he says.

'No, you haven't.'

She wonders if he still does all the things she remembers. Does he still paint his miniature portraits? Tiny pieces of canvas, the size of one of his hands. Does he still like to toss a ball up and down while on the phone? Does he still cycle absolutely everywhere? How can they begin to catch up on nearly twenty years, anyway? *Even if.*

'Anyway,' he says, like he hasn't just told her a horrifying story, 'I was telling you about the debt on the phone. Now you need the next bit. What happened next.'

'Gabe,' she says, and he winces.

'Yes?'

'Do you have an alternative explanation?'

'We're getting to that,' he says quickly. 'I promise we are.'

He reaches for his wine glass. She stares at his arms. Those tanned, black-haired fatherly arms she remembers so well:

opening jars, hanging up paintings, moving quickly in front of her to stop her from running out into the road. They're skinny now, pale, the hairs white. His elbows jut out uncomfortably, too angular, like two squares underneath his skin.

He fiddles with the stem of the glass. 'I drank out of blue plastic mugs for eighteen years,' he says, gesturing to the glass. 'I feel like I'm going to break this.'

'We can get you a mug, if you like,' she says with a smile. An image of her mother's injuries springs into Izzy's mind. God. Is she mad to be here, with this man – convicted by an impartial, dispassionate jury?

'Six weeks before she died, I got this loan,' Gabe says. 'To try and help her out. I didn't tell her about it.'

Izzy blinks. Her father, the old Gabe, would have led into a topic seamlessly, charismatically. This Gabe is a facsimile of him. Some of the same gestures. The same eyes. But faded and distorted, too.

Izzy thinks of the insurance policy. *Foul play.* What if killing her had been his solution to the debt that she had put them in? She shakes her head. No. That doesn't make sense. That is not a normal train of thought; killing is not problem-solving.

'Okay,' Izzy says.

'They wanted to arrange a payment plan, after the two weeks' grace. It was The Money People – you remember them in Luccombe?'

'They're still around,' she says. 'But now everyone gets loans on apps. Wonga. Payday loans.'

'Apps?' Gabe says blankly.

Izzy puffs air into her cheeks. How can she explain what an app is? It would require so much backstory . . . she's not even sure she knows herself. 'Never mind.'

A clock somewhere in the café chimes: it's quarter past seven. She hopes she doesn't meet anybody she knows here. Anybody who could pass it back to Nick, but she doesn't care enough, can't seem to.

Her father puts his wine glass down and inches forward, towards her. 'Let me tell you about what happened with The Money People,' he says.

14

PROSECUTOR: The rows became violent, didn't they? As we heard from the witnesses and the medical experts.

GABRIEL ENGLISH: It wasn't like that.

PROSECUTOR: Okay, then what was it like?

GABRIEL ENGLISH: We had rowed, that's all. It was just a . . . just a normal row. A stupid row.

PROSECUTOR: Just a normal row. For you.

October 1999: four weeks before Alex's murder

Gabriel

Alex had been unimpressed when she eventually found me at 11.30 p.m. in my shipping container. I had left the doors open, to let everything in. The salt and the sea spray and the wind and the rain.

I had been trying to capture the frost on the left-hand side of a telegraph pole – my first real landscape piece – and the sun on the right; the way it lit up the grainy wood. It seemed almost impossible to do, every stroke I added making it worse, not better. I mixed ochre and cadmium yellow. I thought I'd known instinctively that that would be right but, once on the canvas, it wasn't. It wasn't right at all. I'd mixed it with turpentine, that day, and I shouldn't have. The paint was watery, little feathery patterns where I wanted harder edges.

I added graphite grey, instead, mixing it with linseed oil. It smelt sweet and bready. Like play dough. The smell of art. The paint formed satisfying peaks when slopped on to the canvas.

A little later, I added a single white line on the right-hand side of the pole. And . . . ah. It was *alive*. I looked at it for a few moments, pleasure zipping around inside my chest.

I hadn't heard your mum approach the entrance, but suddenly she was right there, at half past eleven at night. I looked at her, and then at the telegraph pole, embarrassed. 'You okay?' I said. She looked tired. Creases underneath her eyes. Make-up worn off.

'Is this what you have done with your evening?' she said carefully.

And I got it. I got her tone, and everything she was saying. She'd recently extended the restaurant's opening hours, to try and make more money. The licence application had been arduous, and annoying, she'd told me pointedly.

It all fell to her. The business, the childcare. Like a weighted dice that would always roll the same way. We fought it, with me being better for a few weeks, loading the dishwasher unprompted, packing your school bag in the evenings, Izzy, but it never lasted. I was crap at anything beyond my remit. A crappy husband. A typical man, I guess. I've had eighteen years to reflect on it, and that's the conclusion I've come to. We're lucky, us men. We can choose to dip in and out of parenthood, housework. Or we can choose to *help*, and boy do we get praised for it.

'Are the clothes ironed? Izzy's ballet shoes darned?'

'No . . .' I said quietly. 'No.'

'Of all the things you could do,' she said. 'You come here.' She tucked a strand of red hair behind her ear. 'Gabe, I don't want to be a killjoy. I don't want to be this way. Why do you make me this way?' Her tone was plaintive, wheedling almost. 'A nag?'

'I don't mean to,' I said. 'I so don't. I just . . . I just got in at ten myself and I wanted to . . . I wanted to come here and paint.'

'What do you think *I* would like to do?' she said. It was a good point. She always went for the jugular, your mother.

'I know,' I said. 'I know.'

I stared at the painting. I'd been experimenting lately, using the cord from my art bag to stipple the paint, making it look knitted and creased in the borders. It was beautiful. It was working. I felt that private satisfaction that comes with creating something good. Something true.

'You always say you understand. But you never fucking show it,' she said. 'You could have paid a bill or two. Renewed the car tax – remember that's due? Done some of the filing. Made us a meal: I haven't eaten. Thrown away the pile of crap you swept up but never quite emptied into the bin. Hung the washing out that's been in the machine since this morning. God, anything, Gabe. Anything except paint a fucking frosty telegraph pole.'

Something bright fired off in my stomach. She could tell it was a frosty telegraph pole! I shouldn't have been pleased about that, but I was. You see, I was there, in my sea-air shipping container, the smell of linseed oil and turpentine all around me, the woman I loved in front of me. It was hard to be sad in that set-up, even when she was angry.

'I couldn't resist it. And, who knows, somebody might

buy this –' I gestured to the painting, 'and then that'll . . . that'll help.'

'You're a fucking dreamer, Gabe,' your mother said. 'Wake up.'

I started a new paint job the next day – a living room in magnolia. I had to take it, didn't I? The woman who rang me was amazed when I said I could start that day.

I was halfway through the first wall when the call from The Money People came. I should have been expecting it, really. The guy had been kind to me so far, in hindsight rather like Hannibal Lecter at his politest. The loan had relieved the pressure for a month. I'd used it to pay a chunk off each credit card, and reserved some for the interest. But the money had run out again, and soon I'd owe interest on that loan, too. I hadn't told your mother. She wasn't sleeping, had lost weight.

I drew a squirrel on the wall with a small roller and looked at it. My magnolia squirrel. I picked up the large roller and dashed over it. It disappeared completely, magnolia on magnolia, like it was never there. It's her bloody debt, I was thinking moodily as I painted. But I knew that wasn't fair. She'd messed up, sure, but it was the only time she'd ever done so. I had messed up hundreds of times. Thousands. So many things missed. Forgotten sandwiches, suncream, passports, tax returns. Other things had been prioritized. Sports. Art. I would be better. I would be a better husband to her. And it started here, in this bland living room. A reckoning in magnolia.

I slopped the rest of the paint on the wall. It was easy to be good at painting a room; it only required uniformity. I was neat, and fast. I'd prepared the walls with sugar soap, cutting in around the masking tape. I had the doors open – French doors, flung out on to the patio – but the acrid smell of the magnolia masked the delicious autumn smokiness. Mushrooms pushed up through the dewy grass. Every now and again a burgundy leaf drifted down from the purple beech tree at the back.

I finished the room in four hours, its character leached out of it. I surveyed it in the amber autumn sunlight. It would have looked nice a deep green, I thought. It would contrast nicely with the brass curtain rail.

We'd stayed in Venice, me and your mother, years back. On a Teletext holiday. You were almost two, and stayed with my parents. The walls of the hotel were teal. Calypso teal, to be specific, if I had been painting them.

I'd unpacked completely, and your mother had laughed at me. 'We're here for three nights,' she said drily, still in her flip-flops and jacket she'd worn on the plane. 'I don't think you need to hang your belts up in the wardrobe.' But she was smiling at me in that way of hers, that indulgent way. Her ears moved up just a fraction when she did it.

'I can pretend we can afford this, then,' I had said, gesturing to the ornate wardrobe. 'Like it's ours.'

She had raised her eyes heavenwards. I saw the white of them flash, but it wasn't annoyance. I'd have liked to paint that affectionate exasperation. I'd have used titanium white, mixed with Mars black: the colour of her black eyelashes fluttering against the whites of her eyes.

We'd been wanting to travel since you were born, Izzy. No offence. We thought we'd pack you up with us; a baby on my back. But it was so much harder than we thought. You were a settled baby, but *only* if you were in your cot at 7.00 p.m. dead on. Our bed count had stalled. 'We have slept in our own bed for five hundred nights, I reckon,' your mother once said to me as we locked up for the night. 'Five hundred and one, soon.'

'I know,' I had said, trying to gauge her mood. But she wasn't down, not really. Just factual. 'We can go somewhere. She'll be fine without us for a weekend.'

'Alright, then,' she'd said, with that look in her eye. That dangerous, impetuous look I'd loved so much. The holiday was booked the next day.

We didn't care about racking up countries. It wasn't that. We cared about what it meant to us to be nomadic. We got it from my parents, I guess. Irish travellers. But you don't want that, I'd told her. The lack of fixed abode. No regular GP, no school for your children. But we did want to go everywhere and feel our full, true selves. We wanted to see New York City – your mother adored *When Harry Met Sally*, she wanted to go to that damn diner – and eat in a shaded courtyard in Provence. But we had no money, no time, and no flexibility, either. Instead, we had started to live out our nomadic dreams in other ways. We were both self-employed. Our own bosses. It was our way of sticking up two fingers to the establishment. We were the next generation, once removed from travelling.

When we got home, she took herself out somewhere. She wouldn't tell me where. She was mysterious, your mother, at times, whereas I was an open book. Three days later, an ornate wardrobe was delivered. It cost £5,000.

'Are you joking?' I'd said, when I saw it.

'But I bought it for you,' she'd insisted. So charming, so childlike almost, in the excited way she presented it to me. But it annoyed me, Izzy. She never *asked*. She never let me buy what I wanted. She bought things for me.

Anyway, the walls of that living room were magnolia, sadly, not teal, but I was remembering that holiday when my phone rang. The Money People. 'Someone will be over in half an hour,' a man's voice said.

'Half an hour?' I echoed.

'For the sum due yesterday.'

I didn't say anything. I couldn't, really. I was too shocked. 'I don't have it,' I said, eventually.

'You need to get it.'

As soon as I hung up, I wondered why I didn't tell him to meet me somewhere else. My shipping container. Your mother was at home. I tried to call him back, but he'd withheld his number.

I had never driven home so fast. I had to sort it.

Your mother was already in when I got home. She was wiping the dining-room table. I guiltily realized that they were my crumbs, from that morning. Her eyes flicked to me as she did it, and I thought of the other Alex, in Venice: carefree. Then I thought of how carefully I had washed up my paints at the shipping container the previous night, and cringed. I cared about them. I was meticulous about them. And nothing else, to be honest.

My reckoning in magnolia was bollocks. I was a shitty husband. I had taken Alex's debt and made everything so much worse by getting a 2,000-per-cent-interest loan. I couldn't admit that to her: more crumbs. More collateral damage of being married to me.

The man from The Money People would arrive in ten minutes. I just had to get her . . . out of there. Upstairs, away from the door.

I should have told her to go take a bath. Go to bed. That

I'd bring her tea and cake. That sort of thing would have worked, in hindsight, but I didn't do it.

Instead, I asked her to go somewhere for me. 'You've just come back,' she said irritably. Two deep gouges appeared on either side of her mouth as she pursed her lips. I could only see them sometimes. Other times, she appeared as she always had, to me: youthful, nineteen-year-old Alex. It was only when I looked back on my paintings of her that I saw the differences. Crow's feet. A gentle sagging of the skin around her jaw. She wasn't any less beautiful, though; she was more so. She was more Alex, somehow.

'I forgot Izzy's lunch stuff, for tomorrow.'

'I'm sure there's something she can have. I've got to make a call, anyway.' She brought her phone out.

'Who to?' I said, stalling for time.

'What does she need?' Alex said. 'I've been at Mum and Dad's. You should've said sooner.'

I stood in the kitchen, in front of the bread bin, hoping she wouldn't open it. 'Everything. Bread. Cheese.'

'So you want me to go out while you faff around?' she said. It was arch, caustic even, but she always was. I loved it and hated it equally. She could be so incisive, so cutting, so funny. I found so much to admire in her. I was a little in awe, I suppose. But that didn't mean she was always *nice*.

I looked at the clock. Six minutes to go. 'Yes,' I said boldly, and she threw her hands up. I walked towards the hallway, trying to tempt her upstairs, at least. 'I don't want to have a domestic,' I said.

'It's not a domestic. It's you appreciating what I do,' she said. 'But no, I'll go buy the sandwich meat. The bread. The fucking bananas.' She found her boots in the hallway and picked them up, then turned to me. Four minutes to go. She was holding the boots in her slim arms, one hand under-neath the heels, like a baby. Just the way she used to hold you. That's what I'd loved most about you being young. You had been half possession and half human, slowly forming into your own person as the weeks passed and the baby fat melted away. And now, where were you? I wasn't even sure. Perhaps, I thought, staring at the boots in Alex's arms, I would paint those arms holding those black boots. Nobody would know what they meant, of course, except me. But wasn't that just lovely?

'Anything else?' she said sarcastically, looking up at me as she laced up her boots.

'No,' I said. I saw a car pull up outside on the drive. BMW. Dark windows. This was it, right on time. I couldn't let her go out. She'd see him. She'd find out. She'd sleep even less. Her face would crease even more. Her beautiful burnt-sienna hair would go grey with the stress of it.

She reached for her bag just as I heard the front door slam.

'Don't go,' I said quickly. 'I'm sorry. I'll go.'

'I'm ready now.'

'I said I'll go.'

She reached for the door, and I had to stop her. I just had to stop her. I reached out to block her path. I grabbed her arm, too tight. Too rough. Her mobile phone skittered on to the floor, its black case cracking.

'Gabe!' she said. She wrenched her arm away from me, but the damage was done. Her eyes stared up at me, two Winsor Green rounds of shock and sadness. Usually, she'd shout and swear. She'd tell me off. But not this time. 'Gabe,' she whispered, wrapping a hand around her upper arm. She winced with the pain. And then she took her boots off and went upstairs. She didn't ever hear the bailiff. I told him to meet me at my shipping container the next day, when I was alone. I got us another month to pay, in the end. But everything was different by then.

Izzy

'I said I'll go,' her mother was saying as Izzy approached the back porch. Her voice was reedy and plaintive. *I've said I'll go, now stop it.* That's what it sounded like. Stop whatever it is that you're doing.

Izzy paused by the back door. Perhaps she shouldn't have come this way, through the back garden and into the porch where neither of her parents knew she could hear them in the hallway.

She turned away from the door, not knowing where to look, what to do.

'Gabe,' her mother shouted, not frightened now.

Izzy raised her eyebrows. Her mother had texted her earlier, saying she was at work. But she was home. Early, Izzy guessed, which was rare.

'Stop being such a drama queen,' her father said nastily.

Izzy closed her eyes, pressed down on the handle, and went inside. Her mother was walking up the stairs. Her father was loitering in the hallway, looking sheepish. Izzy stared at the spot where they'd been standing. What was happening?

She had passed her driving test twenty minutes ago. Eventually, her father arrived in the kitchen. He had a screwed-up ball of paper in his hand, which he threw expertly into the bin on the far side of the room. 'Score!' he said.

'Five minors,' she said.

'Sorry?' He looked clammy, ill even, she realized, looking closely at him.

'Are you alright?' she asked.

'Fine.'

'Five minors. Two for hesitation. The others were just –'

'Your driving test! Of course. You passed?' Slowly, the tension seemed to leave his body as he straightened up and looked at her.

'Yes: five minors,' she said, trying not to be hurt. He had forgotten. All the way home, she had rehearsed how she would tell him. Not out of nerves, but out of excitement. Would she run in, brandishing the pass certificate? Or maybe she would slip it into the conversation casually. Either one a performance they would both remember.

She expected he would be there waiting for her. Nervous, even. Her test had been after school, and he'd have been keeping his fingers crossed for her all day.

And yet, here he was, and he had forgotten. Her mother, too. But it was her father's reaction that she was missing. He was big on emotions, on praise. And now he had disappointed her.

'You're a free woman, Iz,' he said. 'Your life has changed.' And then he reached for her hand and picked it up, raising it in the air and giving a whoop, but it was flat and strange. *He* was flat and strange. But at least he had said it. What she wanted to hear.

Izzy's mother used to take a bath every day. Not at the same time, but every day, regardless of what had happened. Before the lunchtime shift, at 11.00 a.m. When she got in at midnight. Sometimes, during holidays, she would begin and end a day with one. Through winter snow and frozen pipes and summer hosepipe bans, she would take baths. It was always steaming hot, always twenty minutes, and she never took anything in with her. No book. No wine glass. Only a towel.

Izzy was brushing her teeth while her mother was soaking that evening. They were open like that. Nobody minded being walked in on. It wasn't unusual for Izzy to catch a glimpse of her mother dressing in the morning, through a half-open door. That was family life. That was their family life.

Her mother's eyes were closed, her arms draped along the edges of the stand-alone bath. It was a copper tub, its sides mottled and imperfect. Her mother liked it because it retained the hot water well. Its sides became warm, she said.

The sash window was right next to the bath, open just a few inches, letting in the early-autumn air. The windowsill held a bottle of shampoo, a bottle of conditioner, a green cracked soap and a handful of shells from Luccombe beach. Every day, her mother wiped up underneath the soap, but it would soon leave its scummy footprint there again.

'Driving really will change your life,' her mother murmured. 'Sorry we forgot. We're . . . we've got some things going on.'

Izzy glanced at her mother, toothbrush in her hand. Her chest was freckled and her hair was tied up, a few wet strands hanging down by her ears. The bathwater was murky, a steaming pinky grey, the bubbles long popped.

It was unusual for her mother to offer up any sort of apology. She just didn't think to say sorry. Izzy always thought she was modelling how to be. How to be strong.

'Don't worry,' Izzy said, with a mouthful of toothpaste. 'It wasn't a big deal or anything.' She tried to convince herself she agreed with the Izzy who was speaking. But she didn't.

It *was* a big deal. She had taken to driving – her instructor said she was so co-ordinated, and she had blushed and smiled to herself. 'I *am* a dancer,' she had said, feeling full of life and personality, sat in the car in her capacity as a young adult with him.

'Where will you go on your first solo trip?' her mother said.

'Pip's,' Izzy said. 'But I'll be able to run Chris back sometimes.' Chris had so far failed his test four times. Tony and Gabe had been ribbing him over it. Izzy had said nothing, aware of the pressure of it, the repeated failure. She hadn't yet told him that she'd passed first time.

'And how's that going? Pip?' her mother said. Izzy looked back over. Her mother's face had creased into a smile, but when she opened her eyes, they looked sad. Nostalgic, even. 'First love,' she added, which seemed to confirm it. Her mother reached for the soap and began lathering her arms.

'He's fine,' Izzy said. *Fine* didn't sum him up, though, not really. He'd taken her to the beach early on in their relationship. They'd skipped school. Izzy had never been to the beaches as a tourist, as an adult. They'd held hands and let the surf wash over their bare feet. In some ways, he was a lot like her mother: spontaneous, fun, broad-minded.

'How are they all?' her mother said, her tone tentative. Pip's older brother, Oliver, had died over the summer. Diabetes. Pip's mother had often admonished Ollie over his blood sugar readings, his thirst levels, his weight. He'd always been teenage-boy sanguine about it. Telling her his new pump – they'd gone private to get it – would control it for him, not to worry. But he had been wild. Drinking too much. Bringing girls home. They hadn't known what to do with him. Even the high blood sugar readings hadn't scared him into behaving. And then it had been too late.

'A bit sombre at times, as you can imagine,' Izzy said.

She loved the way he'd say, 'Get your ass over here then, English,' when she hovered awkwardly in the doorway of his bedroom. The way he always made her make a wish whenever they were out together and saw the moon. 'Wish on it,' he would say. The way he held her hands all the time: at school, in his bedroom. The way he wanted to know everything about her. No game playing. Just a constant text conversation that had been lasting for a solid seven months now: Izzy's phone bills were horrendous, something her mother privately admonished her about, but paid on the side, without telling her father.

She'd had a Chinese meal with Pip's family the other day. They were richer than Izzy's family, that much was immediately clear, but they also took a care over things that her family didn't. *Ambience*, she guessed. Even after what had happened to them in July.

They were a blended family. Pip and his mother. Oliver and his father. They had a doormat with four surnames on it. Pip's mother's maiden name, Pip's father's surname, Oliver's mother's surname and Oliver's father's surname. It said: *Welcome to the Hill, Talbot, Clarke, Eason Residence.* Izzy's feet had stilled as she'd looked down at it, trying to work it out. She had liked it. That they were proud of how they had come together, even though it wasn't perfect.

Pip's mother had lit red candles all along the dark wood mantelpiece. They kicked out a red wine-y sort of scent which Izzy breathed in deeply. A whole crispy duck sat on the table, pancakes steaming in wicker pots. She poured Izzy a glass of white wine without asking her. Pip's stepfather raised a glass to Oliver. It was nine weeks since he had died.

Later, they retired to a tiny room off the hallway. It had

two sofas in it, soft brown cotton. A log burner between them, footstools covered in plaid blankets. A giant television, facing them. Pip's mother had made hot chocolate for everyone, boozy for the adults. 'Not romcoms *again*,' Pip's stepfather Steve had exclaimed when the credits began to run.

'You need it,' Pip said. 'Rest that academic brain of yours. Romcoms over relativism,' he said, squeezing Izzy's knee.

Izzy fizzed with pleasure. Pip was funny, and nothing drew her in like a sense of humour. She was enchanted by him.

Steve was a lecturer at the Isle of Wight College, in philosophy. He laughed loudly. 'I don't do relativism. It's modal realism.'

'That has less of a ring to it.'

'You can appreciate it on a higher level, anyway,' Pip's mother said to him, and they all laughed. They hadn't been afraid to laugh, even after tragedy.

'They seemed fun at the restaurant,' her mother said.

Pip's family had eaten at Alexandra's early on in Pip and Izzy's relationship. Her mother had surprised Izzy; she'd been courteous and calm, stopping with them for almost their entire meal, delegating the running of the restaurant to other people so she could be with them. They'd all shared a huge cheesecake she had baked especially, with mini eggs on it. She'd bitten into one, while looking at Izzy, and smiled such a sincere, happy smile. As they said goodnight outside the restaurant, Izzy could smell the sea which – since their day at the beach – had begun to remind her of Pip. She looked up at the moon and thought: *we made this happen*. Their families had met because of them. Because they loved each other. It was the first moment she felt like an adult.

Izzy spat the toothpaste out and rubbed some moisturizer into her face. As she went to leave the bathroom, her eyelids heavy, ready for sleep, she saw the mark on her mother's arm.

'What's that?' she said, feeling able to ask, here in the steamed-up, tiny bathroom.

'What?' her mother said, her eyes closed again. Her tone of voice was strange. As though the conversation was over, suddenly.

'On your arm.'

Her mother's eyes snapped open and focused on Izzy. 'Right,' she said, sitting up. Her breasts sagged. Water lapped precariously at each end of the bath.

'What is it?' Izzy said.

'I knocked the kitchen shelves at work,' her mother said. But Izzy just knew she was lying. It was obvious: everything about it. Her mother shrugged, steam rising off her shoulders.

'How?'

'I just bumped into them,' she said.

'It looks sore.' It was red and angry. More a slap mark than a bruise.

'It'll heal.'

Izzy stared at it. It was large. With four distinct striations. Fingermarks, a few weeks before her mother died.

15

'I heard you arguing,' Izzy says now to her father. 'It went on. It got nastier. Didn't it? I remember . . . God. It's all coming back to me now.'

He averts his eyes from hers. 'I don't recall that. She just walked off.'

'I remember it, because it made me stop and think. You said she was a drama queen.'

'I didn't. But she *was*.'

'Was she?'

'She didn't remember about your driving test, did she?' he says snidely, and the atmosphere changes. There's something about his expression. His teeth are gritted. And he's changed the subject. Yet again. Away from the difficult topics, back to things that suit him, that paint him in a favourable light.

'I thought she was just so . . . impressive. She did whatever she liked,' Izzy says. 'That's the biggest thing I've learnt from her. Or am trying to,' she adds, thinking bitterly of the long shifts at the restaurant, the smell of cooking fat in her hair afterwards, the empty feeling of counting down the hours until home time, the days until the weekend, the weeks until holidays. Pointless.

'She had a huge ego,' Gabe says with a small shrug. 'I'm sorry to say. I loved her. But it was a failing of hers.'

'Did she?' Izzy says, but more to herself than Gabe. Maybe she did. Maybe that's why she ignored some of Izzy's achievements. Maybe inviting Pip to the restaurant was more an act of showing off than one of solidarity with her daughter.

She shakes her head. He has distracted her. He *did* call her mother a drama queen. He did. Two truths can't co-exist and so instead their colours run together, muddied and confusing. And he has tainted Izzy's memory of her, too. He didn't need to say that she'd forgotten Izzy's driving test. He just didn't. Her mother is dead, can't defend herself.

She tries to think. Maybe she could contact Pip. See what he remembers of her parents' marriage. If he can verify her version of events. If he remembers these rows that are springing into her mind now, two decades later.

'The bruise looked sore,' she says.

'Right, anyway. You said she'd been at work,' Gabe says, his eyes on her.

'Yes. I'm sure she had, because I remember thinking she was always at work. That she couldn't have an afternoon off even for my driving test.'

'Maybe it *was* work,' Gabe says, shaking his head. 'Maybe it was. I thought she'd been at her mum and dad's. The mind, hey?' He glances at her.

Another inaccuracy. But it was easy to misremember things. Izzy is amazed they can recall any of the details, is thankful for the signposts within her memories: her driving test, her upcoming ballet exam. They help anchor the events.

A tall, muscular man walks into the café, a woman next to him with angular, tense shoulders. His face changes as he sees them. 'You can't be serious,' he says. He stops walking towards Izzy and Gabe. He's in a black coat, blue skinny jeans.

Izzy has no idea who he is.

'Gabriel English, released after murder, and just living his fucking life. Free as a bird,' the man shouts, spreading his arms wide. 'Free as a mother fucking bird.'

'No, no, no,' Gabriel says.

Izzy is surprised by his frightened tone. He seems to fold in on himself, like a snail retreating inside its shell. He bows his head towards the table, his shoulders rounded. She can see the points of his shoulder blades, the bald spot at the back of his head.

'How about we don't eat our dinner in the presence of a wife-killer?' the man says.

Izzy begins to turn away from them, to ignore them completely, but then she looks at Gabe. He's standing up, reaching for his coat and crossing the café before she can stop him.

'Who were they?' she asks, once they're outside.

'Don't know.' He looks furtively over her shoulder.

They begin to walk, unthinkingly, away from the café and down towards the seafront. It's twilight, the sky still a pale blue, but the air is dark, with hardly any light remaining. The moon is up, full, and Izzy thinks of Pip and what happened between them. The moon is gunmetal grey. It's mottled, just like the sides of her mother's copper bathtub. Where did that green soap and those shells go? So much of the aftermath of her mother's death is a mystery to Izzy. Not only the trial, and the exact presentation of the evidence that Izzy can only vaguely summarize, but the practicalities, too. She guesses the house was sold. Its possessions taken. But where to?

The beach is dotted with couples and the sand crunches underfoot. Where in the high season the pier is full of sweet stalls, fortune tellers and fairground rides, now it's empty.

Two figures pass under the boardwalk and Izzy instinctively shifts away from them. In the vacuum of tourism, other trades rush in like incoming tides. Nick says he does so many more drugs cases during the winter and spring months. She briefly wonders if Gabe knows any of these people. These dealers, these people Nick watches and who are quietly arrested in the night.

'Who were those people in the café?' Izzy asks again.

Her father turns to her in the half-light. He looks better in the dimness. Less ill and thin, even though he's clearly feeling the cold, even in the heatwave. 'There are one hundred and fifty thousand people on the island, Iz. Half of them will know what I did. The Isle of Wight hasn't had many killers.'

'I know,' she says softly. It's a fact she's thought of often. A fact she uses to reassure herself. Statistically, there won't be another. She's been safe here on this little island with its small population of people she knows, her father in prison. Nick once said the island was 'surprisingly seedy at times', but she ignored it. She never sees that side of it.

They say nothing, walking on the promenade out towards the sea together. Eventually, she asks him what she's been wondering. 'What's your . . . your plan? For work, and things?' she says. Partly out of concern for him but partly so she knows what he's doing. That he's busy with something legitimate. Something innocuous. Involved and integrating, she supposes.

'I don't have a rule book, Iz. And I don't have a plan, either. That's up to God.'

I don't have a plan. That's what Pip always said to her. He said at the beach that his main aim was to wake up and enjoy every day. So different to Nick with his rigid views and routines. Where is Pip now? Off travelling, she expects. Living in Singapore or something. Learning to surf in Australia. Making some woman laugh.

'Are you going to get a job?' she says. She can't bear the talk of religion. Her funny, easy-going father who once said at a christening, 'What a load of creepy bollocks.' Her mother wouldn't have tolerated it, either. She was far too pragmatic. Her father. Converted to God. To believing. Does he really believe, or is it fantasy? Another story invented to paint him in the best light.

'Trying,' he says. He stops them, there, before they reach the water's edge.

Izzy thinks of conversations she's had with Nick about his cases. True-crime dramas. Nick's always taken one angle – *no smoke without fire* – whether through nature or nurture, she isn't sure. Izzy's always been less cynical. Even more so, now. 'Well,' Nick's always said of perpetrators, of suspects, of protestors of innocence. 'I wouldn't want to meet him in an alley at night, would you?' Izzy's never known what to say to that. Because it's true, isn't it? Once accused, once convicted, they're tarnished . . . Would anybody take the risk? Why would anybody employ a convicted criminal, date one, be alone with one? Everybody has principles, until they're close to home.

Izzy looks at her father, his face pale in the moonlight. But she *is* taking the risk. She is alone with him in the sea-scented night-time air.

'How was it – at Mum's parents?' Gabe says enquiringly.

'It was fine,' Izzy lies, images flashing into her mind. The crinkle of the newspaper as her grandparents filled out the crossword together every Sunday in silence. Being told to stop practising her ballet because it would ruin the wooden floors. They were willing to help her out, so long as she slotted neatly into their lives like a handshake.

She spent her time wondering where the fun and joy of life had gone; spontaneous trips out, and laughter. She couldn't separate her grief from her new living conditions. Everything had seemed bleak, tasteless, mundane. They had been grieving too, she supposes, looking back. But she couldn't see that at the time, not when they shouted, not when they silenced her with a judgemental *shh*.

'You'd better be off. I'm guessing your copper doesn't know.' It's the first time he's acknowledged Nick's job.

'He's an analyst. Not police.'

'All the same,' says Gabe.

'See you,' she says to him, not knowing when she will. The lies in his accounts seem to be growing, multiplying like tumours.

'See you soon,' he says pointedly. He turns away from her and disappears, gradually, up the hill and into the night.

She wonders where he goes. How he gets around. Who else he sees. Where he sleeps at night. *How* he sleeps at night.

By the time she gets home, he has already texted her twice.

Izzy searches for David Smiths that evening. Maybe if she finds him, she can see if there really *was* an alibi in 1999 . . . to see if she made a mistake.

She's been trying to do thirty per night: always the same message. *Sorry to bother you . . . My name is Izzy English . . . Did you used to live at 18 Rainsdown Lane?*

So far, only three out of sixty have responded, all saying no.

Next, she looks at a month of bank statements. She's doing

one month per night. When she can. It's the best way to approach it: logically. Methodically. Tonight is June 1999, five months before her mother's murder. She scans it, digesting the business's financial position. Poor profits. Getting better towards the end of the month, as the weather warmed up, she guesses. It shows nothing. She doesn't know what she's looking for. She's just . . . looking. For anything that might leap out at her. Next, she'll look through the few possessions of her mother's and father's that she inherited.

Before she leaves, though, she opens an unmarked lever arch file. It contains plastic wallets. She opens the first one and a set of receipts falls out. Fuel. A blender purchased in 1999. The paper has started to age, and flakes in her fingers. She turns it over.

And there it is. Her father's handwriting.

Sorry about the glass! Xx

That's all it says. Izzy stares at it. *Sorry about the glass.* Could it be? The thrown glass he referred to? But *he* threw it, and not her mother?

She'll confront Gabe. See what he says. She puts the note in her handbag, ready.

Nick and Izzy are in bed, later, when they hear Thea's window shut.

'Like clockwork,' Izzy comments, to stop herself from telling Nick where she's been.

'Clockwork?' he says.

He has brought his laptop home, and is still typing away, working into the evening as he often does. He should use a screen guard, but says it hurts his eyes. She leans over.

G. Michaels visited the premises on the following dates and times, Nick has written.

'Thea shuts that window every single night about eleven,' Izzy explains. 'She airs the bedroom in the day.'

'How do you know?'

'I just observe her,' Izzy says, but she blushes.

I observe her because I want to be part of a family, she thinks. *Because I want to experience what her children do: being parented when I myself am an adult.*

'You should come work with me,' he says, pulling her towards him. 'You're good at pattern spotting.'

'Maybe,' she says. She leans her head back down on his black T-shirt which smells of their washing powder. If only he knew that just hours before, she was alone with Gabe, at the seafront, in the dark. She shifts closer and closer to Nick's warm body, flinging a leg over his, too, trying to forget the way Gabriel had looked at her.

'What's G. Michaels suspected of?' Izzy says, tapping the screen lightly.

'Human trafficking,' Nick says. 'Owns a load of nail bars. We think he's moving women through them.'

'Like slaves?'

'Yeah. Anyway. Look,' he says quietly. He shuts the laptop.

'What?'

He pulls her nearer to him. His laptop falls off his lap, tipping on to its side on the bed. 'I ordered your father's file,' he says, very close to her ear.

Goosebumps appear on Izzy's shoulders. 'Did you?' she says. She can't believe it. Rule-abiding Nick.

'I thought about the risks,' he says, as if reading her mind. 'But I thought this –' he gestures to her, 'is more important. There's more at stake.'

She nods. That's how he's rationalized it. Still within his tight parameters. Still hyper-logical. She thinks of Pip, for the second time that day, his toes in the ocean. No plans for the next day.

'It'll take a couple of weeks,' Nick adds.

'Will anybody know?'

'No. They put an alert on big files. Celebrity files. Huge murders. Myra Hindley, you know. Not . . . not him.'

'Would you get in trouble if they did know?'

'Don't worry,' he says. 'Protecting you is more important.'

Everybody must do it. Everybody must look people up. Nick certainly isn't stupid. He will have analysed the risk fully.

Izzy catches a glimpse of the moon outside, and decides what to wish for. That this all turns out well. That nobody loses anything. That they emerge unscathed.

He begins kissing her ear. She surrenders to it. For the next half an hour, she is not Izzy English whose father murdered her mother. She is Izzy Gainsborough. Nick's wife.

It is only when, hours later, Nick is breathing steadily next to her, that she realizes what Gabriel said: *There are one hundred and fifty thousand people on the island, Iz. Half of them will know what I did.*

What I did. What I did.

It was a slip of the tongue, she thinks, as she falls asleep. A mistake.

16

Izzy braces herself for visiting her grandmother. Whatever the name of the feeling is that she experiences when she sees Thea, or the Instagram family, her grandmother gives her the exact opposite feeling. Neither feeling has a name.

The nursing home is not far from Matt Richmond's office, just a brief detour on her way to see her father's lawyer. It has red carpets that have faded to a dusty pink. It smells of winter food, even in the relentless spring sun: clammy, cooked potatoes, carrots, meat. The faint odour of urine underpins it all.

Izzy's grandmother is sitting in a green chair in her room when Izzy arrives in the doorway. The television is on, and her head is angled towards it, but her eyes aren't. They're looking out of the window, not really focused on anything.

Izzy's mother's disappearance has taken up residence in the jumbled mind of her grandmother. It's centre stage. On good days, she reminisces about her red-headed daughter – 'Not a single redhead in our family, she came clean out of nowhere' – and on bad days, conversations consist of a steady stream of words associated with that time. Not the time after her mother was found, but rather those two days when she was missing. It's the trauma, Izzy guesses. The trauma of not knowing, of imagining everything. It has embedded itself in every part of her grandmother's brain like rot.

Got a taxi home to be murdered.

Phone call after phone call.
Where's her passport?
The woods.
The woods.
The woods . . .

Her grandmother is in limbo. Suspended in that time, in those two days. Her mother still missing. Still searching.

'Granny,' Izzy says, stepping into the room.

A double serving of resentment and guilt joins her in the room. Her grandmother doesn't acknowledge her. She's working something around her mouth, though there's nothing there. It's a kind of nervous tic. Imagine if Izzy told her she'd seen Gabriel just the previous night. What would her grandmother say?

'I miss Mum today,' Izzy says, instead.

Immediately, her grandmother's eyes swivel towards her. 'Always,' she says. It's as if talking about Alex manages to reach parts of her that normal words can't.

'I keep thinking back to that time, lately,' Izzy says, sitting down opposite her grandmother.

Her grandmother shrugs, a jerking moment. 'Always,' she says.

Izzy nods. It's almost worse for her grandmother. She can remember it so well. Izzy shouldn't try to get her to talk about it, to try and elicit information from her. She should leave her in peace. She stares at her grandmother's hand on the arm of the chair. The skin is almost translucent, stained with age spots. For just a moment, Izzy wishes she was here with a baby. A daughter who'd have fat, plump hands that would be held by those slim, wrinkled hands of her grandmother, crossing the generations.

She glances outside. Already the grass is taking on a

parched, yellow quality. She craves gloom, today. Give her rain and drizzle.

The winter after her mother was murdered was the rainiest on record. The bottoms of Izzy's jeans were constantly soaking and they hung wet around her ankles. Whenever she remembers that time, she gets phantom cold ankles.

She had been living with her grandparents for eight weeks, in the bedroom in the loft where the relentless rain against the skylight kept her up. Her father was in custody in Newport.

They were off one morning to the Shanklin esplanade, to walk along the coast. They were keen, her mother's parents, on maintaining *normality*. They talked about it in hushed tones on the landing. The benefits of *routine*. Fish and oven chips on Friday nights, Sunday roasts. A shared pot of tea after school, even though Izzy hated the tannin taste of their teapot; it tasted like old cupboards and reminded her of caravan holidays. She took it like medicine, the milk jug dribbling on to the floral tea tray. Really, she wanted the things she had always liked. The things she still drinks now. Cheap supermarket lemonade. Banana milkshakes. Instant coffee, weak, with lots of milk and sugar.

Her grandfather was hunched over the steering wheel. He had on glasses which darkened as the sun came out. She couldn't see his eyes behind them. She lived with them now, had lived with them for months, and it struck her, in the back of the Lada Samara car, that she had no idea what he had done for a living. Who was this man in the driver's seat?

'About the trial,' he said. 'Will you testify?'

'Yes,' Izzy said. 'They'll want me to, won't they?'

'I think it would be helpful,' he said, his brown eyes briefly meeting hers in the mirror. 'Especially if you can recall any instances of . . . temper. That sort of thing.' He indicated left, and that was the only sound in the car.

'Right,' Izzy said.

She had been talking about giving evidence for the defence. To give him a fair trial.

That was how it had been, she recalls, as she stands to leave her grandmother's care home, after staying a cursory half-hour. They never argued that her father was guilty. It simply *was* so, just like the nuts and bolts of their weekly routines. Sponge pudding followed roast beef. Your father murdered your mother.

17

At 10.45 a.m., Izzy is parked in her father's defence solicitor's car park. It's a run-down building, a sixties office block that reminds her of school, and she watches a flock of seagulls circle the flat roof, eventually landing in a neat row on a telecoms mast. She waits patiently outside, the car in neutral, the air con on. She has always been good at waiting. She is logical, persistent. She will experiment with different opening hours at the restaurant, different dishes, different special offers. And then she will watch and wait, seeing which works.

A receptionist tells her to sit on the sofa and wait. Izzy's in summer wear, a skirt, and her thighs stick to the leather. She wonders what she will ask Matt, but he arrives in the foyer before she has really begun to gather her thoughts.

He must now be in his mid-forties, but has hardly aged in that time. He is still tall, athletic. Tanned. More expensive looking, somehow, than before. A well-cut suit. A nice watch.

'Sorry, Mrs Gainsborough,' he's saying, as he strides into the room. 'I know you're booked in as a new enquiry but I don't know –' He stops talking. He stares at her, standing still. A loaded pause, like the cock of a gun, and then she speaks.

'English,' Izzy says. 'Isabelle English.'

She watches him work it out, his lawyer brain turning the cogs. He leads her wordlessly into a meeting room which smells of stale coffee and the fetid aroma flowers take on when they're past their best.

He says nothing as she sits down, but his expression is kind. He crosses his legs at the thighs, a strangely female and agile mannerism, and jiggles his foot as it dangles in the air. He has on black shiny shoes and pale blue socks.

'What can I do for you?' he asks.

'I wonder if there is any way,' Izzy says, knotting her hands together, 'that you can discuss my father's case with me. Gabriel English.'

'I know who your father is . . .' Matt says softly. 'You look just like her.'

'I know.'

'I'm afraid I can't discuss his case. I'm sorry, if I had known who you were . . .'

Izzy feels disappointment drop in her chest. Of course not. Confidentiality, integrity, privacy. Her father's right to tell his lawyer his most well-kept secrets.

'Not even now he's been convicted and he's *out*?' she tries.

'Client confidentiality lasts for life,' Matt says. He offers her a kind of smiling apology. 'I'm afraid.'

'I just . . . I'm pretty confused by some things.'

'I know. I remember every aspect of your father's case. I worked with him for several months. And then I kept tabs on every subsequent development.'

'Did you –' Izzy stops herself.

But Matt already knows what she has asked. 'I don't think he should have been convicted,' he says carefully. 'I worked very hard to ensure he wasn't. I hardly slept, during those early months of 2000. I had a newborn. It was one of the very hardest cases of my career. Of my life.'

'If he had told you anything . . .' Izzy says.

Matt says nothing, his cool lawyer's gaze appraising her. He is keeping his powder dry, saying nothing. Waiting.

'. . . could you tell me?'

'Like what?'

'If he had told you he was guilty.'

Matt makes a sudden movement, scooting his chair backwards slightly, raising his palms to her. 'A common misconception,' he says. He leans back towards her, elbows resting on his knees. 'If a client confesses their guilt to me, I would have to stop defending them if they intended to lie in court. All lawyers would.'

'I've been looking at the evidence. There are some things which don't add up.'

'I know,' Matt says. 'He should not have been convicted. Much of the evidence against him was circumstantial.'

'Is that to say you think he's innocent?'

Matt holds her gaze, saying nothing. Looking like he wants to say something, but not saying it. 'What doesn't add up?' he asks eventually.

'Why would he have reported her missing? And why would he have put her . . . where he did?'

'I agree.' Matt leaves a beat before speaking again. 'We never found his alibi.'

'No,' Izzy says. 'I know.' She hesitates, then asks, 'Do you believe them? Your clients who say this?'

Matt purses his lips, showing her those dimples. 'Some of them.'

'He tells me they were in debt.'

Matt looks at her in surprise. 'Yes. From setting up the restaurant.'

'I'm looking into it. Into the case against him. And what he says.'

'Are you?'

'Yes. I own Alexandra's now.'

'Is it the same company?' he says, unfolding his long legs and recrossing them the other way around.

'Yes. Alexandra's Restaurant Limited.'

'In that case, I can help you there,' he says. 'Leave it with me.'

'But . . .' she asks the question before she can help herself. 'Should I be alone with him?'

Matt says nothing again, staring at her. Eventually, he brings a hand to his chin, raises his eyebrows. If it means something, Izzy isn't sure what. But he'd tell her, if Gabe was dangerous, wouldn't he?

Forty-five minutes later, Izzy is handed a box of paperwork from Matt's ex-colleague and partner of another law firm who acted for her mother's company. As the owner, they now belong to Izzy. 'They might not help at all . . .' Matt had said, smiling in his apologetic way, 'but sometimes it's nice to feel you're looking at the primary materials.'

She places the box on the passenger seat in the car park outside the law firm and starts to sift through it, unable to resist.

The restaurant's balance sheets are filed together, in date order, this time. The appointment of her mother as director and shareholder. The company accounts. A few pages later, a letter:

6 September 1999

Dear Alexandra

Alexandra's Limited – Dismissal

I am pleased to confirm that Daniel Godfrey has now been removed from the payroll.

Kind regards
Adams & Co Solicitors

She fingers the letter. Izzy tries to think. Daniel was a waiter in his late thirties who wanted to be an actor. Her mother had always got on well with him. They'd had a shared joke about how much he hated working lunchtimes, that he got up late. 'Alright, alright,' she would sometimes say, 'you can work the evening.'

Dismissal, the letter's subject says. How could this be? And why Daniel? A curly-haired, out-of-work actor. Totally benign, as far as Izzy remembers.

In all of Izzy's research into her mother's running of the business, she had never once let somebody go. Not even the waitress who called in sick thirty-five times in six months. Her mother had paid her sick pay generously, Izzy had noticed the other night while looking at the statements in the loft. Why would she have got rid of Daniel?

Maybe she was sacking people because of the debt.

Or maybe she sacked Daniel for some other reason.

She takes the box home with her. She will look through the rest of it later, out of the heat. It's the best she's got. Better than inscrutable Matt, who gave nothing away. At least she can start somewhere now. She can start digging.

Izzy calls Gabe as she drives to work. Seeing Matt has made her think of alternative explanations. New theories for what might have happened. It's sanctioned what she wants to do: contact him.

'I've seen Matt Richmond today,' she says when he picks up.

'My lawyer?'

'Yes.'

'How is he?' Gabe says, like they are talking about an old friend.

'Secretive,' Izzy says, and Gabe laughs so loudly Izzy has to turn the volume down on her hands-free system. He doesn't seem surprised to hear from her. He seems to take her contact passively, like a stray animal grateful for any scrap at all. 'Mum sacked Daniel Godfrey in September 1999,' she says.

'The actor,' Gabe says immediately, with all of the recall of somebody who lives life entirely in the past. 'When, did you say?'

'September the sixth, 1999.'

'Two months before.'

'Yes. Any idea why?'

'I don't remember.'

'Anyway, that's all I found.'

'Good sleuthing,' Gabe says. 'What's next?'

'I want to speak to the taxi driver,' Izzy says. 'The last person to see Mum alive.' The words she doesn't say hang in the air between them: *except you, perhaps.*

He says nothing, thinking. 'Alice Reid,' he says finally. 'It was Alice Reid.'

'Yes,' she says.

'You going to speak to her?'

'Maybe,' she says.

'Are you looking into it? You know, I can think of nobody better than you – to investigate it.'

'I don't know,' she says, remembering her grandparents talking about Alice's evidence, and the nail it placed in her father's coffin. And thinking of the box of evidence now in her possession, of the bank statements in the loft. 'Maybe,' she says again, more slowly this time, wondering if she's really going to do this.

'You've no idea,' he says, 'how pleased I am that you trust me enough to look into it . . . that you're giving me the benefit of the doubt.'

Izzy says nothing to that. What can she say? Sometimes she thinks he's delusional, manipulative. The police, the State, the CPS used all of their available resources to investigate her mother's murder. What does he think – that she'll find something they missed?

Her father tells her he has to go for another interview and she says goodbye while negotiating a roundabout. She doesn't reach to hang up, and he hasn't, either. She can still hear him, or somebody, rustling around a room. She hears the crinkle of a carrier bag, maybe, and she hopes he isn't taking that to a job interview. She hears footsteps and the thump of shoes being moved on to the floor. And then she hears her father's voice. Speaking. Without knowing she is listening.

18

'Eight weeks. Eight weeks. Eight weeks . . . to go.'

Izzy drives, listening. She knows she should tell him, but she doesn't. Instead, she just listens, her eyes on the road ahead.

'And then – and then . . .'

She hears him scrabble for the phone, loud noises across the microphone.

'Hello?' he says.

Izzy pulls the car over to the side of the road, her head full of his words. His words that don't seem to make any sense. Eight weeks until *what*?

'Gabe?'

'You're still there. I thought I heard your car.'

'I didn't hang up – I was driving. I was waiting for you to do it. What are you talking about?'

He laughs softly, seemingly to himself. 'Oh, nothing,' he says. 'Just how long the Jobcentre have given me to find work before they stop my Jobseeker's Allowance.'

Izzy looks at the road in front of her. She narrows her eyes as he prattles on: he's hopeful about his next interview, anyway. He's pulled pints before, he'll be good, he'll be sure to be evasive about the last eighteen years, this time.

She says nothing, thinking of the way he was speaking. It was almost like a pep talk, to himself. No, not a pep talk. Something else. He sounded fired up. That was it. Like somebody planning something. Setting something in motion.

*

Izzy sends ten more David Smiths messages, then writes to Alice late at night.

Alice Reid is in her early fifties and posts on Facebook every single day about her grandchildren, Theo and Frederick. They've been enjoying ice creams in the heatwave, crab fishing at the beach, and snuggling up watching *Britain's Got Talent* together in the past week.

Izzy wonders if Alice ever thinks of it. That she was a key witness in a murder trial. If she ever realizes the impact she had on their lives.

She begins to type a private message.

I hope you remember me, Alice – though maybe you don't want to. You gave evidence at my father's trial. I'd love to speak to you about it. Please do get in touch, if you're able.
Izzy English x

Izzy goes quiet for a few days, thinking thoughts of insurance jobs and tempers and reasons to kill. She still writes to David Smiths every night, and checks a month of bank statements, but nothing more than that.

She finds she misses her father, after only two weeks of contact with him. Like theirs is an established relationship already. History, she supposes. A diverted river easily becomes functional again, the water flowing freely. Knowing where and how to flow, because of its past.

Paul said you saw him, a text comes through on a sunny Monday morning from Gabe.

I did, she replies immediately.

Communication – intimacy – is her Achilles heel. She could become drunk on it, and it would never be enough. She sometimes imagines Thea watching her as she goes

154

about her day. How good Izzy is at the business side of things. Witty remarks she makes. Even time alone with Nick. She is constructing herself with these parental figures, she knows she is, and yet she can't seem to stop. Doesn't know who she is without them.

What did you discuss? his immediate response comes back.

Oh, yes. That's right. She remembers now. He always replied so quickly.

Within a few moments another text comes in. She can't delete them as quickly as they arrive, in case Nick should ever glance at her phone.

Come to the hostel, won't you? We can talk more. It'll be better than getting shouted at in cafés – better we're not seen.

No, I . . . Izzy drafts and redrafts the text message, politely declining.

Before she can send it, though, he calls her.

'It'll be nice,' he tells her. 'We can have tea and catch up. And we could even watch *Dawson's Creek*,' he jokes.

'I don't know,' she says.

'We can play cards, and just spend time together,' he adds.

And soon she is putting her shoes on, sleepwalking her way out of the house and to the car. Following that rare thing: intimacy. Family. Love, she supposes, as she starts the ignition.

It will be the first time they are alone together.

19

'Welcome to my humble abode,' Gabe says. She has driven to Shanklin, where he is *housed*. That is the term he seems to use, and she has adopted it reluctantly. It's what looks like a B&B set alone on a strip of land between two huge housing estates.

Three teenage boys are standing near the door as she pulls up. Two in tracksuits, one in a shirt and tie, smoking. They stare at her, hostile, as she drives past, trying to find somewhere to park.

She finds a space and walks past an off-licence on her way. It has bars running around the inside of it, like a cage. Not a single bottle of wine or packet of chewing gum can be picked up. The shopkeeper sits there, like a caged lion, watching her warily. Outside, above the sign – *General Convenience Store* – somebody has graffitied the word *cock*.

Gabe is waiting on the steps of the B&B when she walks up. 'It's shit, I know,' he says, raising an eyebrow at the rubbish collecting in the road, at the strange luxurious cars, their blacked-out windows, a cluster of three- and four-year-olds playing football alone over the way even though it is a weekday morning. The youths have moved on, somewhere.

'It's not that bad,' she says, trying to look behind him, hoping the bail hostel is neat, and clean. She can't imagine him sleeping in filth. She just can't.

The smell of marijuana drifts on the breeze.

'What is a bail hostel, exactly?' she says as they step inside.

'It's a room, here, with a load of other . . . well, mostly ex-convicts. Some drug addicts. You get a room – or a shared room, if you're unlucky.'

'Is it . . . can't you . . .' All of the restrictions on his strange little life cluster into her mind. Can he cook a meal? Does he have a sofa? A key?

He ignores her trailed-off question, clearly not wanting to answer, and leads her up a set of brown-carpeted stairs. They have metal nosings on the end of them like they are in a hospital or secure unit of some kind.

His door – dark, cheap wood – jams, and he puts his weight behind it to open it. Izzy has been wanting to paint all of the wooden doors in her cottage white, but she's been waiting to find out if listed building consent is needed. She runs a finger over the splintered wood as she steps into his room.

'Should I be here?' she says. The first thing she notices is the temperature. She starts sweating immediately. The window isn't open, and she looks across at Gabe, but he doesn't seem to notice.

Maybe it's the heat, maybe it's something else, but she jumps as her father closes the door behind them, and they are alone. She is on edge, suddenly wondering if this is stupid. Reckless. The hairs on her arms rise up.

She stares at the closed, single-glazed window, covered in mould and condensation. 'Bit hot, isn't it?' she says, trying to distract herself, but Gabe only shrugs.

'Why do you ask if you should be here?'

'Because you might have . . . I don't know. Rules to follow?'

'I don't have any licence conditions relating to you. Bizarrely, in the distorted eyes of the justice system, you are not a victim of my alleged crime,' he says. 'Only Alex is.'

Alex. He hardly ever uses her mother's name around her.

It brings to mind the things she's remembered and found out about Gabe and Alex. The artefacts of her parents' marriage. That shared kiss in the dimness of the kitchen. Their love notes on the back of bank statements. Their history of counting beds slept in, if that isn't a fabrication by Gabe.

She looks around the room. A neat, single bed. Pink bed sheets. A table. A miniature fridge. A radio on the inside shelf of the wardrobe – the door is missing, and she likes that he has capitalized on that.

She looks again at the mouldy window and removes her cardigan. If he is here – if he is living here amongst the grime, has been imprisoned before this – and he is innocent, she won't be able to handle it. She just won't.

A dog is barking incessantly outside. Six barks, seven. A pause, and then it begins again.

'Staffie left outside all day,' Gabe says ruefully to her. He sits down on the bed and rubs at his temples.

It's a new mannerism. She sees his hair has thinned there, and wonders if he has simply rubbed it clean away.

'Nah, mate,' somebody shouts loudly outside, and Gabe looks up irritably.

She looks at the bed, at the tiny wardrobe containing all of his belongings in a pile on the open shelf – socks, trousers, T-shirts all jumbled up together – and at the coffee ring on the table. Next to that is a small bowl and a single plastic fork, smeared with dried tomato sauce.

She notices a stack of papers on the windowsill. 'What're they?' she says, pointing to them.

To her surprise, his cheeks colour, and his shoulders rise as though he is suddenly cold and trying to keep warm. She has never seen him make such a gesture; the father in her memories is energetic but relaxed, too. Confident. Never tense like this. She watches him, trying to work him out.

'Nothing . . . nothing,' he says with a wave of his hand, but he picks the papers up and he hands them over.

The first sheet is a drawing of a large detached house. He's used coloured pencils on thin, cheap paper that's curled up and stiffened. It has his old flair – a wisp of smoke coming out of the chimney, the green depicting the grass and the hedges. A mobile number is written at the bottom in calligraphic font. *Handyman: No Job Too Small* alongside it.

She leafs through them. The next one is the same. There must be fifty of them. 'You made these?' she says, but as she utters it, she looks again. The house has a blue door. The first one is red. She looks back at the first sheet. They're different. She leafs through them. Different shades of green, slightly different handwriting. They're all different.

'They're not copies,' she says.

'Yes. Couldn't get to a printer.'

'What, so you . . . you just did them yourself? Again and again?'

He shrugs, his cheeks still pink. 'I don't know, Iz . . . I have too much time. Lots of time. It doesn't matter.'

She opens her mouth to tell him about the software she has on her iPad for sketching. About the printer she owns that was £20 in Tesco. The way you can pay a company £5 to print your every Instagram photo, but finds she doesn't know where to start. He probably doesn't even know what Instagram is.

'I enjoyed colouring.'

'Is this the first time since . . .'

He nods quickly. 'I'm rusty. You can tell,' he says, gesturing vaguely to the angle of the first house against the horizon behind it.

'You could've photocopied them.'

'There aren't photocopiers in newsagents any more,' he says. *Newsagents.* Some of the language he uses is so antiquated. What do people say, now? The Spar. Londis. Budgens. They're not newsagents. Many of them don't even sell papers. Does he know that every major newspaper has a website, these days? She supposes not.

'Oh,' she says.

'And anyway, it's expensive.'

She looks at him. For the first time, he's given her a measure of his budget. What would it be – ten pence per sheet? Embarrassed, she gathers up the flyers and straightens them into a neat pile.

'I thought I could be a jobbing handyman again, anyway,' he says. 'No interviews. No DBS checks. Can come and go as I please.'

She nods enthusiastically. 'Yes. Great idea. Some money for you. To spend how you like.' It could work, she is thinking. It could really work. He'd have somewhere to go each day. He could save up, rent a flat. Paint pictures in his spare time. Just like how it used to be.

'I'm going to put them up on the Sainsbury's noticeboard,' he says.

The optimism she had felt in her chest evaporates, leaving her deflated and sad. There is no longer a Sainsbury's noticeboard. This isn't how people advertise themselves any more. She should tell him about Google Places, about Facebook for Business, about TrustATrader. But where would she begin?

'Maybe leafleting people's houses is better,' she says

instead. 'The nice estates in Newport. Maybe the people with scaffolding up. They'll want the finishing touches done. Plastering and painting.'

'Maybe,' he says softly, just looking at her.

She puts the flyers back on the windowsill. They look childish and strange in the light from outside, sitting there on the grubby windowsill, its wood beginning to rot.

'Anyway,' he says, turning his gaze away from them. 'Where were we?' He stands and advances towards her.

She takes a sudden step back, bumping into his wardrobe. She can't explain why she does it. She flushes with embarrassment as his eyes meet hers, hurt. She thinks again of the job interviews. Would she employ him to paint her house, co-exist comfortably with him in close proximity?

'Where had we got to with our discussions?' he says.

'Four weeks before her death,' she says, instead of saying what she is thinking.

'Okay, yes,' he says, sitting down on the bed.

There's nowhere for her to sit so she stands, hovering by the wardrobe awkwardly.

'Next, I need to tell you how I came to send that text.'

'What text?'

'The text the prosecution went to town on. Two weeks before your mother died.'

20

PROSECUTOR: You sent that text to threaten your wife, didn't you, Mr English?

GABRIEL ENGLISH: No.

PROSECUTOR: Your wife wasn't doing as you wanted, was she, Mr English?

GABRIEL ENGLISH: It's not how it looks . . .

October 1999: two weeks before Alex's murder

Gabe

I stopped by the restaurant late in the day. Somebody had scuffed a wall, and your mother wanted me to touch it up quickly. 'With your neat hand,' she had said beguilingly on the phone. She was in the back office when I finished. I walked into the kitchen, on the hunt for her delicious leftovers.

The second I saw it, I stared at it in shock. A massive planetary mixer. Silver. Standing on the work surface like a spaceship. Even through my disbelief, I noted with mild interest that it was entirely reflecting its surroundings. I'd have to use yellow ochre to paint it: it was reflecting my bright, sunshine-coloured T-shirt perfectly. How good that would look, a portrait of a planetary mixer, its owner reflected in it.

'This new?' I said to Daniel, one of the waiters, who nodded, smiling at me.

'Brand spanking,' he said. 'Thousand pounds.'

I turned to him in shock. 'One thousand pounds?'

The receipt was easy to find: of course she'd left it on the counter, folded asymmetrically: £888 plus VAT. My stomach dropped. What the fuck? She didn't need a mixer. She'd never had one, she wasn't replacing one, it was new. *Brand spanking*, as Daniel said.

I called her immediately. She was at the cash and carry. 'What is this mixer?' I said.

Daniel disappeared into the main restaurant area, sheepish, embarrassed by my tone, no doubt.

'What?' she said. I could hear a till ringing up purchases in the background. She loved it there. She went too often. Fucking shopping.

'The eight-hundred-and-eighty-eight-pound mixer.'

'We needed it.'

'That much – on a fucking mixer? Did we need it more than we needed to pay off The Money People? Halifax? Barclays? The Woolwich?'

'You afford your container,' she said coolly.

It was a low blow. My shipping container. My only hobby. My escape. Was that monthly spend foolish? Then call me a fool.

Alex didn't say anything to me after that. I waited a few minutes, but she disconnected.

You will pay, I sent to her, a text which was later picked over, examined, misconstrued in court.

Izzy

It was easy, in the end, to have Pip over. Television had led Izzy to believe that they would need pebbles to throw at windows, ladders. *Telegrams*, Pip had joked. But they hadn't. 'Fine,' her mother had said when Izzy had floated the idea. Izzy had been leaning on the front counter of the restaurant. That was it: *fine*. Fine to have Pip over. Her mother had exchanged a glance with one of the regulars, Marcus with the white-blond hair, who always ate right there at the bar. Izzy had looked at him. 'Teenage romances,' he'd said, and her mother had busied herself at the till.

'So this is your humble abode,' Pip said. She'd never once had a boy in her bedroom, and he looked out of place standing there in his Converse trainers.

He gravitated to her wall of framed black-and-white photographs.

'All the ballet,' he said, running a finger over one. 'Which one is it you're getting into?'

'Steady,' she said. 'I'm not in yet. Don't jinx it.'

'Okay,' he said simply. 'But I'm sure you will. What'll they make you do?'

'Make me do?' she echoed.

'The bleeding toes and the sit-ups . . .' he held up his hands. 'My knowledge comes from shit dance films. Sorry.'

'Who watches those?'

'Steve, of course,' Pip says with a smile. His stepfather always protested at the romcoms, but watched them avidly. 'He's enthralled, look at him,' Pip had said drily last weekend. 'He only wishes *he* could bump into Julia Roberts in a Notting Hill bookshop.'

Izzy always thought she'd want a boyfriend she had lots in common with; someone whose interests aligned with hers, to whom she never had to explain anything. But here was Pip, a strange man – blond, lanky, interested in literature when she couldn't bear the over-analysis, relaxed where she was energetic – and she was fascinated, absolutely fascinated by him. By the way he believed in fate – 'total bollocks,' Izzy had laughed, and he had joined in. And the way he sent her a daily poem every morning. Maya Angelou, Lord Byron, Philip Larkin. All tapped out by him, to her. Love letters, spanning multiple messages that each cost him ten pence. The way he never knew what he'd be doing the next day, how he often 'popped over' to the mainland on the ferry, not letting the Isle of Wight cut him off from life.

And so she didn't mind explaining ballet basics to him. He didn't need to be familiar to her: he didn't need to be like her. 'There are three long classes a day. A nutritional plan. Yes, some sit-ups,' she said.

'Five days a week?'

'Six. And I would still do a quick *barre* on the seventh day. And the rest: darning pointe shoes, breaking the shank – the back – so they show off your arch better. Soaking them in calamine lotion to make them a lovely matte pink, to make the line of your leg to your toes look better.'

'Ballet admin.' He turned to face her. His expression was unreadable. His raspberry-red lips were drawn together, his dark blue eyes carefully watching her. He bit his lip. 'Well, we did it,' he said. 'We're alone.'

She spread her arms wide. This was it. All of the texts and the calls and the *what was the best day of your life; what's your biggest regret?* questions. They had all culminated in this moment: they were finally alone in the way they had been imagining.

Pip didn't make it weird, and that's what she liked best about him. Instead, he flopped down on to the lilac beanbag next to her bed and crossed his long legs out in front of him.

'You should get away, before you go to the military ballet school,' he said. He had been everywhere. Four holidays a year. The hallway in his house was covered in photographs from each trip. Him, Ollie, their parents. Last year they'd been to Thailand for the entire summer holiday. Pip saw himself equivalent to Izzy, she was sure of that, but they weren't. Steve would spend £200 in Sainsbury's, proffer posh chocolates in a box on a regular Saturday night. Izzy's parents spent £20 in Kwik Save, and argued about it.

'Will *you* go away?' she said.

'*We* should.'

Her heart opened. 'Before your literature degree,' she said.

'Yes. Before that. Before you join the ballet Nazis.'

'They're not Nazis,' she said, laughing.

'Those feet have been tortured,' he said, pointing.

She was standing, barefoot, feet turned out, as she often did. Bunions, blisters, over-defined muscles. Her feet looked scary out of their elegant pointe shoes, she had to admit.

'Where?'

'Anywhere you like . . . you can show me pirouettes in Paris. An arabesque in Australia. Wherever.'

'Why English literature?' she said, still standing by the photographs.

'I think it's the way to wisdom,' Pip said in that easy way of his. He leant back, fully stretching out like a cat on her beanbag. Even in here, in her slightly too-cold bedroom, his cheeks were pink. He had just the faintest trace of blond stubble across his jaw. As he leant backwards, she saw a trail of dark stomach hair, which she stared at. 'Besides, writers are hilarious. The shenanigans Lord Byron got up to . . .'

He put his hands behind his head and closed his eyes. 'You coming over, anyway, English?' he said. He opened one eye and looked at her. And, just like that, she went to join him on the beanbag. His left arm enfolded her, around her waist, feeling both as safe as home and as dangerous as fire. The warmth of him. The solidity. The soft cotton of his T-shirt when she tentatively rested her hand on his stomach.

'Well now . . .' she said.

At first he said nothing back, only a deep, thoughtful *mmm*. Then, 'These abs,' he said, his arm around her waist gripping her tightly. 'How many Saturday sit-ups do you do, again?'

'One thousand,' she said.

'Shame about the feet,' he said.

Izzy lifted a leg elegantly into the air and waved her ugly foot at him.

'Like a hag's,' he said, and she giggled into his shoulder. 'It looks like it's been cursed.'

'That's the English student in you,' she said. 'Always looking for a story.'

They lay like that for over an hour before the shouting started.

'It's Mum on the phone to Dad,' she said softly to him as they listened. Her mother had screeched *what?* already.

'Well, at least a domestic might provide a good distraction for me to sneak out,' he said. His voice was intimate by her ear. Only a murmur, really. 'No need to do the meet and greets.'

'True,' she said.

More shouting. *We needed it*, she thought her mother was saying. And then: *no, don't.*

She couldn't make out any more words. She felt her cheeks heat up, regardless. Couldn't they *control* themselves?

They stood and she led Pip out of her room. On the landing, she heard her mother again. 'Shit,' she was saying to herself. 'Shit, shit, shit.'

'Oh dear, definitely time for me to go,' Pip whispered. 'You should've heard mine the other week. Mum went *nuclear.*'

It had put a dampener on the evening, and not even driving could cheer Izzy up. She drove them to Godshill in silence. As they sat outside his town house, the engine idling, Izzy could hear the train line in the distance, and the traffic outside the front of the house. There was a takeaway opposite them that Pip said he sometimes got a naan bread from, to go with Steve's home-made curry, and a music shop next to it that sold guitars and drum kits. It was the opposite of Izzy's suburban seaside house that always smelt slightly salty.

She waited.

Pip seemed to be stalling.

In the end, he kissed her properly.

21

'I had forgotten how much you had started to row,' she says nervously now to Gabe.

He produces a pack of cards and starts shuffling them aimlessly. 'We played so many card games inside,' he says, nodding to them. 'Great way to pass the time.'

'You preferred to play sport at home. Tennis. Badminton.'

'I know. I have come around to the sedentary life,' he says. He starts dealing. 'Here, I'll teach you.'

'I had thought you were happy,' Izzy says, steadfastly leading him to what she wants to discuss.

'We were.'

'But these rows, they're making me remember all sorts of stuff . . . I wish they weren't.'

He shrugs at that, saying nothing. He has dealt them two cards each. 'Pontoon?' he says. They only ever played cards on holiday. The *tap, tap, tap* of rain on French campsites as they played on the wooden decking, sheltered under the porch.

He doesn't mention the rows with her mother again, and she doesn't press. But, as she's leaving, she produces the receipt, scrunched up in her handbag. 'I found this,' she says. 'I was thinking about what you said, that Mum threw a glass at you . . . about *her* temper.'

Gabe takes the receipt, turning it over in his hands. He studies the handwriting, then looks back up at her. 'Yes, she wrote me this,' he says softly.

Izzy swallows. Her mother's and father's handwriting was similar, but not quite the same, and this is his. He's lying to her.

She leaves quickly, looking over her shoulder as she does so. She's a fool. She won't be a fool again. She *won't*. She'll go home and ignore him, from now on.

As she stops in traffic, she sees two men standing in the doorway of a shut-up tourist shop, yet to open for the season. They're performing a transaction of some kind, money in exchange for a small parcel, and Izzy looks away, away from the seedy underbelly of the island that Nick so often refers to.

And then she thinks again of the receipt, her father's lies about the handwriting. She thinks, too, of the wardrobe he claimed her mother bought. But another memory pops into her mind. Him lifting it over the threshold of the house on a borrowed trolley. No. Can that be true? She can picture it perfectly, the curled ornate edges, the wrought-iron handles. She is sure he was wheeling it in, ready to present it to her mother.

And her mother *had* said 'no, don't' on the phone to her father. It was missing from Gabe's account, but Izzy was sure she had heard it. She remembers so clearly because she had a witness. They had exchanged a glance. He was somebody she trusted, somebody she had loved very much, who was with her, alone, for the very first time, who heard it too. He was someone who later stopped loving her.

What's the truth? The discrepancies between her and Gabe's accounts and memories of the events leading up to her mother's death are growing in small but significant ways, like the beginnings of a fault line in the earth itself. His incorrect recall about who had painted the restaurant cellar.

The way his arguments with her mother are tweaked in his favour. It might be misremembering, but it serves Gabe. It always advantages him. It's hard not to be suspicious.

She will go home and, soon, she will read about it, she decides. Properly. Swallow the nausea and read the full accounts of his trial online. The evidence. It is not only that she wants to exonerate him, it is that she wants to free herself of that past.

Of his temper, and what might live within her.

Izzy opens her laptop first thing the next day, as soon as Nick has left for work. He had kissed her goodbye, an unusually full, warm kiss that reminded her of the weekend they met, all that time spent in his tent, laughing at this clever, steady man who'd suddenly become the centre of her life.

She forgets the kiss as she opens Facebook. Somebody has given Alexandra's a five-star review. *Despite its morbid roots* . . . the review begins, and she clicks off it. She sets her coffee down on the kitchen table.

Gabriel is easy to find on the internet. *The Post* ran a full feature in 1999 – GABRIEL ENGLISH: ARTIST AND KILLER. And she's read *The Island Echo*'s story before – RESTAURANT OWNER WIFE MURDERED BY HUSBAND, SURVIVING DAUGHTER TO TESTIFY. Today, she wants something more. She is looking for something outside of herself and her memories. Her own recollections are tangled and incoherent, muddied by the lens through which she views them. She is a melting pot of childhood memories, her grandparents' views, press headlines next to normal family photographs deemed sinister with hindsight . . . She cannot remember what is real.

She is looking for the daily coverage of the trial. All of the evidence, all of the conjecture, all of the arguments. The professionals' views, that is what she wants. Not opinions. But facts. If she reads enough of them, perhaps she can begin to form her own opinion, like taking a handful of different ingredients and making a cake. She can't believe she is here, that she actively wants to read about the things she has avoided for so long.

She types *Gabriel English* into the British Newspaper Archive. It is somehow removed from her father's name, in the way a celebrity's may be. *Gabriel English* is a notorious killer, the subject of tabloid spreads and true-crime documentaries. But her *father* – her living, breathing, soft-bodied father – is somebody who used to like to lick his finger and pick up the tiny splinters of crisps left at the bottom of the bag, somebody who believed in fresh air and long runs, somebody who took seriously the thoughts running through Izzy's mind, and listened to them.

She scrolls down to 1999 in the local press section. The stories begin there, running into 2000, a new one at least every week until the trial was over, then her father's appeal failed and the press moved on. She looks at the most recent articles.

Notorious wife-killer Gabriel English's daughter reopens restaurant in mother's name.

Alexandra's opening – Izzy English – her mother's image.

Izzy remembers the night she opened the restaurant. She was just twenty-one. The money had come from her grandparents, though everybody had assumed otherwise. When you are beset by tragedy, everybody assumes that at least you get a pot of money. Life insurance payouts. Compensation. But she didn't: there was nothing.

She had wanted to open the restaurant without ceremony. Switch the lights on and open the doors one night and see who came by. But her business head had taken over: she needed the press on side. And, of course, they came because of who she was. She avoided the questions, the awkward enquiries, but later that night, when she'd had a couple of flutes of what everybody thought was champagne but was actually Lambrini, somebody referenced her history. She was standing near to the bar, taking it all in, when a man with a DSLR camera slung around his neck came up to her and said, very simply, 'What is it *like*?' His eyes were round and staring as she met them and she saw in them not a journalistic curiosity but a human one. She was *other*. She didn't answer him, just picked up her glass and moved along the bar, but she hadn't forgotten the question. She could never answer it. It would take all year.

After everybody had left, she ran her palm along the bar. She knew she didn't feel how she ought to. There wasn't pride, or accomplishment, or even happiness, really. Instead, she felt the familiar feeling of displacement. *I'm not supposed to be here.* Her mother dead, her father incarcerated, and running a restaurant by herself. It's not where she wanted to be. And so, for two minutes, she let herself transform. The bar became a *barre*. She assembled her feet into first position and did a few experimental *pliés*. But she couldn't continue. She was choked up. Her body was stiff, her memories brittle. She couldn't access her self: her old self. The one who had danced so freely. Before.

She scrolls now to the articles written during her father's trial.

Missing Alexandra English's body found – husband arrested at scene.

Alexandra English: cause of death confirmed.
Alexandra English made phone call plea moments before death.

Izzy feels sick, and clicks off the browser and back to Facebook. It blinks with a new message. Alice Reid has written back.

Hi Izzy, and thanks for writing to me.

I do remember you and your father but I'm afraid I can only remember what I said at the trial. I dropped your mother off at about quarter to midnight. She paid me in cash, got out of the taxi, and in the rear-view mirror I saw her enter the house.

I hope this helps you, Izzy, to perhaps get some peace. I'd rather move on, myself, and enjoy life. And so I'd ask that you don't write again.

Izzy reads her words over and over. *In the rear-view mirror I saw her enter the house.* As she had told the court, she guesses. But could she be sure? In Izzy's and Gabe's recollections there are inconsistencies. Things presumed. How many taxi journeys did Alice make every day? Did she always see her clients enter their destination, or did she just presume – imagine it, construct it around what she expected? What if Izzy went there? Parked up outside? Saw what a taxi driver could see?

'She didn't know,' her grandmother had said at home one night during the trial, to her grandfather, while Izzy sat on the spot on the landing where the pipes crossed and warmed the carpet. 'She didn't know she was going home to be murdered.'

22

Izzy watches the dishes moving around the restaurant. She is not thinking, not doing anything, just aimless. She's remembering her mother, standing here in this exact spot a few days before she died. Black trousers, white shirt, red hair, just like her. What would she think of Izzy? Perhaps she'd be willing her not to see Gabe again: her killer. Or she'd be wishing Izzy would hear him out. And what about that? Who *would* she want Izzy to be careful of? The real killer?

Izzy lets that thought turn over in her mind for a few minutes. The real killer. Not her father. She thinks of her middle-class mother, the restaurant owner, her daughter off to ballet school, her husband an artist. Who would want to kill her?

'Alright?' Tony says to her, walking into Alexandra's and hanging up his jacket. He's come to work the bar. 'I don't even know why I brought that,' he says, gesturing to his coat. 'Sweltering out there. The oysters will be nice tonight, though. I can always smell it in the air when there's been a good catch.'

Izzy hates oysters.

She stares at him. She's not seen him since Chris spoke to her at the pub quiz about Tony not testifying.

'Fancy a walk?' she says spontaneously. 'Before you start?'

It is strange to be walking next to her father's brother along the coast at Luccombe, when she so recently walked with her father along a similar stretch of coast. They have so much in common. Their long strides that she struggles to keep up with. The way they angle their whole bodies to look at the sun and close their eyes, like lions basking. The way they walk with one hand in a pocket. Mannerisms learnt or inherited, but the same either way.

The tide is out, the sand a wide, fawn-coloured expanse, the sky completely blue despite the encroaching evening. Izzy can't remember the last time she saw even a wisp of a cloud. The weather has been reliably the same, every single day, since the end of April. Blue skies. Twenty-five degrees. Zero chance of rain.

'Nice for you to get out at rush hour,' Tony says. 'Costa del Luccombe.'

'Only the boss could get away with it,' she replies with a grin.

She looks sideways at her uncle and wonders about his childhood with Gabe. She thinks of her relationship with Chris, its roots deep as trees', and wonders about all of the things which predated her. Did Gabe and Tony smoke roll-ups outside in the summer and talk about girls? Did they toss a tennis ball back and forth when they should have been studying? What was important to them? How did they define themselves? Music and art and sport? Did Tony ever have reservations about Gabe? What made him conclude he was guilty so easily? She's never asked, never been able to. It would be strange to suddenly want to know why things were the way they were, and had been for decades.

'Did you ever think you might go to see Gabriel?' Izzy says as they look out to sea. The surface of the Channel looks golden, molten with sunlight.

She feels Tony's body language still beside her. 'No,' he says. He turns his face away from her, to the sun.

'Not even for an explanation?'

'No.'

He turns to look at her. He has under-eye circles. He's olive-skinned, too, but his face is more weathered and lined these days. Two fans of crow's feet spread out from each eye. The skin around his jaw is sagging and thin. Izzy feels her face twist into a half-smile: what Gabe said about ageing in prison is true. Gabe looks ten, twenty years younger than Tony. Not healthy, though. Too thin and worn, somehow.

'Why?'

'I felt he could never explain it to me. How could he?'

'I guess even criminals have an *explanation*,' Izzy says delicately.

'You know, Izzy, your dad and me – and Alex. We go back.'

'Yeah.'

'I mean . . . never mind,' he says, with a wave of his hand that is so like Gabe she almost has to stop and ask him to do it again, this facsimile of her father who still has his liberty, his money, who knows what an iPhone app is. 'You don't want to know.'

'I do.'

Tony pauses, hands on hips, then finds a flat rock which they sit on. It's rough with sand and warm to touch.

'He was . . . he was somebody who did exactly what he wanted,' Tony says.

Izzy can't argue with that. He has always been so, preferring to create paintings and make pots when he should have been out earning money.

'He was impetuous, artistic, temperamental.'

'Temperamental?'

'You know, he had this girlfriend, Babs.'

'Who?'

177

'They rowed so much – he was in his late teens then, early twenties maybe. Anyway, the less said about that the better. I thought he was more suited to your mum, but . . .'

'But what?'

'Oh, it's ancient history, Izzy,' Tony says with a finality Izzy recognizes.

'No, tell me.'

'Well, he was . . . Alex could be evasive. And that made him weirder and weirder in the weeks leading up to her death. He was always attentive with her but . . . I don't know. He seemed obsessed.'

'How was she evasive?' Izzy says. She can feel herself frowning. Her mother wasn't *evasive*, was she? Take Gabe, she thinks nastily, but don't taint my memories of my mother.

'She was . . . they were just ill suited, I think. She was . . . I don't know. She did some things I don't agree with.'

'What?' Izzy says.

'She wasn't always honest with Gabe. I can see why,' he says quickly. 'Gabe was so controlling. But she'd tell him things had come up at the restaurant when they hadn't. She would just read a book in the back office, having told him she had to catch up on accounts. She wasn't . . . she wasn't a saint, I suppose. Nobody is.'

Izzy shrugs. She can see why her mother would behave this way.

'Chris said something,' Izzy says, capitalizing on the opening, trying to find answers. 'About the trial.' Tony stretches his tanned legs in front of him and slides his shoes off.

Izzy closes her eyes and breathes in: she can tell exactly where she is on the island by the smell. Down here it is earthy, less fishy than Yarmouth.

'What did he say?' Tony says eventually, turning to her.

Izzy senses his movement and opens her eyes. The sea air is whipping his hair back away from his forehead. God, their brows are identical. Izzy couldn't have described Gabe's until she saw it on Tony: tanned, with that single horizontal line across the middle. The high hairline. She can't stop looking at it.

'That you were going to tell the lawyers something helpful, and then didn't.'

'That's right. I was,' Tony says stiffly, still not looking at her, heels digging two neat divots in the sand.

'Why would you testify for the prosecution?' The words seem to die on her lips, the sentence fading as she finishes it. *Prosecution*. To prosecute. Such a nasty, vicious name for the people who attempted to bring her mother justice.

Tony closes his eyes and leans back on his hands.

'Because he was guilty as sin. But I guess, when it finally came down to it, I just couldn't stand up in court against my brother. You know?'

Izzy nods, but she doesn't know, not this closeness, not family beyond cousins and uncles and aunts, and marriage, which still feels conditional to her. She has no siblings. No parents. The closest thing she has is a family she double-taps too often on Instagram.

'I lost so much fucking sleep over it. Would it help? Would he get convicted without it? Who did I owe the most loyalty to – Gabe or your mother?' He exhales, points his toes, and then puts his shoes back on. 'Anyway. Let sleeping dogs lie, as they say.'

Izzy narrows her eyes. Something feels off. *Let sleeping dogs lie*. Where has she heard that recently? Chris, that was right. Chris had said it. Had they – father and son – said it to each other? Had they made some agreement?

'I'm glad it didn't matter. They got him anyway,' Tony adds.

'But what was your evidence?'

Tony turns to her while lacing his trainers up. 'You don't know?'

'No.'

'The curse of being seventeen, I guess. Nobody tells you shit.'

The dynamic has shifted between them, over the years, from avuncular indulgence to a kind of respect, now that she employs him, and she has always loved that Tony has allowed that to happen. That he isn't stuck in paternity, as Gabe can be.

'Anyway. Enough of that. Lovely weather.' His words are easy-going, his body language languid, but something is still off about his tone. Something feels . . . constructed about it. Perhaps she is imagining it. But perhaps there is more to this than he is going to tell her. It is easier not to testify than to have your story picked apart in front of a jury. Perhaps he has something to hide.

'Nobody told me anything,' she says carefully, hoping to prolong the discussion.

But it wasn't just that nobody had told her. They had become divided. Even though Tony's family and Izzy's grandparents all believed Gabe was guilty, they stopped seeing each other. The split through their family, from what Gabe did, had been too wide.

And so things weren't discussed in the open, because there was no *open* any more. There were no family parties, no meals for ten or twenty, no cold-cheeked greetings outside pubs. Just the splintered remains after everything that had happened. A group of individuals who failed to communicate well, who couldn't navigate the choppy waters of what happened to their family.

'What was your evidence?' she says, frustration leaking into her voice.

Tony sighs and looks at her. 'On the night of Hallowe'en . . . her murder,' he starts, clearing his throat. He stands up and they walk closer to the tide. 'Gabe and I were both at Alexandra's.'

'Yes.'

'And at about seven o'clock he comes to grab me, and says he saw someone coming out of the back office with your mum.'

'Who?'

'He doesn't know. He says she emerged, then someone *else* emerged and went down the back corridor to the door, but he didn't see them because the corridor was in shadow. Your mother was behaving strangely, he said. Fixing her hair. Looking over her shoulder. He went outside to see who emerged but they'd already gone, or gone back into the restaurant, anyway.'

'And so you . . .'

'I didn't tell anybody. No.' Tony stops walking as their feet meet the water.

Izzy dips the heel of her shoe into the tide and watches the sand wash away from it.

'I just thought how bad it looked. For him. And he didn't tell anybody, either. He didn't tell the whole truth in court.'

She looks out to sea and wishes for a moment that her mother had left more behind. That she had a sister, another child, a best friend. Imagine if she could piece her mother back together again. From her university years. From her childhood. From everybody who ever met her. The obstetrician she must have seen. Her dentist. The man she rented the restaurant off. Her property solicitor. Her GP. A patchwork quilt of the woman Izzy barely knew.

'Do you know that I didn't corroborate his alibi?' Izzy

says to Tony, wanting to return the sharing of information. Of intimacy.

'I remember,' Tony says.

'Who told you?'

Tony looks up at the sky, evidently thinking. 'I'm not sure,' he says eventually. 'I just know.'

Izzy stares at her sand-covered shoes, wanting, suddenly, to escape. To cross these seas, and leave the island. Disappear into London. Does Gabe know, too? She can't ask him, can she?

They walk slowly back to Alexandra's. The sand yields satisfyingly underfoot, like freshly fallen snow. Tony says nothing as the restaurant looms into sight. When they reach the foyer, Izzy heads downstairs to the basement. There are a couple of old boxes in the corner next to the wine rack that she wants to look through. More evidence.

Tony follows her.

'I want to investigate some things a bit more,' Izzy says over her shoulder to him. 'What was happening in the run-up to her murder.'

Tony nods in the gloom of the chilly basement. 'Those boxes?' he asks, pointing to them.

'Yes.' The property information lives here, in those boxes, and the financial information and her parents' possessions – those Izzy has been able to track down – are in Izzy's loft.

He shrugs as he turns to leave.

'Was he angry?' she calls up to him spontaneously. 'About Mum and the person in the back room?'

'Yes,' Tony says, glancing down at her and making eye contact. 'He was furious. He thought . . . he thought he had been betrayed.'

*

'This came for you,' Katie, one of the waitresses, says to Izzy when she arrives back. 'After the usual post.'

Izzy takes hold of a letter and heads to the back office. The peculiar not-alone feeling has settled over her shoulders again. The envelope has no stamp. Her address is typed on a sticky label. It's been sealed with Sellotape which she peels off.

She sits on the chair and opens it.

23

A newspaper cutting falls out. One article, folded neatly in half. The top of the paper is jagged, crimped. It has been years since she has read a proper newspaper.

Her hands are shaking as she unfolds it. She is never usually nervous. That part of her has been dulled.

On one side is a political story, but it's when she turns it over that she sees her parents' wedding photograph. They're standing next to a set of fairy lights which shine too brightly, darkening the rest of the photograph. Her mother is smiling at the camera, little happy creases either side of her mouth. Gabe's looking at her, half of his face in shadow. His hair is dark, spiked up. Her mother's is pinned back. It looks auburn in the photo, not bright red.

Izzy stares at the headline: WIFE-MURDERER CHARGED AT SCENE OF BODY DISCOVERY.

It's not unusual for Izzy to get mail of this kind. From fanatics. From people who want to know more about the crime. From people *planning a trip* to the restaurant. But there is usually a note. She checks the envelope, then spreads out the article.

She remembers seeing it for the first time, just a glimpse, the paper removed swiftly from her grandparents' table. Her cereal had tasted bad, the milk sour, her stomach acidic with it. Her mother was dead. Her father was under arrest. He hadn't told them. He had been charged at 4.00 p.m. when her mother's body was recovered, but they found out at 6.00

p.m. from the news. *Husband charged in wife killing*, the Breaking News headline said on the television. That's how they found out he had been charged.

She fingers the faded headline. She had forgotten. She had forgotten that he had never told them himself.

She turns the clipping over, checking there's no handwritten note in a margin. And that's when she sees it. An indentation. Something has been struck out on the other side. She turns it back over.

Alexandra has been neatly crossed out with a black ballpoint pen. In its place is one word: *Izzy*.

Izzy's phone rings, sending adrenaline firing around her chest.

'Hello?' she says distractedly, still holding the newspaper cutting.

'What's the matter?' Gabe says immediately.

She traces the neat line through Alex's name. Hers is written directly underneath it.

'Sorry, I just got this . . . I just got this thing, in the post,' Izzy says, unable to resist the pull of his concern, his tentative tone, his fatherliness. His ability to immediately spot when something is amiss with her, even over the telephone when she has uttered only one word. Even after eighteen years. 'I got this newspaper cutting in the post just now.'

'An article?'

'Yes. About you.'

'Which one?'

'The one with your wedding photo. *The Island Echo*.'

'From who?'

'I don't know. Unstamped envelope. Through the restaurant door. But they've altered the article.'

'How?'

185

'It's got my name. Mum's is crossed out and my name . . . is in its place.'

Gabe says nothing for a few seconds, then says simply, 'God.'

'I don't understand . . . I don't understand who would do that,' she says.

'Nosy people. Judgemental people. Mad people. Like that man in the café. I got a prank call the other night telling me to go back to prison.'

'Oh,' she says, sitting down on the chair and leaving the newspaper cutting on the desk.

'Somebody probably saw us the other night. They're an armchair rescuer, you know. Think you shouldn't be seeing me. Decided to write to you. That kind of thing. The letters I got in prison, Iz . . .'

'I used to get a few,' she says.

'Really. Don't worry. Standard nutcase behaviour.'

'I see,' she whispers. And then, in part to distract herself, without thinking for a second whether or not she should tell him, she says, 'I spoke to Tony about the evidence he didn't give. About Mum being in the back office with a man that night.'

'I'll just come over,' Gabriel says immediately. 'I can explain more easily in person. You free this evening?'

'Okay. I can be. I can leave here, now.' She looks again at the newspaper. 'I want to leave here.'

'Good.'

Her hands are shaking as she folds the newspaper cutting up. 'Where should we go? The café again?'

'I'll come to yours,' Gabe says decisively.

'No, I . . .'

'Let me take care of you. Make you a pot of coffee and sort this out,' he says. 'Without anyone else interfering.'

'No, but –'

'No arguments,' he says.

And, just like that, in the face of the threatening note, her reservations evaporate. The way he cajoles her into meeting. His inconsistent accounts of the past. They don't matter. There are explanations for them. She so wants that to be true.

And so she gives him her address.

She arrives home swiftly, and sets herself up at the kitchen table, which she wipes, then laughs at herself. As if he would judge the cleanliness of her surroundings; her father who shared a cell with a man who smoked Spice.

He hasn't arrived after an hour. After an hour and a half, and three cups of Mellow Bird's, the doorbell finally goes. Izzy looks at the clock in the kitchen. Half past eight. They only have an hour until Nick will be home, and her stomach lurches.

'You took a while,' she says gently to Gabe.

He takes off his jacket. The tag is still inside, dangling off the bottom, and it swings as he bundles it up.

'I walked,' he says.

'You *walked*?' Izzy calculates the distance in her mind. It's five miles, maybe more. As he brings a hand to his upper lip to wipe a sheen of sweat off it, she sees that he is shaking. 'Why didn't you just . . .' the words die on her lips. But of course. He doesn't have a car, and no money either, probably. And yet, here he is. In her hour of need.

'I would've fetched you,' she finishes lamely. She remembers all the times he took her to ballet classes, to meet friends, waited up to bring her home from parties, eyelids drooping as he drove.

'No need,' he says with a wave of his hand. 'Need the exercise. Only done laps of a yard for twenty years.'

'Sometimes walking can help you to work things through,' she says, thinking of Tony's evidence.

'Yes, exactly. Like Elijah fleeing to Horeb.'

'Huh?'

'Elijah fled to the wilderness, in the Bible. There, he found God.'

Izzy says nothing.

Gabe looks around her kitchen. 'This is so . . . you,' he says.

She tells him the story of how they came to buy it. 'And Nick – where is he?' Gabe asks.

'Work,' she says quickly.

He is staring at her iPad which lies discarded – she watches recipes on YouTube as she tries them out. 'An iPad,' he says. 'We had those in the open prison. No internet, though. Just games.'

She goes to speak, then pauses. Eighteen years in prison. No internet. The things he won't know about. It must be like being an alien. Smart phones. Digital SLR cameras. LED light bulbs. Airbnb. Alexa. Uber. Netflix. Broadband. Deliveroo. The demise of landlines, CDs. She shakes her head. She can't imagine.

'Tony told me about the stranger in the back office.'

'The stranger in the back office, indeed,' Gabe says, a weird half-smile playing out on his features. 'That's what I've been getting to. One of the things,' he says, putting his coat on the spare kitchen chair, 'that I have been getting to.'

'What's your theory?'

He shrugs, his angular shoulders lifting upwards and then dropping again. He is this way sometimes. Monosyllabic. Sometimes amazingly eloquent, other times stunted. She supposes it is one of the effects of prison.

'Tony's theory is that you were angry with her,' she prompts.

Gabe blinks. 'I bet. I discussed with Matt why Tony didn't volunteer that information to the police. I knew he'd seen, because we talked about it afterwards. Matt and I thought about calling him to the witness box, to testify about the person in the back room – that it might shine the light on someone other than me – but Matt had, I guess, the same concerns as Tony.'

Izzy shivers. Concerns. That's a mild way of putting it: Tony's evidence gave Gabe a clear motive.

The back door is flung open. She can hear Thea and her daughter out there. She's back now, properly, for the summer. Izzy goes to fill the kettle. 'Tea?' she says, and Gabe nods.

Thea and Molly are sitting at Thea's wrought-iron table. Molly has brought home Indian chai tea, and they're laughing about whether or not to serve it with milk. Izzy allows herself to imagine, just for a moment, not that she is Thea's daughter, but that she is Molly's mother. She's made it: unscathed. She had a child, and the world didn't cave in. She's happy. Fulfilled. Less alone.

Izzy watches them as she gets two mugs down from the shelf. Molly's feet are up on the chair opposite her mother. Thea pats them casually, as she offers to try one cup with and one without milk. It's an intimate gesture. Was Izzy once privy to these things? She can't remember. It's amazing how scant the memories are from before the age of seventeen. As though childhood is only important to the parents, and not the child. Izzy remembers how she felt – safe, happy – but not anything much more specific than that. Did she and her mother share a pot of tea in the garden one time? Maybe. Hopefully.

She turns to look at Gabe. He's staring out of the front window, at the fields opposite, seemingly lost in thought, his face cupped childishly in his hands.

Motives. Izzy's mind is whirring.

Daniel Godfrey was sacked. That is what Izzy is thinking as her father gazes out of the window. Her mother sacked him. What if she had been having an affair with him? Had been in the back office with him?

But even if her mother had been having an affair, does that mean her father would kill her? Of course not: it's a leap for any normal person. For a man who would laughingly draw a caricature of anybody she asked. A man who'd once eaten so many sweets in the cinema that he'd made himself ill.

Izzy watches Molly show Thea something on her phone and thinks guiltily again of her father's alibi that she decimated in one seemingly innocuous police interview.

Perhaps Gabe kills women who betray him.

'He thinks I was angry then,' Gabe says as she sets his tea down in front of him. He shakes his head from side to side quickly. 'But I wasn't. I was confused.'

'I don't understand.'

'Then let me explain,' he says. 'Let me tell you about the night she went missing . . . the night she died. Let me tell you what I *do* know.'

24

PROSECUTOR: And what time did you hear your wife come home?

GABRIEL ENGLISH: I didn't.

PROSECUTOR: And yet a taxi dropped her off, and we heard the driver say she watched her enter the house.

GABRIEL ENGLISH: No . . . I don't know where she went. But it wasn't inside.

PROSECUTOR: Did you murder her there, in the house, and carry her out? Or did you force her into the boot of your car and murder her somewhere else?

Hallowe'en, Sunday 31 October 1999: the night of Alex's murder

Gabe

Sometimes I wonder what would have happened if your mother's car hadn't been in for service. If she hadn't had to get a taxi.

Don't you find, Iz, that when something goes missing, sometimes you focus on the anomaly? A missing wallet, say. You'd switched handbags. You'd check the bags over and over, wouldn't you? Because of a disruption in the routine? For ages, I thought your mother's disappearance was connected to that taxi. To that taxi driver. I was in custody from the day of my arrest, so I had to wait months to find out what each witness would say. I was in the dark. Even after I saw her give evidence – small, slight, harmless – I wondered. I don't know what I think now. My mind roves over the facts, like looking for that missing wallet. I check the same places over and over again. The taxi driver. That night in the restaurant. The debt.

I took you to start your waitressing shift at 7.00 p.m., Izzy, you probably remember. You wanted to drive yourself, but I wanted the car. I came in with you, as I often did. To see your mother. To see Tony, and Chris, too. Is it weird that I have fond memories of that evening? It was the evening before everything changed forever. I guess that's why, in my memories, it seems sweeter – the air had that dewy autumnal quality – and the restaurant seemed to burn twice as brightly on the horizon as we approached it.

You disappeared into the kitchen as soon as we arrived. I ran my fingers over a scuffed wall I'd repainted. It looked good. I was looking for your mother. You know I always was. Looking for that red hair, her slender freckled arms as she handed out plates, took down orders, issued directions. To exchange a glance, a kiss. To join up with her and to be reminded that in all the hard work and tedium, there she was.

She was nowhere to be seen.

'Alright?' Chris said, brushing past me with three stacked plates. One had a smear of gravy remaining which his thumb was resting in.

I didn't respond to him. And that's when I saw what I saw, Izzy. Here is what happened.

My elbows were resting on the bar. I had a perfect view of the back corridor, in shadow, and half of the door to the office. A palette of dark browns and blacks. Your mother emerged, red hair held up by her breadstick. She straightened out her white shirt. Her body language was strange. Self-conscious, I guess, if I had to say. Or maybe guilty: I've seen a lot of guilt.

Her eyes flicked left, and then right – two flashes of white. I watched her move across the restaurant, and that's when I saw the second figure, in my peripheral vision. A man, I thought. Tall, blurred, already retreating down the corridor. A white arm extending to close the door. I froze, stunned. Somebody had been in there with Alex.

And then I followed him out, but it was too late. He'd either come back into the restaurant via the main door, left completely, or gone into the kitchen.

'Everything okay?' Tony said, next to my elbow, as I stood in the middle of the restaurant, getting in the way of waiters and customers. He inclined his head, looking at me, and we moved back towards the bar.

I sat on a red tasselled stool that your mother had bought from a local store – 'It's so impossibly kitsch,' she had said – and I asked him.

'Why was Alex in the back office with someone?'

'With . . . who?'

'I don't know,' I said. 'A man.'

He leant down underneath the counter and grabbed a can of Coke.

'I doubt that,' Tony said easily.

'What, you think I made it up?'

'No need to be upset,' he said, raising his palms to me. His muscles looked defined. So much waiting on tables, I guess, carrying all those plates of food.

'I saw her. And then I saw someone else emerge. They looked . . . I don't know. They looked weird.'

'Probably telling a waiter off. Or dealing with the account-ants. Or any number of things,' Tony said.

I left pretty soon after that. Your mother was busy. I'd ask her later. Turned out, there was no later, as you know: for any of us.

I stopped at the corner shop. I have fond memories, too, of browsing those aisles, piled high with stock, my trainers making squeaking noises as I picked up fabric softener, a few beers, a pizza. Kids in Hallowe'en costumes rushed by me, buying bags of sweets, last-minute broomsticks, a witch's mask. Freedom, I guess it was. The last shopping I ever did. Until I got out.

I'd make the house nice for Alex's return, I decided. Do some tidying. Some useful chores. Then ask her, later, when she was relaxed, who the man was.

It looked perfect by 11.30 p.m. I had always been good at making rooms looks nice. Your mother wasn't. She'd watch films with the main light on, but I knew how to do it. Four or five candles. Lamps. Throws.

For the first time in months, I was looking forward to something. To the winter. To Christmas. To the future, I supposed. We had spent four weeks frantically earning money as The Money People's new deadline approached. Your mother had started operating the extended opening hours at the restaurant under the new licence. I had taken on too many decorating jobs and rushed them but, somehow, everybody was pleased. We had paid off an extra thousand in a month. It would be a tricky few years, but your mother had laughed properly for the first time the previous night. Head thrown back, mouth wide open.

When she wasn't home by 11.45 p.m., half an hour after the restaurant closed, I rang her mobile, but she didn't answer. I walked outside, hoping to see the headlights of a taxi in the distance. She would never pick up her phone to me if she was almost home – she was a pragmatist, just like you – but there was nothing.

'Up late,' David, our neighbour, said. He was loading an end table into the back of a very full removal van. An end table, Iz. Could I really recall these details if I was lying? If I had, at that precise moment, been where the prosecution said I was, murdering your mother, then hiding her body? The legs of the table were white, the top oak, maybe beech. A light wood. Need to know more detail? David had a barbed-wire tattoo around his upper arm. I thought it strange he was in a T-shirt in October, but he was sweating with the exertion of packing.

'Just wondering where Alex is,' I said easily.

'That the old redhead or the young one?'

'The old one, I guess,' I said.

'Not seen her.'

'Right. Don't worry.'

We made small talk for a few minutes more. Afterwards, I rang everybody I could think of. The restaurant's landline: no answer. Your mother's parents: they had no idea where she was. I had a bad feeling, and I'd never been a worrier. But I worried about her, it's why I drove her everywhere, so I called *everyone*. Hospitals, friends, the police. And all the while my phone calls were pinging a mast across the island, lighting it up like a Christmas tree. Incriminating me, with its inaccuracy, without me even knowing. I was in the house, Izzy. Pacing around the garden, at most. That was all. But two different masts lit up. The one near to our house, and the other near to where she was found, a quarter of a mile away. We tried so hard to explain why. That, sometimes, one

195

mast is down, so it re-routes to another. They were always so fucking inaccurate.

But it was no good. It all added up, didn't it?

The evidence.

Izzy

'What time are you in until?' Chris said to Izzy the second she arrived.

Izzy shrugged. 'Ten, eleven? Depends how much there is on . . .' she said vaguely.

'Right, right,' he said, nodding quickly.

She looked across at the bar. Her father and Tony were standing talking.

'Why?' Izzy said.

Chris shrugged, saying nothing. He glanced over his shoulder just as his uncle did, too. Both of them looking towards the corridor. 'Off with lover boy tonight?' he smirked, but Izzy ignored him.

'When will you be back?' Izzy's mum asked.

Izzy tied the strings of her black apron behind her back. 'I don't know,' she said. 'Tomorrow.'

She couldn't believe she was getting away with it. No, not getting away with it, she reminded herself. Couldn't believe that she had . . . arrived. Into adulthood. Spending the night with Pip, with the full knowledge and blessing of all of their parents. Izzy had got the pill from her GP, the green pre-scription tucked neatly into the inside pocket of her handbag. She'd started it eight days ago: she was ready.

Marcus, one of the regulars, was making his way through his lasagne. He always ordered the same thing. 'Too much tomato,' he said. His white-blond hair caught the lamplight.

He and her mother seemed to have an in-joke about the tomatoes on the lasagnes; she'd heard him mention it before.

'Well, let me know?' her mother said, ignoring Marcus.

'It'll definitely be tomorrow morning. I need to pick up my school bag.'

Her mother's expression changed. It dropped. Like, maybe, Izzy didn't need her any more, which was kind of true.

I've got teapots, I've got loose-leaf tea, I've got books, Pip had texted her earlier. They were going to retreat to his annex in the garden, curl up in bed, and read and drink and talk. 'And ignore the world,' Pip had said.

'Okay,' her mother said quickly. 'Okay.'

Chris adjusted his T-shirt. His skin was so pale; he hadn't been away that summer. He looked at her. He would never be permitted by Tony to go and stay at a girl's house. Her mother and Tony often clashed over parenting – Izzy was given such a free rein – and she knew Chris was jealous.

It had been raining all day, and Izzy was privately pleased. Was it possible to be this happy? It seemed, just recently, that life had opened up for her – just completely opened up like a fat, blooming flower. She now inhabited a world full of text messages that made her stomach turn over with pleasure, of shared beds, solo driving, rain on the windows, of doing whatever she wanted. Of being in control, she supposed, of her whole life. It seemed so easy, to build a life she loved.

The atmosphere in Pip's house was sombre, which was why they wanted to sit in his annex and ignore the world. She'd told her mother about Oliver's death but Alex had obviously forgotten, because she'd hardly mentioned it since. She could be this way sometimes. If things didn't directly affect her, they ceased to matter. Her father had asked how the Easons were doing, but he was different. Her uncle Tony had. Chris had. Even Marcus had, after she had told him a few weeks back. But her mother hadn't.

As she left, at just after 10.30 p.m., running out into the sea air, finally free, she saw her mother in the restaurant window, raising a hand to her in a wave. She had her silver phone in her hand and it caught the street lights as she moved.

Pip met her in his little annex which sat forty feet away from the house, down at the bottom of the garden. Izzy's shoes were wet with autumn rain.

'How are you?' she said to him.

'Better now,' he said.

There was a futon in the corner, dressed in a blue-and-white checked pattern. It was piled with cushions and throws. There was a mini fridge in the corner.

'Hey, you're totally self-sufficient,' she said, looking around. 'The world could end and you'd be just fine,' she added.

'*We'd* be fine. More than fine.'

He had a window seat at the far wall. The view wasn't spectacular. Just the hedges at the bottom of the garden and, beyond that, the neighbour's house, visible through the wet leaves. They had a trampoline. But the night was wet and wild, and she settled on to the sill, leaning against the navy-blue mismatched cushions.

Pip came and sat beside her. He folded her legs into his lap. The wall was cold and hard against her shoulder blades, and she shifted slightly. She liked the feel of his hands across her ankles. His grip was firm but gentle. A warm index finger worked its way inside her jeans.

'How're your parentals post-row?'

'They're fine. They're totally fine. They really do like each other. It was just a blip,' she says.

'They met young, right?'

'Yeah, really young. Like in their teens.' She looked at him, but his expression was neutral, his head leaning back against the window, his eyes closed.

She stared out of the window and into the night. Rain splattered the window lightly.

They slept in his bed together. His annex had no curtains on the windows, and every now and then a sweep of headlights from the road illuminated the bedroom, the covers, his sleeping form. She switched her phone to silent and slipped into his arms, forgetting the world around them, forgetting everything except his smell. He did the same, and locked the annex.

'No problems in here tonight,' he said. 'No bullshit, no nothing. And, anyway, soon you'll be up and away, off to the military dance school.'

She had loved him for that. That he could see, somehow, at only seventeen, that there was a world beyond the Isle of Wight, school, their families.

'It really *isn't* military,' she said.

'Sure it is. I bet you ride along on tanks. Wear helmets.'

'You really don't know much about the military,' she said with a smile. 'Helmets and tanks.'

'Hey, I'm a regular English student,' he said. 'Poetry and berets.'

'You'll fit right in.'

He switched the lamp off and they lay in the dark together.

As she was leaving, the next morning, she thought it: perhaps they wouldn't make it. They were seventeen. His brother had died. It was a lot to process. In all the books she read and films she watched, teenage lovers didn't make it. Especially not those under strain. Perhaps there would be no holiday, no long relationship begun early in life.

She stared at the morning mist.

But Pip wasn't like other people. He was good at life. Seemed to squeeze every last drop out of it, like it was fresh orange juice. She couldn't imagine anything that would break them up.

Nothing at all.

She switched her phone on a few minutes later.

25

'So you wouldn't have even picked up her call,' Gabe says softly.

'No. That's what I said, in court.'

'The papers went to town on that phone call.'

Izzy waves a hand, faking indifference. 'They like all that stuff. That *what could have been* stuff.' She used exactly the same phrase when she told Nick about it. It's what she says.

'How often do you think about the call?'

'Hardly ever,' she says.

'Really,' Gabe says, but it's not a question: his tone is musing.

Izzy thinks back to that newspaper article: *Alexandra English made phone call plea moments before death.*

That call. That midnight call, five minutes before she died. Izzy had been in Pip's bed, oblivious. Had she called as she was being attacked, or beforehand – for a chat, to impart some information? They would never know. All they knew is that she pressed 'dial' but that the call was cut off before it could connect.

Izzy sometimes relives the last few moments with Pip, those last few moments before the lights were turned out on her life forever. Their ankles were entwined, afterwards, but nothing else. Their torsos were separate, propped up on his blue pillows, facing each other. It smelt different in Pip's bed to her own: different washing powder. She loved everything about his annex. His guitar standing steady in the corner.

The way they slept on the ground floor, close to the earth, and could hear the rain running down the windows. How surprisingly neat he was: a folded throw at the end of his futon, a little drawer cleared out for her things. It was like their own little flat. Their own world. She felt like she was on holiday. And more than that: she felt like life would follow a different path with him. That the barriers of the island would come down, and she'd be set free.

'And what were you doing at midnight?' the prosecution lawyer said to her.

She swallowed, wishing she didn't have to answer, at just seventeen. 'I was . . . with . . . my boyfriend, I didn't hear my phone,' Izzy said. Pip was looking at her in bed at midnight, she guessed. He was always looking at her.

'And did you have a missed call?'

'No.'

If a stranger attacked Izzy, who would *she* call? She sits back in the chair in the evening sunlight: Nick. It would always be Nick, no matter what.

But that night, her mother hadn't called her husband Gabe. It seemed, to Izzy, to be one of the most damning pieces of evidence against him, though the lawyers brushed it away. *They had been rowing a lot*, her father's defence lawyer had said easily, one hand in his pocket. *Why would you call someone you've rowed with – especially if, perhaps, it's not immediately obvious you're in danger?*

Her mother chose not to call her father that night. Why? Because her father was standing over her, holding the object he eventually murdered her with?

Or maybe just because her mother had chosen to call Izzy for some reason; last number redialled, or for no reason. They'd never know. Sometimes, on days like this, when she is thinking about it too much, or late at night when her guard is down, the night seeming endless and dark, she thinks she might be able to stretch out, far into the past, and find their phones, those almost-connecting phones, and finally answer.

'It's a shame it didn't ring,' Izzy says now.

'A shame.'

She shrugs, irritable, wanting him to stop looking at her. All she can see are the headlines. What if she *had* been looking at her phone? What if she'd called her mother?

Gabe is watching her closely. She tries to blink away the tears, but she doesn't quite manage it.

'It's okay to be sad about it,' he says softly.

'She reached out to me,' Izzy says, her eyes filling again. She finds a tissue and wipes them. 'I don't know if she thought of me as she was dying.' It's absurd that she is confiding in him, but she can't help it. He's her dad.

'I knew I'd get you talking,' Gabe says. 'Close quarters.' He gestures to the kitchen.

'Hmm?'

'All the other prisoners used to confess to me,' he says. 'They'd tell me all sorts. Murders and robberies and money laundering. And then I'd blackmail them with their secrets for extra chocolate.' He lets a laugh out.

'You didn't,' she says.

'I did. I did.' He doesn't look as though he's just told her something unsavoury, something inhumane, and Izzy is relieved when he changes the subject. 'What happened with Pip?' Gabe says now, knowing when to push, and when to change the subject.

'It wasn't very nice.'

'You always seemed so good together. Quite adult.'

'I guess so,' she says, not wanting to get into that, too. 'But I met Nick, anyway . . .'

'What's he like, this husband of yours?'

'He's . . .' Izzy thinks. Suddenly, she doesn't want to describe him as he is. Safe. Steady. Good at facts and figures and at sorting things with a level head. Likes routines. Why? She probes around inside her mind and finds the answer: because she knows Gabe would be surprised to discover she had ended up with such a man. 'He's very funny,' she says, which is the last thing Nick is.

'Oh, good,' Gabe says, his face stretching into a smile that makes him look too thin. 'Funny people take the edge off life. My last cellmate was funny. Nice guy, Keith.'

'Yes,' Izzy says, wanting to change the subject again. 'But the timings of that night. They said she arrived home at just before twelve . . . and that she was dead by the early hours.'

'Yes.'

'But they don't know if she was killed in the house.'

'No. Nobody knows exactly where she died.'

'And the mobile phone masts –'

'I know.'

'Your first call to her pinged the Shanklin mast, not Luccombe.'

'Yes.'

'Shanklin is the nearest mast to where she was found.'

'I know that, Iz. But they were inaccurate then. Not like now. There were fewer masts, so the distances varied . . . I told you.'

'But if you never left the house – if you were only just outside it, in the garden – it couldn't have been you.'

Izzy sits for a moment, thinking of that neighbour. Lost somewhere. An unknowingly important witness. He'd clearly never seen Gabe's story in a newspaper. Had never realized he held the key.

Or . . . he *had* moved days before, just like Izzy thought. He couldn't corroborate Gabe's alibi, because it was made up. Gabe's phone pinged the Shanklin mast because he was murdering her mother right where she was found. She meets her father's eyes as she thinks it.

'Did your lawyer ever trace the removal van? When it was returned?'

'Yes. The first of November.'

Izzy sucks her lip in, thinking. Do you return a removal van the day you finish with it, or a couple of days after – once you'd bought new furniture and transported it home, perhaps? She wasn't sure.

'He gave the house keys to the agent on the first. The agent gave evidence.'

But giving the key back doesn't mean that's when you moved out, Izzy thinks.

'Izzy,' Gabe says suddenly, urgently. 'Forget about David Smith. You were in the restaurant that night.'

'Yes. I was.'

'So?'

'So what?' Izzy says, staring at him blankly.

'Who was there? I want every person.'

Izzy gazes at him as she realizes. 'I see,' she says. 'This is why you're here. Because I have information.'

'I want to know who killed my wife,' he says urgently.

Izzy slides her hands off the table, curling into herself, away from him.

'And yes – you can help.'

'But you have to get me on side first.'

'Are you on side?' he asks.

'Not really. I don't know.'

He turns his hands over in a defeated gesture. 'You know it's about more than what information you have for me, Izzy. Obviously.'

'Is it?'

'Of course.' He holds her gaze.

'Okay,' she says. 'Okay. Chris. Tony. Marcus. Hmm. A couple of other waiters. Was one called Gary?'

'Okay. That's four names. Anyone else?'

Izzy thinks back. She can remember looking forward to going to Pip's, and thinking dreamily of him, but nothing else. The shift has blurred into all of the other waitressing shifts she undertook around that time. There is nothing to distinguish it, so it has faded into oblivion. 'I'm sorry. I don't know.'

'Tony also mentioned somebody called Babs,' Izzy says, watching Gabe's expression closely.

'That's my ex-girlfriend,' he says dismissively. 'Were there any other men there?'

'He seemed to indicate something had happened? With Babs?' Izzy can feel that she is being led away from explanations, towards what her father wants to talk about, but she's powerless to stop it. Perhaps that is just his way. The way he is, has always been: dominant and full of energy.

'He heard us row once. Is all. Took exception to it. Butted in, in the name of *chivalry*, which was actually just stabbing me in the back.'

'How?'

'Oh, said men shouldn't shout at women.' Gabe jumps at a sound.

She follows his gaze, and sees Nick's car pulling up in their driveway. He's early.

206

'You have to go,' she says to Gabe. 'My husband's home – and he doesn't know.'

Stomach acid sloshes around as she stands and gestures to Gabe. 'You can cut through the back garden,' she tells him. He can walk down the shared access and out.

Adrenaline floods her body as she imagines Nick realizing that she's been seeing her father; that he's here with her, a convicted killer, invited into their home. She swallows. She stands in the kitchen, looking at Gabriel, and watching her husband in his car.

'Now,' she says.

He puts his coat on, even though it is warm outside, and leaves without argument.

'Ah,' Nick says as he walks in. 'I wondered if you'd be home already.'

'Yes,' she says, her cheeks burning, thinking of Gabriel, walking down their access way just a few feet from them.

He will have to walk home again. Five miles to her. Five miles back.

It's only once she is in bed, waiting for sleep to come, that the fear joins her, barely knocking on the door of the silent bedroom before letting itself in. That note. That horrible, horrible, personal note. Who could have sent it?

She tries to forget that the last person to hand-deliver a letter to the restaurant was Gabe himself.

26

Izzy goes straight to the attic when she gets home from work the next day. She made an excuse to leave early, saying she had a headache. Chris gave her a look, but she no longer cares whether he believes her. She dithers for a few minutes, looking inside the boxes, and eventually she decides to look through her father's art collection.

She's thinking of affairs and insurance claims. It makes a sickening kind of sense to Izzy. Her mother got her father into debt – debt that was in his name. If she had then been having an affair, too, wouldn't that be the perfect trigger for her father to lose his temper, or to plan her murder, knowing it would solve his debt problems, too? If he believed she didn't even love him, after everything . . .

She opens the box containing her father's pots and paintings, and is immediately assailed by memories. The portraits Gabe used to paint of her mother, all on small canvases, less than the size of a handprint. He used oils – 'Acrylics are for babies,' he would say – diluted with linseed oil, turpentine. Some of them still smell of it, even now. That sweet, doughy smell. It takes her back. He had begun to play with texture, in the last days of his art. Using cording and ribbons to mark the paint. Those are his most accomplished paintings. Her mother's hair, tumbling around her shoulders, stippled and textured by cord.

She disturbs a raft of pots at the bottom of one of the boxes as she removes the portraits. They thump together as she dislodges them – her father was a sturdy potter, making mugs and bowls with thick clay sides and bottoms, never using delicate china – and she reaches in for one. It is a perfectly formed, miniature vase. Big and round at the bottom, like a breast, curving snugly in her palm, then sweeping in at the neck, so slim and dainty. It would hold a single flower at most. It's grey, unpainted, with just the top varnished. The clay has formed a toasted line around the rim, speckled egg-shell brown.

Izzy's mother's dressing table had been covered with pots Gabe had made for her. Ring holders, a necklace tree, pots for her make-up brushes. Odd pots that he'd discarded because they'd collapsed, but glazed anyway for her. Mismatched little dishes, espresso cups, giant misshapen mugs, all stacked. The rejects, her father had called them, but her mother kept them all. She'd had to move them to get to her blusher, to her foundation, to her hairbrush, the things she used every day.

Izzy searches through the boxes, looking for something, anything. A third figure, a man in one of the paintings, maybe. A love triangle depicted. Anger. Something hidden inside a pot. But instead, she finds the exact opposite: here is a love story, chronicled carefully by her father, when he was supposed to be out doing something more worthy.

A portrait of her mother, from behind, customary breadstick holding her hair up, orange tendrils hanging down around it. The details disappear at the neck, her torso left suggestively bare. Her mother looking out across the fields at Luccombe, evening light transforming her hair from red to amber. Her mother bent low over a mixing bowl. Two slender arms along the bathtub, painted from behind. Her mother at the coast, hair whipped around her face by the wind, laughing. Hundreds of portraits of her mother. Of her mother's life. Izzy lingers over them. She had forgotten the set of her mother's eyes, so widely spaced. She had forgotten a particular expression she had when she was amused, a lop-sided smile, indulgent-looking. And then, the most intricate portrait of her feet. Toenails painted pink. *Yes.* She remembers now. It's like meeting an old friend on the street.

Her mother. Here. Preserved by the man accused of murdering her. Izzy's mouth tightens as she tries not to cry.

At the bottom of one of the boxes, she finds dozens of her old pointe shoes. She handles the pink satin carefully, the memories forming. Darning the ends of them, so they didn't slip. They're still dusted with a sticky substance – rosin, kept in a silver tray in the corner of the room. Each dancer would dip the end of their shoe in it, the action like stubbing out a cigarette. Izzy looks inside. She was a purist. Never used padding. The inside is lined with drops of blood from where the knuckles of her toes would bleed.

She puts them back after a while, and looks again at the paintings. She wonders if Nick would paint her this way. *Of course he would*, she thinks guiltily. And what would she paint of him? His long, lanky limbs. His thick hair. The way he makes everything fun; that life with him is never fraught with difficult conversations or unexpected moodiness but instead consists of cheese plates in bed, picking holes in true-crime documentaries – 'That would never happen,' he will say – and knowing he will always be where he says he will be.

God. What is she doing, risking that? Her *marriage*. The most sacred thing in her life. She's been mad. She's got to tell him. Of course she has. She thinks back over the past few weeks: hiding her father's note, the bank statements spread out in their attic, right above where Nick sleeps, without him knowing. Lying about a urinary tract infection. That man who saw her and Gabe together in the café, and who could mention it to anybody. Word can travel fast on the Isle of Wight, as she learnt the day her mother's body was discovered.

What has she been thinking?

She's got to tell Nick.

27

She cooks Nick a proper meal – steak, chips, peppercorn sauce – and prepares to tell him. Her rush of guilt in the loft has dulled slightly. Perhaps she will tell him that she's seen her father, but not that he's been here. Not that they have been alone together. She'll tell him a half-truth, she thinks, as she seasons the steaks.

She has the radio on as she cooks. An expert is discussing the recent dry weather. There have been grass fires by the sides of the road. A hosepipe ban is being considered by some of the water companies. She thinks of her father's boiling, tiny room and turns the radio off.

Nick leaves the door open when he arrives. 'I swear, this is the only house in the whole of Britain that's actually cool,' he says as he arrives. He kisses her forehead absent-mindedly as he goes through the mail. He is always like this. Having a conversation about one thing and doing two other things, too.

'We were invited home this weekend, I meant to say.' He gestures to his phone bearing a string of customary family WhatsApps. 'But I couldn't be arsed.'

'Why? Where?'

'Mum and Dad's. But it's so far and I'm tired . . .'

Izzy's mouth tightens. She says nothing. Imagine skipping a family event because of tiredness, because you couldn't be bothered?

'Cooking in the dark?' he says.

Izzy has let the dusk invade the kitchen, not doing anything about it. Just thinking about how she'll tell him.

'You okay?' he says immediately to her, his eyes lowering as they meet hers.

'I've seen my father,' she says to him as she flips the steaks over.

The air seems to still around them. As he moves back in shock, he stumbles against the open door and activates their outside security light. Goosebumps appear all over her body as she takes in his facial expression, bleached white on one side. His brow has crumpled, but his eyes are on her, wide, wary, not blinking.

'What?' he says quietly.

Neither of them moves, and the light turns off again.

He switches the lamp on. 'When?'

He is information gathering; this is what Nick does before he reacts. In the total silence she hears him swallow.

'Just now,' she says. She doesn't admit the first night. One small step at a time.

'God, why?' he says. Ever rational.

'I . . .' Izzy falters. There's a burst of laughter out back, which makes her jump. William, she thinks. He must have people over. 'He . . . he has told me he's innocent,' she says simply.

'You don't believe him, do you?' Nick's tone is as sharp as citrus.

She wants to answer him honestly, but can't find the words. Her eyes mist over and she realizes: she is upset he has to ask. If there was a tiny chance that his own father *hadn't* killed his mother, wouldn't Nick hear him out? She appraises him, standing in the kitchen in his suit, and finds she can't answer. Maybe he wouldn't. Criminals are guilty upon arrest, to Nick. He has come to believe this. He is a product of a system.

She doesn't ever tell him about the Instagram family, or about how she feels when she watches Thea. She pretends to be fine, inexplicably unaffected by her upbringing, but he must surely know . . . he hasn't taken her at her word, has he? She watches him, standing there in her kitchen, her husband – a stranger. Does he know how she feels, deep down, or has he really never noticed? Or does he know, and it's easier to pretend he doesn't? A memory of Pip springs into her mind. 'What're you thinking?' he would say often. What would he say now, here? He'd be boiling that kettle. Pulling her towards him. 'What's on your mind?' he'd be saying. Izzy can't think about it. Her eyes feel moist.

Nick is silent, his body completely still, looking at her. He's waiting for an answer.

She blinks, then lifts her gaze to his. 'And I think he might not have done it. He seems to act so consistently!' Her voice is cracked and sore-sounding.

Nick doesn't say anything. It is as though her belief doesn't warrant a response; it is so ridiculous. She takes the steaks off the heat but can't bring herself to serve them.

She wonders if – if she let him – he would simply walk into their living room and start his evening. Pretend this conversation hasn't happened. He would like to, of that she is sure. He will pretend not to hear difficult questions.

She dumps the steaks and chips on the plates.

'Don't you think there's any chance he could be innocent?' she asks.

'He was convicted,' Nick says eventually, softly.

His tone is so gentle that her heart breaks and she regrets her previous thoughts. He licks his lips, a dart of pink tongue, and takes a plate. He walks into the living room and Izzy feels with a sudden lurch that he might put the television on. Please don't. Please don't turn the television on. Please don't avoid it. Please don't distract yourself, and consign my feelings to a box labelled *unimportant*.

'Why won't you even consider it?' she says, catching up to him.

'They all say they're innocent, Izzy,' he says. 'Every single one of them.'

Neither of them says anything for a beat or two.

And then Nick says, 'He wants you to hear his side of it, right? From the start?'

'Yes. How did you know?'

'They all say that, too.'

Izzy says nothing for a beat. He's trying to protect her, she reminds herself.

'Izzy. Remember where they found the body?'

'But some of them *are* innocent,' she says, ignoring his question. 'Some of them really must be! Don't you remember the Birmingham Six? Angela Cannings?' Izzy has been reading about them all. She has the Wikipedia page for Miscarriages of Justice open on her laptop, each tab a new name.

'Oh, the Birmingham Six! Here we go . . .'

She's surprised to hear disdain in his voice. 'What do you mean *here we go*? Here we go, my wife is in touch with her estranged, guilty and –' her voice breaks, 'much-missed father? *Here we go.*' She hears the caustic emphasis lacing her words and tries to stop herself. Don't lose your temper. Don't lose control.

'Just because their convictions were overturned doesn't mean they were not guilty,' Nick says, spearing a chip.

'Besides, the percentage is vanishingly small.' He reaches for the remote control.

No.

'But –'

'It's Occam's razor, isn't it?' he says, talking over her, his voice raised. He hardly ever raises his voice. 'The simplest explanation is true . . .' He pauses. Then, 'Where have you seen him? Alone?'

'In a café,' she mumbles.

'Alone?' he persists.

'I didn't know anyone there. But we weren't alone. No.'

'That's so stupid,' he says. But it's not cruel, the way he says it. It's pitying.

'He's not dangerous,' she says now, though she doesn't know that. Not at all.

Nick doesn't say anything, but the expression on his face does. He puffs air into his cheeks. 'You're in deep,' he says, still looking at her. The gel he would have put in his hair that morning has been rubbed out during his working day – he is always messing with his hair – and now it looks dulled and fluffy.

'I'm not in deep,' she says. 'I just think . . . what if he is innocent? Or what if he . . . what if there's more to what he did than meets the eye?' The words seem to ring out in their silent living room. She doesn't know what she expects. For Nick to seriously consider it, for him to ponder it with her, to reassure her, even, that her judgement isn't completely off, that he, too, would feel tempted? But whatever she wants, she doesn't get it. She wants collaboration but, here, she finds defence.

'Izzy . . .' Nick says, his hand still on the remote control, slim fingers curled around its edges.

'I want to hear him out. I want to see him again.'

'You believe him,' Nick says. 'This is why you asked me if I'd needed the file.'

'No. Yes.'

'You've used me.'

'*No*.'

'You *want* to believe him.'

Yes, Izzy thinks. Exactly that. He has articulated it exactly, with the full force of his intellect behind the thought process, but with zero empathy. And is that so bad? The anger has left her now and she's filled with only sadness, instead. How could they begin to raise a family – even if she *was* ready? They disagree on so much. The steadiness that Nick has represented for her, with his even temper and penchant for routine, suddenly feels hollow.

When she hasn't answered for five seconds, Nick finally does what he has been waiting to do ever since he got in. He turns on the television – a mid-week football match he recorded earlier – and sits down.

'How can you be so sure?' she says. 'Of the evidence?'

'You're missing the biggest piece.'

'What?' she says.

He turns to her, fixing her with his gaze, and says, 'It's just that, when a woman dies, it's almost always the partner. When a child dies, it's almost always the parents. That's life.'

'But that's not *evidence*. That's circumstantial.'

He doesn't bother replying.

His words reverberate in her mind as she turns away from him.

Partner. Child. Parents.

It's late, and Izzy's throat is still tight with tears. Unhappiness. Longing, maybe.

She can't stop thinking about how she wanted Nick to react. Their ostensibly solid marriage is being rocked by her family, as she always privately feared it would be. And instead of talking to Nick about it, all Izzy is thinking of is Pip.

Pip Talbot, and how he would have reacted. And how they parted ways.

She types his name into Facebook. It asks her if she means *Philip*, and there he is. Smiling at the camera, skiing sunglasses raised into his hairline, a faint butterfly suntan across his features, the mountains in the background.

He looks exactly how she thought he would. Free and easy. The thought is somehow comforting.

She presses *Add friend*, opens the message box, and begins to type.

28

Izzy wakes with a start. The threatening newspaper article is her first thought, always seeming worse in the small hours. She looks at her phone to discern what's woken her. A Facebook message. Her heart speeds up as she wonders if it's Pip, but it's one of the David Smiths.

Next to her, Nick snores softly.

Afraid I lived near there, but not on that road as I can recall. In London now, David has typed.

Where were you based? Izzy types back to him. *Which road?*

She waits for a long time before it comes back.

11 Dolphin Street, he writes eventually. *Sorry, had to look it up.*

That is nowhere near where Izzy lived. She locks her phone with a sigh. He has become nothing. Another insignificant David Smith in a whole wasted sea of them.

But, anyway, what use would it really be? An alibi might confirm her father's innocence, but that, in itself, would ask a wider question: if not him . . . who did it? And even if – *even if* – she figures it out, then what? She's not exactly going to get peace of mind either way.

She's awake now, at 5.00 a.m., so she goes to look through the bank statements for May 1999. She's moved the statements from their loft and into their spare room, hidden away in a drawer.

She is sitting in the cool spare room, her feet flat against the wall, the folder on her lap, when she sees it. Blackjack Casino: +£1,100.

A credit from a casino on the business account? Izzy frowns at it. Who was gambling? Her *mother*? Gabe? She can't imagine either of them doing so. They never even bought lottery tickets. Never watched horse racing. Nothing.

If her mother had put her father into debt and then gambled – trying to help, but failing – her father's motive would be so clear. Anger. Her mother was gambling with their future, and her father had been angry.

She gets her phone out to text Gabe, but a text immediately comes through from him. Up early, too. He was never an early riser.

I have been thinking of the newspaper clipping, he writes.

I have found evidence of gambling in the bank statements, Izzy types. *Why the newspaper clipping?*

Tell me again exactly what it said?

It had Mum's name crossed out and mine replaced, she replies. *It said 'Alex' was found in undergrowth, but they'd written 'Izzy'.*

Her phone rings and she answers.

'Let me help you,' he says.

'What?'

'You're being threatened. We should try and figure out who it is.'

'Maybe we should just tell the police,' Izzy mutters, wanting to grasp on to the real world. For authority. To avoid being drawn into her father's underworld.

'The police won't help,' he says quickly, easily. 'I think we should meet – but alone. I have a theory. I could come to Alexandra's. After hours?'

'Why?'

Izzy thinks of all of the evidence they have discussed so far. The debt. His lack of alibi. The text he sent to her mother. And the lies he's told, too.

'Don't you think that, maybe, somebody doesn't want us speaking?' he asks.

'Who?'

'The person who did it.'

Something expands in her chest, then seems to click into place. Yes. She wants to know. She's *ready* to know.

'But who?' she asks.

'I don't know . . .' He leaves a significant pause.

'Okay,' she says softly. 'Come by tonight. After eleven thirty.'

She hangs up, thinking of her smart, protective husband's warnings. She is trying to be brave. She is trying not to be scared. Not knowing who to be scared of.

On the way to work that afternoon, Izzy takes a detour. She hasn't been back to her parents' house since she moved out. Not even when it was eventually sold – at half its original value, due to the sinister connection, to a single mother who was pleased by the bargain and intrigued by the crime – and not when it popped back on the market, years later, and there had been an open house. It would have been easy to go, but she couldn't. It was still too soon.

The months after the trial are fuzzy. She guesses the house was emptied and their possessions sold, but she doesn't remember it, or wasn't told.

Rainsdown Lane is a perfectly normal street. A cul-de-sac of 1960s detached houses. Theirs – number 20 – is on the end, by the road, on a corner. Izzy could see the sea from one of the bedrooms. David Smith lived at number 18. It's easy for Izzy to see why he would be the only witness to her father's innocence, or otherwise. The houses are on their own, set apart from the rest, with only a fast main road opposite.

She counts the traffic on the main road as she sits in her car. One car. Two. Three. Three cars in as many minutes. Maybe not a single car went by at midnight that night. There were no witnesses.

Her mother's hair had been found in the boot of her father's car. It was one of the many pieces of evidence the Crown Prosecution Service used to tell their story, Izzy gathered from sitting on the landing and listening to her grandparents, that he had killed her in the house and transported her body, or that he had transported her alive, and killed her near to where she was found.

The defence had evidently batted it away; that evidence was easy to rebut, compared to the rest. *They were married*, the barrister had said, while Matt Richmond and Gabe had looked on. *Your hairs would be in the boot of every single car you'd ever owned*, he had said, gesturing to the jury, who nodded mutely, considering it.

Her mobile phone had never been recovered. The text from Gabe and the call to Izzy were recovered from the provider, but her phone had never been found. The prosecution said her father had disposed of it in a panic, as he knew how damning his communication with her would look. The defence said what they've said all along: that they do not know.

A row of conifers divides the two houses. Gabe's car would have been on the drive, and so the taxi must either have parked where Izzy is, or on the other side of the road. She isn't sure which. She didn't see the taxi driver give evidence and she hasn't found it reported anywhere, either. She is depending on the recall of her grandparents, and Gabe, both unreliable in their own ways.

She looks across at the house. Little details pop out at her that she had forgotten. The three steps up to the front door, worn right in the centre, dipping just slightly from thousands of footsteps. The hook from the hanging basket that used to sit to the left of the door, which is now empty. The two frosted-glass panes either side of the centre of the door.

The door is in plain sight. If the lights were on, Izzy would be able to see the entire hallway when the door opened. She waits for a few minutes, looking at it contemplatively, then moves across the street. The view is the same. The trees might have obscured the door, back then, but Gabe was pretty good about maintaining them. He liked to do it, and was good at it – 'Topiary is art,' he once cheerfully said.

She starts the engine again as she stares at the house. She now has a question for Gabe.

Did Alice Reid ever describe the interior of their hallway?

29

Izzy says goodnight to everyone, as she always does, at eleven thirty, but she hangs around, waiting. She takes her shoes off and hums as she wipes areas of the restaurant she hardly gets to: behind the till, the wooden rack the knives and forks sit in.

Gabe comes at midnight, exactly when she said.

'It's so hot out,' she says as she opens the door to him, still in his anorak. Outside is warmer than the air-conditioned restaurant. The paving slabs are body temperature underneath her bare feet. Like the height of summer. Like being abroad.

There's an amber alert for next week. The unseasonable early heatwave is due to continue. People are being advised to walk their dogs only late at night or early in the morning. The beaches are heaving every day, people covering the sand like ants.

'I feel the cold,' he says.

They sit opposite each other at the bar.

'Any food going spare?' Gabe says, his tone jovial.

She looks at his slim arms, and her stomach flips over.

'Alex used to bring home the most amazing leftovers,' he adds.

'I'll see what I can do. Hang on.'

'Does Nick talk about work much?' Gabe says.

The question comes out of nowhere, and Izzy pauses on her way to the kitchen.

'Not much,' she says carefully.

'Interesting, that you chose to marry a policeman,' Gabe says, his tone light.

Izzy opens the fridge and begins pulling things out, her face hot.

'How're the job interviews?' she says to him. 'And the flyers?'

He laughs, a faint, disbelieving puff of air escaping his mouth. 'They're not interested in hiring somebody whose skillset consists of beating people up and making noodles in a kettle.'

Izzy looks away, embarrassed. This imposter isn't her father. He can't be. She wishes they could wind the clock back, somehow. That he hadn't become this man.

He pauses, seemingly gathering his thoughts while looking around him. His eyes dart to the beams above them, unchanged, and the kitchen behind them, reconfigured and refitted. He runs his fingers over the bar – the same bar her mother had, but painted white – and reaches up for a glass.

'This is huge,' he says.

'Huge wine glasses are trendy now.'

'It'll work itself out,' he says, running his fingers around the rim until it sings, a mournful sound in the silent night.

She wonders if he, too, sees her mother everywhere here, despite the changes she's made. He fiddles with a pot on the bar – he made it, years ago, a tall, thin vase they used to keep breadsticks in but which now houses a bunch of fresh lilies. He taps the top, then smiles at her knowingly.

'I'm sure,' she says, ignoring the fact that she has kept his pot. Ignoring what it means.

'Someone just needs to be brave and hire me,' he says.

She looks at his slim wrists, his white hair; only a handful of hairs remain black, hidden amongst the grey and the white, like the parts of her father from before. To avoid responding to him – to avoid telling him that even she, his daughter, has her phone in her pocket, poised ready to dial Nick quickly, if necessary – she walks into the kitchen and rifles through the fridge.

'Would you like a spare cheesecake?' she says to him.

'Sure.'

'It's a blue cheese cheesecake,' she says, coming back out to the bar. 'Full-fat Shropshire blue.'

She tips it on to a plate and adds an artful smear of balsamic vinegar. Her father raises his eyebrows.

'Blue cheese cheesecake?' he says. He plucks a menu up off the bar and glances at it. He runs his finger underneath each word like a child.

'It's a thing, these days,' she says, taking the menu. 'Don't read, just try.'

He spears a piece but pauses, fork hovering near his mouth. 'We ordered the week's meals every Monday. Inside,' he says shyly.

'What kind of things did you eat?' she says, leaning her elbows on the bar.

'Things that could be cooked in batches . . . kedgeree. Stews. By the time I'd been in there four weeks, I'd eaten every single meal on offer.'

'Wow.'

'We had weird things sometimes, too. Chicken and coleslaw was a popular one.'

'I'd quite like that,' Izzy says, and he laughs.

'People got inventive with kettles. My old cellmate from Belmarsh, Raj, cooked curries in his. He put cling film over the kettle and doctored it so it would keep boiling. He used a tin of mackerel and these Bid Fest spices. Tea tasted awful ever since.'

'Bid Fest?' Izzy says.

'Oh, every Friday we were allowed to order things in. Like an internet shop, except they cost a fortune. A packet of mints would be two quid. They called it Bid Fest.'

'How did you get money?'

'We worked. Stitching up prison uniforms ... cutting people's hair – though only those of us that could be trusted with razors, obviously,' he says with a tiny smile. 'Cooking. Gardening. Building things, sometimes. My best year was when I was doing the bricklaying. Could be out-side more and think. But I earned seven quid a day. It's a different economy, and I got so used to it. Can hardly remember what's normal now. Anyway ...' he breaks eye contact and looks down at the bar, then eats the piece of cheesecake.

'Could you do bricklaying now?' she says.

'Maybe. I've got six months.'

'Until what?'

'Until Jobseeker's is discontinued.'

Izzy frowns, thinking of the snippet she overheard him say when he thought she wasn't still on the phone to him. 'Isn't it eight weeks?'

'No. Six months,' he says, frowning at her. And then his face changes. 'My point being,' he says loudly, 'that you could spend a day's earnings on three packets of mints.'

'How unfair.'

He must have said six months. She must be mistaken. 'Do you have any more interviews coming up?' she says. 'There must be bricklayers needed.'

'You run this place completely differently to your mother,' he says softly, looking up. 'God, this is delicious.'

'Thank you.'

He doesn't want to speak about his job seeking, that much is clear. His gaze drifts behind her and she realizes he is looking for more food. She finds him a roast, cobbles together a few potatoes and a slab of beef. She puts it into the microwave. He eats as fast as a dog, barely pausing for breath, clearing the plate in less than ten minutes. She looks at his ribcage, just visible above his grey T-shirt, and feels her innards twist.

He has mopped up the gravy with a piece of granary bread that Chris made that morning. He makes brilliant bread; she is sure it is because of his huge hands, his muscular arms, and because he puts heart into it, unlike Izzy.

'Do you make a profit?' he says.

'Of course it turns a profit,' she says. 'I thought Mum had it all in hand but she used to spend too much on ingredients. And nobody ever had three courses. Or much wine. She needed to get her ancillaries up.' She feels pleasure bloom across her chest when her father's eyebrows rise. He's impressed. She's impressed him.

'I *see*. Anyway. It's very pretty. Much prettier than when she –'

'People want to Instagram everything these days,' Izzy says, gesturing to a bell jar with a candle inside, to the fairy lights strung up above the bar.

'They what?'

She smiles up at him. 'Never mind,' she says.

He's quiet for a second. She hands him a soufflé that folded in on itself in the oven. It has sat on the side, waiting to go in the bin. 'It's chocolate,' she says. 'It looks rubbish but it's edible.'

'Do you love it like she did?'

'What?'

'Cooking. Dining. Food, I suppose.'

Izzy's skin prickles with his insight. He knows. Without knowing her at all, he knows. He knows about the heavy, dragging feeling she gets in her stomach at the start of the working week. He knows how she sometimes thinks, half-way through a shift, that she could happily bin all of the food she's prepared, and just walk out. He knows.

'No,' she says. 'Her parents wanted me to reopen it . . . to carry it on.'

Her father blinks, looking at her. 'Granny and Granddad?'

'Yes. They wanted . . .' She pauses, trying to be fair to them. 'They wanted it open again. As though . . . I don't know. It was as though it kept her alive. Her name, I guess, too. Her name on the sign.'

Izzy wishes she remembered the moment it happened, but the truth is, there wasn't one. Izzy had offered up her expertise on how long was left on her mother's lease, on who the accountant was, on where she had ordered the food from. And suddenly, as a woman without anything else to do, she was running the restaurant, unofficially and then officially, without truly noticing when one became the other. There was no moment. There was simply Izzy answering everybody's questions, realizing she could make a nice ris-otto and spot when a profit margin wasn't quite right. It had been a welcome distraction, at first.

Nobody had ever asked her. But that was how it was at

her grandparents'. When Izzy asked to turn off the television coverage of the US Open Golf, her granddad simply said, 'Why?' She couldn't justify it, so instead, she said, 'Never mind.' What Izzy wanted – ballet, Pip, travel, all-day breakfasts in a can – didn't matter.

Tears gather in her throat as she remembers those bleak years. Everything good – Gabe's happiness at heading off to tennis, his painting, her mother's delight over an apple pie – was rationed. Life became monochrome. There wasn't even a speck of joy. Not a single Indian takeaway, a morning cup of coffee in the sun, a read of *Glamour* magazine in the hairdresser's. Instead, life was dreary Sundays spent watching *Only Fools and Horses* and the Grand Prix, drinking weak tea and reading classics on loan from the library. Life was functional, lukewarm showers that dribbled, completing puzzles alone in the conservatory, perfunctory phone calls with her aunts and uncles, and a job she came to hate. Her morning coffees were an attempt to ward it off, but they didn't work, not really.

She can't tell Gabe that. It would break his heart.

'I see,' Gabe says, nodding quickly. He stabs the soufflé with a fork. The remaining air evaporates and it folds fully in on itself. 'I'm sorry. You could . . . you could start over. You know. Do what you want.' He catches her eye. 'Whatever that is.'

Izzy can't think about that. About the paths not taken. Ballet school. Seeing the world. Pip. It's too much.

'I visited our old house today,' she says.

His face brightens. He finishes the soufflé and puts his fork down. 'Rainsdown?'

'Yes.'

'I have a question.'

230

'Okay.'

'What exactly was the taxi driver's evidence?'

'That Mum went inside.'

'Was she asked to describe the house?' Gabe is silent, thinking. His jaw clenches. 'Ye-es,' he says. 'She knew about our lamp.'

Izzy's heart sinks. 'Right. The thing is . . .'

'Why were you at the house?'

'Because I'm looking into the case against you.'

His expression darkens and his brow lowers. His eyes dart around the restaurant, looking glittery. 'Are you not yet ready to stop looking into *me*? To look into who really *was* responsible?'

He picks up his fork and she sees his fingers blanch.

'It would be easy for her to make out a lamp through the windows,' he explains. 'She would have seen the glow from it, and could have imagined the rest. I don't think she was *lying* about seeing Mum go into the house. But she could have been mistaken.'

'Really?'

'I wish you'd see,' he says, the fork still gripped, jaw still set. He releases the fork angrily, and it clatters to the plate.

'Are you mad at me?' she says, figuring she may as well ask the direct question.

He rests his head in his hands for five seconds, ten, then says, 'Yeah, you know, sometimes I am.'

'Why?'

'Because of what we had.'

She sees his eyes are wet. She looks down, saying nothing. He doesn't seem angry with her now. Just sad. He'd never hurt her.

'I'm sorry,' she says.

'We were a pretty special father and daughter. Weren't we?'

'We were,' she says softly.

'First day missing,' Gabe says. 'That's next. To discuss.'

She takes a deep breath. They are getting to the worst bits. And she knows he has no explanation. 'Okay,' she says. 'Okay.'

30

PROSECUTOR: What did you do the day after you murdered your wife?

GABRIEL ENGLISH: I didn't murder her.

PROSECUTOR: Were you out looking for her?

GABRIEL ENGLISH: No.

PROSECUTOR: Why?

GABRIEL ENGLISH: I was worried she would come home and I didn't want to . . . to miss her.

PROSECUTOR: Why did you wash her clothes?

GABRIEL ENGLISH: I wanted to . . . I wanted to . . . to do something. Anything. To act. To think.

Tuesday 2 November 1999: one day after Alex's murder

Gabe

She had been missing for twenty-four hours. I thought the worst part would be going to bed without her, consigning her non-appearance from *misunderstanding* to *missing*, but it wasn't: the worst came when the clock reached four in the afternoon. Another eight hours and she would have been gone twenty-four. That was the moment she seemed to disappear, to me.

Cleaning. That's what I thought I'd do, Izzy. I know, I know. But I just needed to move my arms and my legs, and to let my mind *think*. To clean up those crumbs, to make the house nice for her – for her return.

I emptied the kitchen cupboards as I ruminated. What had she been wearing on her feet? Had she put shoes on? We thought a pair were missing, but she had so many pairs, your mother – 'Shoes are life,' she once said to me – that we couldn't know for sure.

I wiped down all the counters, lifting up your mother's herbs and spices and wiping the bottoms of the jars. I wish I'd asked her who that man was. I wish that I had kissed her goodbye, or touched her shoulder just as I was leaving. I was her husband, but I had left so casually. So complacent, so sure that we would have more time, that there would be future conversations and goodbyes to be had, that I could skip one.

I sorted through the washing, picking everything up off the bedroom floor and bundling it into the machine. Load after load after load. Everything she'd worn. Everything I'd worn. *Think, Gabe, think*. Had she seemed angry, melancholy, regretful? Not especially. Maybe slightly distracted, but only with hindsight. Hindsight isn't always helpful, is it? Hindsight, for me, anyway, obscures everything.

Halfway through hanging up the washing, I ran into the bedroom and took an itinerary of my pots. Looking back, that was madness – why would she have taken a pot? – and, anyway, it was impossible to tell, impossible to know, whether or not they were all there. I was scared to go anywhere and scared to stay in the house, not looking, being inactive. She was missing, and it seemed impossible and easy to find her, all at once. We just needed to look harder. But where? Where was she?

I walked upstairs later and looked in on our bedroom. There was my painting of two impressions in sand, hanging crookedly above our bed. It meant something only to me and Alex.

When I was eighteen, my parents – your grandparents – had settled on the Isle of Wight for the longest they'd been anywhere. There was talk of them getting jobs, a house. That summer, we were staying in our caravan on our patch in Norton Green. It had wooden steps and pink curtains. It was one of the first things I ever painted, trying to capture the way my parents didn't close off the outside world the way people who lived in houses did. We'd sleep with the door open, sometimes, the smells of the seasons drifting in. We'd eat outside. We'd have hot drinks before bed on those steps, made from a copper kettle put on the campfire.

Every night during that summer of 1970, I'd walk along the coast between Norton and Yarmouth. In the evenings, when the tide was high, there was just a shabby little stretch of sand; room for only one person's footsteps. I wound my way around there every night.

I followed the path round until it opened up. It was August, and the Isle of Wight festival was in full swing nearby. It wouldn't be put on again until 2002. A group of teenagers was gathered near the waves. They were trying to start a fire, ineffectually poking at the sticks, holding lighters up to them, laughing drunkenly.

Your mother was on the outskirts, wearing a green dress. She threw me a sardonic glance. 'Left the festival for this,' she said. A gesture to the fire. I noticed the effect of the moonlight on her skin. She looked so pale, almost blue. Ghoulish. My little ghoul.

'I haven't the faintest idea how to get a fire going, so I'll bow out,' I said.

'You can chat to me, instead,' she said. She was forward like that. She held a beer bottle up. She couldn't find another, so we shared hers. One sip for her. One for me. Our lips leaving imprints on the rim. We were almost kissing, I thought excitedly. She was wearing an Isle of Wight wristband. She was cold. She kept rubbing at her freckled arms.

We talked for two hours. The sand had two distinct impressions from our arses in it by the time we stood up. Alex pointed to them, and we laughed. 'Look how big they are!' she had said, clutching her green dress to her rear. 'Is mine that big? Tell me it isn't!'

She made me agree to meet her in the same spot – 'By the arses,' she said – the next day. I knew the tide would sweep them away, so I memorized their location, a few feet along from that groyne, just there.

I walked up to the clifftops and took the long way home. I wanted to be alone, away from the crowds. Everything was open late, and the festival's music thudded through the streets. I popped into a newsagent's and bought a packet of cigarettes. Embassy. Filter Virginia. I'd never done such a thing before, had never wanted to. I'd always liked to feel clean air in my lungs. But that night was different. I lit one up and I smoked and smoked, striding the streets alone, little pockets of smoke left hanging in the air where I'd walked. I had become a man, you see, because I had met the woman I was going to marry.

The next morning, she was waiting by the tide for me. 'The sea has wiped our bums away!' she said. She was wearing a denim pinafore, that hair – that fucking glorious hair – left loose and wild and red.

Later, I painted those impressions in the sand and gave the portrait to her.

And now she was missing. And there was the portrait. God, why couldn't the painting of the fucking beach bums be missing, and she be here, in this room, soft-skinned and smiling and alive?

At seven o'clock, I called Tony.

'Fancy a game?' I said to him. We went up to the tennis courts, in the November wind and the rain, and knocked a ball around. We didn't talk about Alex. What was there to say? I didn't know where you were, Izzy. I never even asked, and I'm sorry.

Izzy

He was cleaning everything.

Izzy was sitting outside in the November rain, underneath the apple tree in their back garden. Her back was to the trunk. The ground was uneven and uncomfortable underneath her and the trunk was damp. The rain was pattering on the leaves up above her, occasional fat drops hitting the grass beside her, and she didn't care at all.

She had a view of the other houses, and could listen out for footsteps or cars. It didn't matter that her hands were freezing, that the seat of her jeans was damp. It was like the priorities of everyday life had shifted. Nothing mattered.

She would sit here and wait and wait and wait and soon – very soon – her mother would arrive home. Perhaps injured from an accident. Perhaps casually – 'The hen do, remember?' – and then they suddenly *would* remember, and . . . how they would laugh about it. Izzy looked up into the bright white sky and felt those outcomes so fiercely in her chest they were almost real, almost tangible. She reached her phone out to check for a text from Pip – although God knows, he had enough going on – but then cocked her head, listening. What was that?

She listened harder. The thrum of the washing machine. She rose to standing from her position under the tree and peered through the kitchen window. Her father was doing laundry.

Later, it would transpire that he had washed every surface in the house. Every floor. And everything that he had worn on the night she had gone missing. Even his shoes.

31

'It looked guilty,' Izzy says to her father now. 'That stuff you did.'

He blinks, looking at her in surprise.

He has three empty plates in front of him, all in a row, and he awkwardly arranges his elbows around them to rest his face in his hands. Yes, that's right, that's so right; he used to sit in exactly this way.

'The washing?'

'Yes.'

'But I was *always* in charge of the washing. And, anyway,' he says with a wave of his hand, 'you're looking at it all wrong.' He says it nastily, his lip curling up slightly in distaste.

Izzy steps back from him instinctively. 'Am I?'

'She was missing. Then. But I didn't know she was dead. Murdered. It was just washing then. Just washing.'

'But you cleaned so thoroughly.'

'I've explained,' he says. 'Haven't I? Forget it,' he adds. 'Just forget it, if you're going to give me the fucking third degree.'

'Aren't I entitled to?'

'Forget it,' he says again.

She tries to breathe deeply. Of course he will be defensive. Look at what's happened to him. Rather than rising to it, she removes the plates from in front of him. She will go home in a few minutes: it's late. She needs to write to more David Smiths, though she doesn't want to tell Gabe that now. Doesn't want him to know of her doubts, that her research is concentrated on investigating any possibility of his innocence rather than considering who else could have done it.

'I can run you home,' she says, thinking of the walk he took the other day, to her house and back, all alone.

'No. I like the walk – the fresh air. The space,' he says, giving her a smile she can't read.

He produces his pack of cards from his coat again, and they play on the bar. They share another entire cheesecake – 'I'll get so fat,' Izzy says – and some wine. She beats him ten to five.

'You must be cheating,' he says, throwing his head back and finally laughing, the old him, his lips smeared with balsamic vinegar.

When it's time, she watches him go. For a brief moment, the form of her old father appears before her. Lolloping into the sunlight, tennis racket in hand. Marching off to his shipping container with his burgundy art supplies bag slung over his muscular shoulder.

But just as quickly as he appeared, her new father is back. Her eyes mist over and obscure him from view. White hair, frail form, £12.99 Matalan coat. He eats one meal per day, this father, she is pretty sure. He has only one contact in the mobile phone he doesn't remember to charge – for twenty years, he has been taken care of, hasn't had to organize himself whatsoever – and will likely never work again.

It is after one o'clock in the morning by the time Izzy has finished cleaning. She stands, hands on the bar, thinking that she ought to lock up and go home. She sometimes extends these moments alone in the restaurant. The food sold, eaten, binned. The punters gone home. When it's just an empty building, she can almost convince herself that it's somewhere else.

She's picking up her handbag when she hears it. The soft closing of a door. She freezes, her heart thundering in her ears. *Please be imaginary*, she is thinking. *Please be an animal. The wind.* Something and nothing.

She stands, feeling her heart calm down. Nothing. It was nothing.

And then she hears the second sound. A footstep. Somebody being deliberately quiet. She acts without thinking, ducking down behind the bar, her handbag clutched to her.

A second footstep. A third. This is it. All her foolishness. He's come for her. She will end up like her mother, found days later. He knows that she ruined his alibi. He's angry about that. Or maybe he is just psychotic. Enjoys murdering women. Wants to control them and kill them. Her mind is her enemy, trying to reason it through, and scaring herself even more in the process.

Four steps. Five. Whoever it is, they are not coming towards her, but heading across the restaurant.

Six steps. Seven.

They've reached the basement. She hears the sound of their footsteps change as they reach the stone. Fear thrums through her. The *basement*. Oh God, oh God. She hears the squeak of the old door handle. The slow drawing back of the door. He's going to put her in the basement. The door shuts softly behind him and she stands up, her palms cold and slick with sweat. She reaches into her bag for her phone and gets it out, poised to dial 999. To dial Nick.

But first, she crosses quickly to the basement door and turns the key. It clicks. Air escapes her lungs: she's safe. For just a few minutes, while she works out what to do. She hears movement downstairs. She's poised to call Nick. But what if it's something benign? And then, for nothing, she'd have to tell Nick that Gabe had been here tonight. And then what would happen? Her father would be taken away from her. Again. That warm, safe, hopeful feeling she gets, deep inside, would be destroyed. She stands, frozen with indecision.

'Izzy?' a voice says on the other side of the door.

It's him. She's so sure it's him. It's Gabe.

'Izzy?' it says again, and relief moves through her, just like stepping into a warm room. It's not Gabe. It's *Tony*.

'Why are you in the basement?' she says.

'I forgot to take the wine out of my car,' he explains.

She unlocks the door. He's standing halfway up the stairs, his hands on his hips, a puzzled smile on his face. He gestures to the wine rack where several bottles are sitting on the floor. 'I was up when I remembered – rather do it at one in the morning than get up early to come round.'

That's right. He's a night owl.

'God,' she says, relief making her unburden herself, forget her reservations. 'I thought you were him. I thought you'd come for me.' She leans forward, placing her hands on her thighs like a runner just finishing a race.

Tony comes for her, his arms open. 'No, Izzy – no,' he says softly.

She stands, enfolded in her uncle's arms, feeling sick, her legs shaking.

She can't resist looking in the cellar the next morning. She doesn't know what possesses her. Something about Tony's body language. His tone had been relaxed. His words, too.

But there was just something . . . something in the set of his jaw. Something a little too practised about his confused expression.

She hates going down into the cellar. It's one of the reasons Tony sorts the wine. It's half the size of the restaurant, with low ceilings and a damp smell, like sour washing. She hardly knows what's down here. She has made many discoveries over the years – that is often the way, when you inherit a working organism like a restaurant. She took it on passively, reluctantly. She has reworked it piecemeal, over the years, altering the menus, the prices, the wages, the layout of the main room. But she's never really overhauled it fully. She hardly goes into some areas – the little store cupboard off the kitchen, which is *still* full of plates from the 1990s, and the basement.

She can see immediately that the wine rack has been fully stocked. Red at the bottom, white up top. The surplus is left standing along the wall.

She walks upstairs, leaving it be. She's almost at the top when she looks back and notices. The wine rack is at an angle. Just slightly. You'd never be able to tell if you weren't looking for it.

She crosses the basement again and approaches the side, which is sitting a couple of inches out from the wall. She peers down behind it, but the wine rack has a solid back, and so it's completely dark. She gets her phone out and finds the torch, then shines it behind the rack. It glints off something. A small door?

Izzy blinks, then drags the wine rack out further. She stares at what it reveals: a safe.

32

A memory pops, fully formed, into her mind, as she looks at it.

Her mother putting things in the safe. Yes, of course. How could she have forgotten? It had a double-sided key. An old brass thing, more like a cross than a key. It's funny how she remembers the feel of its weightiness in her palm exactly.

She gets her phone out and calls Gabe, the man she thought had come to murder her last night. God, how foolish she was. Why would he? She's his daughter. But then, Alex was his wife.

David Smith pops into her mind, but she leads him back into the box and locks it. That's nothing to worry about. It's not. It's just not.

'I've found something,' she says when Gabe picks up. 'It might be nothing, but –'

She stops speaking as she tries to consider whether she should mention Tony. No. Not yet. She'll try and open the safe. Withhold her judgement. And not worry Gabe about his brother in the meantime. And then she'll see what she finds. And if it leads her to Tony, then . . .

'It's a safe.'

'A safe?' Gabe says.

'In the basement. Behind the wine rack.'

'Oh!' Gabe says. 'Oh, wow.'

'It's locked – I don't have a key. I don't know where Mum's set went?' she says.

'You know, you could really be on to something here, Iz,' he says. 'The police never really searched Alexandra's. And they certainly wouldn't have bothered tracing keys.'

'Why?'

'Because they had their suspect.'

'I see.'

'Has anybody else had control over these premises?'

'No, not really. Granny and Granddad did come here – before I became the owner, properly – and Chris and Tony have always worked here.'

'Those people are all so convinced of my guilt,' Gabe says lightly.

'Hmm,' she says, thinking of Tony's easy manner last night.

Gabe seems to be thinking.

'So it hasn't been opened in two decades?' he says.

'Probably not. Not by me, anyway. What do you think's in there, Gabe?'

'I don't know. But if your mother was keeping secrets, might she not keep them in there?'

'Do you think she was keeping secrets?'

'Aren't we all?' he says.

Izzy suddenly feels cold, down here alone in the stone cellar.

'What should we do, then?' she says.

'We should hire a lock picker,' he says decisively. 'I know a few. Guys who've served time. Great burglars.'

Izzy doesn't laugh, though she almost wants to. 'Don't use those,' she says. 'I'll find one.'

'Right,' Gabe says. 'But where were we? In our chats?'

'Day two, missing,' Izzy says. 'The day they searched your shipping container.'

33

PROSECUTOR: Who had the key to that location?

GABRIEL ENGLISH: Me.

PROSECUTOR: How many keys were there?

GABRIEL ENGLISH: Just mine. One.

PROSECUTOR: One?

GABRIEL ENGLISH: Yes.

PROSECUTOR: Had you checked it when your wife had been missing for two days?

GABRIEL ENGLISH: No.

PROSECUTOR: So you had a sheltered place where somebody could be.

GABRIEL ENGLISH: Yes.

PROSECUTOR: And you decided not to check it at all during the time your wife was missing until the police prompted you to do so on the second day?

GABRIEL ENGLISH: No. Because I . . . I knew she wouldn't be there. She never went there. I was looking. I *was* looking for her.

Wednesday 3 November 1999: two days after Alex's murder

Gabe

They – this is how I had come to think of them, the police – were checking my shipping container in the morning, and so I accompanied them with the key. We walked. It was less than ten minutes from home, you probably remember.

My relationship with them had become strained, like a couple not yet ready to admit it was heading for divorce. Still sharing a bed, still watching television. Uneasy silences and small talk while each assessed the other.

What do I remember about that morning? I remember the way the light hit the pale sides of the container, that honeyed autumnal light even at nine o'clock in the morning. And I remember the way I felt, the way I'd felt for days, like I was full of anxious poison.

They let me unlock the two doors at the back. The sun blinded me as I did so, and I fumbled with the key. Earlier, they had asked me who else had access to the container, and I'd told them nobody. Not even the man I rented it off. He had given me the only set; he'd joked he was 'a good sport that way'.

The container opened up like a pair of French doors, two together. It smelt of art. That's the only way I can describe my container. Art, and home.

Do you know how much your mother hated that container? Even before we were in debt, she hated it. Treated it like a competitor, a rival. When I packed up my art bag to go there in the evenings (I was always transporting oils around, because I was never not painting) she'd raise her eyebrows, but say nothing.

But sometimes she liked it. When it suited her, I guess. If I left my container late, she liked me to give her lifts home from the restaurant. So much so that I'd started surprising her. Turning up when she didn't expect it. She would always be delighted. She'd turn the heat up, take her shoes off, curl her legs up on the passenger seat – no seat belt – and doze.

She said it was the only time of day when she wasn't in charge.

The two police officers – one short, one taller and thickset – stood like sentries as I opened the doors. The container was undisturbed since the last time I had been there. An easel to the left housing a half-finished painting which their eyes roved over. I closed my eyes and breathed in the smells from before. The sweet, Play-Doh smell. That's the oils themselves, Iz. Then the mellow, doughy smell of the linseed oil I used to mix them with, the paint becoming gluey, forming stiff peaks like your mother's meringues. And then the acerbic cut of the turpentine I used to wash the brushes with. A kind of citrus mouthwash, that's how it smelt. All together they were . . . they were me.

'This the extent of it?' one of them said to me as he walked towards the back of the container.

'Yes,' I said. 'Just a little spot to paint and store my things.'

They poked around for a while, lifting things up, removing them.

It was right before we left that I realized it was missing. My hand was on the double doors. I blinked. Looked, then looked again. Where the fuck was it? It must have been at home. It *must* have been at home.

I didn't say anything. I was too scared to, Izzy. They were already questioning me closely. That would make it all so much worse.

Later, I told the court I hadn't noticed. But I had. That's the truth. It wouldn't have saved her, anyway, if I had spoken up.

She was already dead.

Her father left with them, to go and look in his art shipping container. There was something off about his body language. She knew him well, and she knew what his hunched shoulders meant, what his stiff walk signified, as they left the driveway and turned on to the street.

She knew he didn't want them to be looking there.

She stared at them as they disappeared from view, her hand against the cool windowpane. He hadn't glanced back at her, not once.

Pip rang her after that.

'Any sign?' he said immediately, his voice soft and comforting down the telephone to her, like being pulled out of a stormy sea and deposited on warm sand.

She removed her palm from the glass and it left a misty mark that slowly faded, leaving just the grainy film of her fingerprints.

'No,' she said sadly.

They didn't find her mother's body that morning, but they did find one of the clues that would lead them to her killer.

Or rather, they should have. The clue was, as is often the case, in the absence of something. Something that should have been there, but wasn't. Something belonging to her father, kept in a place only he had access to.

34

'You thought I looked . . .' Gabe says.

Izzy is sitting on the bottom step of the basement, holding the phone to her ear, and she stretches her feet down on to the floor.

'I thought you looked like you knew something. That day, you looked like you didn't want to go.'

'I didn't want to go anywhere, Iz. I didn't want to leave in case she came home. I didn't want to check places where *bodies*, not *people*, would turn up. And I didn't want to waste my time. She wasn't in my shipping container. She was . . . away. She was on a weekend away we'd forgotten about. A restaurant management course. Something.'

'Yeah. I remember feeling that, too.'

'And they were checking the container because they were focusing their efforts on me – the suspect. When I wanted them to be finding her.'

'I know,' she says.

'Or finding my alibi. You remember him, don't you?'

'Yes,' she says carefully.

She hangs up shortly after that, making excuses. Before she goes back upstairs, she calls a lock picker. He's booked up until June, but she takes the next slot.

She shouldn't have called Gabe. She was excited about the safe. She forgot herself, and all his lies. But she's *glad* she called him.

This is what she does: she vacillates. She is suspended in

indecision. She is frightened of her father but offers him meals, company . . . what next? Money?

As she drives home, she looks out to sea, and thinks of the first eerie autumn–winter spent with her grandparents. Tony would visit often, but conversations were shut down like closing doors whenever she tried to discuss his brother with him: 'That's enough, Izzy. Let's talk about someone worthwhile.'

He had never before been so proprietary, so dictatorial, and hasn't since.

Why? What was he hiding?

The thought arrives before she can question it, examine it. Guilt? Why was he so insistent the case never be talked about, picked over, examined?

Was he worried what Izzy might find out? About her father . . . or about him?

Izzy lets herself in through the front door, and at first she thinks Nick isn't in, even though his car is on their driveway. The lights are off, and it's getting dark. She feels relief – her shoulders relax, and her heart lifts as she thinks of pottering around the house by herself – but then she hears the sizzle and crack of something frying in a pan. She shakes her head. *Nick*. This is Nick. What's happening? Why is she thinking like this?

She pushes open the door to the kitchen and breathes in: sauces, fried onions. A set of hot-dog buns on the counter. The ketchup out, ready. Hot dogs.

'Making your favourite,' Nick says.

His tone is so easy, his movements so fluid, she wonders if they could forget the person who is dividing their relationship in two, and remember each other. Can Izzy remember him? Nick with his steady, self-sufficient ways, his brilliant memory. She hugs him from behind, their first physical contact in a while, and Nick slowly rubs a foot up the inside of her ankle.

The sausages begin to burn in distinct stripes as they stand there, and the onions are on too high a heat, the fat splattering the silver hob in messy globules, but Izzy doesn't say anything.

Tiredness overcomes her as she sinks into the kitchen chair. She almost fell asleep on the drive back, the tail lights of the cars on the roads blurring hypnotically as her blinks became slower and slower. In the end, she opened the window and let a blast of air stream in.

Nick's work laptop is open on the table, the screen dark.

'How's work been?'

'Oh, fine, fine. Same old.' He hardly ever elaborates. He turns the sausages instead of saying anything further.

It's only when they're sitting opposite each other, a bottle of red open, a plate of sausages in front of them with a pair of tongs neatly lined up next to them, that Nick says it.

'Look. I wanted to talk to you about it. Him.'

'What?' Izzy says, one delicious bite in.

'I looked him up on CRIS.'

'What's CRIS?'

'The crime reporting system we use.'

'Okay,' she says. She sees now. Her favourite meal. He is sweetening a blow.

She doesn't ask. He will tell her. She swallows, wanting to delay the moment. The moment that he tells her he's found something. God, what's on the crime reporting system? All of the things that convicted her father rise to the surface but she pushes them down again.

'Will you get in trouble for it?' she says, stalling for time.

Nick seems to consider her question. He has ketchup on his thumb and he licks it off. 'No,' he says. 'I don't think so. My activity isn't monitored. It's not ideal, but don't worry about that: it's my decision.' *For you* he has added silently, she can tell; the subtext sits heavily in the air between them.

'Okay.'

He finishes his hot dog and lays his hands flat on the table. His thumbs are gripping the underneath of it, like he is about to turn it over. He seems to consciously drop his shoulders, like he's just been told to relax. 'So . . .'

'Okay, just say it, please,' she says, putting her hot dog down.

The sausage flesh inside is pink and oozing and her stomach turns over with nausea.

35

'He has a previous conviction,' Nick says quietly. 'It wasn't disclosed at the trial because his lawyers got it excluded.'

Izzy's mouth turns dry. A previous conviction? A criminal record? Her *father*? Her shock is ludicrous, of course. Her father has the pinnacle of criminal records. But this previous conviction is from before she knew him. Before she existed. How could it be? In her mind, the night he killed her mother, her father *transformed*. But this would indicate he was always dangerous. Always, therefore, pretending. The thought chills her.

She can't believe that just yesterday she was suspecting Tony. And why? Because a wine rack moved? She has been so foolish.

'What for?' she says, her voice dry and brittle-sounding.

She finds she is holding her breath. Her brain throws options into the nothingness, and she wishes she could stop it: a caution for a drunken fight. A speeding ticket. Theft of a supermarket trolley. Affray, on a stag do. Not returning money a bank deposited in error. Over and over again, she thinks of *acceptable* crimes. Victimless crimes. Identity fraud, sending phishing emails, accidentally leaving Tesco with a packet of toilet rolls. Oh, please let it be one of these. Let it have an explanation. Let it not be violent.

'It's for domestic violence,' Nick says. He pushes the plate of sausages to one side and reaches for her hands. 'The victim was his girlfriend.'

Babs. Izzy knows it before he tells her. The woman her uncle told her about.

'What . . .' Izzy says. Saliva fills her mouth. She really may be sick. She can't look at the sausages, and she pushes them further away from her so she can't smell them, either.

'I'm sorry,' Nick says. 'I brought a printout, hang on. I knew you'd want to see.'

He strides into the hallway and comes back holding a piece of paper. It's A4, plain paper. 'Page 1 of 1' written in the top right-hand corner. She scans it.

Assault occasioning Actual Bodily Harm contrary to s47 Offences Against The Person Act: suspended sentence (12 months). 15 May, 1969.

She looks for his name at the top and, sure enough, there it is: Gabriel David English.

'What did he do?' she says, staring at the paper in shock.

This was it. This was all of it. Everything they'd accused him of. Domestic abuse.

The behavioural patterns. Charming behaviour. Controlling her mother. Keeping tabs on her. Spying. *Escalation*. Hitting her, they said. Verbal assaults. That text. That bruise on her arm. Frightening her. He denied it all, but look: she holds the paper in shaking hands, the black text blurring as tears fill her eyes. Look. Here is evidence. Real evidence. Not her half-remembered memories. Not her father's false accounts of his.

Domestic violence. She thinks of the newspaper cutting and her stomach turns over again. Oh Jesus. She needs to get away from Nick. She needs to think about this, this foolish thing that she has allowed to happen. That she has done.

'I don't know much yet – that's all I've got. The file will come soon. But I wanted you to know . . .'

His body language has changed. She looks at him, trying to pinpoint exactly what it is. He puts his plate on the kitchen counter and asks if she's okay. She nods quickly, not wanting to discuss it. That's it. She realizes as he walks out of the kitchen. Those shoulders are up again. The chest puffed. He is . . . triumphant. He is *right*.

Rage starts off like a Catherine wheel in Izzy's stomach. How dare he use this to score points against her? Her jaw clenches and she stands and opens the back door and breathes in the scented garden air. *Don't get angry*, she tells herself. *Don't lash out, or you'll be just like him, like Gabe.*

She doesn't share her cheese and biscuits with him, later. She eats them alone, in the kitchen, standing in the light of the refrigerator, thinking of the newspaper cutting, of her father's betrayal of her, of how stupid she might have been. Of course her father's memories have convinced her. They are not, after all, his memories, but his own accounts of his memories. The difference is subtle but vital. He has had almost twenty years to construct them. His own case. And look: he's lured her in.

'I'm sorry,' Nick says later, as she climbs into bed.

She thought he was asleep.

He opens his eyes in the half-light and looks at her.

She says nothing.

'It's so understandable,' he says, his tone softer.

Finally, finally: here it is. The sympathy. The understanding. *It is easy to give it when you are in the right*, Izzy thinks bitterly, unfairly.

'The way you are is . . . I'd be the same,' Nick adds, clueless about her nasty thoughts.

The way you are. Izzy is vulnerable, exposed, as if she has been cut open, there on the bed, and everybody can see all of the things she does to try and cope with what has happened to her. The Instagram family. Watching her neighbour too closely. Keeping people distant. Wanting approval from anybody senior: doctors, teachers, even the health and safety inspector at work who wore reading glasses and a kimono.

'I wanted him to be good, I suppose,' she says.

'Wanting something to be true doesn't make it so,' Nick says. He looks up at her, his head in between their pillows. His eyes are soft and wet, too.

36

Izzy sleeps on it.

When she wakes, she has a text from Gabe: *How're you?*

She blinks, reading it, then closes the messages app on her phone. He's an abuser. Her father assaulted one woman, then murdered another.

But what if . . . ?

Her mind idles over the possibilities. He was young. He has an explanation. Neither is an excuse. But she wants to know. She can't just leave it, loose ends and all.

Should she at least hear him out? Ask him about it? She sits on her bed, looking out over the fields across from her house, thinking.

Does she owe it to him?

No.

She wants to ask him. That is the truth, she realizes, as she unwinds after a busy evening at Alexandra's.

She wants to dislodge this unhappy stone and replace it with the other feeling that's been bubbling up through her recently: hope. She's not felt it for decades. It isn't *coping* or *making the best of it*. It's the belief that there is something better on the horizon.

She thinks of the newspaper cutting. Who could that be from? Not him. Why would he do that? That is something she can't fathom. Why would he threaten her? And even if he is a killer, a sociopath, why would he kill *her*? She thinks of the alibi she ruined for him, but dismisses the thought again. The truth is, if he did kill her mother, she doesn't know why. And so she has no idea of the danger she's in. If any. He might be a monster, but he's definitely an enigma.

So maybe it's from somebody warning her about him. But does anybody truly know him? She knows him better than anybody, after all.

She wants to ask him about Babs, and so she will.

She dials his number. Turning to him – even after nearly twenty years' absence – feels natural. Like she is a normal thirty-something with a broken boiler, a picture that needs hanging, the oil in her car topping up. She calls her father like thousands of women have done before her.

Something in the back of her mind is calling her foolish. Reckless. Looking for parents in the wrong places, chasing down danger, but she doesn't care.

'Your previous conviction,' she says, her tone icy. She can't help it.

She closes her eyes, and wishes she hadn't called him. That she could see his eyes. Those eyes of his that are nothing like hers, except the way they both squint at the sun; like just-woken animals. She remembers a photograph of them skiing, taken back in 1998. They were both looking at the camera like meerkats.

'I . . . oh,' he says.

She can imagine his mouth moving, forming an O. He will be pulling a hand back through his dark hair. No. She corrects herself: his hair is white now.

There's an awkward pause.

'I'll tell you about that,' he says, recovering fast.

She shouldn't be telling him, shouldn't be on the phone to him, she thinks.

'But in the meantime, in your entire childhood – which is *after* Babs – was I ever violent?'

'No.'

'Short-tempered?'

'No. Mum was,' Izzy says, feeling guilty.

Her father was always easy company. 'Don't worry about it,' he said of various misdemeanours, changing the TV channel and offering her a Quality Street. 'The things I did in my youth . . .'

'Right,' he says now. 'And anyway, we've got a good thing going, haven't we?' He waits a beat. 'I'm so enjoying this, Iz. I . . . I missed you. I waited thousands of days for this, and . . . God.'

'Don't,' she says, her throat tight. 'Don't guilt-trip me. Don't manipulate me.'

'But didn't you miss me?'

'I couldn't,' she says. 'I wasn't allowed to.'

'*Allowed?*'

'Granny and Granddad, it was . . . it was tough. *They* were tough.' Izzy looks down at her jeans, embarrassed. She wasn't merely taken away physically, she was forced to take sides. Pulled away into her mother's narrative. A tragic woman murdered by her husband. A husband who wouldn't tell anybody where she was. A husband who then put every-body through a trial. It was easier, in the end, to take a side.

'How so?'

'Your case was off limits. They didn't . . . I don't know. They didn't care about me. They didn't let me do anything, or talk to me. It was dark, I guess.'

'No,' Gabe says. 'Please don't say they made it worse for you.'

'I never wanted to say.'

'I thought you'd be well looked after.'

'I was. I was never hungry, or cold, or whatever.'

'But you didn't feel loved,' he says softly.

'No. I guess not. Not for *me*. I had to fit in with them.'

'Well, I love you,' he says.

Izzy closes her eyes and leans in to the words. She is drowning in them. She is choked up, unable to speak. He loves her.

'Anyway. Babs,' he says. 'I was seventeen years old.'

She steps out into the garden and holds the hot phone to her ear. The paving slabs underfoot are still warm, even though it's nearly midnight. Birds are nesting in the trees just beyond her garden, the bushes shivering with their movement.

'I had this girlfriend, Babs,' he says. 'God, I loved her.'

She immediately thinks of Pip, and how much she had loved his floppy hair, his raspberry lips and his adventurous spirit. 'What happened?' she says.

'She was *cool*,' he says. 'Smoked. Bell bottoms. Liked art, liked *me*. But, Izzy, we were a disaster. The best, when things were good, but we were awful communicators. It was pretty volatile. She lived in this little flat above a greengrocer's. I always used to take her up an apple, as a joke, on my way through. We'd paint and chat. She loved The Beatles, had this huge poster on her wall of the *Help!* album. Used to quote their lyrics all the time. Anyway, one day we had one of our rows – the kind that start off about one thing and end up being about things said during the row. Tony witnessed one, once, but this time, someone in the greengrocer's called the police.'

'Why?'

'We were shouting. I was louder, I guess. My voice

261

carried. She scratched my face. I bent her arm behind her back.'

'Oh,' Izzy says. 'Why?'

'She came at me. But more than that, I was angry. It was wrong. But she was . . . we'd have these rows where she wouldn't let things drop. I'd say, "Leave me to calm down," but she wouldn't. She'd come after me. She brandished the hot iron in my face once, as a threat.'

'So you intended to hurt her.'

'I lost my temper,' he says measuredly. 'As did she.'

'But when men hit women . . .'

'That was a two-way street. She hurt my face as much as I hurt her arm.'

'It doesn't work like that now,' Izzy says tightly.

'Anyway, it went all the way to trial.'

'What – she accused you?'

'No. But the police came, and she was honest.'

'Did Mum know?'

'Of course,' he says quickly. 'And my parents. Go and see my mum, if you want.'

'She's on your side, right?'

'Yes, she is. But she has an interesting perspective. It might help you.'

'Maybe I will.'

Izzy thinks of the worst of her behaviour when she was seventeen. The way she would career around roundabouts while texting, no regard for lives at stake. The way she would sometimes hoard a hundred mouldy mugs in her room without thinking that her mother had to collect them up, had to take out the rancid, stiff herbal tea bags. That time she kicked her bedroom door when she hadn't been able to understand her chemistry homework. The faintest of dents was evident, afterwards, which she was ashamed to look at. Could she have ended up in a similar situation, given the right circumstances? An awful row, recorded forever?

She screws her nose up in frustration. Was she trying to twist the facts to suit her? It felt like it, sometimes; like they were malleable, changeable. Like she might be looking at things through prisms that refracted and misdirected the truth, over and over. She couldn't tell. Who could? She could only go on how she felt, here in the garden, her father explaining himself patiently, quietly, on the end of the phone to her. Her father telling her that he loved her.

'Why didn't you tell me? Even when I asked?'

He pauses, thinking, she guesses. 'How did you find out?' She doesn't answer that and, eventually, he says, 'Do you know why people exclude previous convictions at trials, Iz?'

'Not really, no.'

'It's because if there is even a hint of a defendant having done something in the past, the jury can't move beyond it.'

'Yeah.'

'They convict. And, I guess, I didn't want you to do the same. It's not relevant. I was a different person then. As you are different to the teenage you.'

'But it *is* relevant.'

'It's not to me. Because I'm not a murderer.'

She looks across at Thea's garden. Her kitchen windows are open and she can hear the chink of cutlery. The sound of footsteps on wooden floors.

'It was just me and crazy Babs. Being teenagers.'

It makes sense to Izzy. His explanation feels authentic. Exactly how she would be if she were accused: defensive, trying to hide things that seemed relevant, but weren't. She can feel her mind coming around to his version of events, like the slowly turning Isle of Wight tides: she is starting to believe him.

'Would you say you have a quick temper?' she says.

'No. But I do think everyone has a limit. And nobody's perfect.'

Izzy is glad he says that. She is glad he isn't delusional.

'So whose fault was it?'

'It was both of our faults.'

'That's called victim blaming in today's parlance.'

'Well, it was what it was.'

Izzy doesn't respond to that. Instead, she looks up at the sky and wonders who has the answers for her, and if she will ever find them. Her mother, her father . . . and God, she supposes. Gabe's God.

'We split up, afterwards. Which was just as well,' he adds.

'Pip and I split up, too,' she says, though she is still thinking about breaking points and tempers.

'What happened?' he asks. He's asked before.

He keeps asking, and she wishes he wouldn't.

'Nothing,' she says, sitting down on the bench in her garden.

She and Pip used to discuss babies. It seems immature now. But she felt so sure they would make it. 'I like the name Gigi,' she'd said once. 'No. Pole dancer's name,' Pip had said, which had made her laugh.

She and Nick never discuss it. Izzy knows her own reasons: how could she be a mother? She has no idea how families work. The idea of giving birth to, and then leaving hospital with, a life she is entirely responsible for fills her with horror. But what about Nick? Sometimes, she thinks he merely can't be bothered to have the conversation, and that thought fills her with sadness.

'Nothing happened,' she says again. 'Just the usual.'

'I'm sorry, Iz. I liked him. First loves, hey? I guess it was too much – with his brother and everything?'

'I guess so. Where are you?' she asks quietly.

'In the hostel. Hey, I'm on cooking duty tomorrow.'

'Me too,' she says with a smile. 'I've swapped shifts.' He says nothing but, somehow, she can tell that he is smiling too, down the telephone line to her.

The next night, at Alexandra's, as she dices an onion which makes her cry, she doesn't think of his hostel, or that he has to perform chores in order to have a bed. She thinks only of him chopping an onion, eyes watering too, along with hers.

37

Three days later, Izzy is on a ferry to Portsmouth. She's moved her shifts again. Work seems to matter much less than Gabriel.

She doesn't leave the island often; the ferry will forever remind her of that trip to Belmarsh. The sea is calm and flat, like a freshly made bed. She stares at the neat line of the horizon.

Her father's parents eventually settled in London. She wasn't permitted to see them when she lived with her mother's parents and, after she moved out, it seemed, somehow, to be too late. Things were easier left. Life went on, she told herself, as a way to compartmentalize, to avoid, to bury.

She is struck once again by how little she knows about where she has come from. It is as though she sprang into being with no context for what came before her: her parents' marriage, their history, their lives before her. Now, she wants to know it all, absolutely all of it. It is the bedrock upon which the crime is founded. There is an answer somewhere, deep in the past; she can feel it. It's not hidden in the police evidence – missed by some negligent copper, as Gabe fantasizes – but in the personalities of her parents. Who were they? Why did they do the things they did? And how did that lead to one of them being murdered? The answer's here, on this ostensibly happy, sunny island with its seedy underbelly. She can feel it. The pieces are coming together.

The train has no air conditioning, and the air outside is

still, with barely a breeze. She eases the train window open a crack. The air here smells different; she likes the scent of it, especially in this freakish summer-in-spring. Hot city air. The smell of cigarettes and takeaways and stale beers and street food.

A car sits outside her grandmother's drive in Tooting. It's a green Nissan Micra, old. A postman is just leaving, the gate clanging behind him, and he nods to her. It's so strange to think she's never been here: her grandmother's house.

It's a normal residential street. Dropped kerbs. Pebble-dashed houses. Porches with white uPVC doors. Funny how, even though they travelled all over, living so differently to others, they ended up here. In London suburbia. They had no choice, she guesses. Once Gabe was convicted, they fled to anonymity. A kebab house is opposite, and a tube sign is nearby, but otherwise, it could be any city in Britain.

Her grandmother answers the door, and Izzy should be struck by her appearance – stooped, her hair dyed a sort of pearlescent white, age spots across her tanned cheeks – but she is too busy studying her grandmother's reaction. There is an emotion present that she can't read. It's the same emotion she heard on the telephone when she arranged to come, but she can't quite grasp it. It might be sadness.

Yes, maybe.

There is nothing of her other grandparents' fusty tradition in this house. Nor does it reflect their own travelling past. It's clean and modern. White walls, blue carpets.

Her grandmother steps aside and lets Izzy enter the living room first. She presents her with a mug of green tea without asking and Izzy cradles it in her lap.

'You look so much like her,' her grandmother says. She

has the same soft Irish accent as her son, but her voice is weaker now. She is old, unable to project quite as much, and the effect is a reedy, watery sound. 'You don't look at all like Gabriel.'

'No. I'm sorry it's been so long, I –'

'So you've seen him,' her grandmother says, waving away the apology.

'He's back on the island.'

'Yes . . .'

Her grandmother surprises her by taking the seat next to Izzy on the pale fabric sofa. Her eyes – even into her eighties – are alert, scrutinizing her. They're the exact same colour as her sage-green trousers. She doesn't look much like Gabe, save for their darker complexions.

'. . . he can't leave it, now,' she says. 'He can't visit us. Terms of his licence.'

So he's stuck there, on the island, the sea a moat around him.

'He tells me he's innocent,' Izzy says.

'He tells that to everybody,' her grandmother says. 'Because he is. I'm seeing him soon. I need to get over to him.'

Izzy places her tea on the coaster sitting on the largest of a nest of tables. Izzy can hear paws skittering on the floor. A dog, maybe, shut in the kitchen. She can't help but imagine a parallel life running alongside hers. One where she's here all the time, with Gabe and her mother. She knows the dog's name. Life has an infrastructure of grannies and granddads and birthday visits and holidays to France on which they all bicker. Trivial Pursuit. Barbecues. Mothers and fathers and grandkids.

This grandmother thinks the exact opposite of the other.

How can two women – two mothers – hold such different views? They have taken opposite sides of the same case, but one of them must be wrong.

'But he's very charming,' Izzy adds. 'I like . . . I like seeing him.'

'Yes, he did always have the gift of the gab.'

'But I don't know what to think. What he says . . . it . . . I don't know. It makes sense to me. Sometimes.'

'Yes.'

'I think I . . . I think I *could* believe him. I think I –'

Her grandmother holds a hand up. Her teacup rattles on its saucer. 'You want to believe him,' she says quietly.

'Yes,' Izzy says, her eyes budding with tears. She nods. 'Yes.'

It's exactly the same sentiment that Nick expressed, but it is kind, and not harsh. There's no judgement. It's fair enough that she should want to believe her father, her grandmother is implying. Nick did the opposite. Something rises up through her; a slideshow of all of the worst parts of their relationship. His refusal to understand where she's coming from. His avoidance of all things tricky or difficult. Sometimes, she thinks nastily, sadly, he just wants a companion. Somebody with whom to have sex and dinner and nothing more than that. Anything deeper is hard work, to Nick. *No.* She forces the thoughts down. They aren't true. They can't be true, not these disastrous thoughts about her marriage.

She tries to think of the good things about him, but her mind draws a blank. *He's a safe man*, she finds herself thinking.

'We wanted to believe, too,' her grandmother says simply. She places her cup down on the table with a clatter. 'So we did.'

'Was it that easy?' Izzy asks.

'Yes, and no.'

Izzy waits patiently. She's good at waiting.

'The first few years were rough.'

'Yeah?'

'The accusation of domestic violence. Those text messages . . . his temper. Her injuries.'

'And Babs,' Izzy says softly.

'Babs was a problem,' her grandmother admits. 'She was my first thought when your father was arrested: *again?* But, it was . . . Two things occurring together do not mean escalation, Izzy. I had to . . . to broaden my mind. Look.'

She stands up, hands on her slim legs, and brings down a photograph from the shelf. It's in colour, her parents standing in front of Alexandra's on its opening night. Gabe's arm is around her mother's slim waist. Her hair is up, a green hairband contrasting with its redness. Her head is thrown back, laughing at Gabe. Tucked into his chest is her hand, clutching her phone, a black pebble in the palm of her hand. Yes, that's right, her mother had spent the entire day in the run-up to the opening on the phone, and moaning about it.

'Look,' her grandmother says, still holding the photograph out with shaking hands.

'What?'

'Love.'

'I went to live with Granny and Granddad,' Izzy says, taking the photograph in her hands.

'I know.'

'Well, they –'

'I know. They wouldn't let us see you, either,' her grandmother says.

Izzy nods. 'It was . . . it is all black and white to them. But now I see . . .' Izzy looks at the photograph again. 'Now everything is muddy,' she finishes lamely.

'Sometimes, somehow . . .' her grandmother says. Her eyes become damp.

Izzy wonders what the tears are for. Time served by an innocent man? Or the never-quite-knowing situation they find themselves in? Never a hundred per cent; only as close as they can get. Eighty. Ninety. Ninety-nine. Do they feel fully safe, themselves, around Gabriel? If he makes a sudden movement? If he raises his voice? He's like a dog that's bitten once, maybe. Izzy never feels completely sure or safe.

'You find you don't really *need* to know. You just believe,' her grandmother finishes.

'I'm not there yet,' Izzy says.

'Well,' her grandmother says, 'it's different for you. You've more at stake, I know.'

'Did you ever think, if it wasn't him, who else it might have been?'

'Yes. Often.'

'But you've no idea?'

'No. We never figured it out. Nobody ever got to the bottom of it. The reality is, only *he* knows for sure that he didn't do it. So only he really *wants* to know.'

There is a scratching at the door.

'You like dogs?' her grandmother says.

'Sure,' Izzy says.

She rises unsteadily to her feet, knees barely straightening, and two Schnauzers rush in. The larger one licks Izzy's hand. His tongue is surprisingly soft.

'Would you have said they were happy? My mum and dad?' Izzy says.

Her grandmother's face forms a strange, unsure expression,

her bottom lip pulled downwards. 'You know, they ought not to have been, but they were.'

'Why?'

'I think, having had decades to think about it, I think they were just very different people. Your mother thought the stuff of life was hard work. Gabe thinks – well, Gabe just wants to have fun. But it worked. It shouldn't have, on paper, but it did, in real life. They liked each other so very much.'

'I see.'

'It comes down to two things, anyway, doesn't it?' her grandmother says. 'Whether Gabe did it, which nobody knows. Not the judge,' she says, as the smaller dog jumps up at her, 'not the jury. Not us. Not your mother's parents. And secondly: if not him, then who? Both are mysteries. But you can, in a way, choose to solve the first one. You can decide, yourself, what you think about it. And, really, only that matters. Your thoughts are all it is.'

'Yes,' Izzy says.

Her grandmother makes it sound simple. But is it? A life was lost. But if her father *is* innocent, what happened to him is almost as bad as what happened to her mother. Two lives lost needlessly.

'But I do know one thing. Although the evidence against him is . . .'

Izzy waits patiently as her grandmother chooses the right word. She knows *what* the evidence is, but she doesn't know what it *means*. She could never serve on a jury, she thinks, gazing into the clear green tea. She would believe everybody.

'. . . compelling,' her grandma says.

Izzy's heart-sinking reaction tells her all she needs to know.

'Although it is compelling, I know him to be good. He *is* good,' she finishes, looking straight at her granddaughter.

Izzy drives off the ferry, metal ramps clunking under her wheels, and heads for home. She's bone tired, as she often is when she leaves the island. The sunlight is low, and she has the windows open, enjoying the salted breeze in her hair.

As she turns off the A-road, she catches sight of something in the rear-view mirror. A black car, close to her. She turns left at a roundabout, then right, then takes a side road. It drops back a few cars, but still tails her. As she turns on to her country track, it drives past her. A few seconds after she parks, and just as she is locking the car door, she sees it circle around again, driving slowly past her house. She stares at the windows, but they catch the sun at just the wrong moment, whitewashing her view of the driver.

She stares and stares as the car retreats, trying to make out a form. The car turns left at the end of her track, and she sees him. A man. Older than middle-aged.

It's nothing, she tells herself.

It's nothing: what else could it possibly be?

38

Izzy sits at the desk in the back of the restaurant and opens Google. Earlier, she made a list of the names of the men who worked at the restaurant regularly.

Tony, Chris, Marcus the regular, Geoffrey Adams, a waiter. She adds Daniel Godfrey, too, the waiter her mother sacked.

If her mother *had* been having an affair, then maybe there is an explanation other than Gabe's jealousy, Gabe's debt, Gabe's temper. The prosecution wanted the jury to believe that she meant nothing to him. That he was controlling, that she had got him into debt, and that he killed her in a temper. But what if one of these other men had killed her – or knew something about who might have?

She gazes around the office. The walls know. The walls know who was in here with her. And her mother knew. And whoever was with her knew – if it was anybody, and not another one of Gabe's lies. But nobody else. How can it be this way? Something happening, deep in the past, and leaving zero imprint, zero trace. It wouldn't now, Izzy reasons. There's CCTV in the corner, just up there. Her phone is probably recording everything she says and sending it to advertising companies.

Last night, Izzy finished checking the 1999 statements. She still hasn't found the extended licence or seen any evidence of it having been paid for. Why? Was her mother lying to Gabe about having applied for it? Or was she merely disorganized, and the application was lost somewhere in the swathes of paperwork?

Izzy googles Marcus, Daniel and Geoffrey. There's nothing of note. Charity JustGiving pages. LinkedIn profiles. That's all.

She looks them all up on Facebook. Marcus isn't on there, but Daniel is. He's still a jobbing actor. Was in a mobile phone advert a few months back. Geoffrey might be on there, but his profile is locked down, the profile picture a white figure on a grey background.

Chris walks into her office and she closes the laptop guiltily. His eyes linger over it, but he says nothing, as is his way. 'Charger needed,' he says, waving his phone, then plugs it into the socket at the bottom of the wall, sitting on a spare chair and looking at her. 'How's the boss?' he says.

'The boss is tired,' Izzy says, rubbing at her eyes.

'You could never hack it,' Chris says with a lopsided grin. 'Sleepover wanker.'

Izzy laughs. That's what he used to call her when she'd fall asleep before midnight and he'd have to stay up watching horror alone. *Sleepover wanker.*

'Nick brought these in for you,' Chris says, producing a tiny bag of chocolate coins.

Izzy takes them, not saying a word. Chocolate coins. She has always loved them. The cheap, plasticky chocolate. She only ever has them at Christmas. Here they are; a love note from him to her.

39

Izzy visits Gabe at his bail hostel the next day. He is insistent that they meet in private. Alone. It will be easier, he says. They will be undisturbed.

'The humble abode,' Gabe says as he opens the door to his bedroom and welcomes her inside.

She looks around his room. Eight cans of beans are in the wardrobe next to the radio. She stares at the neat row of them, labels facing out. There's a deck of cards on the bed, which he sits down next to. His bedroom at home was nothing like this. It wasn't functional or plain. He was messy. He had old sports trophies on his bedside table which her mother used to tut at as she dusted. Paintings everywhere. Little pots he'd made. Canvas paintings air-drying.

There's nothing in this room. Just the radio and those tins of beans.

She tells him about her visit to his mother's.

'I'll go soon,' he tells her, though his tone doesn't match his words.

He can't. He's not being straight with her about that, but she knows he can't. She shrugs, uncomfortable under his intense stare. There's nowhere to sit down other than on the bed next to him. He used to sit on the edge of her bed, just the way he is now, and read her bedtime stories. He'd act them out with her row of cuddly toys. He'd always have the window open, in all weathers, and she liked to think of their neighbours overhearing those quiet, private moments of theirs, as she listens to Thea's.

She looks at the beans again and thinks of everything an innocent man could have lost. His freedom. His house. His wife. His daughter. And more than that, somehow: his zest for life. Endless pottery and ball games and fine art and opinions on Tracey Emin and Damien Hirst and Tottenham Hotspur and Pete Sampras. Marvelling at the patterns fat summer raindrops made on the patio – 'They look like inkblots!' – and the way he loved the smell of linseed oil and turpentine – 'It signals the beginning of pleasure,' he once said to her.

Gabe clears his throat. 'There's a whole history of miscarriages of justice, you know,' he says. 'It's not that uncommon.'

'Who?'

'The Guildford Four. The Cardiff Three. Sally Clark. Jesus.'

'Jesus?'

'Untrue charges from the government. Betrayal by his friends. False witnesses. Anyway,' he says, looking at her expression, then seeming awkward, 'we need to talk about the day . . . the day they found her.'

She says nothing. The religious talk has set her on edge. Comparing himself to Jesus.

'How' they found her,' he adds.

She drops her head.

'I know it's the worst part,' he says.

She looks across at him. 'Okay,' she says. 'Let's talk about it.'

40

PROSECUTOR: What is your explanation for where your wife was found?

GABRIEL ENGLISH: I don't have one.

Tuesday 2 November 1999: the afternoon Alex's body is found

Gabe

The call came from my brother Tony. Not from the police. Not from your mother's parents. And not – as I had hoped, *God*, how I had hoped – from your mother herself, to say that she was alive and well. It came from Tony.

'There are a lot of police here, Gabe,' he said to me that afternoon. 'Twenty. Thirty people. Forensics. I think you'd better come.'

I left the house while still on the phone, hurriedly unlocking the car while trying to ask exactly where they were, the phone wedged between my shoulder and ear.

'The woodland near me,' he said.

Woodland.

Woodland.

Forensics.

No.

I wish I had waited, had slowed my steps. Had enjoyed that milky autumnal light, the russet of the trees, my final moments in limbo, in purgatory. Because that was better. Better than where I was headed. Towards the end of Alex. Forever.

Sometimes, even now, twenty years on, I'll catch myself thinking a certain way. Thinking that I'm about to see her. I'll mentally store things up to tell her about. And then, after hours of normality, it'll hit me. I'm not *ever* going to see her again. Not as the Gabe I am now. Maybe in heaven, maybe in the afterlife. But somehow I don't think it's that simple, do you? As Luke says in his Gospel: 'Today, you will be with me in paradise.'

But paradise isn't here.

I drove towards the woodland near Tony's house. And that's when I saw them: more police than I could count. Four squad cars. CID. A cordon, already set up – oh, my heart, Izzy, my heart when I remember this stuff and when I tell it to you. The cordon was manned at each entrance by an officer. There was a crime scene tent, and the forensic team in their bright white suits, ready. They began moving across the wood like a formation of birds, moving en masse, stealthily, inevitably, towards the end of my life.

They wouldn't tell me whether it was her, and they wouldn't let me in, so I could only imagine her. They wouldn't tell me anything, as though I was just another dog walker, passer-by, rubbernecker.

We'd shared a bed for twenty-nine years and here we were, separated by a hundred coppers who later would accuse me of murder. They'd galvanize themselves. They would utilize all of their money, and all of the powers available to the State, and accuse me. Police officers, solicitors, barristers, all intent on doing a job: prosecution. Me and my lone lawyer didn't stand a chance.

I couldn't reach for your mother's hands, to feel her grasp one last time, to smell her shampooed hair, to observe the curve of her back, her small, girlish hands. That's what they robbed me of, more than anything else. Those final moments with my wife, my lover, my best friend, to see her and to close her eyes and to hold her and say goodbye. Those dignified moments in what was – to me – your mother's death.

Instead, they read me the police caution and, later, told me about the bag.

My bag. My art bag, from my container, a place only I had access to. The bag her body had been found in.

Embroidered with my initials on the inside.

Izzy

She hadn't yet gone back to school, though people were trying to encourage her to. And so she was in her grandparents' house when it happened. They were fussing over cleaning out the teapot. Her grandfather was saying they shouldn't use soap – they had the same conversation every day, without irony or self-awareness – when the doorbell rang.

She knew immediately. The sight of the police car. The formal, shifting dark shape of the officers in the frosted glass as they respectfully removed their hats. She had seen enough television dramas to know.

What she didn't know was the full extent of it, of course.

That her mother had been found in her father's art bag.

That she had been wrapped in a sweater belonging to him.

That he had strangled her with the rope cord from the

bag – it had always been covered in paint, but he said it worked *just right* for his art, and he didn't want to buy a different cord – then buried her body in the woods, so that it would take the police time to find it, and so that some of the forensic evidence would be corrupted by exposure.

That he had then reported her missing.

That in the purple bruising covering her mother's neck was the printed pattern of the cord from her father's art bag. That he had branded her, just as he had marked his paintings with his signature style.

41

Her father sits back heavily on the bed, his back against the wall. 'That was the last moment I thought she might still be alive,' he says. 'She was already long dead, by then, apparently, but I still think of that as the last time . . . the last time that I saw her. Even though I . . . even though they wouldn't let me.'

He reaches a hand up to wipe at his face. His fingernails are dirty – Izzy winces – and he rubs at his eyes. She isn't sure if he is crying until he brings his hand away and she looks at his eyes. They're red and watery. She has never once seen him cry. Not ever.

She sits next to him on his bed. It yields too much under her small frame. It must be horrible to sleep in. Spongy and cheap, like a waterbed.

'I'm sorry, it's just . . . they made me relive it, all the time, back then. But not so much recently. I just said I'd done it, and was sorry, in my parole hearing.'

'Nick said you would have.'

'It was the least worst option,' he says.

Izzy stares at him. He seems to be sadly used to rocks and hard places. To having *the least worst option*. But she's glad he has been honest with her.

'Makes sense,' she says.

Izzy continues to looks at him carefully. The black car has been playing on her mind. And the presence of her uncle at the restaurant on the night her mother died. Something is niggling somewhere, in the corner of Izzy's vision. She can't even say what. So she suspects Tony? Is that what she's saying? She doesn't know. It's ridiculous, but it was ridiculous to Izzy that Gabe killed her mother, too.

'During the investigation . . . was everyone else looked into?' she says.

'Do you have a theory?' he says, looking across at her, his elbows on his knees.

'Well, it was probably someone she knew.'

'I guess.'

'Chris and Tony have always been so adamant about your guilt. And everybody – Mum's parents, as well – is so closed about it. I wonder. Isn't it logical to wonder if anybody has anything to hide?'

'You suspect them?' he says, his eyebrows raised, his eyes narrowed, looking at her thoughtfully. His tone isn't sceptical but respectful, instead. He admires the conclusion she's come to; the care she's taken over it, the thought that she has given to it. 'Tony was . . . he was with Auntie Julia. And her parents were with each other.'

Izzy winces under his gaze. She can't tell him about Tony. Not until there's something certain to tell. Her father has already lost too much. 'No, I just . . . I'm just keeping an open mind.' She swallows down the distaste of suspecting another relative of hers. Wouldn't that be just as bad?

'Maybe that's why he didn't testify,' Gabe says thoughtfully.

'Was it in his nature to do you a favour?'

Gabe pauses, then says, 'No. He was pretty black and white, really. If he felt it was the right thing to do, he would have done it. But I don't remember his exact reasons in the . . .' he waves a hand, 'in the mess of it all. Anyway . . .' Her father looks at her, biting his bottom lip.

'Well . . . ?'

'Matt told me you went to see him.'

'I am investigating,' she says, throwing him a weak grin. 'You still see him – Matt?'

'Yes. He cares about me, I guess. We get on.'

Izzy nods. Perhaps she had taken Matt's loaded silence for suspicion, when actually it had been professionalism. Confidentiality. Loyalty.

'I wondered, you know,' he says. 'For years, inside. And nobody would discuss it with me. Nobody. Everyone said to move on. *Do the time.*' He pushes his hair back from his face, widening his eyes. 'And now you're here. And you're listening. And it's not just me and God any more. I was in my own head for so long, you know? Hard to know what's real. But reliving the truth of it is hard, too. The messy truth.'

'The truth of it,' Izzy echoes.

He nods, and the flimsy bed bounces up and down. Their legs are almost touching. There is a photo of them together, like this, somewhere, sitting on a stone wall in a French campsite. Her legs half the length of his, little red T-bar shoes on her feet, white socks, grubby at their tops with sand from the beach. He was swarthy next to her pale skin. Spanish-looking.

'How could I explain the messiness of it to that bloody parole board? That I don't *know* who took the bag, and who put her in it in the woods? It makes no sense to me. Death doesn't, but especially not your mother's. It's a riddle I haven't been able to solve for eighteen years. Nineteen this October.' He starts to say something else, then stops, his words subsumed by proper tears. A rogue *sorry* escapes through his hands.

Izzy says nothing, watching him, her heart pounding.

'And then the questions,' he says, 'and then you.' His sobs have subsided into a gentle stream of tears.

His face is wet and Izzy is ready, she is so ready, to reach over and wipe his tears for him. This is how it should be. He cared for her when she was young, and she should care for him now he is old. This is the cycle of life. She shifts closer to him.

'Me?'

'And then I lost you. I didn't care about liberty. I lost her, and I lost you. In the same day.'

There is something about the tone of her father's voice that makes Izzy's body still. The pain marbled through his words like watercolours. She stops moving completely, sitting there on the bed next to him.

'And maybe you did nothing wrong,' she says softly.

She appraises his tears, the self-conscious way he wipes them away while apologizing. There is something authentic about it. She stares at his shaking hands. He couldn't fake that. He *couldn't*.

Those tears. They count for something, despite the evidence. Despite her father's DNA underneath her mother's fingernails – signs of a struggle, the prosecution said. Despite where she was found, and how. Despite his lack of alibi and his phone call having lit up a mast near to where her mother was found, despite him washing all of the clothes he was wearing that day immediately, guiltily.

Despite all of that, those tears count for something. The tears and the other things: the way he told her about the last day he saw his wife. The shape of his body when the sobs overcame him. A million unmeasurable things: the tone of his voice, the things that seemed to be important to him. Not the loss of liberty, but the loss of his wife and daughter. She can't explain it, but something has shifted.

She could believe him. She can feel the truth of it like a tangible object inside herself. She could do what his own mother has done, and choose.

Izzy is ready. She is ready to help him.

'I made a list,' Izzy says, after a pause. 'Of everybody at the restaurant that night.'

And, just like that, he moves his hand from his forehead and places it on her knee. She lets it sit there for a few moments, just like the photograph of them that was taken all those years ago.

It is the moment. It is the moment she chooses to try and believe him.

42

Izzy spends her time in the shower thinking of the black car. As she lathers shampoo into her hair, she wonders if she should have told somebody about it. Her father? Nick? Somebody who could help. But what was it, really? Her father has enough to worry about, and Nick . . . God, she doesn't want to tell Nick. Doesn't want to open up that topic again, doesn't want to have to answer his questions about how often and why she is seeing her father. But she's not stupid. She can see what's happening. Her marriage, constructed so carefully during her twenties . . . it's crumbling, like cliffs exposed to the elements.

She turns her mind away from it, away from that possibly benign black car, away from how seldom she and Nick entwine their ankles in bed, and thinks instead of the men at the restaurant. There must be something hidden in her memories.

Marcus. White-blond Marcus with his pale blue eyes used to come in every Friday. She racks her brain. What else? What else? But there is nothing. The things she knows about him – that he liked lasagne, that he spoke very basic French – she can't remember how she knows. They are just facts that exist in a vacuum, the background information rubbed out, leaving the knowledge but none of the context.

She thinks of Daniel Godfrey, the waiter who was sacked. He had a motorbike. He used to bring a McDonald's into the restaurant at the start of his shift, which irritated her mother. But that's all she has on him.

As she is towel-drying her hair in the bathroom, an image springs to mind.

Daniel waiting for her mother to finish serving somebody. He wanted to book a day off. Yes, that's right. He was standing by the end of the bar, just watching her.

As her mother turned to leave the table she was waiting on, she took two steps, then stopped. Seeing Izzy. Two steps, a pause, then her mother resumed, the pause infinitesimal, and continued towards him.

She hadn't wanted Izzy to see them interact. That's it. That's the impression she got.

Izzy hasn't thought of it for years, has dredged it from her memory through sheer force. But when was it? There is nothing to anchor it to.

But, nevertheless, it is something. Is it? Or was it just a pause, just an innocent pause? All of her memories are littered with this – this detritus, these loose ends. When somebody dies so suddenly, they leave things behind that don't make any sense. Ordinary occurrences loom large and seem extraordinary, and it's hard to tell if the past is littered with mere clues or coincidences.

When she goes downstairs to lock up before bed, she sees Nick's laptop on the pine kitchen table. He must be working from home tomorrow.

The thought appears in her mind uninvited. *I could look anybody up on that.* She knows he'll leave it unattended at least once, the next day. He always does.

No, she thinks. She's not that desperate for information. She wouldn't do something like that.

*

288

Before she goes to bed, she checks her Facebook inbox. Her message to Pip remains unread, the friend request still pending. Perhaps he's not logged in since. Or perhaps he just doesn't want to hear from her. Perhaps, once again, she is reaching out, inappropriately seeking intimacy, when she ought to keep her counsel, become somehow self-sufficient.

She clicks around on his profile. She idly searches his friends for Talbots and Easons. There are a few hits. Carly Eason. Jemima Eason. They must be cousins or something. Steve Eason is the last. His father. How must it feel to be Facebook friends with your own father? To see him casually for barbecues and at Christmas, to phone him up, to trust him.

She brings up his profile. And there is his smiling face, holding up a philosophy book written by him. The familiarity of that photograph makes her open the message box. She writes quickly, before she can change her mind.

I'm trying to get in touch with Pip, she says. She leaves her mobile number.

As she ascends the stairs, she thinks of her father. Imagine if he was innocent. How light she'd feel. She would go out shopping. Hold her head high. Take the ferry to London. Visit Liberty and Jo Malone and Abercrombie & Fitch. Take a ballet class, just for kicks. She'd be . . . free.

She performs an *arabesque* on her stairs, in the quiet, in the dark. Nobody sees, but she feels it: her body remembers how to do it. She is still good.

She is woken by a text in the night. She has been programmed to wake up when she hears the tone, in case it's a David Smith, and now Pip or Steve. In case it's information.

DO NOT REPLY is who the text message is from. She

opens it, half-heartedly expecting some junk text – about free pizzas, or two-for-one burgers – but her hands still when she swipes to reveal its contents.

You might think you're safe eating dinner with your father in the restaurant, but you're not. You're not safe at all.

Her body is covered in goosebumps, the hairs raised.

You're not safe at all.

Izzy hesitates, in the morning, deciding who to show the text message to. She slept because she knows how to sleep when terrified. She did it for years.

Her choice doesn't even make sense to her. Izzy is a mystery to herself. The risks she is taking. But something in her gut is propelling her in this direction. It feels right: to tell her father. To tell him is as natural to her as it is for a child who has fallen over in the street to look for their parent.

He answers the phone on the first ring. He understands immediately. He understands the position they're in.

She reads out the text to him, and he says, 'Somebody doesn't want us meeting. They're trying to scare you. That's a threat. The clipping was *weird*. But that's a threat.'

'From –'

He doesn't miss a beat. 'The person who did it.'

'But what do we do?' she says. 'Should I tell someone?'

'What do you want to do?' he says quietly.

'I want to know who's doing this to us. But I don't want to be threatened.'

'I know. But what if we work it out?'

Izzy's in only a vest top, the morning sun warming her skin through the kitchen window, but inside she feels cold. She hasn't slept well, and her eyes are gritty from tiredness and worry. Her father suggests they meet at Nettlecombe

Farm Lake, the only lake on the Isle of Wight. Izzy pictures the holiday cottages dotted around the green sloping hills and, sunken in the centre, the expanse of water, reflecting the blue of the sky. The idyllic location and the sunshine through the window are incongruous to Izzy, who is freezing cold with fear. What if she's followed again? She will be vulnerable, driving alone –

'Look,' her father says, cutting across her thoughts. 'Don't go to the restaurant today. Meet me at the lake, and we'll discuss my arrest. The only way to find out who did it is to keep talking. The only way out is through.'

43

PROSECUTOR: What was Mr English's response when asked if he had murdered his late wife, Alexandra English?

DI BOTHAM: He said, 'No comment.'

Wednesday 3 November 1999: two days after Alex's murder

Gabe

'Gabriel English, you do not have to say anything unless you wish to do so . . .'

They arrested me at the scene. Of course they did. Your mother's body was recovered within and surrounded by my possessions, with what they regarded as my *mark* left imprinted around her neck.

The police caution flooded my ears. The woodland seemed to shimmer a kind of grey colour. I blinked, but it stayed that way. Shock, somebody later said. I bent double, was sick, before they had finished speaking. The handcuffs were around my wrists and for the first time in my life – the very first time, Izzy – I was not in charge. In any other area of life you can say: *enough*. You can quit jobs. Get off public transport. Stay in bed.

But not when you're accused.

I was taken to the station in the back of a police car while my wife lay dead in the undergrowth. I hadn't slept for two days and I was to be questioned imminently. A lawyer would be called. My possessions searched and taken from me. My human rights meant I was allowed to ask for a cup of tea, but that's it. How fucking British.

The car wound its way across the island to the station, with me in the back, the world still a gunmetal grey, and meanwhile, the killer was still out there, and everybody had focused incorrectly on me, their gaze narrowed to a single point.

Press were already gathered on the steps of the police station in the November wind and rain. A grey umbrella turned itself inside out, revealing a grey woman underneath it with a BBC microphone.

I was sick again in the cell, then drank my tea and waited for the lawyer and stared at the wall.

My lawyer, the man who was supposed to explain away this whole mess, to put it right, was an uninterested guy who couldn't have been over twenty-five. His gaze kept sliding to the door while I was talking. 'Okay, okay,' he kept saying, once I was finished. 'Okay, okay.' He wrote the date on the top of a grey legal pad. His handwriting was huge and childish. I later sacked him and hired Matt.

'Tape running: six thirty p.m., Tuesday the second of November,' Detective Inspector Botham said.

He was a slight man, dainty looking, quite short, with shaved hair.

'Gabriel English,' Botham said. 'Please state for the record where you were on the night of the thirty-first of October, running into the early hours of the first of November.'

'At my home,' I said, rattling off the address.

'And was there anybody with you?'

'No.'

'Where was your daughter?'

'At her boyfriend's house,' I said. The part of my mind that hadn't been blown apart by the discovery of my wife's body thought: *God, we sound like delinquents. Our daughter in the bed of a boy whose surname she had only mentioned once.* But the thought was obscured in the dimness: the lights were off in that functional part of my brain. The spotlight was on your mother. She was the only thing not grey, to me. Vibrant, red-headed Alex.

'What did you do that evening?'

'I told you all this when she disappeared. Was she killed that night? Or later?'

God, *why* hadn't I checked my container before the police did? Sometimes, it sounded reasonable: she had never been there on her own, and only I had the key. Other times, it sounded like the most unreasonable thing in the world, like somebody who was looking for their house keys and checked everywhere except the lock.

'Tell us again.'

'I went to the corner shop, I went home, I watched television, I spoke to the neighbour at around eleven forty-five for half an hour.'

'And then what?'

'I checked around the house for her. Looked in the car. Called her mobile. Called the garage who had her car, but got no answers.'

'And you were in your house making these calls?'

'Yes.'

'The mobile phone records say you weren't at your house.'

'Well, I was. And then I waited for her. I thought she'd . . .

I don't know. Got distracted. Forgot to come home. Gone somewhere *en route*.'

'Why didn't you use the landline?'

'We just didn't. I always favoured my mobile . . .'

'So when did you worry?'

'I guess after twelve.'

I was trying to sound composed, but my mind disobeyed me. It needed to be clear, to map out my evening neatly for the detectives, but I was shrouded, instead, in memories. *My God*, I kept thinking. *She is dead. She is dead she is dead she is dead.* Never again would I see her clear green eyes open, first thing in the morning, fluttering into comprehension. Never again would I see the curve of her bottom, bigger since childbirth, and want to paint it a luminous white, using big, arcing strokes. She'd hate that portrait, but I thought it should be celebrated, that bottom, and its middle-aged bigness.

In my mind, Alex turned to smile at me while we walked around Venice together, on that weekend break. The backs of her calves had caught the sun. They were red and blotchy and beautiful.

'Why didn't you check your container? It's another space that you and Alex owned, one where she could have gone. Mr English, you didn't check it once – until we did.'

'I . . .'

'How often would you usually go to the container?'

'Most days. But I didn't feel like . . . I didn't feel like painting.'

Alex triumphantly winning a game of mini golf, a few years ago, her arms raised at the final hole after she putted her ball. She'd worn a hoody and I'd laughingly pulled the hood up. She'd made a face at me, her ears sticking out.

'Painting. Right. So in those two days, it never even crossed your mind to check it?'

'No.'

'You were concerned for her welfare.'

I swallowed. *Concerned.* How I would long to be *concerned* now. She was dead. Dead. Could it really be? The facts, the truth, kept rolling over me like thunderclaps, and all I could do was startle in surprise, standing in the rain, waiting for the next one.

'What *did* you do?'

'When?'

'When she was missing.'

'I worried about her. I called her. I spoke to everybody she knew. Her parents. Her friends. Old colleagues.'

'Who?'

'A few waiters and waitresses. A few customers. Everyone who knew her. I called the accident and emergency departments of all the hospitals.'

'And so we require just a little more detail about your movements on that night. What did you do between ten thirty and twelve thirty?'

'Is that when you think she died?' I said, my head snapping up to look at them.

God. She had died immediately and been put in there . . . She had been in those woods for two damn days. My wonderful wife who loved shoes and telling me off and spending money. My wife, not next to me in our warm bed but murdered, out in the cold. Left alone, her body chilled and crawled over by insects and discovered by a dog walker.

'I . . . I didn't do much of anything really.'

The opening night at Alexandra's, the speech she gave,

bronzed champagne twinkling in her glass, the whites of her eyes bright. Hair a burnished red in the lamplight.

'Which?'

'Neither, none. I didn't do anything,' I said, sobbing, looking at the grey table and my grey hands and my grey tea. What if the world never became colourful again? 'I paced.'

Alex reprimanding me, holding up a blue shrunken jumper from the washing machine. 'This is the size of a cat's jumper!' she had said. 'Cats don't wear jumpers,' I'd said immediately. And *God*, her laugh, her laugh, her laugh.

'Did you go out?'

'*No.*'

'Why was a mast near to your container and the wood-land where her body was recovered pinged by your mobile?'

'I don't know.'

'Bit of a coincidence, isn't it?'

'No.'

I felt, rather than saw, my lawyer shift uncomfortably next to me.

'Okay, so can you prove you stayed in your house that night?'

'Well, I . . .'

'Did you call anybody on the landline?'

'No.'

'Did you have anyone over?'

'No. But the neighbour saw me.'

'Who?'

'David Smith.'

'Can we contact him?'

'Yes. Definitely. We talked for around twenty minutes, and then he was in and out of his house all evening. He can confirm my whereabouts. That I didn't go anywhere.'

'So what time did you go to bed?'

'I don't know . . . after I called the police. Three? I didn't sleep.'

'Had you discovered something, that evening, Mr English? Something that angered you?'

'No.'

Alex with a towel wrapped around her hair, emerging from the bathroom steam with a bright red face. 'I've been exfoliating,' she would say to me with a grin. Alex holding you for the first time, when you were just born, covered in vernix, and our lives had been changed for four minutes and an entire lifetime. Alex sucking the end of a ballpoint pen, blotting her lip, during that crazy first month when the restaurant had just opened.

I had never experienced death. I'd been lucky. But now, at over forty, I found I couldn't wrap my mind around it. Where was she? Not her body but – *she*?

Alex was still missing, in a way. She was *in absentia*. Elsewhere. But where? Maybe I could find her. Be the first human ever to do so; to find somebody in the afterlife. I closed my eyes. Maybe I could paint her home. If I captured her likeness so *completely*, she would be delivered back to me.

'Gabriel, we are just simply trying to work out why somebody would behave this way,' Botham said, his expression earnest, his brow wrinkled.

I had never felt somebody concentrate on me so intently. I was a grey specimen in a grey lab.

'I didn't behave in any way,' I said tightly.

'Where was the key to the container?'

'On my keyring.'

'The whole time?'

'Yes,' I said, and I could see, then, that they thought it was me. They were closing in, surrounding me on all corners. There was no escape.

'Anybody borrow it?'

'No.'

'Where was the bag?'

'I don't know.'

'Surely you noticed it had disappeared from the shipping container?'

'No.'

I don't know why I lied, Izzy. Actually – *that's* a lie, too – I do. Because I felt like they were on to me, and there was nothing I could do to stop it. The freight train of the police, the prosecution, the State. And let me tell you: when the State wants to put you away, they make sure it happens.

'Why did you choose the woods?'

'I didn't. I can't answer your questions. It wasn't me. I don't know. I don't know. I don't know. I don't know.' The world was darkening now, grey to black, and I was surrounded by Alexes, all the Alexes I'd ever known, pale skin, red hair, green eyes. 'Somebody else must have, because I didn't put her there,' I said through my fingers, through my sobs.

At that point, my lawyer held his hand up, halted the interview, took me next door and advised a 'no comment'.

I took his advice. I wasn't in a fit state to do anything else.

Later, they told me that she had been strangled. Strangulation. One of the most painful and traumatic ways to die. No doubt she looked at her attacker as they did it.

The world regained its colour eventually. But nothing else was ever the same again.

Identifying the body did not fall to Izzy. Her grandparents did it. She waited for them in a side room painted entirely pink.

There was no morgue. No unveiling of the body dramatically from beneath a sheet. Later, her grandparents told her they'd simply been shown photographs of her mother's body. Izzy didn't ask to see them. She knew she would never forget them.

They came into the room with the pink walls and pink chairs and sat down next to her. All it took was a nod from her grandmother. Izzy didn't know what she was supposed to do, so she nodded back.

'It's her,' her grandmother said.

'Okay, then,' Izzy said.

She knew she sounded dispassionate – uncaring, even. She didn't mean to. She just simply didn't know what to say, sat there in that little pink room. She stood up and looked at her grandparents with their iron-grey hair, their matching beige slacks.

'Izzy. There's more.'

'What?'

'She was found in your father's art bag, in the woods.'

Izzy said nothing. She couldn't say anything. Her mind was skittering, her thoughts crawling over themselves like ants in a nest.

'Did she look like herself?' Izzy said eventually; a sentence she would recall for years afterwards. A strange thing to say. So disconnected from what she had just been told.

'Yes,' her grandfather said, after a brief look was exchanged with her grandmother. 'Yes, don't worry about that.'

Later, she saw the photographs for herself, after one of the prosecution's medical experts came to her grandparents' house to relay his findings to them.

Her mother had been strangled and her arteries compressed. Blood strangling, not airway strangling, the pathologist called it. Clear marks, striated in tones of mauve and purple and green and yellow, like a gruesome sunset.

Her eyes were open.

44

She finishes speaking. They're sitting on some decking over-looking the lake.

All she is thinking is: *he knows*. He knows about the alibi. Why else would he mention David Smith's name so specific-ally to her?

'I've never thought how traumatic your interview would be,' she says, deliberately not asking.

'Nobody thinks about the accused, and rightly so, for the most part,' Gabe says with a sad shrug. 'But it was . . . it was a trauma. I think something happened to my brain that day. I've not been the same since. Not even now, when so much time has passed. And I'm no closer to being Gabriel again. No painting. No sport. No joy in life, either.'

'You painted your flyers.'

'I coloured them in. And I hated every minute of it.'

Izzy sighs. Her father was never the type to turn posi-tives into negatives. She thinks about his failed job interviews and his cans of beans, and her heart seems to drop in her chest. It *is* all hopeless. He can see it, and so, too, can she.

He is not Gabriel. Gabriel is somebody from the past who he aspires to be.

'I mean . . . none of it makes any sense. Why would you use your own bag to dispose of her body?' she says.

'They say it was a crime of passion. That we were at the shipping container or in the house and I lost my temper.

That I wasn't thinking straight. Or that I forgot about the initials. That the art bag was identifiable.'

'I see,' Izzy says, looking out over the lake, its surface a flat, opaque blue, not a single imperfection or ripple on it.

She thinks of David Smith, and all the strangers she's written to. She takes a deep breath and decides to ask. To be brave. To confront, rather than avoid.

'I ruined your alibi,' she says to Gabe. 'They didn't include my evidence at your trial because I wasn't certain. But I told the police.'

'I know,' he says.

'How?'

'Police told me. Later on, via my lawyer, that you hadn't corroborated it.'

'I'm sorry, I . . . I thought he was . . . he said goodbye to me, a couple of days before, and he drove off in the van.'

'I know. He didn't return the van until the first. There was much made of that, at my trial. All sorts of people were called to say some people keep the vans for days after moving to buy new furniture, and some return them as soon as possible . . . but they couldn't trace him. They tried so hard, Matt tried so fucking hard, Iz, but David Smith rented the van registered to his Isle of Wight house, and he gave nothing more than his full name. Paid cash. Bum luck, that's what it was. The whole damn thing.'

'I'm sorry. I was asked without warning. I was –'

'You were seventeen,' he says tightly. 'It's fine. It's just . . . that was one of the things which began all the suspicion. Sadly.' He shrugs, saying nothing more.

She fiddles with a loose spindle of wood on the decking, the silence hanging between them.

'I know, but I spoke too soon, maybe . . .'

'Don't,' he says, pulling off his shoes and socks, ready to dangle his feet into the water.

'It'll be freezing,' Izzy says.

He ignores her warning.

'I didn't know. He was probably just saying goodbye to me in case he didn't see me again.'

'Iz, it's fine,' her father says, turning his head sideways to her.

His expression is unreadable, and she narrows her eyes, looking at him. The scent of summer is in the air. Lurid smells, flowers that have bloomed too quickly and are now dying in the heat. A kind of fetid greenness. 'Really,' he adds. 'It was bad timing. It all is. Death by a thousand cuts.'

'A thousand cuts?'

'A thousand small, innocent things, done at the wrong time, adding up to – well, to this,' he says. He swishes his feet in the water. 'I haven't been submerged in water for twenty years. Do you know how that feels?'

'I can't imagine,' she says.

'No.' He says it softly, non-judgementally. 'Nobody except a prison guard has touched me for years.'

It's an unusual admission from her usually stoical father. Izzy scoots closer to him, saying nothing.

They look out across the lake, then he gets to his feet. He leaves wet footprints on the decking. A thousand childhood holiday memories assault her. The slap of his feet around a swimming pool as he taught her how to dive. Sitting together, sweating in a sauna, and arguing over their Desert Island Discs – he had included Puff Daddy on his, which she thought was *bizarre*. That time they had gone jogging together, one Christmas Day, and had spent the entire time laughing so hard their stomach muscles hurt. The way those tanned, elegant feet of his became paint-splattered in his shipping container in the summer as he sat on his stool, perfectly still. Sometimes, she'd go and watch him paint, a spectator sport. Eventually, he kept a second stool there, and got it out whenever she arrived. It had a brown leather top.

She looks out over the calm blue water. It's a kind of greyish blue, a bland background to the cyan-blue sky and the green leaves on the trees.

'So that's everything,' she says.

'That's my side of it, anyway.'

'Why was your DNA under her fingernails?'

Her father looks across at her, his expression quizzical. He picks up his coat, discarded a few feet away, to sit on. 'We were husband and wife.' He gives her a significant look. 'We loved each other.'

She nods, not saying anything. So here it is. Every memory, laid out. And nothing has changed. What did she expect? Evidence, she supposes. Missed evidence that would exonerate him – a message from David Smith, maybe – or more concrete evidence that would underpin his conviction. What she really wanted, she guesses, was for them to *crack the case*. For their memories to inform each other and to hit upon something. Something missed. Something significant. But there's nothing. Her father is right: it's just a mess.

'I really thought we might get somewhere,' Izzy says.

Her father shrugs and sits down next to her, putting his feet into the water again. 'You can't prove a negative.' He crosses his legs at the ankles. She can see only his shins, disappearing to a blurred nothing in the murky water. 'That's the thing. That's been the thing this whole damn time. Once you're accused, that's it. You can only try to tear down their suspicions. Tell them, again and again, that you don't know where she went. That you don't know who might've seen her.

And hope that you can chip away at their evidence. But you can't ever disprove it. And you can't ever stop them thinking it. Because they make their minds up, and then everything – absolutely everything – you do looks guilty. If you stay put, you look guilty. If you go out and look for her, you're covering your tracks. If you don't check the shipping container, it's because you knew where she was. If you do check it, it's to get in before the police and dispose of evidence. It's endless. The skewed perspective. I was guilty from day one.'

'Yes,' Izzy says, thinking of the men – and women – she sometimes sees on the news. Parents accused of murdering their children. Outliers of society accused because they *looked weird*, were in the wrong place at the wrong time. Lynch mobs forming, based on nothing – on conjecture, on judgement, on gossip. Even when they're exonerated by DNA or cast-iron alibis or the real perpetrator having been caught, they are ruined. What do they do, these people, in the afterworld? The world that exists after such a serious allegation? What *can* they do?

'Who visited you?' she asks.

'Inside?'

'Yes.'

'Paul. My parents. That's it.'

'Wow.'

'To be honest, nobody visited *much*.'

'Why not?'

He lets out a sigh; a sad, melancholy sound like a pipe being let down. 'That's lifers for you. I may as well have emigrated. People move on. They have to move on. I would never encourage them not to. I *told* them to.'

'Did you?'

'Yeah. They can't wait around for twenty years. Especially not for a waste of space.'

'Don't say that,' Izzy says, her hand fluttering to her chest. 'No, you're not a waste of space.'

'Oh, but I am,' he says, looking at her, eyes dark in the shadow of the sun. 'Anyway,' he swings his feet out of the lake, showering them both with cool water droplets, 'I was going to take a walk to one of the nice estates. You want to come? Deliver some flyers?'

'It's a nice day for it.'

Her father looks up, as though noticing for the first time. He puts his trainers on, then hands her half of the flyers, crumpled from his coat pocket.

'There's no name on it. Just a number,' she says, studying one.

His expression stops her saying anything further. Of course. Of course he hasn't put his name on them.

They walk out of the farm and turn left down a long, wide street. The grass verges on either side have been highlighted by the sun, their strands a honeyed yellow. The trees are in full bloom, shaggy and green like it's July, and even in the dappled shade it isn't cool.

'Are you just going to post a flyer through each letter box?'

'I guess,' he says.

They stand at the bottom of a bungalow's long driveway. The walls are white, the sky a Persian blue behind it.

'Know what this reminds me of?' he says, looking up at the house.

'What?'

'Your paper round.'

She smiles. She'd taken on a paper round when she was fourteen. She'd thought she'd enjoy the early mornings, the sun on her shoulders, walking around the neighbourhood.

Sleeping houses, dogs at letter boxes. A glorified walk, and more money to spend on ballet shoes. But she hadn't. The bag had made her arm ache. It had taken hours, for hardly any money, in all weathers. In the end, her father had come with her, before her mother got up. He held the bag for her, and they'd chatted.

She supposes there aren't paper rounds any more.

'That one has scaffolding,' Gabe says, pointing down the road.

'Go, ring the doorbell. It's worth a shot,' she says. She gives him an encouraging smile, just the way he did to her when she was delivering her papers.

'No, they ... I don't know. They won't want to be disturbed.'

They begin walking slowly towards the house.

'Go and give them your leaflet,' she says. 'They're beautiful.'

'Okay,' he says. He takes a steadying breath and walks up the driveway which bends and curves out of view.

She hears the doorbell ring out into the afternoon. She turns away, looking back down the street, her lower back sweating, her arms warmed by the sun. She hears nothing for a moment, then his footsteps, his light tread, on the driveway.

'Let's go,' he says, appearing on the pavement next to her.

'Go?'

'I can't do this,' he says, and she sees his hands are shaking. He thrusts the flyers into her hands.

'What – what happened?'

'Nothing, nothing,' he says, ushering her down the street. 'Shit, come on. They've probably answered by now.'

'You didn't wait?'

'No.'

'Why?'

'Oh . . . I just can't. I just can't do this. I . . . I'd have to buy the equipment.'

'I can buy the equipment.'

They are walking back to her car. He continues as though she hasn't spoken.

'I'd have to be there on time and bring a . . . bring a lunch? I haven't made a lunch for eighteen years. I'd be alone and . . . How do I paint a wall again? I don't know how. I'd have to pay my taxes and National Insurance. Do they still have that? And buy a car and . . . I can't, I can't, I can't.'

'It's fine, it's fine, let's just . . .' Izzy looks at her father. He's breathing shallowly, his eyes darting around. Anxiety, she guesses. 'Let's just . . . sit,' she says, leading him a little way down the road and sitting down on the kerb. It's a quiet road, and his breathing seems to slow in the silence.

'Let's take it one step at a time,' she says. 'You remember how to paint – you do the sugar soap, the masking tape.'

'Yes, yes,' he says. His head is in his hands, little white strands of hair curling around his fingers. 'It's not just that,' he says. 'It's everything.'

'What?'

'I don't know.'

'Can you speak to your probation officer?'

'Maybe I should. I just don't know where to start.' He swallows, and she sees his eyes are wet again. He reaches down and begins pulling at the straw-like grass. 'Why do you think people go to prison, Izzy?'

'Because they have done bad things,' Izzy says, picking up a tiny hot stone with squared-off edges from beside the kerb and rolling it between her forefinger and thumb.

'To protect the public. To punish the person. To deter other members of the public from committing crimes. Right?'

'Right.'

'So inside, they make my meals for me. They lock me up. They stop me voting for my MP. They socialize me with people who have done similar things to me. They stop me working. They don't give me access to normal people. They parent me. Mobile phones aren't allowed. My own clothes aren't allowed. They don't let me have access to a television unless I behave in an exemplary way. If I'm really, really good, I can earn points to play on a PlayStation – old games, non-violent games. And they seriously think, they seriously fucking think, that people don't mind giving up everything. That they'd knowingly choose to trade it all – seeing their wife, their kids – because they get a PlayStation inside. An easy life. That it isn't a punishment.'

'Yes. Some people do think that.'

'So,' her father leans back on his hands, looking at her, squinting in that way of his, in the sunshine, 'at the end of it. When it's all been done. The public are protected from me. I am punished. People are deterred, right?'

'Right.'

'But what about me?'

'What do you mean?'

'Well, what do I know how to do?'

'I don't know,' Izzy says quietly. There is something belligerent about her father's tone, like he is giving a drunken political speech at a dinner party where nobody has asked for his opinion.

'I'll tell you what I know how to do: I know how to smuggle heroin into prison using drones and dead pigeons.

I know how to start and stop a fight. I know how to make a knife out of a broken razor blade and refrigerated tooth-paste. And what do I *not* know how to do?'

'What?'

'Well, vote in an election. Pay my taxes. Rent a house. Trust that my neighbours aren't plotting to kill me. Catch a bus. Send an email on these flat things you have that you call tablets that look like kids' toys to me. Cook a meal not in a kettle. Attend an interview. Be a part of society.'

'So . . . but you can learn. You know you can.'

'I can't, Izzy. It's not that I don't know how to do these tasks. It's that I don't know how to organize my life. The system has gobbled me up and spat me out. I've served my purpose. I've deterred people. And now they've disposed of me.'

'So what are you saying?'

'Do you remember our postman?'

'Er . . . not really,' Izzy says, confused.

'Well, I do. He was called Ray. You know, I saw him most mornings. I thought nothing of it. We used to talk about football – he was a Newport fan.'

'Yes.'

'Well, anyway. I avoid my postman now.'

'Why?'

'Because I can't deal with it. For eighteen years, every single one of my relationships has been divided into two things: officer or fellow inmate. I don't know how to talk to him. I don't know how to have normal relationships.'

'You're managing with me.'

He looks sideways at her. Even now, in the sun, in the middle of the longest heatwave for years, he looks sallow. He says nothing. Doesn't need to, perhaps.

'It's just life, Iz. I've not cooked a meal or posted a letter or worked for a non-prison employer or taken a walk or set my own bedtime or driven myself somewhere or been really, truly alone for nearly twenty years. I don't know how to *do* life. I'm so fucking angry about that.'

'It's okay to be angry,' Izzy says softly, speaking before she's even thought about what she's saying. But it is. It is okay to be angry. She's been so phobic about it for all these years, and with no reason. She's not a monster. She is good. And maybe he is, too.

He sits on the pavement, puts his head in his hands, and cries. The sobs echo in the quiet street.

After a while, he pulls his deck of cards out of his pocket. They play pontoon, wordlessly, father and daughter, by the side of the road in the sun. It helps them to forget.

She loses herself in it.

It is only on her way home, in her car, that she truly lets herself think of it. So he knows. He knows about the alibi. Where previously she'd thought there would be a dramatic moment, a confession, a showdown when he found out she'd ruined his alibi, here, there was nothing. Just a quiet admission that he already knew.

And that he wasn't angry.

Or was he?

She replays the set of his jaw when they were talking about David Smith. He had looked angry. He looked irritated, to her. She is sure of it. She thinks again of her mother's debt, her alleged affair and thinks: this is a man who bears a grudge, and it is only when she's alone that she can fathom it. When she is with him, all she can see is him, like he is the sun, and everything else is left in shadow, starved of light.

*

Izzy stops for petrol on the way home. A familiar figure is filling his car up in front of her as she queues. She wonders why she recognizes the set of this man's shoulders, his fluid movements. For a second, she wonders if it's Pip, but it's not: it's Steve, his stepfather.

She stares at him as he fills up, her eyes roving over him, willing him to see her and to ignore her, all at once. She's amazed she hasn't seen him before: the island is so small she sees people from her childhood all the time, but never him, until now.

There's a movement in the passenger seat. She leans forward, squinting. She can just about make out a blond head. Pip. It's Pip.

Steve opens the passenger door and he and Pip go into the shop together, laughing at some newspaper headline or other. Izzy's eyes burn as she looks at them in the queue. Pip is still slender, his shoulders tapering to a neat waist. He still has the same walk, too, a kind of cheerful gait. He's dressed youthfully, in faded jeans and a grey hoody. Izzy is surprised to feel a lurch of desire as she looks at and remembers his body.

Steve smiles and claps Pip on the shoulder right before they pay, and Pip selects a bag of Maltesers at the last minute. Yes, that's right. He liked the same sort of foods as her. Cheap chocolate.

As they approach their car, Steve seems to sense Izzy's eyes on him, and he turns to look at her. She raises her eyebrows, her hand in a wave, but he turns away from her. He says something to Pip, who keeps his eyes downcast in the exact way people do when they're told not to look. As they drive off, Pip's eyes meet hers, just briefly, just once, through his window. There's an expression on his face she can't read.

Pity, she realizes as she pays for her petrol. It was pity.

She must have been looking at them too intently. Contacting them. Looking for families. The island leper.

Nick is waiting for Izzy when she gets home. If he is wondering where she has been, he doesn't say. He keeps it inside; a metaphorical evidence file of her misdemeanours, this man that she loves. He looks over his shoulder at her as she arrives in their kitchen. Something about the expression on his face, or maybe the dim lamplight, takes her back to the night they moved in.

They'd completed late in the day, and most of her boxes were still at Chris's. It was just the two of them in their empty kitchen. 'Domino's, then?' Nick had said. They'd always had pizza on Friday, and moving house was no reason to vary a routine, to him.

They'd ordered it and observed its progress on the app on the kitchen counter, like new parents watching over a baby. And she'd had this feeling: how many more evenings would she spend with this man? The rest of their lives. She was so lucky with him, her new family, with their unlimited, bountiful days stretching out in front of them. Thank God she was here, and not back there amongst the aftermath of her mother's murder, alone.

And now. Well, now what? She believes her father, and she supposes it's time to tell Nick that.

'Glad you're back,' Nick says to her with a brief smile. 'I have your dad's file. I think we should talk.'

45

Nick smells freshly showered. His T-shirt has damp patches where the material is clinging to his still-wet skin. She breathes in his minty smell as he walks past her, into the living room, and she follows him.

'You've got it with you?' she says to his square-shouldered back.

'Yep,' he says. He looks back at her again.

His face is in profile and she stares at it. His long, straight nose that she knows as well as her own. The atmosphere feels awkward, somehow, strained. Perhaps he doesn't want to be poking around in police files. Perhaps he wishes he was with an easy, uncomplicated woman, the kind of person he used to think Izzy was.

He sits down in their living room. All of the windows and doors are open, but it's still stuffy.

There is a pale pink cardboard folder resting on the arm of their sofa. It looks innocuous, like a geography project or household filing. It's unmarked. No name on it.

'I photocopied some things and brought them home in a blank file,' Nick says, watching her.

Her arms become goose-fleshed the longer she looks at it. Here it is. A file brought home by a police analyst. Contraband. A file whose contents up until now existed in the police station and the courtroom. A file that means the State expended money, time, resources on capturing and incarcerating her father.

'There are about twenty files. I've been doing a bit each day and adding to this folder. There are two key things in there.'

'Right,' Izzy says. He has been doing it every day, and only now he presents it to her. How can he be so calm, so measured – so calculated?

There's something strange about his body language. It's angled away from her. He keeps looking out of the window, over her shoulder.

'Well . . . what?' she asks.

He turns to her, taking the file off the arm of the sofa and opening it. His fingers are long and elegant and he thumbs through the papers slowly.

She sinks down on to the chair she's been sitting in every evening lately – when did they stop sitting on the sofa together? – and looks at him. He's dimly lit by the lamp in the corner of the room. Half of his face is illuminated amber, half in shadow. She can't make out his expression. It looks distorted and strange.

'The lawyers got the previous conviction excluded . . .'

'Yes.'

'I read it in full. Her account. Barbara Johnson. He strangled her, Izzy. Exact same method. She'd cheated on him.'

Izzy's mouth goes dry. She can hear her heart in her ears. Her stomach coils immediately into knots. He told her he bent her arm behind her back. He lied. Her father has strangled two women. Women who have betrayed him.

She thinks of the newspaper article. She thinks of the time spent alone – increasingly isolated – with her father. She thinks of that alibi. Oh, please don't say she has been foolish. Please don't say she is in too deep.

'And there's something else.'

'What?' she asks him.

'He said something to a young PC, at the scene where your mother's body was recovered.'

'What?'

'It was excluded by his defence team because he wasn't under caution. I asked around . . .'

'What did he say?'

'He knew how she had been killed. Before he saw her body.'

46

Izzy feels her jaw slacken. The goosebumps disappear and are replaced by something worse: a stomach churning, a kind of rocket launch in her body that she can't control. The fear rises up through her, unchecked. Please, no. She has been so stupid. So naive to let herself be alone with her father. To have trusted him. To have given him a space in her lovely little safe life that it has taken her so long to rebuild.

'What?' she says to Nick.

Her vision has tunnelled, narrowed to just a point: the bundle of pages he is holding out to her. It looks like it could be nothing. A note of a long meeting. An abandoned manuscript. A tax return. Bank statements. Nothing. Just nothing. But it's not nothing: it's everything. Gabriel has lied to her. She thinks of his previous conviction, untold until she found it. Until *Nick* found it. And now Gabriel hasn't told her the whole truth about it, either. Are all of his memories lies, concocted over the last eighteen years? Or just altered, distorted to suit himself? Tweaked here and there to shine him in the best possible light, key details – knowing how her mother died, his previous conviction – being removed, and replaced with made-up anguish?

'He was called DS Perry. There was a legal battle over excluding it but, eventually, they managed it. The jury never knew.'

He passes her a piece of paper bearing the word CRIMINT across the top. She stands up and takes it from him, her eyes scanning it.

'This is an intelligence report. It couldn't go on the record because it's a statement made to a police officer not in the context of an official interview.'

She reads it, her eyes scanning quickly. It is signed and dated: 2nd November 1999. It is signed by Perry and sworn. An affidavit.

> On the 2nd November I attended at the scene of the recovery of the body of Alexandra English, who had been missing for two days. I was tasked with guarding the cordon and preventing entry by members of the public.
>
> At around 4.10 p.m. Gabriel English arrived. He was very distressed. We were standing around one hundred feet from Alexandra English's body which was inside a tent. There is no way he could have seen her.
>
> His exact words to me were: 'Strangulation – that's an awful way to go.'

Izzy stares up at Nick, this stranger in her living room. 'Did you know?' she says. 'Did you ever know about this?'

'Not until tonight, today,' Nick says. 'He got a really good lawyer. Bal mentioned that.'

'A good lawyer?' Izzy says. She narrows her eyes as she looks up at him. He doesn't mean a diligent lawyer, a hard-working lawyer.

'A shark,' he says. 'One good at getting people off.'

Izzy nods, then swallows. It's distasteful. That's what it is. Her father has distorted the truth, removing his statement from evidence presented to the jury, acting like it was never made. The truth was wilfully deformed by Gabriel, and the defence team he paid £350 per hour to get him off. And hasn't he done the same with her? He has rewritten history, painted his own picture, the way *he* wanted to portray it.

The room seems to swim as Izzy thinks of all the ways she has been foolish: suspecting her uncle, her cousin, wondering about Daniel, a man to whom her mother merely stood too close. The bank statements she has sifted through. The David Smiths she has tried to find. The time and energy she has wasted.

Pointless.

Her mind skips forward to the consequences of her naivety, of how gullible she has been.

The times she has been alone with her father.

The threats that she has told him about. The newspaper clipping. The text that said that she's not safe. She thought he would be able to help her more than the police. But her father is a murderer. And he is angry.

Izzy presumes she sets the piece of paper down on the arm of the sofa, because that's where it seems to land. Nick in front of her, his brown eyes level with hers. 'I see,' she says softly.

'Yes,' he says. He's nodding. Her focus has narrowed just to his eyes. He has completely straight eyelashes. She has always loved those.

'He never told me he strangled Barbara. He said he bent her arm backwards.'

'Well, he didn't.'

'And he said he was *informed* how Mum had died in his police interview, by the police. He told me so vividly.'

Nick reaches over to touch the piece of paper just lightly.

'He's a liar,' she says.

Nick is staring at her, saying nothing.

'He said he arrived at the scene and broke down. It was

the moment . . . he was so, so convincing. It was the moment I started to believe him.'

Something like sympathy crosses Nick's features. 'How many times have you seen him?'

'A few.'

'But the previous conviction I got from CRIS, I thought that would . . . that alone would make up your mind? Izzy?'

Izzy blinks, tears filming over her eyes. Everything she had thought has been incorrect. The nebulous gut feelings that told her that she was supposed to be seeing her father, hearing him out. The way she chose to turn to him rather than to Nick. The way she thought they would figure it out together. Naivety. Wishful thinking. Constructing a partnership where there was nothing.

'I got that for you . . .'

'I know. And this, too. I *am* grateful,' she says. On top of everything, she doesn't want her husband to think that she has used him.

'How far has it gone?' he says.

Suddenly, she doesn't care what he thinks of her. She doesn't need to try and cover it up any more, because it has been exposed. Her inner shame. Her inner child.

'Really far,' she says thickly. 'It was . . . *he* was like a magnet for me.'

Nick blinks, saying nothing, looking at her. He sits down next to her.

She leans into him. 'I miss it all so much,' she says, a sob escaping.

He puts an arm around her shoulders, solid and weighty. 'What?' he says quietly.

'Every day I think about people with families, you know? Your WhatsApp group with your sisters, Thea, this woman at the Chinese takeaway who always has her toddler there with her . . .'

'Mmm.' Nick rubs her back.

'And I just wish . . . I just wish it was *me*. I wish it hadn't been taken from me. I wish I had that,' she says, her eyes wet with warm tears that Nick rubs away with his other hand.

'I know,' he says.

'Do you?'

'Of course I do.' He rests his forearm on her knee lightly. 'Yes.' He leans into her. His body is warm and sweet-smelling: her Nick.

'You seemed surprised I wanted to see him – my dad.'

Nick folds his lips in on themselves, dimples forming either side of his mouth. 'I have always known how much you want a mum. A parent. It's obvious. It makes me sad how obvious it is.'

Izzy closes her eyes. All this time, she's been thinking she had kept it hidden, but she hasn't. Not even close.

'But I guess I trusted that you're . . . level-headed. About your dad. You only visited him once in eighteen years inside.' *Inside*. He uses the same terminology as her father.

'I'm not,' she says. 'I'm not level-headed about him.'

'No.'

She leans against Nick and lets him brush her hair away from her face rhythmically. 'Don't worry,' he says. 'Don't worry.'

Izzy nods, not saying anything. He always knew. He always knew she needed a parent, and yet – did he help her? Did he get her to talk about it, the way Pip would have? No, he didn't.

She won't always feel this way, she tells herself. Surely she won't. Surely, one day soon, the pain and the destruction that her father has inflicted will stop, like an overflowing river spreading and spreading and spreading until finally it dries up.

'We'll sort it,' Nick says.

And so here it is, the truth she has been searching for. Of course: Occam's razor. The evidence against him.

Her father had been convicted of domestic violence in the past. He had sent a threatening text to her mother.

He had no alibi for his whereabouts that night, and the last place her mother had been seen was walking into the house he was waiting in. He spent the time while she was missing cleaning the clothes that he had been wearing.

Her mother had been found murdered by and buried in an item belonging to him, taken from a place only he had access to.

He knew how she had died before he had seen her body.

If the simplest explanation is true, then her father is a murderer. What other explanation is there?

And here is another truth: her husband loves her.

Unconditionally.

She deletes Gabe's number that night.

47

Izzy's eyes feel black the next morning. Her father has texted her – of course he has – but she has ignored it. Nick hasn't gone to work. It must be serious, she thinks, as she opens the door to the back garden from their kitchen.

She will have to tell him about the newspaper article and the text. She knows she will. It's just a matter of when. She wants to drip-feed it, as though she can control his judgement that way. He was sympathetic, last night, but he also abhors people who make silly mistakes.

She stands outside and looks at the sky. The exact same blue as yesterday, when her father had cried by the side of the road. She thinks of his tears, of his reliance on her, of his fake, gilded memories, fabricated over eighteen years. Perhaps he believes them himself, like a truly insane person. He's lived with his lies for so long he has become them.

Nick comes up behind her. His hair is messy, his belt undone. She loves all of his guises. When his hair is neat and his ears look bigger and his face leaner. And now, when his hair is messy and he looks like a hipster. That's what Izzy likes most about the terrain of a long relationship; all the forms she sees her husband take.

'Look,' she says. She clears her throat self-consciously. 'The other day I received a newspaper article. I don't know . . . I didn't tell you . . . it was about Dad. And there's been a text.'

'What was it?' Nick says, releasing her.

She misses the warmth of his body, feeling suddenly cold in the sun.

'It was about the crime, and stuff.'

'Right.'

'But where my mum's name was written had been crossed out – and mine was written, instead,' she says softly.

Nick says nothing. The only way she can tell he has heard is because his nostrils flare, his upper body tenses, as if ready to fight.

'Right,' he says. 'Can I see them? What did the text say?'

'Yes.'

She goes inside and fetches her phone and the newspaper cutting from her handbag.

'I see,' he says, when she passes them to him. He looks directly at her, the weak sunlight lightening his dark eyes to a lion-like gold. 'Did you tell Gabriel about these?'

She drops her head. 'Yes,' she says. 'Yes,' she whispers. 'That's why he suggested being alone more . . . because somebody knew. Somebody knew we were trying to solve it.'

Nick closes his eyes. 'Izzy,' he says softly.

'I know,' she says. 'I know.'

'Okay,' he says, exhaling.

'You think he's sent them.'

He pauses, looking thoughtfully up into the sun. Running that mind of his over the facts. 'Two things spring to mind.'

'What?'

Nick's eyelids flutter. 'Somebody who knows he's guilty could be warning you.'

'But . . . who?' Izzy says, her mind racing.

'Often an inmate.'

'Oh.'

'Someone who spent so many years with him . . . they sometimes write to family members. Or get someone on the outside to write, to warn them.'

'But they wouldn't know he'd seen me.'

'Unless he told them.'

'Oh. What's the other explanation?'

'Well, sometimes people with form like Gabriel . . . well, they might play games.'

'What games?'

'Cat and mouse,' Nick says quietly.

She turns to him. His slender hand is raised to his forehead, shielding the sun from his eyes. 'It's, you know. Pretty typical.'

'Of what?'

He looks directly at her now, removing his hand and placing it back on his hip. 'Abuse.'

He says it factually, which she's grateful for, though she allows her mind, for just a moment, to imagine another Izzy, here with him. Izzy who complains about her parents interfering in her life. Who is utterly different to this Izzy. Never needy, never shameful, never jealous. The Izzy to whom this didn't happen.

'He wouldn't do that,' she says.

They'd ridden everywhere on their bikes the summer before her mother had died. Izzy's ballet teacher had suggested some extra cardio, and Gabe had obliged. He'd bought her a bike he'd seen advertised for sale in the paper, from a blue-green shed a few streets down from them. He should have been working, she thinks now, looking back, but she didn't care then. Not at all. They had cycled to the coast. Her thighs had burned, but they had reached the clifftop. They could see Portsmouth in the distance. It had been worth it, especially when they had cycled down again. They hadn't gone fast. Her father had led her down a slow, winding path, past a patch of bluebells so vivid they seemed to move and shimmer. The sun on her bare arms. The wind in her lungs. Her hair trailing out behind her. She had felt as happy as it was possible to feel, as though a fizzing tablet of pleasure had been dropped down her throat and into her stomach.

She blinks, looking up at Nick now. She can't explain that, especially not to him.

'He wouldn't do that,' she says again, but she knows her argument makes no sense, is illogical. He would murder, but he wouldn't threaten her. *Sure*, Nick would say.

Abuse, she tells herself. Violence. Violence against women: against vulnerable women. Killings, strangulations, disappearances, lies, mind games. *That* is who her father is.

'Are you going to tell work?' she says.

He looks at her, brows lowered, his mouth forming a thoughtful pout. 'Maybe,' he says easily, but doesn't elaborate.

She wonders what would happen if the police needed to look into her father. His licence conditions. His past. They would get the file, surely. They would see it had been retrieved.

'I'll sort it,' Nick says, catching her worried expression.

'But won't th –'

'Leave it with me. I can speak to his probation officer.'

'Okay,' she whispers.

'Then if he's done *anything* . . . he'll be back to prison for life. Proper.'

She thinks of her father's eight cans of beans. Single key

to his single room. His single pink bed. Of their shared memories, their shared grief. The way they understood each other. She is abandoning him to the abyss; to loneliness, forever.

No. Stop it. He is a murderer. He is sending things to her house, designed to scare her. This sympathy, it is misguided: a poison.

48

Izzy gets up in the middle of the night. She has two missed called from Gabe, and three texts.

Nick stirs, but doesn't wake, and she walks across the deep, soft carpet of their bedroom and downstairs.

In the kitchen, she stares out at the blackness of their garden. The fronds of the palm trees are completely motionless in the still, humid weather.

There's movement outside. Izzy thinks of the text and the car and her hands go cold, but then she sees that it's just Thea, letting herself out across the access and into her own garden.

Izzy unlocks her door and follows suit. It's after two, and she throws Thea a look of surprise that she manufactures in the moment.

'Can't sleep,' Thea says. 'Just trying to cool down, but it's impossible, isn't it?'

'It is,' Izzy says, wishing that was all that troubled her: a bit of summer heat.

'How are things?' Thea says slowly. 'You were saying – about your dad . . . ?'

'Oh, I think we can forget about that,' Izzy says.

Thea nods, standing on her little patio, her feet bare on the flagstones.

'I just felt . . .' Izzy starts to speak, the warm, close night air and the darkness a kind of safe embrace, enabling her to unburden herself. 'I was taken in by him, for a while,' she continues. 'I guess I just so wanted – a family. Like you have.'

'Oh, Izzy!' Thea says in surprise.

Izzy looks across at her. She's in a towelling dressing gown of the kind not sold any more. It's sage green, the belt double-knotted around her waist. Her face bears the expression of a slow realization. She is no doubt cycling back through the things Izzy has done, the way she has imposed herself upon their family, dropping by too casually, too often, full of excuses about why she was there.

'But you can make your own family,' Thea says, taking a couple of tentative steps towards her. 'Now that you're an adult. You can leave it all behind you.'

Izzy steps towards her and – unthinkingly, it seems to her – Thea holds her arms up and Izzy steps into the embrace that she's craved. Thea doesn't smell like her mother or feel like her mother but she is a warm body and her grasp is firm. She stands there with Thea for just five minutes.

Five motherly minutes.

Later, still not asleep, she finds the printout of her father's previous conviction and scans for the name.

Barbara Johnson.

She types her name into Facebook and scrolls and scrolls until she sees what she's looking for.

Barbara Johnson. Profile photo: a woman in her sixties, wrinkles around her eyes, sunglasses on top of her head.

A redhead.

Izzy sits up straight in bed the next morning. She has been woken by something, though she doesn't know what. Only that it is something.

Nick has gone to work, and she sits for a second, listening to the complete silence of their cottage.

They had made love last night, Nick's dark eyes on hers.

She peers out of the bedroom window. It was just a fox. Her entire body relaxes.

They often get foxes in their garden. They were both up early a few months ago. It was a misty spring morning, a chill on the soles of her feet as she made coffee. As she flicked the kettle on to boil, the light of it glowing blue in their kitchen, Nick came up behind her, and pointed outside. 'Look,' he said. It was their first spring in the cottage, and they were still learning about it. How to run the Aga; what grew, and when, in the garden; the noises the ancient floorboards sometimes made.

Izzy followed his gaze.

There was a fox in the garden asleep, inexplicably, on their garden table.

'Oh!' she said.

'And look,' he said, pointing again.

There was a second one, in the grass. It ambled up, on shaky legs, and headed for their back gate, where it must have come through.

The other fox remained sleeping on the table as they watched it. She couldn't stop looking at him as she poured the water into their mugs.

'What's he up to?' Nick said, poking his head into the kitchen later, and they stared at the fox for a little while longer.

It had been one of those mornings, she supposed. One of those mornings that stood out because it hadn't been ordinary. But there was something else, too. The warmth of his body next to hers. The way he touched her hip to get her attention. The way they had laughed at the foxes, and they had texted about them throughout the day. *Will he still be there when we get back?* she had asked as she ate soup at the restaurant, and he had responded immediately: *Hope so!*

It had been sweet, sipping her soup and smiling at text messages from her husband.

When they returned home, the foxes had gone, of course. And they had never been back. But Izzy has never forgotten that day. It had been right somehow. Just right.

It was just a fox.

But that's when she hears the noise again. Footsteps.

There's somebody downstairs, in her house.

49

She remains sitting up in bed, listening, her body flooded with adrenaline. Should she call the police? Should she wait it out?

She hears nothing for a few seconds, then the same thing again. Light footsteps.

She grabs her phone, pulls her dressing gown on and walks downstairs slowly, trying not to make any noise on their ancient wooden staircase.

She emerges into the kitchen, her breath held, her muscles tensed.

There's nobody there. She checks the living room, then the hallway. There's definitely nobody there.

But she heard somebody. She did. She spins around, and that's when she sees it.

The kitchen door, swinging uselessly.

The lock burst open, the wood caved in, like it's been hit with something, injured, the wood splintered and buckled, its insides spilling out.

'I'll make sure he's spoken to,' Nick says on the phone. 'I'll make sure his accommodation is searched. If it's him, we'll find out.'

'What then?'

'If it's him?'

'Yes.' Izzy fingers the broken lock. A splinter pierces her

finger and she removes it, wincing. 'I don't want another trial.'

'There's no trial for recalled lifers who've breached their licence.'

'Really?' she says, surprised.

'No. We just investigate it. And report them, and then they go back.'

'So who decides if it's true?'

'The police.'

Izzy tries not to let her mind unpick that particular injustice.

That night, she dreams of her father's shipping container. Had he taken her mother there, alive, or dead? Or gone there to collect the bag and then headed back out, premeditated?

She dreams of her mother, and of herself, dying in exactly the same way. Strangled, the breath squeezed out of her neck, her lungs.

As she lies half-awake, covered in sweat, she realizes. If her father murders her, he'll deny it. And in another twenty years, some poor redhead will believe him, with his brown eyes, his easy manner, his charming texts, his skinny elbows and his vulnerability. They'll be lured in, and it will happen again, and again, and again. Memories and falsehoods and lies and charm. Strangulation and paintings and death. Izzy has been fooled. Everybody can be fooled.

They have to stop him. Nick will stop him. He will do it for her, her husband who has kept her safe for all these years.

They'll ensure that Gabriel can't do it again to anybody.

That he is locked up, recalled back to prison immediately. Public protection, punishment, deterrent.

But until then, her father hangs like a spectre over her, her body imbued with fear even as she tries to sleep. She will never be free from him, not really. He lives inside her. She is half him.

50

It is only a matter of days before he turns up at the restaurant. Of course, of course he arrives, right when he used to, at close to midnight, just as she is hanging the glasses up, warm from the dishwasher. It is just like the first time he arrived. The fear is just the same.

His face is at the window, just how it was, all those weeks ago, when this whole business began. He is framed in one complete window, a floating head. He looks thinner than before, if that's possible, his brow creased, his hair whiter. He must be motioning for her to open the front door, because she sees a movement in the night, his arm flapping in his Matalan anorak.

God, he really is too thin. She can see his cheekbones, like he's wasting. She could invite him in, feed him up – really, what's changed? He's never tried to harm her, never.

No, she tells herself. She recites the evidence against him in her mind. She will be strong. She will not let him in. She turns away from him and back to the dishwasher.

He raps on the window.

He knew how she'd died.

He moves to a second window, presses his face to the glass.

He'd done it before.

Izzy busies herself in the kitchen and, eventually, he shouts her name, ringing out clear in the warm night.

'No,' she cries out, wanting, childishly, to put her hands

over her ears, for him – for this dilemma – to go away forever.

She walks to the letter box and prises it open with her fingers, the metal cool on the tips of her hand. 'Please go away,' she says, out into the night. A stream of warm air drifts inwards.

'Why?' he says. He comes to the letter box, too, and his eyes meet hers, framed in the rectangular box.

'I know about what you said as Mum's body was found. I know about the strangling, I know it all,' she says. 'Don't contact me again or I will call the police.'

She lets the metal slam shut, removing her fingers just in time. The sound seems to reverberate around the restaurant. She shivers, wrapping her arms around her body, wondering if her mother had an encounter exactly like this, right before she died.

Izzy doesn't get frightened often. She's never allowed herself to be. Where some people may spend the rest of their lives living in fear after something like her mother's murder, Izzy never did. The worst had already happened, she reasoned. Or rather, the worst *could* happen – the very worst – so there was no need to rehearse it. *Move on*, she used to say to herself, always parenting herself inside her head.

But now, standing alone in the kitchen, too frightened to even reach into her handbag for her phone, too frightened to move, staring at her father, his face once again framed in the glass window, Izzy is frightened, after eighteen years of peace.

She is frightened for her life.

51

It is a few days later when a man emerges, in the early summer sunshine in the car park of her restaurant.

It is her father's best friend, Paul, the man she met nearly six weeks ago in his house, when she was right at the beginning of this mess.

'He sent you,' she says to him now as she walks to her car. She ought to be frightened, but isn't. It is hard to be frightened when faced with a benign relic from her past, as familiar as a duvet cover not seen since the 1980s.

'Yes,' Paul says. He spreads his arms wide. They're tanned, the hairs on them still dark. He removes his sunglasses and looks at her properly. His eyes are a vibrant blue in the sunlight.

'Why?'

'To protest his innocence,' he says. 'That's all he ever wants to do.'

Izzy looks down at her shoes, knots forming in her stomach. 'Don't you think twice about this stuff? Being sent to defend a murderer to me?'

'No.'

'I'm his daughter,' she says, looking up at him. 'But I want to move on. I've lived with it for so long.'

She doesn't tell him of the threats she's been receiving. She doesn't tell him of the fear she has felt every night for weeks as she locks up the restaurant, as she walks alone to the bank, as she locks her car on their drive. She doesn't

338

tell him that, for the first time in her life, she just can't take the risk. That, even if he is innocent, it almost doesn't matter to her because she never wants to feel as threatened and pursued and confused as she has for the past six weeks. She doesn't bother to say any of it. She shouldn't need to.

'Okay. I just need to tell you one thing,' he says. 'Then I'll leave.'

'Why would you do him a favour?'

'Because of Megan,' he says. Paul's daughter, born much later than Izzy. She can only be twenty or so now. Izzy hardly remembers her. Little details spring to mind: a brown-haired tomboy. She wore trainers with bright blue laces.

'Right,' she says faintly in the car park.

A cloud of mosquitoes blooms, just to the left of Paul, gathering and then dispersing in the evening air, coming from nowhere, disappearing to nothing.

'I've spent the last few weeks thinking about our chat. And all the things that made me think your dad was innocent. I remembered another thing.'

Izzy shrugs, saying nothing.

'He called *me* when he was first arrested,' Paul says. 'So he got allocated the duty solicitor. He was naive, I guess. They let him have his call and . . . it was me.'

'Right,' she says.

Paul pauses, straightens his shoulders, then breathes in and out. 'I remember his exact words. I always have. I never told you, because they're not evidence. He always said to just leave it – to leave you in peace. But they are . . . something.'

'To leave me in peace?' Izzy says quietly.

'Yes, he never wanted me to contact you. I think he thought you had been through enough, I suppose. That you should be left alone until . . . he always said to me that he would speak to you when he was out.'

They are like the two contrasting sides of a coin. Tails: the father with the previous conviction, who planned to murder her mother and who covered it up. And heads: the father whose best friend unequivocally believes in him, whose parents stand by him, who waited for the best, most opportune moment to attempt to reconcile with his daughter, who did it gently, compassionately, slowly. They are night and day, these two men.

'What did he tell you on the call?'

'I'm getting to it.'

A greenfly lands on her arm and she brushes it away irritably.

Paul crosses his legs at the ankles and reaches a hand out to steady himself on the roof of his red car. The sun is heating the back of Izzy's neck. She will get burned if she's not careful. Her mother used to wear factor 50 year-round, and still went pink in the sun.

'I guess I always believed him because none of the things they were saying were a surprise to me.'

'What things?'

'The conviction . . . the text messages. The temper he sometimes had.'

'No?'

'No. I have known him since we were eighteen. He's always been the same. Reliably wild.' Paul smiles a nostalgic, private smile. 'He was the liability on nights out, you know? Always ended up in a shopping trolley. Would threaten to lamp someone at the bar for rudeness.'

'But then he killed someone.'

Paul inclines his head, like, *you might think so.*

'He wasn't a stranger to lying, too,' he says. 'To suit himself. He'd tell me he'd sold paintings for more than he had. Ego, I guess.'

'So he's violent and a liar.'

'No, he's mildly temperamental. And he's never lied about anything big. He's not immoral. He's just human. And those human traits loom large when you're accused. I see those pieces of evidence for what they are: props to the prosecution's case. They weren't the substance of their case. And we all have something, if brought out in court, that would make us look guilty.'

'Do we?'

'I know I do.' Paul shrugs.

It's a strange gesture, here in the car park, as they discuss her mother's murder. Izzy thinks of Nick. What if he were found murdered? He'd been looking into the police file for her. They'd been rowing. What if he'd been killed with a knife that looked like it had come from her kitchen – the bread knife that's been missing for several years? It could happen. And she *would* look guilty.

She finds her mind wants her to keep opening this door, to keep probing, so she does. What if she had been accused of something years ago, when the restaurant was first reopened? There'd been that waitress she had to sack, that awful, awkward exchange – 'I'm just not that happy with your work' – oh, but what if that waitress had been found somewhere? Would Izzy have been questioned? Definitely.

'He said she'd been strangled, you know, at the scene. Before he saw her.'

'Who says?'

'A cop.'

Paul almost laughs. 'Why don't you ask Gabriel?'

341

She is tired of debating this. Tired of taking the same set of facts and looking at them from this angle and that. Tired of trying to make them fit one version or another. The truth is messy, her father said, and he's right about that.

'What did he say in his phone call to you? From the police station?' Izzy asks again.

'He said, "Paul. Izzy's going to think it was me."'

Izzy says nothing.

'That was his big fear, his *only* fear, that you were young and impressionable and that you'd think it was him. He didn't care about the rest. The conviction. The jail time. It's only ever been about you.'

Paul is looking at her intently.

She says nothing in reply.

Izzy is serving a customer – late for their eight o'clock reservation – and taking a pashmina and hanging it up when he arrives. A man in his early twenties in a green T-shirt.

'The safe?' he says.

'The safe?'

'I'm here to unlock the safe,' he says in a bored tone. 'You booked me for tonight.'

'Oh . . . it's fine,' she says, moving away from the bar with him. She appraises him – maybe he's in his teens, actually – and he stares back at her, unblinking.

'You paid online. Where is it?' he says.

Izzy apologizes to the woman she was serving. 'Downstairs in the basement,' she says. 'Behind the wine rack. Door's over there.' It is easier to let him do it. 'Sorry,' she says, turning back to the woman. 'This way.' She shows her to a table, her mind reeling.

Once they're seated, she heads to the basement. She had better supervise him.

She can't see what the man in the green T-shirt is doing with his lock pick. He hasn't checked that she owns the restaurant, or asked her why she needs it doing. It's not exactly above board, she guesses.

It takes him less than five minutes. Izzy stands awkwardly at the bottom of the stairs, her hands across her body in the cool, musty air; a nice respite from the summer heat.

'All done,' the man says neutrally to her.

He leaves up the stairs, not seeming to want her to see him out. She moves towards the safe, repeating his words inside her head and trying to gauge his tone. What's he found?

She reaches for the little green door that her mother touched a hundred times, and opens it.

And there it is.

The evidence she has been waiting for.

52

She picks up the bundle of notes and fingers their papery outsides. They have Edward Elgar on them, the font curly. Old twenties. Unusable now, she guesses.

There are four bundles, clipped neatly together, held firm. She flicks through them, not moving the clips. It must be ten thousand, fifteen, twenty, she guesses. Hidden for all these years in that tiny safe that, she is sure, only her mother knew about. And maybe Tony. Did he know about this cash, sitting there? It's clearly her mother's: it's old money. But why was he trying to move the wine rack?

She focuses instead on the banknotes.

It is *evidence*. Finally. Not historic previous convictions or an unsupported alibi, but real, tangible evidence. And it is evidence that something *else* was happening. Something not in keeping with the narrative of the prosecution – or, she supposes, of the defence.

It is new.

She sits there, cross-legged on the bottom step in the basement, and wonders who to tell. Who to trust.

She breathes deeply, her nose in the notes and, amongst the dust and the old papery smell, she thinks she can smell her mother's perfume.

Izzy decides to tell nobody. She will keep it to herself: she knows she can trust herself.

She avoids Nick, coming home late, going to bed even later. She tells him she's swamped with annual accounts.

He knows it's not her year-end, but he doesn't say anything. She guesses he thinks she's going through a kind of grief, a second mourning period, and leaves her be. She hears the clink of his knife against their cheese plate in the bedroom, which makes her eyes mist over.

In the restaurant the next day, during the lunchtime service, she takes a blank piece of paper out of her printer and makes notes of what her mother could have been doing.

Money, she writes along the top, then underlines it in red.

Sex.

Fraud.

Selling things.

Favours.

Blackmail.

The list goes on and on. The sordid words run unchecked from her ballpoint pen.

Prostitution.

Assassinations.

They seem to get worse the more she writes, as though she is descending steps into the underworld itself.

She sits back in her chair and stares at the depraved piece of paper, thinking.

If there was money, her mother can't have been acting alone. Either she was giving somebody the money, or she was receiving it. Basic economics. Supply and demand.

She thinks of the list of names again.

Suddenly, she knows what she is going to do. She almost doesn't care about the repercussions. All roads have led her here: her father getting in touch, their shared memories,

Nick agreeing to get the file for her, the lock picker. And now here she is. Alone, still not knowing whether her father is guilty or not, or who killed her mother. Not knowing what happened on the night of Hallowe'en almost twenty years ago which has come to define her entire life. Only knowing one thing: that she is going to put the name of every single person who came into contact with her mother into Nick's Police National Computer over the next few days, when she can. That surely one of them will have done something with their money.

Something naive.

Something foolish.

Something suspicious.

Something illegal.

She drives to the coast. She needs to be alone for this. Away from Nick. Away from the restaurant. Away from anybody who can overhear her or judge her as she takes the plunge. What she is doing is either clever or foolish, but she wants no witnesses: she needs to feel as though she is at the end of the world.

She parks at the Devil's Chimney car park. The steps are carved into the rock, narrow and dark, and it suits her mood. She wants to bury herself in the forest, in the path carved through the cliff. As she descends the stairs, she thinks about all of her messages to all of the David Smiths in London. They would be able to corroborate her father's innocence, but that isn't what she's doing any more, not really, not with this. It isn't about whether or not her father did it. It's about what happened. The messy truth of it.

The stairs are covered with ivy, waving in the breeze, so

green it shivers, moving like it's alive. When she's right in the middle of the forest, completely on her own, she retrieves her deleted messages, and calls her father.

He answers immediately, jumpily, in that animalistic, startled way of his, his brain always scanning the horizon for hazards.

'Hi, hi,' he says. 'Hi.'

'I got into the safe,' she says.

Izzy takes a deep breath. She counted the money last night, when everybody had gone. She doesn't know where to keep it, so she's separated the bundles and put one into each of her locked desk drawers.

'And?'

'And there was eighteen thousand pounds in there.'

'Shit,' her father says, not questioning her silence, her estrangement from him, her doubts. '*Shit.*'

'Look, were you involved in something with her?'

'No.'

'I need you to tell me the truth.'

'*No.*'

'Right, then. Well, then the money was hers. Hers alone. And I guess . . . I guess it is a clue.'

Izzy sits down on a moss-covered rock and feels the heat of her phone against her ear, like another person really is here with her. She breathes in the cow parsley wafting around her, the verdant, sensual summer. The sun is warm on her skin in dappled parts, but the rest of her is cool in the shadows. It's finally set to rain tomorrow, ending several weeks of drought. A storm and flash floods, they're saying.

She hears her father blow air into his cheeks, then expel it slowly.

'So she was buying or selling something,' he says.

She closes her eyes against it: like father, like daughter. The same thought processes. The same phrases. Oh, please let this be something. Please let him be innocent.

'I think I'm going to try and look up some of the men on Nick's computer.'

'I think that's a good idea,' he says. 'Money changes hands. Someone else was involved.'

'I will,' she says.

'Look, I'll come over. We can go through everything. You can explain properly. Show me the cash. I think we should look at the bank statements again. I . . . I have a theory.'

Izzy hesitates for just a second before she agrees. He hasn't harmed her yet.

53

'Where are the statements?' he says. He's standing in her kitchen, holding a cup of tea – the most middle class of drinks – and the bundle of likely illegal cash. He's flicking through it.

'In my loft.'

'I like small spaces. Used to them.' He passes her the cash.

He climbs the ladder quickly, arriving next to her in the hot loft. She retracts the stairs up with them, even though Nick isn't due back for hours. The hatch closes, and she clicks the light on, and here they are, in the tiny, hot loft, alone, together.

'There,' she says, taking the lid off one of the box files and passing it to him. 'Accounts and wages.'

'What's that one?' he says, pointing to the second box.

'Property stuff – the lease. Insurance documents.'

Her father leans back on his hands. His upper lip is sweating.

'You know, sometimes I forget you're no longer this scrawny seventeen-year-old ballerina with a boyfriend with a daft name. The Izzy of then.'

'Yeah, I know,' she says, thinking of the Gabe of then, too, and all that they have lost.

'You're all grown now, and so smart.'

'Thank you.'

'You never finished telling me what happened with him. Pip?' There's a question in her father's voice.

349

'He fucking ghosted me,' she says bitterly.

'Ghosted?'

She rolls her eyes. 'You need a twenty-first-century translator,' she says.

'Be mine,' he says. He always was so charming.

'He blanked me. Three days after Mum died. Later, his dad, Steve, emailed me. A fucking email. Said it was too much for him, with his brother dying and then my mum. That he was depressed.'

Izzy winces as she recalls seeing them in the petrol station. She wishes she hadn't messaged them. The scorned ex, from years ago, getting in touch even with his father. She blushes as she thinks of it.

'People,' her father says.

'Yeah. But then two weeks later, my first time venturing back into town after everything, I saw him. He was fine. Out drinking. As soon as he saw me, he turned his whole body away from me.' Izzy could still cry when she thinks of it, even now, almost twenty years on; a fact which embarrasses her.

'Well, depression's invisible, you know.'

'I know. But even so.'

'Yes. Owed you a text at the very least.'

'Yes.'

'I've lost track of the number of people who "ghosted" me, if it helps.'

'I bet,' she says with a bitter smile.

'Are you ready to discuss it yet?'

'What?' She shifts, uncomfortable on the hard floor, and her father passes her his Matalan coat. She lifts herself and sits on it. It's warm from his body heat.

'The strangulation. Your mum's and Babs's. I can explain them.'

'Try, then.' She looks at the money, a tangible little pile of purple notes that anchor her to something else. To his innocence, she supposes. To an alternative explanation. To the messy truth.

'I did put my hands around Babs's throat. I didn't tell you because I thought you'd do what a jury would do – conflate the two. That I had done such a thing so foolishly, once, would mean I would do it again. That I . . . that I liked strangling people, I suppose.'

'You lied to me, and you excluded it.'

'Yes.'

'Is it fair to exclude things from trials?'

'It is if you think they'll lead to a miscarriage of justice. I wasn't trying to kill Babs. But it was a . . . loss of control.'

'A loss of control.'

'I was angry with her. She'd cheated on me, and I had *just* found out. I didn't tell you because I knew how it would look . . . It was wrong, obviously. I stopped almost immediately. Tony is prickly about it because he thought he ought to have stopped it. He heard one of our bad rows, before that one, and warned me.'

'I would never do something like that. I would never do that to Nick.'

'No. But . . . I don't know. Some of us do. And we're not monsters. Just human. Fucking fools. Young foolish men.'

She says nothing to that, not agreeing, not disagreeing, wondering if he is deluded. But one thing is for sure: he wants to find out. That is what he wants. And that is what she wants, too.

'And the confession . . . They insist on calling it that,' he says. 'Let me tell you how it really was.'

54

Tuesday 2 November 1999: the afternoon
Alex's body is found

Gabe

There is the cordon and there is the tent and there are the forensics. And she is dead and she is dead and she is dead.

I thought of the things I'd never see again. The soles of her feet. The way they curled up behind her as she walked, her catwalk model walk. I'd never see those feet again, those toes, the nails always painted pink. 'Pink clashes with my hair, but I don't care,' she had once said, in a fake Liverpudlian accent: *hurr, curr.*

The crook of her elbow. She rubbed this Vaseline cream into it. She had dry skin, eczema, burned easily. Both sun and windburn. Sensitive skin. I'd never see those elbows again, never see her twisting her slim torso to rub it in, never be able to take over and rub it in for her.

The back of her ribs, her spine. Bending over forward in the bath – God, she loved the bath – to rinse her face. A satisfyingly straight, neat row of spinal nodules; her perfect form.

Her easy, crinkled smile, the way she laughed at me sometimes, good-naturedly. I'd never taste her tomato and garlic sauce again, nor plunge a spoon into a chocolate pudding of hers.

Those bright eyes of hers, catching a slice of sunlight: the restaurant faced south, and she always had the curtains open, shielding her eyes with her hand as she served people.

The smell of her perfume in the crook of her neck.

How much she loved to buy shoes. Buying shoes and ridiculing me: her main hobbies.

The world had turned to grey but my hearing seemed acutely heightened. I could hear the crunch of the leaves underfoot as the forensic team descended. The murmur of shocked spectators' voices. The rustle of the tent.

And then: more than a murmur. A person addressing me. 'Looks like she'd been strangled,' a man said, making a gesture around his own neck. The man who found her, I thought.

And it's so funny, the things you think . . . the things you think when you finally find out what happened to your wife. All I could think about was this fucking documentary I watched where someone who was strangled was actually still alive, and they were resuscitated because the paramedics realized in time.

I screamed something. That she'd been strangled. That it was painful. I'd seen that on the same fucking documentary, and couldn't get out of my head how much pain she'd have been in.

Later, the dog walker denied ever saying anything. He sold me up the river. Worried he'd get into trouble with the police, I suppose.

Like all of us.

55

Izzy looks at her father and thinks of what he said to Paul when he was in custody. And his lies and his shady behaviour – they don't fall away. But something else joins them: love. She loves him. Of that she is sure.

That is the evidence. That is the truth.

'It was stupid,' he says now. 'I'm ashamed to say I wasn't thinking of you, my baby girl, and I should have been.'

'You were thinking of her. Understandably,' she says.

'There should be laws against using statements made at the scene, or questioning me so soon, Iz. I was in a shock so deep that it took me . . . well,' he gives a tiny, sad little laugh, 'I don't think I ever did come out of it. Not yet, anyway.' He reaches for the money again, like he is tying himself to the present, to the evidence that might exonerate him. 'Anyway. It *was* my fault. Not legally, but . . . I failed her.'

'Who was the dog walker?'

'Oh, I don't know. Once Matt got it excluded it didn't matter.'

'Was it easy to get it excluded?'

'Easier than the previous. It was a remark made off the record to a police officer when I wasn't under caution.'

'I see.'

'It was like falling down a well, that day. I thought I would disappear from the grief and the shock . . . just disappear. The world transformed. I was not fit to be making any statements to any police officers,' he says. 'Not one little bit. That's why we got it excluded.'

'Did Matt believe you?' she says. She can't help but ask.

'Maybe. He always said he did. But he was being paid to say that, I guess. All his clients say that. That's the thing, Iz. They all say it.'

'But you really didn't do it.'

'No. I didn't.' He doesn't break eye contact.

'How have you lived with it?' she says. 'All these years.'

'With the conviction?'

'No. With not knowing who did it.'

'I don't know. It was . . . I was suspended, in there. I shelved it. Until . . .'

'Until what?'

'Until I could come out. And see you.' He gestures to the money. 'You've found this, and you've told me about those three men. Your memories of the events have informed mine. Together, they're more than the sum of their parts.'

Izzy sits back, in the silence of her hot attic, saying nothing. Her father breaks the silence. 'What happened to your dancing?' he says.

'It's kind of tied up with Mum's funeral,' Izzy says.

'Tell me.'

56

Tuesday 7 December: the day of Alex's funeral

Gabe

I was not allowed to attend her funeral. That is what they told me. I sat there, my senses dulled, on remand, in Wandsworth prison, and instead, I imagined it, amongst the noise and the chaos. A white coffin, as pale as her skin. Pink roses, to match the polish that would remain on her toenails, unless they removed that, in the morgue. *Who knows?* I thought, staring at the wall of my cell.

A fight broke out right outside, interrupting my thoughts. One prisoner was beating another up, to repay a debt owed to somebody else. They rhythmically thumped against my door while I watched it, not thinking much. One landed a punch, caused the other a nosebleed, and blood splattered the toughened-glass window of my door.

The guards took a while to come.

Izzy

Izzy pulled a pair of black tights on.

She had not worn ballet tights for eighteen straight days during November, when her mother was lost and then found. The audition had been at the end of November, and her mother's funeral was now during the first week of December.

It took a while to bury a body that was the subject of a homicide case, an insensitive police officer told her.

She had attended the audition, wearing pink tights that had a slight stain around the ankle. She was selfish, she thought, as she performed the first *barre* exercise, *pliés*. Her soft block shoes squeaked against the unfamiliar wooden floor. She was selfish to miss such a materialistic thing – to angst over not having perfect pirouettes. It ought to have been unimportant in the face of her mother's death, and yet, the piano music and disappearing into her own body were as important to her as the three meals her grandparents made her eat, as the sweet tea the police had made her drink, as the sleep she took pharmaceuticals to get.

Her teacher had once said to her that if a ballerina missed one day, they noticed. If they missed two days, their partner noticed, and if they missed three days, the whole world noticed. Izzy had often wondered how true that was but, on the way to her audition a week ago, she could feel the truth of it in her bones. The way she walked was different since her mother's death. Her balance was off. Her back ached more. She'd lost her suppleness. But she went. She got through it. She didn't stumble or fall over. She hoped that the years of training would act as a kind of safety net for her, raising her standard to acceptable.

So here she was, seven days after the audition, and on the day of her mother's funeral, wearing tights again. Black ones.

She dried her hair with the hairdryer until it lay fluffy around her shoulders. The attic room at her grandparents' was cold, the tartan bedspread unwelcoming and strange, like perpetually living in a B&B or as a lodger. She had tried to unpack some things into the wardrobe last night but had stopped halfway through, her balled-up socks lined up in rows that simply ended. The rest were still in the bin bags she'd hastily stuffed her clothes into, the night she'd been taken away.

She wondered what her father was doing right now, as she often did. Was he allowed socks, hairdryers, any possessions at all? Probably not. *And he doesn't deserve them*, she thought.

Izzy performed an impromptu *arabesque*, once she was ready. She'd hear any day now, about the audition. And if she got in – she looked around the attic room – she'd be able to leave. She'd be living in London.

Maybe she wouldn't tell anybody who her mother and father had been.

At two o'clock, at the wake, she escaped the clutches of a morbid aunt and walked to her old house, now – officially, finally – no longer a crime scene. She rifled through the post that lay scattered in the hallway, but there was nothing for her.

A week later, her grandfather broke it to her: she didn't get in. It would be fine, he said. She could help with the restaurant. Life wouldn't always be this sad.

57

'The messy truth,' she says, throwing her father a sad smile. 'It's fine. I guess I'd be retired now, anyway.'

'So you stopped dancing then? Forever?'

'Have hardly danced a day since.'

'But why?'

'I don't know.' She tries to gather her thoughts to explain it. 'I guess I feel like ballet is . . . freedom, I suppose.' She blushes as she says these words to her dad. The honesty of them. She is not used to it. She is used to hiding behind special offer stands in supermarkets when she is recognized. She is used to pretending everything is fine. 'And I've not been free. Either.'

'I understand that more than anyone,' he says.

She glances up, and sees his eyes are filled with tears.

'It just goes on and on, doesn't it?' he says.

She shakes her head, not trusting herself to speak. She knows exactly what he means: the losses. His eighteen years in jail, their lost decades. Her lack of parents. Pip, even. She wonders how her life would truly look now, if none of it had happened.

'It's done,' she says tightly.

Her father picks up a bundle of the money and flicks the edges of it.

'Pass me the bank statements, then,' he says, in a weird tone. Upbeat. He wants to solve it, she guesses. 'Though I can't remember the last time I added anything up.'

'1998/1999,' she says, handing him a stuffed lever arch file. She holds up a manila envelope with a red frank mark on the top. 'Then there's this, but it's nothing. A few menus. A health and safety form . . . here's the letter confirming Daniel was taken off the payroll.'

'The waiter she sacked?'

'Yes.'

Her father scans the letter, his finger following each word just like he did with the menu at the restaurant. 'It's very specific wording,' he says. 'Taken off the payroll. Not *sacked*, actually.'

'So?'

'What's this?' He's pointing now to one of the statements she's highlighted.

'She went to a casino,' Izzy says.

'Oh yeah, you said you'd found evidence of gambling . . . I remember now. It doesn't make sense.'

'I know.'

'She would never do that. She'd say it was pointless,' he says, running a finger over it. 'She'd rather buy a pair of shoes.'

'None of it makes any sense.'

'Yes, it does,' her father says slowly. 'Izzy. The problem wasn't that she had too little money, eventually. Look: it was that she had too much.'

'What?' she says, baffled, shaking her head at him. It's hot and dusty up in the loft. Claustrophobic.

'It's criminal,' he says.

She shivers with it. His shady past. His dalliances with the law. His knowledge of crime. He is changed, her father, whether or not he is guilty.

'How?'

'I'm looking at a classic money laundering structure.'

'Huh?'

'She earns this, right?' He picks up the notes. 'And probably more. And she buries it.'

'How?'

'Okay: listen. I shared a cell in my Category B prison – the one before my release. I should have moved from a B to C and then to an open prison, but there wasn't room.'

'Right.'

'With a man called Gary. He embezzled money from HSBC. And then he had to launder the money. He told me all about it.'

'Okay,' Izzy says, trying to withhold judgement.

Her father is now a product of a system. That's all. He would never have chosen to spend time with embezzlers and murderers. He was forced to.

'Scenario one,' he says obliviously, 'restaurant makes £20,000. Salaries are £10,000. So profits are £10,000. Okay?'

'Okay,' Izzy says, watching him scrawl the figures on the back of the letter. Seeing his handwriting takes her back to seeing his letter, all those weeks ago. Those looped *L*s.

'Scenario two: restaurant makes £5,000. You make £15,000 from some other source. You put £5,000 in as takings, and get rid of £10,000 paying wages not on the books. Profits are £10,000. Looks the same. Right?'

'Right,' Izzy says, nodding.

'They're called black salaries,' he says. 'Daniel wasn't sacked. He was taken off the payroll, but still working.'

He unclips the lever arch file and starts leafing through it. 'Look. June to August. The takings go down two thousand a month, but the wages go down, too. See? So the profits are no higher. She probably never got the extended licence. Because she wasn't opening longer. She was doing something else.'

361

'I see,' Izzy says, reaching for the bank statements. One of them has a coffee ring on it. Izzy traces it with her fingertips and wonders if it was her mother's coffee. If maybe just one molecule of it might contain her mother. She'll never know.

'She loved coffee,' her father says.

'Mum?'

'Yeah, drank four or five a day. Nerves a-jangling.'

'Same as me.'

Izzy looks back down at the statements, thinking. So that's why she couldn't find the extended licence: it had never existed. Sometimes the evidence wasn't to be found in the presence of something, but rather in the absence of it. Something slotted into place. Finally. Finally. Things were making sense.

'*And* . . . and,' her father says, flicking the paper triumphantly, 'Iz, I can't believe we didn't twig this, he was still there when I found that receipt for the mixer. Daniel was still working there right before she was murdered. It was right there, in our memories.'

'Really?' Izzy says, trying to remember. Yes, yes, that's right. Daniel had said the mixer was new. *Brand spanking.* She had focused on the mixer, and on her father's anger, that text – *You will pay* – as the evidence, when really she should have focused on Daniel himself. He was being paid, but he hadn't been an employee for weeks. He was contraband.

'Right. Second scenario. Casinos. You make, say, £2,000 from selling something. You need to clean the money, right?'

'Right.'

'You take it to a casino. You put it all in. You play for ten minutes. You take it all out. It looks like casino winnings. You ask for a cheque from the casino, though you originally paid cash. It's classic. Classic money laundering.' He meets her eyes. 'She was making huge money from something – from somewhere – and burying it in the restaurant.'

'I . . . see,' Izzy says. 'The planetary mixer. That's how she could afford it. She wasn't being reckless. She was burying cash.'

'Yes.'

'But . . .' Izzy says, 'how did she end up dead?'

'I don't know,' her father says, not breaking eye contact. 'But I know that *this*,' he holds up the cash again, 'is illicit.'

As he flicks through it demonstrably, theatrically, something falls out and drifts to the floor. Izzy and Gabriel reach for it at the same time, and there it is: a receipt, from Timpson's, for a key cutting. The key to Gabe's shipping container, no doubt.

Her mother had made a copy.

58

The cash.

The money laundering.

The spare key.

Her mother was doing something, maybe at the shipping container.

When Izzy had asked her father, he said he didn't know what had happened to the container. He guessed the lease had lapsed, and knows the container isn't there any more.

Izzy agonizes over it for three days. She's sure that the men who were at the restaurant on the night her mother died will provide an answer. That she was embroiled in something.

It could get Nick into trouble if she uses the computer to look people up. That is what whirls around and around her mind, like a spinning top. It's not his fault. It might be the police's fault – and the computer does belong to the police – but it isn't Nick's fault. There must be another way, she has thought many times. But there isn't.

Izzy realizes, when sitting outside with Nick one evening, that she cares more about what happened to her mother, and about exonerating her father, than anything. She will risk anything to find out. Her parents are the bedrock upon which she is built. Until she knows what happened between them, who is she? Logging on to his computer is a necessary act, she thinks, taking a sip of strawberry Nesquik – Nick is drinking red wine – and appraising him in the evening sunlight.

It isn't right. But she can't help it.

No, that's not right at all, she thinks later, in the shower, while using his mint shower gel and breathing in the peppermint steam. It's an unnecessary act of betrayal.

The truth is, she realizes, as she gets dressed the next morning, she is going to do it. And so she can agonize over it, or she can get on with it. Make the mistake. Implant it firmly in the past. Take it from anxiety to regret, if necessary.

It is a further three days before Nick works from home.

Izzy tidies the living room around him, wiping the flagstone floors, making dinner. She has listed the names in order of who she wants to look up first. She has the list in her mind and is poised, ready for her opportunity.

Nick has a screen shield on, but leaves his work laptop unattended while he goes to boil the kettle. She only has a few minutes. She thanks God for his meticulous tea-making skills. He always leaves the bag to brew for a couple of minutes.

She reaches over and looks at the laptop, then slides into the chair Nick's been sitting on. It's warm from his touch.

It's just a normal laptop. Windows. Outlook is running. Funny how it looks like any mundane office computer. He could be an accountant or an IT manager or an admin assistant.

She minimizes Outlook.

There it is, in the corner. An application – CRIS. That's what he said, didn't he?

She opens it. There are five fields, and *name* is the top one. It looks ancient, like a computer program from the 1990s, the text blocky and strange.

There, she types them. One by one.

Daniel Godfrey.

Nothing. No hits.

Geoffrey Adams.

Nothing.

Marcus Scott. The blond restaurant regular.

She presses 'enter'.

The program seems to stall, this time, loading something where before it had responded instantly.

Izzy isn't prepared for what pops up. She has been thinking about affairs. Falsifying the restaurant records, maybe. Fraud, sex, tax evasion.

Anything but drugs.

59

Arrested on suspicion of possession with intent to supply. 14/07/2002. Police bail. 15/07/2002. Not charged.

Izzy blinks. Drugs.

Not charged. She frowns at that.

She has Outlook back open and the laptop on the table by the time Nick comes back in with his tea. He has made her a cup of coffee.

'What are you even doing?' he says, sounding mildly amused.

She jumps, her heart thumping, even though she's no longer at the laptop.

'What do you mean?'

'You're just . . . I don't know. Faffing about, being weird,' he says with an easy grin.

Izzy ignores him. A man who'd been at the restaurant on the night her mother was murdered was involved with drugs. Her mother had almost twenty thousand pounds in cash hidden in a safe. It couldn't be.

Could it?

She takes a walk and calls her father. For once, he doesn't have the answers. His silence is shocked.

'Drugs?' he says, eventually. And then, *'Drugs.'*

'Is this . . . is this even possible?' she says.

'She never even smoked a cigarette. Barely drank. No. She was a bit – spontaneous, sometimes. But no. Not drugs.'

'Why would she?'

'It could be something and nothing,' he says. 'A coincidence.' And then he adds, 'Leave it with me. Do you remember Marcus Scott? I honestly think I never met him.'

'He had such distinctive hair: white-blond.'

'Will you have a think? About what else you might remember. Maybe we can work out if it's a dead end.'

'Okay,' Izzy says. And then something occurs to her. 'Maybe Mum ensured you never met him,' she says.

'Maybe.'

'Anyway, anything I remember might just be because I'm trying to remember things.'

'I know that well,' her father says.

Izzy has reached the public footpath into the fields that sit opposite her house and she lets herself in at the kissing gate and on to the parched, yellow long grass.

She thinks of all the small things she can remember from back then. Contextless childhood memories.

One ballet class from a non-specific time when the ceiling had sprung a leak; she can't remember whether it was summer or winter, nor how old she was. All she remembers is the way the pianist slowly stopped as the drips began, his fingers stuttering on the keys as the melody became fragmented.

Izzy remembers fingering her necklace – a St Christopher given to her by her mother that she never much liked – as she walked to her GCSE geography class. For no reason at all, she guesses, she remembers particularly that day the feel of the warm metal disc in her fingertips, the chalky smell of the maths classrooms as she walked by them.

She remembers more easily the events leading up to her mother's murder. They have been amplified and emphasized because of the legal system, the police and the media, as though the universe has underlined them for her. She remembers checking what time the sun would set on that day – the day her mother would die – because she had read somewhere that it got earlier by one minute per day in the autumn, and she wanted to check. She did so on the dial-up internet, before school, and it had made her late.

None of these things are significant, and yet she remembers them all. How is she to trust that she would remember something sinister, especially if it was hidden, concealed from her by her father – or her mother?

'How was Mum around this man? How did she seem?'

'I don't know,' Izzy says now.

'Scared?'

'I don't think so.'

'Hmm.' Her father's tone is irritated.

Maybe it's just that, she finds herself thinking. The oldest explanation in the book. An affair. A lover. A violent man, perhaps. Unsuitable. No drugs. Not then. He was arrested three years after her mother's death, after all.

Or perhaps her father knows all this, and killed her himself, another voice inside her speaks up. Her mother's mobile phone was never recovered. Perhaps her father discovered something on it. Perhaps he found the cash.

She sighs. No matter how much she decides to trust him: there it is. The doubt. Never reasonable, never proportionate, but always there. He has almost convinced her. Only a speck of doubt remains, like a stain that's been washed and washed and only the wearer can still see the outline of where it once was. His guilt is fading, fading, fading fast . . .

'How old was he?'

'About forty,' she says. 'Not old. Really not old.'

'Hmm. Nothing else?' he says.

'He wasn't even charged. I think you're right that it could be nothing.'

'I know. And the police can get the wrong man . . . it was just an arrest,' her father says, like being arrested is quotidian. And she supposes it is, to him, on the other side of a life sentence. 'But the money.'

'Yes. What if she got caught up in . . . something. Something really dark?'

'I know,' he says softly.

Izzy wonders at what point her mother knew. At what point she realized who her attacker was, and at what point she realized she was going to die. Or perhaps she never had? Perhaps it had happened too quickly. She tries to imagine herself as her mother, the rough feel of the rope around her neck, the feeling of her body going slack, numb, the buzzing in her head as she struggled for air. She'd read about asphyxiation on an ill-advised Google search late one night. Apparently, it felt like your lungs were burning, and then like you were falling asleep. That was all.

'I don't know,' she whispers to her father. 'We've got almost nothing, haven't we?'

'No,' he says quietly. 'I know. But will you do me a favour?'

'Sure.'

'One thing I learnt in prison was the power of the mind. To idle. I spent almost all of the first year in my Category A prison in solitary – voluntarily. And I thought about all sorts. That's when God came to me.'

'Right.'

'Next time you're . . . whatever. Dancing. In the shower, or reading in bed . . .'

'I don't dance any more,' she says.

'What, not even . . . ? I thought you'd always dance. *Tendus* by the kettle,' he says with a smile in his voice.

She feels her heart twist in pleasure. That's right. He had learnt all of the ballet lingo when she had been learning. '*Fondu*, to melt,' he had said proudly one evening when she got in. '*Frappé*, to strike.'

'When the kettle boils, while you're driving, cooking, will you just think about this man?' he says. 'In those quiet moments. You might find you remember something about him.'

'Okay,' she says. 'I will.'

'Trust me. Your mind will start to throw things at you. Anyway, is that everything the computer said?'

Izzy looks out across the fields. The landscape is completely different. Where previously it was green, it's now yellow, like a desert. The grass is crunchy and parched underneath her flip-flops.

'Yes,' she says.

'Can you find more – like, why they didn't charge him?'

'I don't know, I only had two minutes. I mean, it's Nick's –'

'Yes, yes,' her father says, not dismissively, but sincerely.

He has no connection to Nick. They have never met. Not shared a Sunday dinner together or played a game of tennis, toasted each other at Christmas . . . all of the things Izzy has done with her own in-laws, and missed seeing the inverse of with Nick. It is another thing she doesn't have, she supposes. Will never have, probably.

'I don't know his password, otherwise I could look when he's out. I can only use it if he's in and leaves it unlocked.'

'I see.'

'Maybe we could speak to Marcus, instead,' she says.

'Are you serious?' her father says immediately. 'He'll be rough as houses.'

'He might know something.'

'Who do you think the threats are from?' her father shoots back, quick as a flash.

Of course. The texts aren't from her father, or someone warning her off her father. They might be from Marcus himself. Whether or not he murdered her mother, he knows something about it: he knows who did. He might be threatening her. Goosebumps appear over her bare legs and she turns around, looking at the deserted field. It's like a wasteland. Blond grasses, pale blue skies. Nobody around.

Marcus wants her to stop.

And he's a criminal.

His politeness and his well-cut suits take on a sinister tone in her mind. What was her mother involved with? She was in too deep, in whatever it was, and ... she didn't survive.

Somebody had been in Izzy's kitchen. Busted the lock. Threatened her by text.

What next?

60

Memories, unknown time frame

Izzy

A blond man ordered a lasagne from Izzy in the restaurant. She was waitressing that night. She was sixteen, seventeen maybe. Her skirt was tight across her stomach. She was worried about weight gain. Hoped it was just muscle.

He ordered a lasagne. 'And don't put the tomato on the top,' he added.

'Not a fan?' she said wryly, finding a strange thrill in transacting with an adult in this way. That was right: she wasn't yet with Pip. It must have been 1998 at the latest.

'Horrible, wet things,' he said.

That was all. The memory of taking him the lasagne, once it was cooked, must surely exist, somewhere in her mind, but she can't access it; can't grasp it.

They had a singer in the restaurant. She lasted two nights. Nobody liked it; people couldn't hear conversation over it, and the microphone kept squeaking. It was amateur-sounding, Izzy told her mother coldly. She can't remember why she was in a bad mood that evening, but she was. Her father had said nobody would like it, but her mother hadn't listened, booking her anyway, talking about needing to diversify.

'Pretty loud,' Marcus said to her mother.

She heard him in a break in the music. Her mother nod-ded, looking tense.

Marcus was the only person left in the restaurant.

'Go on home,' her mother had said, waving Izzy away, even though the tables needed wiping, the dishes washing.

'It's fine,' she said, mopping up around Marcus.

He was a tidy sort of person. His clothes were precise: a suit with neat creases down the front like they'd been freshly pinched into place, immaculate, shiny shoes. He had, too, a neat way of sitting, with his feet looped behind the step of the stool, his wallet exactly square on the bar.

'Your mum says you do ballet,' Marcus said to her, and she'd nodded.

Her mother had reiterated it, then. 'Really, Iz, go, you're up early,' she'd said.

'I want to keep busy,' Izzy had said.

It wasn't long after Oliver had died. That's right. She remembers.

'Her boyfriend's brother died,' her mother said quietly to Marcus.

'His name was Oliver,' Izzy said.

'Oliver what?' Marcus had asked, and she had liked that: that Oliver was a full, rounded person to him.

'Eason,' she said. 'His name was Oliver Eason.'

Izzy had left then. She doesn't remember where she was going. The context surrounding the memory disappears like smoke.

'These are great,' her father says to her on the phone a few days later. 'Keep thinking.'

'They're meaningless.'

'Keep thinking. Drugs rings never operate in isolation. There's always a chain. Think who he spoke to.'

'Okay,' she says. 'I will.'

Later, in the shower, she closes her eyes and tries to think, but no more memories will come.

61

Nick issues an invitation to the cinema by text the following Saturday. *Tomorrow?* he writes. *Your pick.*

A second later: *And your pic 'n' mix x*

Izzy flushes with pleasure as she scrapes a leftover roast dinner into the bin. 'Flirting with the old ball and chain?' Chris says wryly, looking over her shoulder.

Love to, she responds to Nick, ignoring Chris, and appreciating the normality of it all the same in the chaos that is investigating her mother's murder, and not yet knowing if her father is innocent.

The next day, she spends all afternoon getting ready, just like she used to, in the early days of their relationship. She takes a long, oily bath which smells of lavender. She blow-dries her hair properly, so it's bouncy and straight. Yes, this is right, she thinks, as she applies her mascara in their bedroom. She has missed this. A date with her husband. Banter with her cousin. Just mundane, ordinary things. Looking forward to wearing a black, well-cut blazer, dark eyeliner. Looking forward to pic 'n' mix and holding hands in the dark.

'Two secs,' Nick says when she arrives downstairs holding a glittery bag. 'Hot stuff,' he says, glancing briefly at her, then opens his laptop.

He types his password in front of her. She catches the first six digits:

IS@BEL

'Right, just . . .' Nick says, navigating to something and typing. He looks at her. 'Done,' he says. He closes the laptop.

The words leap out of Izzy's mouth before she can really consider them. No, not the words: the lies. 'That didn't send,' she says. 'You logged off before the sent bar finished.'

'Did I?' Nick opens the laptop again, and types.

She watches carefully, afraid to even blink.

IS@BELLEENGL1SH^

There's a mother in the movie that they watch. She is exactly Izzy's type: reading glasses perched on the end of her nose. An artfully draped, expensive-looking top. She spends the film making roast dinners for other people and worrying about them.

As Izzy watches her, she thinks of the mother she misses. Not her own mother, exactly, but some maternal emblem. Somebody to tell about house purchases and arguments with Nick. Not everybody has this, she reminds herself. She is just fine. Fine, she thinks, as she tries not to wipe her eyes, so that Nick won't notice.

How could her mother get involved with *drugs*? How could she risk everything – risk leaving Izzy – for that? Her mother was capable, firm, in charge. So sometimes she expected too much. She worked too long hours at the restaurant. But she was *good*. Wasn't she?

But then perhaps her mother was trying to solve a problem. A problem she had caused: debt. She wanted to give Izzy the things that she deserved. The cash in the envelope for the ballet audition. Not saved up, as Izzy had presumed, but dirty money, passed to her. Her mother had good intentions, maybe.

Izzy remembers her happy, softer mother now. When life parted just enough to let her in. She'd cook Izzy steaks, home-made chips salted with garlic, tenderstem broccoli. She'd ask her about her ballet class and about Pip. 'Finish it all,' she'd say, nodding to the steak. 'I made it specially.'

Later, Nick takes her to bed, just the way he used to.

The password is almost forgotten by the time they are entwined together, their heads on her pillow, eyes closed. But, on the cusp of sleep, Izzy recites it again to herself, so that she doesn't forget it.

62

Monday rolls around and Izzy pretends everything is normal, going to the quiz with Chris even though ... even though what? Even though she and her father are on the brink of something, she supposes. Even though she is waiting to illegally log on to a police computer. Even though she doesn't care about any of this stuff, except finding out the answers.

Halfway through the music round, she says it. 'I wanted to ask you something. About Dad.'

'Your dad?'

'Yes.'

'What?'

Britney Spears blares out over the sound system and, to her surprise, Chris puts his pen down and walks out, gesturing for her to join him.

It's warm, but the beer garden is empty. The early days of the heatwave, when everybody was barbecuing and drinking outside, are over. Now, it is just life, in all its inconvenience. People are irritated that they can't water their gardens or run a bath. That strips of road are melting, causing roadworks. That trains don't run on time and nobody can sleep during the warm nights. The promised rain still hasn't come. It's moving later and later, like a delayed train that will eventually be cancelled.

She sits at a picnic table, under a Carling parasol, and looks in at the quizzers.

'We'll lose if you're not quick,' Chris says lightly, kicking the side of the bench. He stands, looking at her, hands on his hips. 'What do you want to know?'

She takes a deep breath. How can she explain it all to him? The whole journey? All of her digging in the bank statements? That they are – she just *knows* it – on the cusp of figuring it all out?

She rolls up the sleeves of her denim jacket and lets the evening sun warm her wrists.

'Come on, English. Left my Coke and my phone in there,' he says, shifting his weight from foot to foot.

'Do you remember a man at the restaurant called Marcus? He was a regular.'

'No . . . I don't think so.'

'He had white-blond hair.'

'Oh, yeah – I do remember him!'

'Well, he got arrested for dealing drugs.'

'Right?'

'And Mum was . . . Well, there's evidence she was laundering money through the restaurant.'

Something in Chris's expression closes down. 'Laundering.'

'Yes. Some things inflated. Some people taken off the books – black salaries.'

'Who's told you this?'

She looks up at Chris. The sun is behind him, his face is in shadow. He's moving the gravel with the toe of his trainer, steadfastly not looking at her.

'I've worked it out myself.'

'Worked what out?'

'Well . . . that. There was all this extra money in the business.'

'She was working hard,' Chris says shortly. 'She extended the licence.'

'No, but she . . .'

'When was the drugs conviction?'

'July 2002. But he wasn't convicted.'

'Right. Three years after. Hardly relevant, then.'

'I think it is.'

'Your father murdered her, Izzy,' Chris says, sitting down gently next to her and taking her hand, which she withdraws. 'I'm so sorry, but he did.'

'He didn't. I really think he didn't. I think there's been a miscarriage of justice.'

Chris says nothing, shaking his head, almost to himself. Izzy thinks about the newspaper clipping and the threatening text, about the people she suspected: her grandparents, her uncle, her cousin. And all along it was somebody else. Somebody involved with a dark world Izzy hadn't even considered. Drugs. Money laundering.

'You need to forget this, Izzy,' Chris says.

'Why are you being so short with me?'

'I'm not.'

Izzy thinks of Tony's behaviour, coming into the restaurant in the night, and the wine rack having been moved. 'Did your dad know about the money?'

Chris's next sentence tells Izzy everything she needs to know. 'No, he didn't know about the *money*,' he says. The emphasis is placed upon the word before he has consciously realized it.

'He was in the basement, near the safe, acting . . . strangely,' Izzy says.

Chris says nothing, evidently weighing it up. 'Okay,' he says eventually. 'Okay.'

'Okay what?'

'It doesn't have anything to do with your mother's murder.'

'What doesn't?'

'Dad . . . he tried to get me to help him get into that safe.'

'But why?'

'Don't freak out.'

Izzy says nothing, making no promises.

'Something happened between my dad and . . . and your mum.'

The air seems to still around them. The noise inside the pub retreats stage left and all Izzy can hear are her own thoughts.

'It was nothing to do with what happened . . . what happened *to* her. Though maybe it motivated your dad, I don't know.'

'What do you mean – what happened?'

'They slept together.'

A palm tree rustles in the distance. Her mother. Her fearless, outgoing, strong mother. Sleeping with her husband's brother.

'How do you know?'

'He told me. He's been trying to get into the safe because . . .' Chris puffs air into his cheeks. 'She told him she kept a second phone in there. They'd been using it to communicate. And he knew you'd started to look into it. He panicked. He knew the police wouldn't check behind the wine rack, but he thought you might. He checked it to make sure it was locked. No key.'

'A second phone?'

'I know. He doesn't know why she had it. But he used it to – I think it was . . . I think it was a mistake, a one-off, but he used it to text her on. She kept it in the safe, and he was worried everyone would find out. And see his messages to her . . . which were, I think, a bit forceful.'

'He knew she had a second phone, and he never told anyone?'

'I know,' Chris says. He looks at her, his eyes red-rimmed. 'I think that's horrible. So that's why I'm telling you.'

'There wasn't a second phone in the safe.'

'Then I don't know where it is.'

'Did your father have something to do with it? What happened to her?'

'No – *no*,' Chris says quickly. 'I think he's just . . . ashamed. About trying to cover it all up.'

'I can't believe she'd do that. This whole time – it's like I didn't know her.'

'I know.'

'If she had a second phone, that fits with the drugs. God.'

'No, it doesn't,' Chris says. 'Doesn't it make more sense that she had an affair, and your dad . . . well, you know.'

Izzy looks at him, properly this time. She has been suspicious about Chris's motives, about his and Tony's staunch belief in her father's guilt, in mud sticking, just like her father said. Everybody seemed so sure, but now she sees it for what it is: faith. Faith in the justice system. Faith in a conviction. And faith in the establishment, too, in the status quo. In self-preservation – the lies we tell ourselves.

63

Izzy's life has divided into two.

Two days ago, she and Nick were standing in the kitchen, looking at the back door. Three weeks since the break-in, her diligent, methodical husband still hadn't reported it to the police, as he'd promised to do. 'The thing is . . .' he said, biting his lip.

'I know,' she said.

The thing was, if he reported the break-in, it would all unravel. They'd look into her father's case. And they'd see it. Files checked out. Things looked up on systems. Every piece of information that he'd found for her. Everything he'd done for her. He'd lose his job. Maybe worse. It was an imprisonable offence, what he'd done: he had googled it.

'So, what do we do?' she says. 'We deal with it ourselves?'

'I guess so,' he said. 'That's all we can do.'

She had stared at the tap, glinting in the morning sunlight, as he had said it. But it wasn't the only thing they could do, was it? He could come clean. It was easy to think, to expect. Harder to actually do, she knew.

Besides, running parallel to that was Izzy's other life. The one where she was still seeing her father, without Nick's knowledge. The one where she was on the verge of figuring it all out.

But, she thought, looking at the back door, its brand-new lock: she was running out of time.

Somebody was trying to stop them. Somebody was coming for them.

And that's why she does it. The second he leaves the house to go to his sister's early on Saturday morning.

She opens the lid of his laptop, types the password, and within moments, all of the information Nick has access to as a police analyst is accessible, right in front of her.

She looks for the CRIS icon on his desktop, but that's when she sees it: the folder.

Name: *Gabriel*.

She opens it, not thinking of what it means. Not wanting to think.

64

It contains one Word document. It is what seems to be Nick's investigation of her father's case. All date stamped. So organized it is like reading a timeline.

General notes: June

Alex dragged after death – jeans rolled up in classic folds, which indicates dragging – but forensics noted that Gabriel English could have easily carried her as he is over six feet four. Query discrepancy?

PC Bryan Michaels said on 03/11/99 (early hours) that Gabriel English displayed clear symptoms of denial. He kept asking, over and over, whether Alexandra English could be resuscitated. He spent the night sobbing in his cell, banging on the door, and asking them to try and resuscitate her, that some people have been known to be revived after minutes and hours. He suggested a defibrillator.

Izzy has to stop reading that part. Her eyes are filmed with tears, her throat tight. Her father, in deep denial, in shock, crying in his cell over the woman he had loved so much.

After a few moments, she begins reading again:

No David Smiths were traced.

June 24th

Address of home entered on to database: no hits. Address of restaurant entered on to database. An entry was thrown up but it was shielded in 2002.

June 28th

Passed the file on the restaurant by colleague.

Witness statement (whistle-blowing) of Rudy Morris, 2002: he was distributing drugs, with Marcus Scott the head dealer. Rudy claims Marcus had been trafficking heroin through the restaurant premises during 1999. Paying the owner to turn a blind eye, to cut it and clean up – commercial kitchen so cleaning easily explained.

Jason Brewer was approached for a statement in 2002: he saw a transaction take place on Sargisson Avenue at 11.30 p.m., 1 August 2001.

Malcolm Graham was approached for a statement in 2002: a friend of his, Ralph Thompson, had bought heroin from Rudy Morris in August 1999.

Steve Eason was approached for a statement in 2002: his son, Oliver Eason, died in 1999 from complications after taking heroin. He confirmed this to be true but had no knowledge of the restaurant being a venue for trafficking and had never been there himself.

Drugs ring investigation collapsed when the dealers being watched destroyed the drugs and evidence before police could get the warrant.

That's all it says. She sits back in the chair in shock.
Pip's stepfather?
And her husband, working it out . . .
But not telling her.

65

Izzy collects her father from his bail hostel – he's waiting outside – and brings him back to their house. She has explained briefly already, on the phone on the way over, but her hands are shaking as she shows him the Word document. Nick. Nick. Nick. Her mind thrums with his name. What was he doing? He was collecting information in support of her father's innocence. And trying to find out who else might have done it. Just as she was.

But he was telling her the opposite. Why?

Her mind is spinning with it, trying to work it out, her stomach clenched. No David Smiths traced. Her father crying in his cell. Nick's betrayal, Nick's betrayal, Nick's betrayal.

And . . . her mother. Her mother who seemed so smart, so together and vibrant, wrapped up in stuff that was so sordid. An affair. Sex with her brother-in-law. And now – separate from Tony, it seems to Izzy – drugs.

'So,' she says, 'Pip's father gave evidence in this – whatever this was – this investigation, that there were drugs moving through the restaurant.'

'Why would *he* know?' her father says, still standing, his coat folded over his forearms, a puzzled expression on his face.

'Oliver. The brother. He died. We thought it was diabetes but it was actually heroin.' She traces a finger over Nick's notes. 'But listen: he said he never went to the restaurant. But he did. We had a whole meal there. Mum served us. Remember?'

Her father swallows, his eyes wide. He seems rattled, distracted. He met her on the steps of his bail hostel, kept looking over his shoulder up at the house. 'So he lied to the police.'

'Exactly. And why do people do that?'

'*Generally*,' he says, an eyebrow raised, 'because they're guilty.'

'But not always,' she says.

Her father hides a smile.

'I don't understand this,' she says. 'I don't understand why these people were asked. How the police knew to ask Pip's father. Why they didn't look at your case again.'

'This all happened in 2002,' he says. 'My appeal was in 2000.'

'Yes, but . . .'

'It's a covert operation,' her father says quietly, almost to himself. He puts his coat down on her kitchen table – her heart turns over at such a familial gesture, like he's just here for a chat – and puts a hand to his chin. 'The lads inside were often caught on these things.' His voice is tight, his brow lowered. 'It's ring-fenced. Because there would have been a lot of convictions at stake – every dealer, every supplier – they open a secret file.' He taps the screen. 'Looks like your husband got the details on the restaurant from a colleague involved in it. It's historic, so I guess it was easy.'

'Start at the beginning. Explain this to me,' Izzy says, looking up at her father.

'Okay. A dealer blows the whistle on an operation. On a drugs chain. Marcus was selling, with Mum – apparently – and then with others, in different locations. Then it's distributed to smaller dealers who sell to consumers. They start to investigate, maybe watch the dealers involved, interview people, like

Steve, who might have some evidence. They were trying to get as much evidence – covertly – as possible, but it collapsed. Somebody must have alerted the dealers, and so, by the time they arrested them, the evidence was destroyed.'

'Right. But why hasn't it affected your case?'

'That's covert ops for you. The information will never, until Nick took an interest, have crossed over on to my file. No officer who investigated my murder would have *any* idea about this stuff. Chinese walls. And it happened so long after I was sent down.'

'But . . . it's so unfair.'

'Well, the restaurant's involvement was historic. And my case isn't open. And it's not cold. I was convicted. The police trust the justice system above anything else.'

He walks to the sink and helps himself to a glass of water. His forehead catches the light from the kitchen window; he's sweating.

She continues to look at him while she thinks about Tony. So he wasn't involved with the drugs. The police would surely have found out if he was. His affair with her mother was incidental. Just an unrelated thing, discovered because she had died. What would they find if Izzy died? A bunch of liked Instagram posts of a family none of them had heard of. Nobody would know what that family meant to her, because they are a private obsession.

Her father is gulping his water. She appraises his slim frame, his prematurely white hair, his prisoner's pallor, and thinks: he's lost enough. She won't tell him about Tony. It's kinder not to.

'Are you annoyed?' she asks.

'No.'

'I am. It seems so unfair.'

'There's only so much injustice you can take before you stop caring,' her father says. 'This doesn't surprise me at all. I don't give a shit.'

'I can't believe Mum was wrapped up in all this,' Izzy says eventually. She blinks. Her mother isn't Thea. And she isn't like the Instagram family, either. She's herself. Her flawed self. But perhaps she was trying to do the best for Izzy. To get them out of debt and to help her off to ballet school.

'I know,' he says, his tone softer now. 'I know. But . . . I get it.'

'Do you?'

'She was always a misguided businesswoman. Wasn't she?'

Izzy thinks of the cheap wine, sold on at extortionate prices. At how amateurish her mother was at running a restaurant, but how swiftly she'd thrown herself into it, getting everyone into debt before she even knew it would work.

'I don't understand why the debts remained, though.'

'You have to launder money slowly,' her father says. 'The cash was sitting there and, month on month, she'd launder it through the restaurant. And then, when I was inside, the house was seized to pay off the creditors.'

'Oh,' Izzy says. 'Do you think . . .'

'What?'

'Do you think she did it – this – because . . . because of how much she loved us? Because she wanted to do the best for us?'

'Without a doubt,' her father says quickly. 'She loved you so fucking much, Iz. I guarantee it.'

'And you,' Izzy says simply.

'And me. But, you know, relationships are . . . She was

reckless. Wild, at times. And so she forced me to be the safe one. I loved her, but that wasn't always easy.'

'I get that,' Izzy says, thinking how the exact opposite occurs in her relationship. 'So . . .'

'It seems to me that Steve is at the centre of all of this.'

'Yes,' Izzy says, thinking of the way he looked at her across the petrol station forecourt. 'I think so.'

'Then it's time to speak to him. Isn't it?'

Steve hasn't moved since Izzy used to visit Pip.

'Everything's so easy, these days, isn't it?' her father says when Izzy types the postcode into her phone to navigate them there. 'That little thing can do everything.'

Steve's house is a Victorian terrace with a blue door which has no knocker or bell. Izzy stands on the steps, her father just behind her, waiting. Wondering if they are being foolish, to do this alone. Wondering if it's all a mistake. Wondering at his precise involvement in her mother's death. Will he lead them to what happened to her? Does he even know himself?

Izzy knocks softly on the wooden door. Steve answers after a few minutes, wearing shorts and a T-shirt, one brightly-coloured flip-flop on, one in his hand. He looks harassed.

'Steve,' she says to him, not knowing what else to say.

He stares at them both, saying nothing, his eyes moving from her to Gabe and back again.

She is just wondering how they ought to play it when her father speaks.

'We've seen the police report about your statement from the restaurant. We know how Oliver died. I think we had better come in.'

His face drains of colour.

She's read about that happening many times, but she's never seen it before. His cheeks lose their redness. His eyes go dark, becoming red-rimmed against his white skin. Little dots of sweat appear on his upper lip, which he wipes away. His lips turn a whitish blue.

He steps aside, both hands dropping to his sides. The green flip-flop falls to the floor. Izzy stares at him. He's not acting like somebody who has information. He's acting like somebody who's done something. Who has something to hide.

As soon as they are inside, the door shut behind them, her father, always two steps ahead of everyone, says it. 'It was you, wasn't it?'

Steve stares at them, in the darkness of his hallway. And then he speaks, his voice hoarse and cracked. 'How did you know?'

66

Izzy stands there, her whole body buzzing with shock. It was him. He killed her mother.

The hall is huge but empty. Izzy looks at the floor. It used to be scattered with boys' trainers and school bags, but there's nothing now.

The only sign he's ever had a family is a framed black-and-white photograph above a corner table by the door. Pip. There he is. She takes a step closer; she can't help herself. He has lines around his eyes. A receding hairline. The man who ghosted her when her mother died.

'I don't care any more,' Steve says, standing at the end of the hallway. He turns away from them, his frame heavy underneath his too-small T-shirt, and leads them into his kitchen, though Izzy knows exactly where it is, knows to step down and turn to the left as they enter.

They sit at the table. Izzy can see Pip's old annex out in the garden. She can't stop looking at it.

Steve seems to dither over offering them a drink, then sits with them instead, his hands empty. 'I want to tell you everything,' he says. He runs a hand though his hair. It used to be dark, where Pip's was golden, but now it's almost all white, like her father's. 'I don't care what happens to me.'

'It was you,' Izzy says, unable to stop looking at him. 'And you let me think it was my dad.'

Steve had been looking at her intently but, at that, his

gaze slides down to the table. He says nothing for a few minutes. 'Pip really loved you, you know,' he says.

More memories. Watching movies in the snug together. Steve making cinnamon hot chocolate, with far too much spice in. It had been disgusting. 'Who's going to tell him?' Pip had said, and they'd all laughed.

And then, without saying anything else, Steve leans forward, puts his head in his hands and cries. His back shakes, his elbows rattle the wobbly table. A spoon falls from its perch across a sugar bowl and on to the surface.

Izzy watches him, not sure what to say. Her father's hands are knotted together, she notices, the bones showing.

Steve lets out a kind of frustrated sigh, almost a shout. 'I knew this would come,' he says. 'I knew you'd come. I'm relieved you're here. I have been in prison, just like you,' Steve says, a kind of manic elation in his voice. 'Waiting for this to happen.'

'What happened?' Gabe says. His tone is short, that clipped tone he sometimes uses. He's sitting straight, still with his Matalan coat on, staring at Steve, who opens his mouth and begins to speak.

Haltingly, hesitantly at first.

And then louder, and clearer.

'I never meant to kill her,' he begins.

67

Hallowe'en, Sunday 31 October 1999:
the night of Alex's murder

Steve

'I've been following you,' Steve said to Alex. 'I've been following you for weeks.'

'Sorry?' Alex said, squinting into the gloom. She was in the shipping container, where he knew she'd be. He could see her red hair and her white face, but nothing else. He moved towards her and saw the precise moment she recognized him.

'Hi,' she said. She drew a little package into her pocket, out of sight.

'I've been watching you.'

'Watching me?' she said, bringing a pink hand to her chest. She was wearing a coat, but had it unbuttoned, exposing her white skin to the winter air. She reached for the key to the container, lying on Gabriel's stool.

'The heroin is delivered to Marcus. He brings it to the restaurant every Sunday night, late, when nobody's there. You cut it. How right am I?'

Alex swallowed. He watched her thin neck tremble, the pulse flutter. 'Very. But it's not . . . I never intended –'

'You keep the heroin in the safe, don't you?'

'Yes.'

'And the money.'

'Yes.'

'And then you cut it, bit by bit, and Marcus filters it down to his dealers. But now . . . you're getting greedy, aren't you? Cutting it with cheaper stuff? Diluting it with kitchen ingredients. Flour.'

'Right,' she whispered.

'Trying to turn more of a profit, aren't you?'

'Yes. Look, I . . . I got in deep. And now I can't get out.'

'Only, the flour can cause a pulmonary embolism, did you know that?' he said, talking over her. He'd been waiting to say this to her for weeks and weeks.

'No,' she said, her eyes widening.

'Say, a diabetic injects the first go of heroin. Just a kid, wanting to experiment. We never found out what possessed him. It causes a pulmonary embolism. It renders them unconscious. They have an insulin pump and it continues – automatically – to pump out insulin, bringing the blood sugar down, low, too low, until he ends up in a diabetic coma. And dies. Your son.'

'Oliver. The diabetic.'

'Yes. Ollie,' he said. His son's lovely name – *he looks gentle, like an Ollie*, his wife had said after giving birth to him – sounds wrong uttered to this woman. His indirect killer. Steve would ensure they all paid for it, soon; once he had enough evidence. The head guy, Marcus. Each dealer. But first, Alex: a mother herself, and connected to his son via Pip and Izzy. How *could* she?

'And then, what's this now – you're getting greedier? You're dealing yourself?'

'No, I . . . Marcus texted just now, as I was in a taxi home, to ask me to use the shipping container to do just one drop-off. Just one. I've only ever done one.'

'Why?'

She waved an old phone around. 'The punter wanted this location. It's right by my house. I got the text as I was leaving the taxi, so I walked here. I told Marcus I'd do it . . .'

'Well, guess who the punter is?'

'Who?'

'Me,' Steve said with a harsh laugh that echoed in the night. 'Why would you do this? Our children love each other.'

'I . . . I'm in so much debt. You have no idea.' Her face had paled. She started talking faster, panicking.

'I think you'd better tell me how it began,' he said, standing in the doorway of the shipping container.

All around them were paintings of her. Twenty other Alexes were looking at him, too. Over their shoulders. Alexes in the bath. An Alex drinking a glass of something sparkling. It was unnerving. The real Alex was frozen, standing inside the shipping container, Steve outside.

She was still clutching the key, appraising him, like a wild animal about to bolt. 'How do you mean?'

'From the start. I only want to understand. Did you see Ollie?'

'No.'

'Do you know why he was buying drugs?'

'No. Are you going to go to the police?'

'I don't know,' he said. 'I don't know yet.'

Alex took a deep breath. She paced backwards a couple of steps, stumbling over Gabriel's bag. She was assessing, Steve thought, how much trouble she was in. She thought she was going to prison. And maybe she was. Maybe she ought to. He really hadn't decided yet. Hadn't been able to see past this point.

'I was cleaning up the restaurant one night, and I found a bag of white powder,' she said. 'I was so scared. I was shitting myself really. I had a daughter, a reputable business. But there was a lot of it – two, three hundred grams, I'd say now – underneath the table in one of the booths. I couldn't get rid of it. I'd owe the dealer. They could come back, looking for me. So I put it in the safe in the basement.

'Then Marcus came in the next day, enquired about having lost his glasses. He gave me a meaningful look, so I asked if they were expensive. He said *very*, so I took the risk and got it for him. He gave me forty quid, just what he had on him, for my trouble. For staying quiet. I paid some interest on one of the credit cards with it.

'The next day, he came back, late. He ordered a lasagne and asked me where I'd stored his glasses until he picked them up. I couldn't . . . I couldn't argue with him, or lie. He was a criminal. So I told him: the safe. He laughed then – a weird, quiet kind of laugh – and said he had never thought before how perfect a restaurant would be for moving drugs. I had a working safe. We had to do a big clean-up every night. And we had ingredients here that we could order in bulk, without suspicion.

'He said he could come once a week, drop off the heroin, and all I had to do was keep it. For now. He wouldn't deal from here – too many known dealers in one place would alert the police. But we'd use it as a base.

'I got in so deep. I never meant to,' she said, her voice wobbling. 'He said I could earn more if I started cutting it with him. And we agreed I might do the odd drop-off in the future. It wasn't a request. It was an order.'

'Oh, Alex,' Steve said. 'What a fucking fool.'

'He was asking and asking how to make more money, so we started cutting corners. Lacing it with flour. Nothing harmful. So we thought.'

So we thought. Steve was watching her closely. Her eyes were on him, the keys clutched tightly in her fist.

'We've put less flour in it this time, but I . . . I said to Marcus we need to make it pure or I'm out, but he said he'd shop me, so I . . .'

'Why . . . ?'

'I don't know.' She started crying. Lips quivering, nose reddening. 'You have no idea how deep I've got, just from a fucking bag left in my restaurant. Just a single . . . one single bad decision. But what could I have done? Destroyed it – and got myself killed? I had no choice. I had a family to support. A daughter who needed me.'

'You always have choices.'

'But then, when Oliver died, I . . . I had no idea flour would do that –'

Her words seemed to ring out in the sea air around them.

'You knew?' he said. His mouth had filled with saliva. *She knew.*

Anger began to bubble in his veins. He wondered if Ollie felt like this, the day he died. Like his veins were on fire. His little boy. His little boy whose first steps had been so assured, like he had just decided to master walking on those short, fat caramel-brown legs, no nonsense, no stumbling needed. He wondered if he knew he was dying; that, the longer he stayed unconscious, his insulin pump was slowly killing him. If he knew he wouldn't get to university, that he wouldn't get married, that he'd never remove muddy boots again and take a shower or bite into some pink candy floss or dance drunkenly to 'Don't Look Back In Anger'. If he knew his parents' hearts were breaking.

'We . . .' Alex said, wringing her hands. 'We always hear . . . if there's been a death of one of our customers. We always hear. Someone leaks it, somewhere along the chain. I knew from Izzy that Oliver had died. But we found out along the chain that it had been the heroin.'

'And yet you . . . you just kept on selling the heroin?'

'I . . . I . . . I . . .'

It was too much for him. Her prattling. Her nervous talk. Her excuses. That she was still dealing. It was too much.

He reached for the first thing to hand: the cord from the art bag. She tried to make a phone call as he reached for her, but he disconnected it.

Afterwards, his hands shaking, shocked at himself, he tried to clear his mind. Damage control. He took her phones, one black and one silver – a burner phone, he guessed – reasoning there was no way he could leave a trace of himself. He took the drugs, too, which he flushed down the toilet.

He buried her in the woods. He wasn't in great shape, and he had to drag her, half-in, half-out of the bag.

As he dug a shallow kind of grave, he saw the initials inside the bag. That was right: her husband. *GDE* embroidered on it in gold.

It was a sign: the perfect way to cover it up.

68

Izzy looks across at her father. His face is wet with tears.

It wasn't him. The truth hits her right in the stomach. The doubt. The reasonable doubt. Eradicated.

Izzy can't observe the scale of it. It's as though she's arrived at the edge of the world, and she's peering over into blackness. Infinite blackness. Steve murdered her mother. Then let her father serve time for it. Framed her father, really. Here he is. The man who robbed her of a mother. The man who couldn't control his temper. The man towards whom all of her malicious, angry, guilty, sad, remorseful thoughts should have been directed over the years.

'I couldn't believe myself,' Steve says. 'I couldn't believe that I had killed somebody. I was living in one world and then . . . quite another,' he says, rubbing at his forehead. 'I've never even had a temper. It was so shocking to me. Like an episode, or something. Like a breakdown.

'I went home and tried to pretend. But after three days, I hadn't eaten or slept . . . my wife begged me to tell her the problem, so I did. By then, Alex had been found. We decided to tell Pip. Otherwise he would've carried on seeing Izzy. We had to keep it secret forever, between us. She agreed to give me an alibi if it came to that. But it never did.'

Izzy closes her eyes. That's why. Pip. Three days after her mother's death. He had no choice. It was a family secret. Just as her family's secrets were cracked open in the courtroom, Pip was forced to keep his hidden, against his will. But how could he do that to her? Would she have done it to him? She really doesn't think she would have. She thinks of the way his eyes met hers when he was leaving the petrol station, and the betrayal seems to rise up through her.

He let her believe he didn't want to be with her any more, despite how much they loved each other. Despite all of their promises.

He let her believe her father murdered her mother.

But how could he have done anything different? He couldn't tell her: she would've told the police. And then his father would have gone to prison. And wouldn't Izzy protect Gabe in just the same way?

Izzy looks at Steve, her eyes glazed over in shock. How can *he* feel sorry for himself, when he has taken everything from her? He was robbed of his child, so he took her parent. It is a cruel kind of vigilante justice he has imparted, for no logical reason.

'Why her?' Gabe says.

Outside, the rain begins. It's so sudden and so strong that it sounds like hail on the roof. Izzy looks out into Steve's tiny garden. Rain begins bouncing off the crooked paving slabs.

'I was just going to talk to her,' he says. 'Confront her. And then I was going to get proof and shop the others – maybe her, too, I don't know. But then: she knew. She knew about Ollie and was still dealing the same stuff. God, I just lost it. And then I had to hide – obviously. I'd killed somebody. I went totally dark on the whole thing. Until the police knocked on my door a couple of years later and asked me if I knew anybody who had dealt Ollie heroin. I had to give a statement. Otherwise they might've suspected.'

'So you lied again. Said you'd never been to the restaurant.'

Steve blinks, looking surprised at how much they know. 'Yes,' he says.

'Did Pip ever . . . want to tell me?' Izzy says tentatively.

'Yes. Oh, yes,' he says earnestly. 'I've lived in fear of it for twenty years. I've lost everything over it. My wife left. Pip is often withdrawn now. Will only see me on his terms. They kept my secret for me — but at the cost of *everything*.' His shoulders shake, as though his body is still crying when his eyes have stopped, and looks at Gabe. 'What're you going to do?' he says.

Her father says nothing, fiddling with the cuff of his coat. He doesn't seem angry like she thought he'd be. He seems listless, melancholy.

Izzy is studying Steve. So her mother wasn't killed by somebody involved with drugs. Or a man with whom she'd had an affair. But instead . . . by somebody who, like herself, was grieving. And grief isn't logical. Izzy started to run a restaurant that she hated, gave up ballet. She did things which didn't make any sense, too. They were just *self*-destructive: internal not external.

'I guess you'll tell the police,' Steve says.

Izzy swallows. The police. Nick. He has betrayed her. He'd solved most of the case, he was only missing one piece: the knowledge that Steve had lied, but even without that he suspected her father's innocence. But can Izzy betray him? If they tell the police the truth — unless Steve confesses everything — Nick will lose his job, or worse.

Steve pushes his fists into his eye sockets and sucks in a ragged breath. 'I'm sorry. I'm sorry. I'm sorry. I wanted him back. I thought it'd bring him back. If I punished her. But instead, I just took her from you.'

'Yes,' Gabe says.

Steve wipes his eyes and looks at Gabe. 'If I could go back . . . I'd never do it. I'd stop myself. I wish I could go back.'

69

'We could tell the police,' Izzy says simply to her father when they leave.

They haven't said much more to Steve. What can they say? They've left it open-ended, messy. The only way they know how.

'Why would we?' he says, standing outside, his jacket clutched to him. He puts it on immediately and pulls the hood up, pulling the drawstrings tight so that only his face is visible.

'To make him pay,' she says over the noise of the rain. The road is a river, already, moving and shivering like a snake.

Her father's eyes flicker. *Contempt*, she thinks.

'Since when does making people pay help anyone?' he says, looking at her levelly.

All along, she thought he held a grudge, had a vendetta against her, but he doesn't. Not at all. Not even after everything he's been through.

They start walking to Izzy's car. He's fiddling with his phone, holding it up, and she wishes he would stop.

'But he . . . all the damage he's done –'

'Is done. Besides, what're we going to say – that we hacked into the police computer? Get your husband sacked?'

Izzy doesn't say anything to that. They reach her car and get inside. The steering wheel is hot to the touch; it was only a few minutes ago that it was sunny. The windows steam up as they sit there, rainwater evaporating off them.

'Then what was it all for?' she says to her father. 'We did it – we *actually* did it. We found out who and . . . Will you stop texting?'

Her father puts his phone in his pocket immediately. 'It was for you,' he says.

'For me?'

'So you knew.'

'That you were innocent,' she says.

Her father looks thoughtfully across at her. 'That your father didn't murder your mother,' he says. 'I wanted to lift the burden of that story off you. Make it untrue. That's all I wanted.'

'I see,' Izzy says quietly, thinking.

'Anyway – look. Can we go to Alexandra's?'

'Okay,' Izzy says. 'Why?'

'You know, it wasn't me. But it kind of was, too,' he says, not answering her question, as she pulls away from the kerb.

'How?'

'Why was she dealing?'

'Because of money,' Izzy says.

'Exactly.'

'But it was her debt.'

'Oh, yeah, the debts were her fault, maybe, but the context is . . . our marriage. I could've worked harder. Supported her better. Definitely. Then she wouldn't have had to resort to all that.'

'She loved us enough to risk everything to get us out of it,' Izzy says firmly.

That is what she has chosen to believe: it is medicinal optimism. Just like the cups of coffee during the bad times, so too is this belief. Her mother wasn't reckless with their lives. She was selfless. Misguided, maybe.

'Did you ever think we'd do it?' she says.

Here he is, her father. No molecule of guilt remains. The stain's been lifted. He never did it. Never would. Izzy can't even begin to think about the time lost. The suffering inflicted upon him during the miscarriage of justice. No, she thinks pragmatically – the way she always has. They will move forward, past this. To dwell on it would only let it take more. She concentrates instead on what's been left behind: love.

'I knew you would,' he says. 'It's all down to you. And finding that safe.'

Izzy swallows. She won't tell him about Tony. What good would it do for him to know the woman he loved cheated on him? That his brother sold him up the river, willing to hide evidence so his own affair wouldn't be exposed? No. She'll let him think that his relationship, her mother's love for him, was pure.

He's already lost too much.

'Look, Izzy,' he says, breaking her thoughts, 'I want to tell you something, but I want to do it at Alexandra's. Where I first saw you again.'

'Okay,' she says, looking sideways at him.

But his tense tone matches his facial expression, his fidgeting. She stops at a set of traffic lights and looks at his eyes. They're apologetic. He is somebody about to give bad news. What is it? That he knew, already, what had happened on the night Alex disappeared?

They pull up outside the restaurant. It's mid-morning, not yet open for the lunchtime rush. It's as quiet as it was at midnight when he arrived to share more memories with her.

Her father gets out of the car and crosses to the front of the restaurant. Izzy opens it and they go inside, out of the

407

rain, sitting opposite each other. The Alexandra's sign that he painted twenty years ago squeaks as it swings in the gusts coming in off the sea. Izzy looks out: it's wild. Waves breaking on top of each other, several feet high, sea spray being flung at the windows.

'Imagine,' Izzy says, turning away from the window and sitting down on a bar stool. 'Imagine if we'd just figured it out then. If I'd heard you out. If the police had done their job in 1999.'

'Don't, Iz.'

'Why not?'

'I can't think of it,' he says, looking across at her. 'It breaks my fucking heart. You have to stop running this place,' he says to her. 'It's not your thing. It was your mother's thing.'

'It's fine – it's just a job.'

'You never talk about it,' he says, shifting his weight next to her. 'You don't love it.'

'No,' she says. He's right about it. But what else can she do?

He runs a hand through his hair. 'Okay,' he says. He breathes in and then out. She sees his chest rise. 'Okay,' he says again. 'Anyway.'

'Okay . . .'

'When you told me about the police file on the phone . . . I did something,' he says softly, sadly, to her.

He reaches for her hand. 'We've figured this out, Izzy, and now you are unburdened.'

She likes nothing about the tone of this conversation. It seems utterly wrong, somehow. He looks wretched, telling her, in what should be a happy moment, sitting out of the rain inside her mother's restaurant.

'Yes,' she says. 'What did you do?'

'I wrecked my bedroom.'

'You wrecked it?'

'Yes. It's ruined. I swung the bean cans into the wall, cracked the plaster. Snapped the table in two.'

'Oh, Dad,' she says, the word leaving her mouth before she has time to consider it.

He looks at her, just briefly, his face stretching into a sad smile. He squeezes her hand. It is the first time he has heard her use the word in twenty years.

'You were upset,' she says. 'Understandably.'

'No, I wasn't upset. I knew it wasn't me. I've always known it must have been someone else. And so I wasn't upset.'

Izzy pauses, dumbfounded. 'Well, then . . . why?'

'I've just been texting my probation officer to tell her what I've done. And where I'll be: here.'

'What? Why . . . ?'

'Because, Iz, I want to go back.'

'Where?' she says, looking at him frantically, her eyes desperately scanning his features.

'Home,' he says simply.

70

She shakes her head, not understanding. And then, all of a sudden, she does. She understands exactly what he means with a sick certainty.

'No,' she says. 'Not now. You can't leave me now.'

'They're coming for me.' He doesn't break eye contact as he rubs his hand over his face. Eventually, he looks down at his feet, then back up again at her. 'They're going to recall me, Iz. It's criminal damage. I *ensured* it met the threshold for criminal damage. My landlord found it. I confessed. They're on their way.'

'You could get out of it. I've got money. We could get you a great lawyer . . .' Her voice trails off as she recalls Nick's advice to her: there are no trials for breached licence conditions. They just get recalled – for life.

'It's not too late,' she says. 'I can say it wasn't you. That you were with me. We can fix it.' Her voice is high and panicked. Please not now. Please don't take him away now, not now he is – finally – innocent. She takes his rough, leathery hand in hers and brings it to her face, and her tears wet his skin.

'It's not about that,' he says. 'No, please don't cry, my love.'

'No.'

'You know what it's about. You know why.'

'I don't.'

'Nobody will hire me, Iz. My reputation is shot. I can't

work a computer. I can't figure out how to scan my shopping in Tesco. I don't know how to cook a meal or register with a GP or . . . I don't know how to have a life. I'm supposed to remember to cook three times a day and shop once a week and sign on at the Jobcentre and fill in my benefit forms and collect the mail every day and remember to take my mobile phone everywhere and lock the front door and clean the bathroom and . . . Iz, I just can't do it any more.'

'Is it the stuff that's passed you by? The new technology? New cars?'

'No, not really. It's the . . . it's the infrastructure of a life. I don't know how to do it. To have one. I don't enjoy anything. I don't eat. I don't *paint*. Life is still in grey, for me, baby girl.'

'No.'

'I've been inside for a third of my life. The most vital third. My prime.'

'No. It just takes time. To adjust. Move in with me,' she says spontaneously. 'I'll help you.'

'Iz,' he says, looking straight at her. 'They're going to recall me to prison for the rest of my life sentence.'

'No,' she says, the tears coming fast now.

'You'll visit me, won't you?'

'You can't go back,' she says through sobs. She can hear a siren in the distance, outside. 'You're innocent. You were always innocent.'

He swallows as she says it. 'Yes,' he says. 'I was. But . . . it happens. It's happened. It's over for me, Iz. Remember when you heard me on the phone? When I hadn't hung up?'

Eight weeks. Eight weeks. That's what her father had been saying, to himself, in private. Nothing to do with the Jobcentre at all. 'Yes.'

'I was saying that because that's how long I was going to give it. If we hadn't figured it out after eight weeks, I'd let myself go back. It was my own time limit. To stay sane.'

'But you could stay out. Start over.'

'I can't,' he says. 'When something like that happens, you . . . you can't be accused and convicted of a violent crime without your life . . . It has ruined my life,' he settles on, eventually. 'It's beyond repair. I'll hang myself if I stay out. I can't do it. I can't. I can't. I *won't*.'

'Please,' she says, her voice hoarse and strangled from crying. He is going to leave her for a second time, an hour after she found out he is innocent, and she can hardly stand it.

'Do you know how many lies I told you, trying to protest my innocence? How twisted is that?'

'I know,' Izzy says quietly, thinking of the glass her father likely threw, of the wardrobe he bought and pretended her mother had, of the decorating he said he'd done but really it was Tony. All things said – invented – out of desperation to seem better than he was. Being accused, and convicted, had made him defensive. 'They made you look more guilty,' she says simply.

'And that's what it's like to be accused,' her father says. 'Every no comment interview you give. Every defence. Every excuse. If there *are* things in your past you're ashamed of, you try to hide them. To obscure the truth.'

'But it's over now,' Izzy says. 'You're innocent.'

'But I'm not perfect,' he says.

Izzy thinks about his previous conviction. His lies. His temper. No, he's not perfect. But he is innocent. They are not the same thing, after all. And Izzy isn't perfect, either.

She can lose her temper, and scream and shout, but she won't ever be a killer. She is good enough. They both are.

'Jesus had to hand himself over,' he says.

'Not the religious stuff.'

'But it's true. And it helps me. That little prison chaplaincy that I went to every Sunday. It . . . it gave me hope.'

'Of release?'

'No – of *acceptance*. Some people don't get the life they think they're going to get. I've been out for near enough eight weeks, to the day, and we solved it. We solved it. The second I knew you'd seen enough on the computer to solve it, I did it. And now *you*,' he says, holding her hand between his cool palms, 'you can get on with your life. Knowing your father didn't kill your mother. That's all I wanted. That's all I ever wanted. Your burden was heavy, and I halved it. You lost your mother but not your father. Not me.'

'I have lost you, though. I am losing you.'

He says nothing, wiping his tears away with his rough Dad thumbs, wiping and wiping even though more fall. The sirens get louder and Izzy's body begins to shake.

By the time the police arrive, he has a blotted mark across the shoulder of his Matalan coat, from her tears.

She rushes outside with him to see him being driven away in the police car, his face framed in the window, looking at her, just as he had done all those weeks ago when he first came to find her.

Izzy's marriage ends with four words.

Nick tells her that he traced the text and Tony was behind the threats all along. Izzy nods. Of course. Of course he was. Trying to save his own skin. That's how the person had her number, her address, knew intimate details of her life. Tony arrived at the restaurant five minutes after Gabe left: he knew she was seeing him, and that's why he sent that text. He was worried she'd find the phone.

Nick stands with his hands on his hips, looking at her, not telling her the rest of it.

In the end, she asks him. 'And the drugs? The covert operation?'

Nick's eyebrows rise in shock.

'I looked at your laptop,' she says.

He takes a step back from her, and she can tell. She can tell he's going to do it. He's going to turn it back around on her.

'At my work laptop?' he says snidely.

'Why didn't you tell me?' she says, unable to stop a sob escaping with the words.

Her husband. He could have given that gift to her – the gift of an exonerated father – but he chose not to.

Nick begins fiddling with the teapot on the work surface. He pulls at the china lid, which rattles in the hole. He turns it around and around, the chinking noise the only sound in the kitchen. 'Look. You know now,' he says.

'That's not the point. You didn't tell me, Nick. I . . . I really don't think I can forgive this.'

Nick, his status quo challenged, finally panics. 'When I started to look into it, I found other evidence . . . evidence that didn't support the prosecution. But I was so worried. I thought he'd charm you. I was still so sure he did it. And I was jealous, too, I guess. He meant more to you than I did. So I hid it. But more and more came out, and by then it was too late to backtrack.' His voice is wobbly. He finally leaves the teapot alone.

'How could you do that?'

And then he says the four words that end it.

'It was easier to,' he says sheepishly, shamefully. 'I might've lost my job,' he adds.

Izzy sees Nick for the real person that he is, finally. A coward. Somebody content to deceive his wife rather than have a difficult conversation. Somebody who was willing to eschew fatherhood rather than ask his wife what her issues were with motherhood: to work through them.

He avoids her gaze while she stares at him.

Epilogue

4 May: one year later

'We'll finish it, then come and curtsey,' Izzy says. She looks at the clock. Five to seven. She's teaching the Advanced 1 RAD ballet class on a Saturday night. As she often does, these days, she looks at the clock and wonders what she might've been doing a year ago. Starters, probably. Slicing cucumbers. Half-heartedly making soufflés she would never choose to eat herself. Tonight, although she is looking forward to getting home and eating Angel Delight straight from the jug, she is happy here, too. Before, life began when she left work for the day. Now, it's the other way around.

She checks her phone during the curtsey. Nothing from anybody.

She has lost her father and her husband, and yet – here, in the ballet studio – she is happy. She doesn't check up on the Californian family on Instagram any more. She doesn't need to. They – *parents* – are no more empowered than she is. All adults are winging it. Parents or not. Nobody is in charge: nobody knows what they're doing.

And here she is, teaching ballet. The night her father was recalled to prison, she stayed at the restaurant, looking at the stools they sat on in the small hours, took off her shoes, and began to dance. She performed *arabesques* and pirouettes unself-consciously in her own restaurant, her feet sticking slightly to the floor in the heat. She enjoyed the expanse of the room. That she could do a *grand jeté* without hitting anything. She was finally free and able to express herself – happiness, sadness – in dance.

She didn't have the part in the middle – the ballerina career – but, she thinks, looking down at her feet in their ballet shoes, that would've ended by now anyway. Like her father, she has simply intermitted. Eighteen years, misguided, in the wrong direction, but she's back on track now.

'Thank you, Miss English,' the students chorus.

And here they are, the new generation of islanders. None of them knows who she is. Who her mother was. Where her father is. Some of the parents know, but Izzy finds she cares less, these days: she knows the truth.

'Thank *you*,' she says to them. 'You all did so well.'

She's going to the pub quiz tonight with Chris, just as soon as this class is over. They've switched to a Saturday quiz. She'd tried to show him the bank statements, in the autumn, after Gabe was recalled, but there wasn't enough evidence. It was all on Nick's computer, and born out of the memories she and Gabe shared over the spring. There was nothing tangible. She won't ask Steve to confess. Chris rebutted it all, like a conspiracy theorist with an answer for everything. She hardly sees Tony now, either. Izzy avoids him, and she suspects he knows why. She does the quiz and they talk about other things. It isn't perfect, but it is something. It's family.

Chris runs the restaurant now. She said goodbye to it, running her hands over the tables and nodding to her mother's sign as she left for the last time, but the truth is that she's back often. For visits, for meals.

A father of one of the little students walks in. Izzy stills. God, he looks just like Pip. He isn't Pip, but the resemblance is there. The floppy hair. The languid smile, sort of sarcastic, even though he hasn't spoken. She checks: no wedding ring. She looks at him – brown eyes, not blue – and casts about inside herself. Yes. This is what she wants. Not cowardly, smart, complicated Nick who – when it came to it – didn't love her enough. Not somebody who was perhaps a choice born out of the psychology of murder, of thinking her father was no good, a waster. A coward, too, in his own way.

Someone new. Someone with whom she could be her whole self. Izzy the ballet dancer. Izzy the woman who likes fish finger sandwiches and who once solved a crime. The Izzy who can lose her temper with abandon and never worry about it. No longer the Izzy who needs parenting, who chooses a safe man because she needs anchoring. She smiles shyly up at him.

She could find him: someone she could love with all of herself. As much as her father had loved her mother.

She calls in to see her grandmother on the way home. She has deteriorated over the past year. She often doesn't recognize anybody. Today, though, her eyes look clear and bright. She turns to face Izzy the second she walks in through the door.

'Alex,' she says, 'you look lovely.'

Izzy's eyes fill with tears, but she nods, saying nothing. Letting her grandmother believe it, that Alex is alive and well. That she never died. That she is here, with her: with her mother.

Later, at home, still thinking of the man she just met, Izzy lets herself into her house.

'Hi there,' Thea calls from her driveway.

But Izzy only waves. She doesn't need her any more. The validation she sought from Thea and women like Thea wasn't because she was missing a parent: she was missing herself. She validates herself now, embracing her flaws. She likes to eat crap food, and doesn't wish to run a restaurant: and so what? It's her life.

'Are they treating you well?' she says to her father the following Monday. Visiting hours are two until four, and she hasn't missed one yet.

'It's home,' he says softly.

His body language has changed. He is no longer stooped. No longer skinny. He's pasty, but healthy looking. There is fat in the places there ought to be – in his cheeks, no bones prominent – and on his arms, which look strong again. He is fed and warm and clothed, and he is happy.

It's nothing like the first time she visited him, when she had just turned eighteen. No shouting, no anger, no depression, from him. He belongs here, now. He had to change, to survive it, to adapt, but then he couldn't change back.

At first, she used to pretend it was a nursing home and that she was visiting an elderly parent, as so many children had done before her. But now she thinks nothing of it. He lives here: it is his home.

'I've been teaching a little art class,' he says.

She blinks, trying not to let him see how she truly feels. In prison, he is diminished – speaking joyfully of being able to get Sky Sports in the east wing while the west wing of the prison lie about, bored – and of laundry duties and lifting weights in the yard. He doesn't enjoy the summer weather or the seasons or Christmas or Easter. But it doesn't matter, to him. Here, he is able to teach an art class. He didn't pick up a paintbrush on the outside.

Here, now, however unfair it is, he is at home. At rest. And she is here, to visit him. Because they love each other. No matter what.

'Fancy a game of pontoon?' he says.

She deals. They play for an hour, father and daughter. In companionable, familial silence.

This is family.

In all its fractured forms.

Six months later

1 January

Sorry for the late response. I was indeed your father's neighbour. I had no idea about the trial. I do remember seeing him: we chatted for about half an hour and I remember he didn't leave his house all evening.

If I can help at all, please do let me know.

David S.

Acknowledgements

I dedicated this novel to my agent, Clare Wallace, but really every novel should be. No author could manage much of anything without their agent, but only she knows why this novel specifically warranted a dedication. To the fantastic rights team at Darley Anderson too, who continue to sprinkle my inbox with translation joy, and to Camilla Bolton who read and gave notes which assisted me so much.

It's hard to believe that here I am, writing my fourth acknowledgements section, three bestsellers under my belt, when in many ways I still feel like the bewildered drunk-on-luck woman I was the day I got my publishing deal. It is very charmed, this life I lead, and I owe that to Maxine Hitchcock, Tilda McDonald, and the whole team at Michael Joseph. So many people go into making a book successful. Sarah Kennedy, Shân Morley Jones, and the tour de force that is the Michael Joseph sales team: I'll forever be indebted to them all.

As ever, I bothered a number of experts over email this past year. Dr Alison Malkin who very cleverly and carefully helped my diabetes and drugs plot. Imran Mahmood who is always on hand to help me with legal queries. Officer Jimmy (who would rather not be named) who met with me for an afternoon in a pub and talked me through typical days in prison while I made frantic notes. And Officer Peter Green, who let me come and give a talk at HMP Spring Hill in exchange for a tour of the open prison. That afternoon vaulted my book from a work-in-progress to a novel with a heart and soul and I will forever remember standing there in the spring sunlight with my father (of course) as I realized that this novel is really about institutionalization and the catastrophic effect of being accused of a crime. Special thanks go, too, to ex-cop Alice Vinten, who plugged away with me at my covert ops plot, trying and trying and trying to avoid the cliché of 'the police missed this piece of evidence and got the wrong man'. I think we managed it, and it's all down to her. Narbi Price, an artist whose guidance (and advice to go out and buy linseed and turps was right on) and descriptions gave Gabe colour and realism. To DB and to Marigold for the house buying anecdote. And to Dave Matthias for the religion help.

To my close and small circle of author friends, Holly Seddon, G. X. Todd, Claire Douglas and Lia Louis. I'd be lost without the four of you. To Sara Pietrafesa for regularly bringing me back from the brink, and to Joanna Houghton for the text anecdote (where lzzy and Nick met), and to Alice Reid who won a competition I ran on my Facebook page to have a character named after her in this novel.

I can't begin to do justice to the help my father gives me in planning, writing and editing my novels. As my hobby has morphed into my job, he's gone from amateur to professional with me. Our plotting sessions are more formal now: we've gained whiteboards and timelines but there's still tea and laughter. Some things don't change. He's so good at it that my author friends wish to hire him to discuss their plots with . . .

And finally, as ever, I must acknowledge (though he would never expect such) the stoic man in my life: David. My books are imbued with love because you marinate me in it every day. Every interesting character I write has elements of you. You are all I know, and all I ever want to know, forever.

The new book from

GILLIAN McALLISTER

Coming 2020

Read on for a sneak preview . . .

Prologue

Zara

London, Highbury Grammar School, August 2018

The air is warm against Zara's legs as she strides across the football pitch. It is strange to be at school in August, like she is at the beach in the off season or in a closed shop after hours.

She is thinking about the new school term as she walks from the pitch to the surrounding fields, dry clumps of yellow-green grass littered like balled-up socks on the lawn. Specifically, Zara is thinking about stationery. She bought new pens today, a pack of three wrapped in cellophane. Blue, black, red. She'll never use the red one – isn't it rude to write in red? – but she likes the collection, the three together.

It's already dusky, at eight o'clock, but the evening stretches out in front of her. She can go to bed late, get up whenever she wants tomorrow. And so tonight is going to be spent in a delicious frenzy of unpacking new stationery. Four stiff cardboard folders. Slippery A4 plastic wallets. Sticky tabs. She'll return to school, to year ten, a new woman, she has decided. She doesn't quite yet know who she will be. But it won't be who she was before.

When she first hears the noise, she thinks it's nothing. An unexplained shout on a hot summer's evening. Her pace is slow and relaxed across the empty field, the sky a high

429

lavender dome above her, little dried tufts of grass stuck to her trainers.

It's only when she hears the second shout, then the third, that she stops, a fine layer of sweat on her lower back slowly evaporating as she turns, scanning the horizon for the noises like an animal looking for its predator.

Her eyes land on the bandstand. It's been having its roof repaired over the summer. Each week, on the way home from her piano lessons, slightly more progress has been made. She squints now in the half-light. That's where the noise is coming from. Two men. One on the stage, another halfway up the steps.

She paces forward then stops, maybe twenty feet away. Something's happening.

Goosebumps appear on her arms as she moves back across the field to one of the greenhouses nearby, lets herself in and breathes in its familiar, hot-musk-tomato smell. She had spent so many hours in here over the spring, growing organic and non-organic lettuces for a biology experiment. She would re-pot them in her break times, moving from small pots on the windowsill to fat grow bags outside. She would lie awake, sometimes, worrying about her frilly-leaved lettuces out in the cold, which her mum had laughed at. 'Classic you,' she had said, a strange expression on her face.

Concealed by forgotten, spindly, grey-green plants, she looks carefully through the leaves and into the bandstand. She can see the figures clearly. Two boys, a couple of years older than her, maybe sixteen. Not men, as she had first thought.

She shifts her weight on her feet, poised to intervene. But no. She can't bring herself to. To leave the safety of the green-house. She puts a hand on the windowpane, just looking.

She watches it unfold, staring so hard her eyes go dry and

430

painful. Something horrendous is happening, but something important, too, and so Zara forces herself to keep looking, not glancing away for even a second. She counts, instead. One second. Two. Three.

It's over in ten.

Lauren

London, Islington, November 2019

Lauren watches Zara walk into the kitchen. She's wearing a white blouse and a black skirt. Her legs are long now, somehow gamine, like a deer's or an antelope's. She seems to have grown since witnessing the crime last summer. Taller and more womanly, but more adult in a nebulous way, too. The way she holds herself. She's poised. Her daughter is so beautiful, just standing there in a patch of November sunlight, that Lauren feels pride bubbling right up through her like pink lemonade.

'Feeling okay?' she asks. Zara's role in today's trial has become part of their lives this past year. Piano lessons, their jobs, walking the dog, and the various meetings associated with Zara's evidence as a witness. At each one, she has seemed to mature even further. Speaking up, giving opinions, organizing the family. 'We're at the solicitor's at seven, remember,' she said once, and Lauren thought: *who are you?* This brave, bold girl with principles and a superb moral compass. Her daughter, the almost-adult.

Zara shrugs and Lauren waits. This is what they do. Lauren asks, Zara shrugs, Lauren waits, then Zara speaks. She is as circumspect as her absent father, who left Lauren before Zara was even born.

'I mean – it's the right thing, isn't it?' Zara says.

'It is *absolutely* the right thing,' Lauren replies as Aidan walks into the kitchen. He is always running late, and today is no exception. His belt is undone, shirt untucked, a pair of socks in his hand.

'But,' Aidan adds, raising his head in a sort of backwards nod at his step-daughter, 'you don't have to do it. You don't. It's not too late to say no.'

'No,' Zara says on an exhale. 'I'm ready.'

They ride in an unmarked police car, on the advice of their solicitor, Harry. 'More anonymous,' he had said lightly. 'And all three of you in the back is best. Harder to distinguish you that way.'

Lauren has been impressed with his dedication since Zara gave her statement about that night to the police. Not a single slip-up. Zara's identity has been protected by an injunction, by redacted documents, by law. Today, she will enter the courtroom through a back door shown to them last week, and give evidence from behind a screen, known to the jury and the public only as *Girl A*. And why? Because she was the only witness to a brutal murder. Her daughter, who Lauren shielded from swear words on the television and *scenes of a distressing nature*, witnessed a man being murdered when she was just fourteen.

Lauren is almost intimidated by this version of her daughter. So self-possessed. So sure. Lauren hasn't been sure of anything for years.

'Scarf on,' Aidan says as they do a slow loop behind the Old Bailey, ready to be deposited at the back entrance. 'Face covered.'

Zara obliges, wrapping a black scarf around her head, saying nothing, her dark eyes – so like her father's – the only visible feature, scanning the world outside.

As Lauren looks at her, all grown up, ready to testify in

court, she feels a dropping sensation in her gut, like they have just driven over a low bridge, though she knows they haven't. She stares at the weak November sunlight darting out from behind buildings, across at Aidan's profile, and down at her lap. Zara's hand is still in hers. It has lost all its childhood chubbiness, around the knuckles, in the past year. Lauren explores the unpleasant sensation within her. Similar to grief. Time's passing: she hasn't felt it for years, not since Zara was tiny and Lauren's days were punctuated by joy and sadness commingled; the potent ingredients of new motherhood.

It's just because she looks grown up, she tells herself now. But really, she knows it's more than that. Something is coming. This, her stomach is telling her, is the last time they will be here, relatively carefree, together, the sunlight on the backs of their necks. She squeezes her daughter's hand tighter, just for a second, not wanting to frighten her, not wanting to admit it, not even to herself.

2

Aidan

London, The Old Bailey, 2019

Aidan watches as Zara is led, an animal to slaughter, into the witness box in the empty courtroom. He is not sure that this is the right thing for her to be doing, but his voice has been lost in the crowd. The Crown Prosecution Service do not have her best interests at heart – of that he is sure – no matter what they might say. To them, she is a commodity. She has knowledge, and that knowledge is going to be extracted from her, and then she will be discarded. They have placated Aidan with promises of anonymity, with assurances that she is doing *the right thing*, but Aidan thinks, rather, that it's the right thing *for them*, but not for her.

The curtain is drawn tightly around her by an usher, secured by Velcro, which Aidan cannot resist reaching out to check. The usher glances at him, and he shrugs helplessly.

'You'll be in the public gallery,' their solicitor says to them. Harry's young. Mid-thirties. He drinks bright-green matcha lattes and he gets on with Lauren, but then everyone does. They're both fast thinkers, fast talkers, gesticulators. Aidan feels like a Neanderthal in their meetings.

Harry runs through Zara's account with her once again, quietly. He perches like a flamingo behind the box, one leg against the wall's wood panelling.

Aidan and Lauren hover in the corner of the courtroom, talking quietly.

'It should be quick,' Lauren says. 'I think.' She runs a hand through her ashy-blonde hair. His wife is sometimes beautiful and sometimes plain, though he would never say so. Aidan finds her fascinating in this way. Her features are slightly irregular, somewhere around the nose and mouth. She is *interesting to look at*, he once said while drunk, which he regretted.

'She'll be okay,' he reassures her, though he doesn't mean it, isn't sure. How could he be? He stares up at the windows above and wishes that they hadn't done *the right thing*. That they had done the wrong thing. The easy thing. That Zara had closed her eyes and walked away. Pretended it had never happened.

Zara is almost at the end of the questioning. She has told the jury – from behind the screen – what she saw. About the two sixteen-year-old boys, youth football team players, who surprised a homeless man sleeping in the bandstand during the school holidays. She's told the courtroom in her clear, precise way that she used to know Jamie, the victim. That she would wave to him whenever she walked by him, some- times on the street outside school, sometimes in town, depending on when he was moved on.

She has told the courtroom, too, about the discarded roof tile the defendant, Luke, picked up, while his friend – accused only of perverting the course of justice – watched on. She tells them about how Jamie lay helplessly, covering his head, asking him to stop, until he was silent. Aidan dreams about what she saw. A bloodied man, a murderer standing in the twilight. He wakes itchy with sweat. Zara doesn't know how much this thing will affect her, later. Her teenage brain hasn't caught up yet. He wishes he could take this thing she's seen from her, and the nightmares that will surely follow, and subsume them into himself instead.

'One final question,' the defence barrister says. He has a pink mark on his nose from pushing his glasses up with his knuckle, which he does every few minutes. 'Can you talk me through the movements of the defendant, his co-accused and the victim?'

'The movements?' Zara's disembodied voice asks from behind the curtain.

'The victim died on the steps at the front of the bandstand, you say. Yet by your own account, the defendants surprised him while he was sleeping in the far corner.'

'Jamie was backing away from Luke,' Zara says.

'I see,' the barrister says, leaving a drawn-out pause. Aidan looks across the public gallery at Luke's parents. He feels a morbid fascination with them. They are parents whose child has done something unthinkable. Parents desperate to believe it isn't true: not their kid. Aidan knows that feeling well, or, at least, a watered-down version of it. One Christmas, his daughter from his first marriage, Poppy, called him an unimaginative twat because she didn't get the £500 pair of trainers she wanted. He ate his Christmas dinner alone, heart in his feet, thinking: *I messed it up. She was supposed to grow up to be nice: humble.* That's what children don't realize. They don't realize they are avatars of their parents. Like Aidan has taken his heart out of his chest and has to watch it walk around outside his body. And the heart doesn't even know. The heart wants Gucci trainers.

'So – Girl A,' the barrister says. 'Why would Jamie have come towards the front, when there were steps all around the perimeter of the stand? Why wouldn't he have run *away* from the defendants, rather than towards them?'

437

'I don't know.'

'But he did?'

'Yes, he did.'

'Was he facing you, or was he facing the other side when they approached him?'

'I don't know.'

'Did he stand up at any time?'

'No.'

'And yet you say he ran away.'

'No. He did – he did run away.'

'Right. And so – here's what I think happened. The boys disturbed Jamie, who then retaliated. That's what went on, isn't it?'

'No.'

'He stood up, confronted them, and, in self-defence, the defendant reached for the roof tile. Isn't that correct?'

'He did stand up but . . .'

'Do you know Jamie has a history of violent behaviour and that Luke does not?'

'I don't know.'

'He did confront them, didn't he?'

'Not really,' Zara says, her voice a whisper behind the black curtains.

Lauren turns to Aidan. She's frowning at him, his wife who is at the moment in her beautiful guise. She doesn't look away, not even as the barrister labours the point, and then – like a gun going off – he realizes what her stare means. *Zara has lied*, her eyes are saying. *Zara is lying.*

He just wanted a decent book to read ...

Not too much to ask, is it? It was in 1935 when Allen Lane, Managing Director of Bodley Head Publishers, stood on a platform at Exeter railway station looking for something good to read on his journey back to London. His choice was limited to popular magazines and poor-quality paperbacks – the same choice faced every day by the vast majority of readers, few of whom could afford hardbacks. Lane's disappointment and subsequent anger at the range of books generally available led him to found a company – and change the world.

'We believed in the existence in this country of a vast reading public for intelligent books at a low price, and staked everything on it'
Sir Allen Lane, 1902–1970, founder of Penguin Books

The quality paperback had arrived – and not just in bookshops. Lane was adamant that his Penguins should appear in chain stores and tobacconists, and should cost no more than a packet of cigarettes.

Reading habits (and cigarette prices) have changed since 1935, but Penguin still believes in publishing the best books for everybody to enjoy. We still believe that good design costs no more than bad design, and we still believe that quality books published passionately and responsibly make the world a better place.

So wherever you see the little bird – whether it's on a piece of prize-winning literary fiction or a celebrity autobiography, political tour de force or historical masterpiece, a serial-killer thriller, reference book, world classic or a piece of pure escapism – you can bet that it represents the very best that the genre has to offer.

Whatever you like to read – trust Penguin.